FLASHOUT

ALSO BY ALEXIS SOLOSKI

Here in the Dark

FLASHOUT

A NOVEL

ALEXIS SOLOSKI

FLATIRON
BOOKS
NEW YORK

FLASHOUT. Copyright © 2025 by Alexis Soloski. All rights reserved. Printed in the United States of America. For information, address Flatiron Books, 120 Broadway, New York, NY 10271. EU Representative: Macmillan Publishers Ireland Ltd., 1st Floor, The Liffey Trust Centre, 117–126 Sheriff Street Upper, Dublin 1, DO1 YC43.

www.flatironbooks.com

Grateful acknowledgment is made for permission to reproduce from the following:

When The Music's Over
Words and Music by John Densmore, Robby Krieger, Ray Manzarek and Jim Morrison
Copyright © 1967 Doors Music Company, LLC
Copyright Renewed
All Rights Administered by Wixen Music Publishing, Inc.
All Rights Reserved   Used by Permission
Reprinted by Permission of Hal Leonard LLC

Designed by Susan Walsh

Library of Congress Cataloging-in-Publication Data

Names: Soloski, Alexis, author.
Title: Flashout : a novel / Alexis Soloski.
Description: First edition. | New York : Flatiron Books, 2025.
Identifiers: LCCN 2025004248 | ISBN 9781250883643 (hardcover) | ISBN 9781250883650
   (ebook)
Subjects: LCGFT: Theatrical fiction. | Thrillers (Fiction) | Novels.
Classification: LCC PS3619.O4374 F53 2025 | DDC 813/.6—dc23/eng/20250228
LC record available at https://lccn.loc.gov/2025004248

The publisher of this book does not authorize the use or reproduction of any part of this book in any manner for the purpose of training artificial intelligence technologies or systems. The publisher of this book expressly reserves this book from the Text and Data Mining exception in accordance with Article 4(3) of the European Union Digital Single Market Directive 2019/790.

Our books may be purchased in bulk for specialty retail/wholesale, literacy, corporate/premium, educational, and subscription box use. Please contact MacmillanSpecialMarkets@macmillan.com.

First Edition: 2025

10   9   8   7   6   5   4   3   2   1

For my mother and my teachers

When the music's over
Turn out the lights
Turn out the lights
Turn out the lights
　　—THE DOORS,
　　　"WHEN THE MUSIC'S OVER"

FLASHOUT

1972, NEW YORK CITY

The subway car gobbled the track, lurching, shrieking. I would not stumble. I would not fall. My mother, her voice high and tinny in the dorm receiver, had made me promise that I would never ride the subway at night, never set a single loafered foot into Times Square without a proper escort. Nice girls didn't do such things. But I wasn't nice. I was greedy, keen. And if my mother knew how much a taxi cost, she would have dropped the kitchen handset and fainted right there. So I wrapped my fingers around the silvered pole, warmed already by other hands. I stood tall.

The tickets themselves were criminal. Ten dollars each, more than a balcony seat at a Broadway show. But that year, I had a part-time job in the campus mail room and a part-time habit of holding the thinner envelopes up to the light and scanning them for cash, which could be extracted from a corner of the flap with a sewing needle. I didn't take the cash often. Just often enough. Last week, I had palmed a twenty.

So when Stavros phoned the floor and left a message telling me there was a show I had to see, that this show would change my life, I had the money for a ticket. Two. Because while it killed me to agree with my mother about anything, I knew I shouldn't brave Times Square alone. Two tickets, then. One for me. One for Rachel.

The car bucked again. Its windows were scarred with paint, the tunnel was black beyond them. Then the black fell away to gold. Our stop approached. My eyes found Rachel, her hand clutching a strap, her head half buried in the day's paper, glasses slaloming down her nose. A thick man in a tan coat let the train pitch him closer to her, until his zipper was flush with her back. I saw Rachel stiffen, freeze.

The doors opened. I lunged for her, stamping hard on the man's instep, careless of the consequence. Then we were away, laughing, screaming, the newspaper lost and fluttering behind, out onto the platform and up the stairs into the cool spring dark, past the peep shows and the hamburger stands and the marquee bulbs that flashed in time with our feet. Blocks away, breathless, we leaned against the window of a pharmacy. Rachel wiped the steam from her glasses as I fixed my skirt, and I remember wondering, Did I want my life to change?

Well, hadn't I flown across the country—away from shimmering light and wavering palms and air that smelled like oranges and suntan oil? Hadn't I indentured myself to the older girls, the dark stars of the art department? Hadn't I come to Times Square? Times Square at night! I was young then and so hungry for experience that some days I could taste it like blood in the back of my throat. This is what I will admit: I wanted it. All of it. I did this to myself.

Stavros met us at the corner of Forty-Second and Tenth Avenue, as he had said he would, his limbs like sticks against the darkened sky, his curls a forest. "Hello to you, Allison," he said. He swept his arms out wide, like he could hold the whole city. "And to your friend. Welcome to this night."

"Thank you," I said. "This is my roommate, Rachel Stein. Rachel, this is Stavros Makris." On that filthy street corner, I made the introduction politely, just as I'd been taught at Saturday cotillion.

"Pleased to meet you," Rachel said. She didn't sound pleased. Stavros stuck out his hand, but she kept hers in the pockets of her tweed overcoat, so he had to pull his back unshaken.

"Well, yes, here we are," he said.

But where were we? And what were we to see? Stavros, when I'd reached him at his own dorm, had prescribed only the corner and the time and how much money to bring. When I had asked him about making curfew, he had laughed. "Oh, Allison," he'd said. "You are so funny." And I'd had to pretend I'd been joking.

"So, yes, you will come," he said. He turned and led us farther down the block to the doorway of a low-rise brick building where a cluster of people had gathered. Some of them wore hooded cloaks that cast their faces into shadow. Past the door, I handed my money to an elegant man, all in white. He reached beneath a folding table and brought out two more cloaks, undyed burlap, and gestured me back outside. I wanted to ask him for a program, but I did not want to seem unknowing. Instead I pulled on one cloak and handed the other to Rachel, who was waiting near the curb.

Rachel shrugged on the cloak, sighing theatrically, then put two cigarettes in her mouth and lit them both, glamorous with it or trying to be, passing one to me. I inhaled, working not to cough. I didn't like to smoke—not then, not really—but only a baby would decline. After the judder of the subway and those hectic sprinted blocks, this waiting felt unbearable. The burlap itched my wrists. I wanted to be inside, in my seat, facing whatever Stavros thought was so extraordinary. Because this time, maybe it would be extraordinary. Maybe it would change my life. Begin, I thought. Change me. Form me. Teach me what I am.

Then suddenly, right there on the street, it started. A chime sounded, and a woman with wild hair, her cloak finer than mine, shot through with metal threads, pushed through the crowd and bent toward the gutter. There was water there, reflecting back the streetlights in murky rainbows. I stepped forward, past Rachel, and watched as the woman straightened up, a wicker basket in her arms. From the basket, a baby wailed. No, not a baby. A forgery of a baby. A cassette player, wrapped in blankets, shrieking like a newborn.

The woman walked on. I followed with the crowd, pushing to stay in front. The basket disappeared. A boy walked beside the woman, then a man, tall, Black, with a dancer's gait. Another man appeared. The first man pushed that second man down, then ran. I ran, too, for blocks it seemed, until my sides hurt and there was iron in my mouth and we were back at the building. Was that all? No. Fingers pointed up. And there, on the third floor, in a lit window, a different woman, naked, beautiful, with brown hair that fell nearly to her waist, washed and dressed herself. I watched her, my breath coming short, glad now of the hood. Then we were running to a parking lot, where a fire burned inside a trash barrel. It was cold that night, and the fire warmed me, pinking my face, beading my forehead with sweat.

A voice boomed out. From somewhere. From everywhere. "I am that I am," the voice said. "I am that I am. I am that I am." Music blared—guitars like a wave, a bass that thudded in my chest like a second heartbeat. The crowd danced around the fire. I danced, too—my loafers kicking against the blacktop. Shrouded in the hood, unknown, I let the rhythm take me. I could not have said where the world ended and the show began, or where the show ended and I began. I would not have wanted to.

A man approached me. A man from the show, cloaked in a mourning dove's gray, the hood shadowing his eyes. "And who are you?" he said. He said it into my ear so that I could hear him over the music. His mustache tickled, and I felt it in my stomach.

"No one," I said. I might have yelled it. "I'm not a part of this."

"Oh, I think you are," he said. Then he was gone, whirled away by the dance.

Rachel was there, grabbing for my arm. "Fuck is going on here?" she rasped. The words fell out clumsily, the way they always did when Rachel swore, when she tried to swell herself into someone tougher, more worldly. "Is this about the war?"

"It's the Bible," I said. I'd worked out that much. "The Old Testament. Don't you know it?" I'd never before felt grateful for those listless hours spent at Sunday school. I felt it now.

"Nope," Rachel said. "Never." Which I should have known. I'd spent the recent spring break in Westchester with Rachel's family, and despite my mother's fretting over my immortal soul, they had never gone near a temple.

"Guess you should have," I said, wresting my arm back, running for the fire, running for the dance.

When the music ended, we were handed paper masks—mine was green, a frog's face—and brought together around a car, a Buick, like the one my father drove, but older, dented. A man, the man who had whispered to me, knelt on the roof, shirtless now, in a funny sort of crown. The crowd jeered at him. Some people threw things. A beer can, a cigarette pack.

A change was wrought, in me, in everyone. I felt it as I leaped, as I shouted myself hoarse. The man was right. I was a participant now; we all were. I saw the show with a kind of double vision. There were the base elements—the car, the masks, the dirty street—and then there was the wonder those elements had made. And I was among it—fevered, free, outside my body and still somehow deep within it, a sensation I had only ever felt at home, as a child, in church on hot mornings when the censer swung and the candles smoked and the choir chanted and the air went heavy and strange.

Someone poured blood—or colored syrup, more likely—on the man atop the car. A doll was thrown to the ground. The killing of the first-born. The man vanished. Red fabric unfurled all around us, but a path was forged, and the crowd, led by that first man, that Black man, took the path, and then we were out of the lot and on the sidewalk again, whooping, hollering, forcing passersby into the street.

I ran on. Back to the brick building and up the stairs now, to a great, shadowed room where a party had begun, the music so loud I felt it shake the floor. Furniture was pushed aside. A curtain made of block-printed sheets stood partly open, revealing mattresses beyond. Bare bulbs, strung on thick wires, made hazy circles of light. There was a bin for the cloaks. I left mine there. Then a flyer was thrust into my hand, with the title of the show, *The Exodus Project*, and a list of names below. I folded it, cleanly, and put it in the pocket of my coat.

I knew that I did not look like I belonged here, in my plaid skirt and loafers. And even in the dim glow, the squalor of the place took me aback, made me want to pull on my mother's pink dishwashing gloves and set to work. But I was alive here; I could feel every hair as it brushed against my face, each bit of cloth that covered my skin. That skin was febrile, burning. Slipping farther into the room, I looked for Rachel, for Stavros, a familiar face that might return me to myself. I saw Rachel by the makeshift kitchen and stepped toward her, but no, it was a different woman, that first woman, the light from a bulb turning her neck and shoulders gold. Her arm was around the waist of the woman I'd seen naked in the window, and they were dancing together—sultry, slow, out of time with the music, right there where everyone could see. I wanted to be that woman. Either woman. I turned away, snatching a bottle of wine from a low table so that I would have something to do with my hands.

"Any left for me?" a man asked. I recognized him. The man from the car. The Pharaoh, he must have been. He seemed shorter now, denuded, even though he wore more clothes—a white shirt unbuttoned past the breastbone, corduroy pants that flared at the ankle. But there was a strength to him, I thought that night, a sturdiness, as though whatever had gone into his making had more substance than ordinary flesh and bone. His hair was wet, combed back from his forehead. He must have showered the blood away. For a moment, I imagined myself in that shower with him. I blushed, like neon inside my skin. And he saw it. That startled me. I was good at hiding then.

I pushed the bottle at him and looked down, away. What a baby I must have seemed. What a schoolgirl.

Then there was a hand on my face—his hand—tilting my chin up to meet his eyes, which seemed so welcoming, so kind. "Nothing to be scared of," he said. His lips kinked into a smile, rustling the mustache, which curled as it dried. The yellow, I saw, was shot through with gray. I'd thought he was in his twenties. Forty was more like it. He might have been my father.

"What's your name?" he asked, letting my face go.

"Allison," I said. "Allison Hayes."

"Alice," he said. In all that time I knew him, I never asked if he misheard me over the music or changed my name deliberately. This was what gods did. And men. They named things. Renamed them. He called me Alice. And I answered.

"What did you make of the show, Alice?" he asked.

I didn't have words then—I barely have words now—for what it had made me feel, fused with the crowd, one with the night. I would learn that the company considered the show, stitched together hastily during a residency in Mexico, a residency they had been made to leave, a miscarriage, a failure. But it had loosed something in me. I took back the bottle, enjoying the shock of his fingers against mine, and drank from it, not even wiping the lip first. It ran down my throat, bitter, sharp.

"It was Exodus, right?" I said. "But you ended it early. You didn't do the mountaintop, the commandments."

He stepped toward me. It would have taken a knife—a small one, sharp—to cleave the space between us. "No commandments," he said. "No laws. We don't believe in them. But you were into it, right? It was good, right?" I could hear the need in his voice. What I thought of the show, it mattered to this man.

"Yes," I said. And I meant it. "So good. Like nothing else."

Rachel came for me then. I had forgotten her. "We have to goooo," she said, stretching that final word into a whine. "We'll barely make curfew as it is."

I hated her for reminding him how young I was, how in thrall to rule and order. But he liked us young, I would learn. He liked us blushing. I gave the bottle back. "I have to leave," I said.

"Okay, Alice," he said. "That's cool. But come back, all right? We do open rehearsals here on Wednesdays. It's how we make the work. The work, it's the gift. It's like nothing else."

I thought he might kiss me then. The men I knew, the boys, they didn't bother talking to you if they didn't want something—a kiss, a feel. Instead he took his thumb and pressed it, hard against my lips, tracing their outline. Then he pressed that same thumb to my forehead, like a priest would on Ash Wednesday. I felt that he had marked me, that I would stay marked. This, at least, was true.

"Go on," he told me. "Back up the rabbit hole."

I didn't move. I didn't want to.

"Allison," Rachel urged, pushing her glasses back up her nose.

Then we were down the stairs and hurrying east, as quickly as we had come. It was colder now. These first blocks were far from the flashing lights, and sometimes you couldn't even see a man until the cherry of his cigarette cast him into silhouette. I wondered what those men thought of us, of what we were running from.

The train wouldn't come and wouldn't come, and then finally it did. But it went so slowly, halting at every local stop. It would never return us in time. I could feel a headache coming, a stabbing pain behind my eyes, and a sense of loss that made me want to weep. I'd had a chance at some other life, and I hadn't grasped it. I'd been too frightened, too beholden to the college's rules. I slunk down into the seat, hating my cowardice, hating also the greedy, heedless part of me that wanted and wanted and wanted.

"Well, I didn't get that at all," Rachel said as we transferred to a second train. She was shaking her head. The mist had frizzed her curls. She was talking fast, as though she'd drunk an entire urn of coffee. "I mean, thank you for the ticket and everything, but God, ridiculous. And so loud, right? Anyway, I still think it was about the war. I'm sure of it. All that red at the end." I had always liked her chatter—brash, cynical, outspoken where I was quiet. But that night, I would have pushed her onto the tracks just to shut her mouth.

"I'm sure you're right," I said. It was easier with Rachel to let her win, to let her think she'd won. I shut my eyes and canted my head back, feigning sleep.

The campus was in darkness when we came up the walk, the street-lights spilling onto the lawn in dim pools. We had missed curfew by half an hour. But the lounge's leftmost window had a broken catch, so I led us there and pushed it open, tensing as it squeaked. Rachel went first, my hand on the seat of her blue jeans, boosting her up. I heaved myself in after, slopping onto the window seat. Rachel giggled, shrilly, a hand over her mouth.

"Sorry," she said, between fingers.

She laughed when she was scared. I couldn't fault her. When I was scared, I did worse.

We couldn't risk the elevator, so we tiptoed, shoes in hand, past the night girl, already dozing at her post, into the stairwell and eight floors up, panting by the end. The stairwell door opened noiselessly and, with the scrape of a key, so did the door to our room. We parted then, her to the bathroom to wash her face and me to change into my night things and hang my coat and skirt. I fell into bed, and by some miracle, I slept undreaming.

The next morning, I woke late—I knew it by the light—and kicked the bunk above. Rachel had already gone. Snatching the compact, the gold one, from her desk drawer, I checked my face in its mirror. Eyes clear. Forehead smooth. Like the night had never happened.

But it had. The flyer proved it. I took it from my coat. Smoothing out the creases, I read it properly for the first time. At the bottom was a name: Theater Negative. It was a name I knew. A lot of people knew it then. They were famous in their way. Anarchists. Rebels. Athletes of the heart. Dr. Broussard, the professor of a course I'd taken in the fall, had lectured on a few of their adaptations. And in high school, at the gas station where we sometimes snuck away for snack cakes and bottles of Coca-Cola, I had peeked—disgusted, fascinated—beneath crinkling brown paper at the scandalous magazine cover they'd shot, all nude except for flowers.

I'd thought that they were finished somehow. Or off in Europe, on some never-ending tour. But they must have come back. Their shows, I knew, were drawn from legends—creation stories, mostly. *The Exodus Project* was one more. In the classroom, in the abstract, the company hadn't made much of an impression on me. It had seemed too lawless, too sweaty. Back then, despite my occasional nights downtown, I still believed that theater didn't really count unless the seats were numbered and the curtains heavy and velvet. Now I'd seen behind those curtains. It had been like staring at the sun. I folded the flyer and transferred it—solemnly, like an altar boy preparing the gifts—to the top dresser drawer.

After changing into day clothes, I took the grinding elevator to the ground floor. Mrs. Pritchard, the dorm matron with a face like a toma-hawk and a body that jiggled like one of my mother's Jell-O salads, stopped me in the hall. "You didn't sign in last night, my girl," she said.

"Didn't I?" I made my face go innocent, blank, a doll still in its card-board box, though inside I felt white-hot. "I'm sure I meant to. I came in just before curfew with my roommate and a crush of other girls and when the elevator finally came we all ran for it because you know how it takes forever to go up and come back down and I must have just for-gotten. I'm so sorry. Forgive me?"

I could see Mrs. Pritchard studying my face, scanning each pore for signs of a night's debauch, finding none. "Your roommate said the same," Mrs. Pritchard said. "I'll let it go this once, but you see that it doesn't happen any time again. I have eyes on you, my girl."

"Yes," I said, nodding in a steady beat meant to convey seriousness. I was picturing what it would feel like to push her to the ground, to put my foot into that wobbling stomach. "I know you do. It won't happen again. I promise."

I took the shortcut toward the snack bar, light with the feeling of having gotten away with something. In truth, I hadn't gotten away with anything. More than a decade later—in a different state, with a different name, with so many of the company already dead—I would understand what I had missed that first night. In a Santa Ana church, at one more funeral, searching for distraction so that I wouldn't scream or cry or admit I felt nothing at all, I would take a Bible from its seat-back pocket and read the whole of Exodus.

The Exodus Project hadn't included the Ten Commandments. Had omitted them deliberately. I'd known that. The mustached man had said as much aloud. But this is what I would realize: Their absence meant that we had drunk and danced and rejoiced in the service of a false god. Back then, everyone in Theater Negative would have told me that there were no false gods, no true ones, no gods at all. I had learned better since. A person could absolutely worship the wrong god. A person could pay for it with her life.

2

1997, LOS ANGELES

C lass, your attention," she said. She blew a shrill note from the pitch pipe around her neck and stood poised, statue-still, with enough disapproval in her posture to let them know she meant it. Conversations quieted, backpacks were shoved under seats, beepers powered down.

"Yours, too, Kyle," she said, her mouth a thin smile. "The weed dealers of the world can wait until last bell."

"Mrs. Morales," Kyle said, pocketing the device. "I'm, like, very offended."

"Dude," his friend Patrick said, clapping him on the back, "at least there's one girl here who gets you."

"Not a girl, Patrick," she said. "A credentialed professional twice your age. Just for that, you can take us through the warm-up today. And after, we'll continue with our classical scenes. If you're not off book already, make sure you have everything memorized by the end of the week. The language won't open up until you've learned it all by heart. Are we clear?"

She waited for their nods. Then she placed her hands on her hips and nodded back. "Okay. Some of you have been asking me about the winter play. *Asking* is the nice way of phrasing it. Really, you're very annoying. But since you are also my favorite class"—she paused here, taking the temperature of the room, watching the students tip forward in their seats—"well, I can tell you first. I will be staging *A Midsummer Night's Dream*. I know it's out of season"—a slight lift of the eyebrow—"but it's about a group of young people who refuse to do what their parents say and party in the woods all night on psychedelic drugs instead. I'm guessing that at least a few of you can relate to this, summer or no. Isn't that right, Kyle?"

Kyle ran a hand through his sun-streaked hair. The shells at his wrist jangled. He was the son of a prominent B-movie director and could usually be found on the lunch terraces, fooling with a camcorder. "Oh, I wouldn't know anything about any parties, Mrs. Morales. You know me; I live by the three Ss: sun, surf, and—"

"Shakespeare," Patrick finished for him. "You meant Shakespeare, right?" Patrick, a water polo player with a chest like a file cabinet, seemed to have found his way to the drama classroom by accident. But somehow he had stayed. "And not so many woods in the Valley," he said. "Mall parking lots. Maybe."

"And psyche—what now?" Kyle added, hand on heart. "I am shocked at the suggestion."

"Adorable, Kyle," she said. "We'll have auditions next week, with sign-ups posted on the door on Monday. Please memorize a speech from the play of about fifteen lines, and now would be a good time to decide if you see yourself as an Athenian, a fairy, or a rude mechanical. And yes, Naomi, if you're raising your hand to tell us that in this case *rude* only means 'unfancy,' you are quite correct."

The girl, Naomi, put her hand down, hid behind the curtain of her hair. Naomi was a goody-goody. A kiss-up. She knew that type. She had been that type.

Another small smile. "Any further questions?"

There were none. Although she could have answered them, even in her fitful sleep. This would be her second time staging *Midsummer* since she had come to Greenglade. She knew it line for line. Institutional memory was short here, departmental oversight lax. Theater was an afterthought, something to placate the industry parents. This meant that she could repeat the same plays every five years or so—a limited repertory of *Our Town, Grease, Once Upon a Mattress, As You Like It, The Crucible,* and so on. A classic in December, a musical in March, sometimes a contemporary play in June, if a student director had ambitions. The students, who cycled through the upper school every three years, didn't notice. The other teachers, who blazed their own shortcuts, weren't paid enough to care. The parents never complained. A few with multiple children at the school even seemed to enjoy it.

"That girl was perfectly fine," a mother would say. "But not nearly so good as Margo." Or Andrew. Or Chrissy. Or Jack. And she would smile back, a finger to her lips, a confidence shared, even though she couldn't remember what Jack had looked like or if he could act his way out of a basketball uniform.

Early on, she had made more daring choices—*Godspell*, *The Misanthrope*. She had even once staged a deeply expurgated version of *Hair*. She would not make that mistake again. No communion for her, no ecstasy, no aspiration to a whole greater than the sum of its shuffling, mumbling parts. The students could have *You Can't Take It with You* or, God help her, *Twelve Angry Jurors*, and they could like it.

"Okay, then. Circle up."

Some grudging, some eager, they moved to the center of the floor and circled. "Close your eyes lightly and breathe in through your nose," she said. "Good. Hold it. And then out your mouth." She wondered for a moment what it would be like to lead them through the old warmups, the chanting, the mirroring, those strange and sinuous dances. But she would never dare it. "And again," she said. "Let me really hear that exhale. Patrick, the floor is yours."

As he took them through twists and toe-touches, her gaze wandered out the back windows. Even in early October, the sun, high and unforgiving, goaded the temperature toward eighty. Here, at the edge of the campus, sere grass and low, starved shrubs clutched the lip of the canyon. The lawns, of course, stayed emerald all year, tended by sprinklers that misted them at dawn and dusk. So much water, feeding grass that never should have grown here, while the chaparral curled and browned. Sunlight like this should have seized on every blemish, should have made the people and the place less secret, more real. But nothing in Los Angeles was entirely real. It was an easy place to hide, once you knew how.

Then eyes were on her. She could feel them. The warm-up had ended. She turned back to the circle and let her lips broaden into something like a smile. "All right," she said. "Paired stretching. Partner up with whomever you think is the cutest."

At the last bell, the campus emptied, abruptly, as though a clogged drain had suddenly worked loose. A scramble for the buses, a slip-knot of cars at the gates. Then only birdsong, far-off traffic, the purr of the HVAC system that stilled the air at sixty-eight degrees perpetually. At the classroom's terminal, she input the day's attendance in a few clumsy keystrokes. Then she collected her bag, locked the door, and climbed toward the main hall for the weekly faculty meeting.

The blinds were lowered there, the fluorescent lights buzzing. She waved at Linda Darling, the senior biology teacher with hair like clouds before a storm, and took the seat that Linda had saved for her, at the row's end. The announcements came—SATs, PSATs, a reminder to flag any student who seemed to be struggling. The girls' volleyball team was to be congratulated.

The headmaster, Dr. Daley, leaned over the lectern. His skin had reddened, as it always did when he spoke in front of a crowd. "And now," he said, "for some even more exciting news. As you know, Greenglade joined the World Wide Web at the start of the year, and I'm told by our technology teacher—thank you, Mr. Ko—that we're seeing a steady increase in traffic, with more admissions inquiries coming in through the online portal. Which is fantastic news. In the coming years, parents will be looking for schools that can equip their children to succeed in this changing world. And our website shows that they need look no further.

"But we must keep moving forward. So in addition to our website and the attendance and gradebook features—thank you again, for your adaptability, old habits die hard in secondary education, I know— we are adding a new component: electronic mail. Each of you will have a specific address, that's your first initial and your last name and an @ symbol and then greenglade.edu. So, for instance, you would write to me at ddaley@greenglade.edu. You can use it to send messages to each other and to me. Parents will also be able to communicate with you in this way. From now on, that's how we'll announce any global schedule changes and so on, so please check your mailbox each day. Your electronic mailbox, I mean. Though yes, thank you, Ms. Noakes, you should still keep checking your box in the lounge. Anyway, I'm told it's completely secure, and the best part is, we'll save some trees, just like my daughters are always telling me to do. Stop by the lounge on your way out and you'll find a packet with everything you need to get started. We expect you to be up and running by the end of next week. Any problems and you can call Mr. Ko, and he'll be happy to sort them out for you."

She looked over at Mr. Ko, his arms folded, his lips slivered.

"Okay, that's it. See you all on Monday. Don't do anything I wouldn't do!"

"If I ever do anything that man might attempt, may God strike me down," murmured Linda. And then, in a louder voice, "We're cooking out on Sunday. Come by?"

"Thanks," she said. "Maybe. But I have to prep auditions." She liked Linda, as much as she liked anyone. Liked her partner, Darlene, too. She was careful to socialize just enough so as not to seem unfriendly, but not so much that any intimacy was expected. The best way to lie, she had found, was not to say anything in the first place.

She stood to leave, but like some shabby conjurer's trick, Dr. Daley was suddenly at her side. "Mrs. Morales, a word, please?" He turned cleanly on his heel—his bluff, sturdy body had an unexpected grace—and she followed, down the hall, her shoes clacking on the terra-cotta tiles, past the outer office and through to his inner one, its blinds also drawn.

She made her face smooth. But underneath, she felt that sick excitement that never left for long. Had she been caught? Found? Finally?

"Am I in trouble?" she said, voice unwavering.

"Always," he said.

He sat in the rolling chair behind the heavy desk and gestured for her to join him. She set her bag down and sat astride him. One hand sought her breasts through her blouse. The other rummaged under her linen skirt and then, with some adjustment on her part, into her panties.

"Wet for me?" he said into her chest. She was. Fear aroused her, some strange sensory confusion.

"Not for you," she said. "Just wet."

"Take off your glasses."

"I like to see what I'm doing, Dan."

He was young for his job, but not that young anymore, and from her vantage on his lap, she could see the red of his scalp through thinning blond hair, the dwindling of his bland handsomeness. She had never desired him exactly, but she enjoyed how power flowed between them. His wanting. Her capacity to meet that want. His influence over her job. Her knowledge of the kind of man he truly was. It was better than attraction.

He unzipped his pants, huffing his breath, and she straddled him fully, pulling her panties aside until he was inside her. He lifted up her blouse and pushed down her bra, taking one nipple into his mouth and then, after a considered interval, the other, because he was the kind of man who would have told himself that he was nothing if not fair. She arced her back and moved as he moved, like a horseback rider posting to the trot, trying not to notice the flab of his belly, the sweat. He came quickly, eyes slitted, teeth clenched, and seemed to deflate almost instantly, shrinking back into the chair, his penis sliding marshily onto a thigh. She had come for him, once, that first time—in the cramped back of her Celica that shuddered as they moved—so that he would know she could. And never again.

He gestured, as he usually did, to the box of tissues on his desk, and she tidied herself as he zipped his pants. The rods implanted beneath the skin of her arm, flooding her blood with synthetic hormones, would prevent any further consequence. She wouldn't need to replace them; she would be too old for that. She threw the tissue in the trash.

She had asked him once, in their early days, if the janitorial staff might notice the tissues, their stickiness, the bleach-like scent. "The janitors don't even speak English," he had said. Which made the whole affair easier. She would not have to complicate it with any liking for him.

"There really is something we should talk about," he said as she smoothed the wrinkles from her skirt. "It's out of my control and miles out of yours. But something's gone wrong with the endowment, with the way it was invested. Something to do with the Asian markets. Maybe you saw it on the news?"

She shook her head. "You don't pay me enough to invest, Dan. I don't watch the finance stories."

"Apparently, we've recovered some value, but not enough. Unless something changes, something big, we're looking at a very different budget for next year. Lotta belt-tightening."

"I'm guessing most of those notches concern the art departments?"

"I'm afraid they do."

"What does this mean for me?" She was standing straight now, her spine traded for a ship's mast.

"Nothing," he said, wheeling his chair closer to the desk, looking down at some papers. "For now. But if things don't improve, we may have to pause the theater program for a year or two. We can still use you in English, of course. Though maybe only part-time."

"I can't do part-time, Dan," she said. Her voice had gone lower, harder. "I have expenses. My mother's care. I took this job mostly for the benefits, and I don't get them at part-time."

"It won't come to that," he said. "We'll get a donation or the accountants will figure it out or maybe we can talk one of the older teachers into retiring. But I had to tell you. In case you want to start looking around for something else. Marta Jensen, George Thibodeaux, I'll tell them next week. I'd be sorry to lose you, all of you. But I would understand."

"Would you, Dan?" She felt herself rousing again, a heat in her belly, a tightening of her skin. She leaned over, putting her hand against his zipper. But he shook his head and lifted that hand away. She felt the shame of that rebuff.

"You know me," he said. "I'd do anything to keep you here. But I can't be seen to play favorites. People will talk. I'm lucky they don't talk already." He looked up at her now. "If I were smart, I would have ended this years ago."

"But you're not that smart," she said.

"The thing with you is I never know when you're joking."

"Oh, I'm always joking," she said.

"Well, I'm sorry," he said. "Really. If I could do anything, I would. I mean, I will."

"So what does this mean for now? Is the winter classic still on? And what about a technical director?" The last one, Robby, had left in June. Gone to Ojai to farm oranges on some commune. Even a commune probably paid better. "The kids can't hang the lights themselves. Not on our insurance policy. Can we still afford a new TD?"

"Yes, yes," he said dismissively. "The play's fine, and the ad's up. Should have someone for you soon." He murmured something about needing to get home, then repeated that same unfunny line: "Don't do anything I wouldn't do, okay?"

"I will, though," she said as she took up her bag. She pulled out a pale lipstick and felt him watching as she ran it slowly over her lips, the bottom, then the bow of the top. She snapped its cap back on. "I'll do everything."

She left his office and circled back toward the faculty lounge, keeping her steps even, her face empty. She was used to this, projecting calm when underneath all she wanted was to scream, to hit out. She'd learned it first in her father's house and then again, years later, when any protest would have been seen as selfish, individualistic. Besides, Dan was most likely right—the markets would correct themselves or some parent with deep pockets would be persuaded to reach inside. Probably he had only told her because he wanted her scared, wanted her beholden to him for her rescue. Next week, she would confer with Marta, who oversaw studio art, and George, who directed the music program. They would work this out together.

From her mail slot, she took the stapled sheets of pink paper—the instructions on how to set up electronic mail—and a disc in a cardboard case. Something else remained, a single sheet of paper, folded and folded again. She uncreased it. Most of the page was taken up with a black-and-white picture, which looked as though it had been put through a copier a few times. It showed a girl with dark lips and light hair, in a see-through shift that barely covered her, trapped like an insect in amber beneath a spotlight. Underneath that, in block capitals, were the words, IS THIS YOU?

"Rosa," she whispered, although only the dust and the sour coffee, cooling in its carafe, were there to hear her. She imagined Rosa's hand, fingers pruned and river-wet, pushing that paper into the slot. "Rosa, are you here? Did you find me?"

She would not think of Rosa. She would not think of anything. Abruptly, she shoved the paper down into her bag, then forced herself out of the lounge and into her car, swerving out of the parking lot, then onto the freeway and off again, windows down, babble on the radio, driving fast enough that her mind emptied. Streets blurred past. The light deepened, muting into a yellowed gray, slashed with orange, and she had to pull over for a moment, lowering the visor and scrabbling in the glove compartment for her sunglasses. That pause returned a memory to her, another night, another race, through narrow streets, in wooden shoes that slid and slapped against the wet stone, blood on her skirt, blood on her hands, and it made her feel something like gratitude for this ugly, rusting car, because a car meant that you could run so much faster.

When the tank ran low, she headed for a gas station, but stopped instead at Lucy's for two green chile tacos and a Coke that was mostly ice, which she swallowed in the front seat, ravenous now, licking the sauce from her fingers, the sugar and the peppers the only things she tasted. And then she was driving again, gas forgotten, toward the bar on Santa Monica, though she had told herself she wouldn't come here again so soon.

Parking a few blocks away, in a space that wasn't entirely legal, she applied new lipstick, burgundy this time, like cherries underfoot, and walked toward the entrance. She glanced to either side, watchful, alert. There was nothing wrong with wanting women. She knew couples, like Linda and Darlene, who were more or less married and didn't care what anyone thought about it. But having lived with secrets so long, she couldn't bring herself to tell them now. It was better that Dan didn't know. That no one at school knew. They couldn't fire her for a thing like that. Not anymore. There were protections. But they could make it hard for her. Unless your intimate arrangements looked like a commercial for salad dressing or detergent, private lives were meant to stay private.

It was dark inside. She removed her sunglasses and made her way to the bar. The bartender poured her a glass of wine that could have stripped the polish from her nails. She drank it down. A woman with short hair and a flannel shirt bought her another, and she drank that, too. Then she was on the checkerboard dance floor, the music moving through her. A girl circled her, hips tucked into squeaky leather pants. The girl, a round-faced brunette, was pretty but barely formed. She looked young—the lady at the door must have flicked her flashlight back and forth across her license—and lit up by the kind of nerve that only the young have.

They danced for three songs, maybe four, then they were outside on the patio, grinding against the trunk of a desiccated palm. She was loose from the wine, sloppy with it. What her lipstick must look like.

The girl paused for breath and asked her to come home, trying to be aloof with it, failing.

"Do you have roommates?" she asked. "I'm too old for roommates."

"No roommates," the girl said. "Just an asshole cat."

"Fine, then."

"My name's Shereen," the girl said. "Means 'sweet.'"

"I'll follow you. I just have to get gas first."

The girl had a motorcycle. Which went a long way to explaining the pants. She trailed the bike first to a Shell station and then over to the 101 and away again, arriving at a dingbat in brown stucco. She parked beneath the overhang, and they went up the stairs and into the apartment. Shereen darted a hand toward the switch.

"No," she said. "No lights."

They tumbled together onto the couch, in the dark. The girl's skin, lit by a wide window, was smooth and ghostly, like pooled moonlight. Time hadn't marked her yet, hadn't scraped at her luster until it flaked and fell away. So she dealt with her gently, using her fingers and then her tongue until the girl cried out. Then she put Shereen's hand between her legs and held it there, showing her what to do, until she felt herself rising, falling, once and then again, tipped over a cliff's edge into something like peace. The girl fell asleep—they had moved into the bedroom by then—and she left without waking her, stopping only to pee and to pocket a small succulent, an aloe, from a collection on the bathroom windowsill. She never saw the cat. In the light from the open car door, she squinted at the Thomas Guide, then shut it, driving toward Encino, the plant nestled on the passenger side, spilling grains of soil with every turn, dirtying a seat that had never been clean as long as she'd had the car, that would never come clean again.

3

1972, NEW YORK CITY

The college had no theater major, just a vague collection of courses referred to as the concentration in the arts. And even if they had, my father would never have allowed me to declare it. So on the necessary papers, I was an English major, supposedly intended for law school, a career path that my father, who occasionally dealt with lawyers in the conduct of his novelties business, could understand. But theater was what I loved. I had been a liar, always, and onstage lies were beautiful, necessary. They told a kind of truth.

My parents would only entertain a women's college. ("I just feel that you'll be safer there," my mother had said, stitching a hem that had come loose in the back of some boy's car when I was meant to be in the library.) And while they might have preferred Scripps or Mount St. Mary's, I had chosen this one, thousands of miles away, because of its proximity to Broadway—thirty-six theaters, cinching the city at its midline like a spangled belt. A belt can be too tight, of course. A belt can strangle.

I saw so much my first year. Sometimes the student center had tickets at a discount. At other times, at matinees, I would plant myself outside of the theater, making my eyes wide, hoping that someone would offer me an extra seat. Sometimes someone did, though after a performance of *Hay Fever*, during which I spent the whole second act frozen as a hand crept up and up my leg, I took tickets only from women. From the older theater girls, I learned about standing room and second acting. But there were some plays I had to see all the way through, like *Home*, with John Gielgud and Ralph Richardson, too, even if it meant paying full price for a balcony seat. I saved that ticket stub and mailed it to my mother.

This was what I thought I'd longed for: Broadway theaters with their red curtains and plush seats. But there, among the well-dressed people—the ladies with furs, the men with shoes that glimmered in the lobby lights—I never felt at ease. The whole of it seemed false, fake, void. The worst of it was *Oh! Calcutta!* I saw it that first spring, at a Sunday matinee, bringing Rachel, whom I knew then only as the frizzy-haired history major in the adjoining quad. How daring we felt as we took our seats, how adult. But the show made me flush and cringe and wish like anything that the actors would put their clothes back on. Later, on the long tramp back to campus in the failing sun, Rachel and I had walked in silence, too sunk in embarrassment to even joke about it.

Hair was better, of course. I knew its songs by heart, and each note sounded richer live at the Biltmore. But were those notes too rich? I felt that I had missed something—some truth, some danger. I should have seen it in '67, maybe, before the wildness had gone out of it. I did not know if the problem was me or Broadway or if everything was the problem and I should make a sign, like the girls in black, who would stand on the campus lawn and protest just about anything. Inequality. Discrimination. But also in favor of bagels. They had won the bagel protest. The snack bar carried them now. What those girls were really protesting was their own helplessness, their own bad timing. They had missed the upsets of '68. The signs let them pretend they hadn't.

I liked a bagel. I had one for breakfast sometimes when I allowed myself anything more than coffee and an apple. But I would never join those girls on the lawn. They were too conspicuous. A black turtleneck and a sign marked you out, put people on their guard against you. What those girls should have understood was that cotton blouses and plaid skirts were better camouflage. A person could hide a lot under a skirt, especially a pleated one.

In the fall of my second year—after a grim, aimless summer, assisting in my father's stockroom and borrowing the car at night to drive the twenty minutes to the beach and sit, safe behind locked doors, drinking a strawberry milkshake and feeling sorry for myself—the older theater girls deigned to bring me along on some of their outings. They took me to shows in coffeehouses, in churches, in a cement-floored room that had recently been a body shop and might one day become a body shop again.

Once, an actor wearing only a G-string nearly sat in my lap. Once, a woman sang—sweetly, wrenchingly—for an hour and then took off her wig, because she wasn't a woman at all. One night, at La Mama, a pianist walked offstage in apparent disgust. A long pause followed—terrible and ugly. Then someone from the audience, a skinny Black boy, took a seat at the piano stool, studied the sheet music, and the show began again. On nights like these, I felt close to something fine, something real. But then the girls would hustle me away, onto the bus or into a taxi, and home in time for curfew.

Still, none of those shows affected me the way that *The Exodus Project* had, none of them made me feel a part of something greater than myself. What remained of it now? Just a creased flyer and a memory of a thumb against my lip. I wanted more. I longed to tell someone of what I'd seen. Someone who might understand. I was like a girl in love, desperate for any mention of her beloved.

On Monday, I crept down a narrow hallway to the office of Dr. Broussard, who had taught Theater: Then and Now last term. She was the most elegant woman I had ever seen—I think this is true even now—with long, center-parted hair and a wardrobe of jewel-colored dresses. Her glasses, on a resin chain, dangled at her breast.

I sat opposite her in a hard-backed chair, and told her about the show.

"They're back?" she said. "Really?" She brought the glasses to her nose and studied me more closely. Her voice was low, like wind through sycamore. "I thought they couldn't come back. There were charges, last I heard, warrants outstanding. Perhaps that's all settled now. To the work, what you describe, it sounds imitative, honestly, cannibalized from the early experiments, from the time before they had a theater. So it makes sense in a way. But it's disappointing."

I felt small then and angry. "I wasn't disappointed," I said, brave with it. I didn't often disagree with teachers.

"No," she said. She smiled with something like pity. "Of course you weren't. I only wish their work had progressed, that they'd transcended cheap spectacle. But to someone encountering them for the first time, it must have been exciting. Was there much nudity?"

"No," I said, lightly scandalized. "A few men with their shirts off. Is there usually?"

"Oh God, yes. Once at the Academy of Music, a colleague of mine, a professor at Hunter, he stripped and ran onstage and joined them. They have that effect on some people." She tilted her head. "Did they have that effect on you?"

I could feel the blood rushing to my face, which was an answer of its own. I took a breath, clasped my hands primly in my lap. "I think I might want to write about them. For a class I'm taking." I hoped that she would not ask which class. "Can you tell me more about them, please? I remember your lecture, but I'm interested in their process, how they make their shows."

I was hungry and Dr. Broussard fed me, telling me how Theater Negative had begun as a literary theater devoted to the European avant-garde, then veered into a more experimental mode. They were communitarian, she said, and worked without hierarchy, developing story and script together. Everyone wrote. Everyone directed. Everyone designed and performed. Sometimes there were puppets. Sometimes there were pageants in the streets. Instead of blackouts, they favored flashouts, turning the lights on full and dazzling. They had toured Europe several times and were regulars at Avignon. In the late 1960s, they had spent time in Mexico. There had been several arrests, stretches in jail.

"For what?" I asked.

"Oh, well, let's see. In Mexico, I want to say it was corruption of some kind. Or obstruction, maybe. Indecency. Public nuisance. God knows. Years ago, they had some problems with the city. With permits. That's how the theater downtown went."

"Was it?" I said. My palms were damp. I dried them against the wool of my skirt.

Dr. Broussard sat back in her chair. Her neck was long, a swan's. "I can guess what the show might have meant to you," she said. "I felt the same a dozen years ago when I saw *Blood Moon and Jaguar Night*. The possibilities. The expansion of what theater can be. Is your interest truly academic, Allison? Or is it personal?"

"Academic," I lied. "Honestly." My mother had once told me, in a rare flash of anger, that I lied as easily as I breathed. But it did not feel easy now.

Dr. Broussard let the glasses dangle again. "I'd leave them alone, if I were you," she said. "They're fascinating. There's no denying it. Or they were some years ago, before they went to Mexico. Back then, they swore that they'd never return. America was no longer the land of the free, they said. Well, neither was Puebla, I suppose. But listen to me: They don't live like other people. They don't work like other people. I've known actors who joined Theater Negative, more than a few. Some of them—the younger ones—it did something to them, used them up somehow. And not only the younger ones. That man from the Academy, he isn't a professor anymore. He's . . . well, it doesn't matter now. I understand your curiosity, I do, but if it's anything more, I would urge you to give it up. You're what? Eighteen?"

"Nineteen?"

"That's too young."

"Yes, that's good advice," I said. I did not take it. I did not see myself as young. Ducking my father's rage, despising my mother's submission, I had grown up fast and sure. One more visit to the loft would not shake that. I would dare it. Alone this time.

On Wednesday, I chose my outfit carefully, brushed my hair until it shone, and bullied Rachel into agreeing to fake my signature on the sign-in sheet if I didn't make it back in time. She had tried to talk me out of going. She never liked it when I did anything without her. I ignored her. I ate dinner—or rather I didn't eat it, just pushed what might have once been steak around the plate—then jogged all the way to the subway entrance. But at the turnstile, some internal resolve collapsed, leaving me mortified and sick. I hauled myself back up the stairs. Rachel was waiting at the gates. She must have known I wouldn't go through with it.

"Changed your mind, huh?" she said. "Not gonna spend the evening with the crazies?" She was smiling. I imagined backhanding that smile, how the blood would look against her braces-straightened teeth.

"I forgot I had a paper due," I said lightly. "Can you believe it? Eight pages, too. And I haven't even started."

"Oh yeah? See you in the library, then."

I went to the dorm for my satchel, but paused instead at the phone booths, hungry for the voice of someone who loved me. "Allison, what's wrong?" my mother said when she picked up. She knew the rhythm of my calls. Knew this one had come too soon. "Lamb, are you all right?"

"Of course I'm all right," I snapped, irritated at the babyish endearment, irritated that I had phoned at all. "I just wanted to talk to you. Is there a problem with that?"

So we talked. About my classes. About the summer. She had already mailed the airline ticket that would fly me home in early June. She suggested that we could all go away somewhere. To Ensenada, maybe. She hadn't been to Ensenada since her honeymoon. "Oh, wouldn't that be fun?"

I could picture it. The suffocation of the drive. The cheap hotel. My mother pretending gaiety as my father drank. I murmured something she might have taken as agreement. And when she asked if I wanted to speak to my father, I invented an excuse and replaced the receiver. The call hadn't worked. I felt more lonesome than before.

I promised myself—that night, in bed, eyes shut and hands clasped—that I wouldn't lose my nerve again. And on the next Wednesday, as good as my word, I took the train downtown. Outside again, men called to me, leering as I hurried past the porno houses: "Hey, mama." "Hey, baby." But I was nobody's mother. And that night, shuffling down those streets, I was no one's child. At a corner store, I stopped and bought a bottle of Coca-Cola, drinking it as I closed the last blocks. The bottle was a kind of armor, a shield between the world and me. It was also a weapon. I could break it if I had to.

I found the building without trouble and searched for a bell to ring. There were none. But the door opened to my touch. Climbing the stairs, I felt suddenly unprepared. I should have come bearing some token, a box of chocolates, flowers in crinkling cellophane. I had only myself to give. The entrance to the loft stood open. Music was playing. Candles flickered. An affectation? Or evidence that the power company had turned the lights off? Both, I would discover. The heat, dispersed by clanging radiators, was nearly tropical. And there was a musky, herbal smell that I thought at first was incense. A dozen people, mostly bare-foot, had gathered in the room's center, on a sofa and the threadbare carpet beneath it, sitting legs crossed ankle over knee in what I would be taught to call lotus position.

My eyes fixed on the blond man with the mustache, then darted away before he saw me looking. There were other faces I recognized from the show. And Stavros was here, too—I was annoyed at this, as though I had been given a sweet and then been forced to share it—leaning into a black-eyed man. Jorge was his name, I would learn, a living souvenir of the company's residency in Mexico. Everyone else looked older than I was, except for a child, a boy, barely out of diapers, peeking out from behind the flowing skirts of a broad-hipped woman

with red-gold hair. I stepped out of my shoes and placed my May Company coat on an arm of the sofa. The rug was strangely soft. I sank into
it, worried for a moment about the dust.

Then dust was forgotten as the blond man turned his gaze all around
the circle. When it fell on me, like rain on parched ground, I had that
same sensation that he could see into me, see through me. And that he
liked what he saw. We would begin, he said, by chanting together. The
woman in the Indian-print skirt came and joined him. She opened her
mouth wide, like she wanted to swallow the room, and then she pursed
it in a perfect O and released a single syllable, arcing toward the ceiling,
an "Ommmmmmmm," long and low.

Other voices joined hers, and I joined, too. Within a second, less, I
couldn't tell where my voice ended and the others' began. One syllable,
one keening note joined us. I'd never had an interest in Eastern matters,
in yogis or Sufis or the Hare Krishna dancing on the beach. But there in
that shadowed loft, chanting and moaning, I wept, the tears speeding
down my cheeks, because this is what I must have wanted in all those
sleepy mornings at Mass, in all those crowded afternoons on Broadway, to
feel held by something larger than myself. Holy. Whole.

Then the note ended and there were hands on me, stroking my hair,
drying my tears. The red-gold woman, she stood apart, watching me,
but another woman, one I had seen that first night, threw her arms
around me, let my tears wet the bodice of her dress. Her skin was warm
through the cotton.

"I'm sorry," I said, though I wasn't, not at all.

The blond man was at my side. "Hey," he said. "It's cool. It's what
happens when you open yourself up to the universe, all right? In all its
joy and pain. You should cry about it. We should all be crying."

"Okay," I said. "Thanks." I let go of the woman and sat back down.

He turned his body out and away. "Friends, this is Alice," he said.
He remembered me, however wrongly, and this was like honey on my
tongue. "Welcome her." They did, waving, smiling, shouting back the

name that wasn't mine. I did not care. I would become this other girl if she were welcome here. We went around the circle then. Besides Stavros and me, there were a few other newcomers recruited from the show, but I sensed, rightly, that they were only tourists, here for kicks alone. They might last another week or two, then disappear.

"Welcome to you all," the man said. "As most of you know, these are our open rehearsals, our playtime; they're how we develop new work. *The Exodus Project*, which you were in or which you saw, we made it this same way. But we won't be performing *Exodus* again, not here. A show all about getting free and they got us on the fucking permits again. For a parking lot no one even uses if they don't want their car windows smashed in. That's America for you. Never found anything she couldn't outlaw, couldn't fence.

"Besides, it's time we were working on our next piece. We don't know what it will be. Maybe something else from the Bible. Or the Bhagavad Gita. Suzanne"—this then was the red-gold woman beside him—"has been studying Sanskrit. Or we might take another tradition. Origin stories, that's our thing. How the world came to be. To begin, anyone who's new, go on and tell us a story, something from childhood, something that made you who you are. Alice, start us off?"

As his eyes held mine, I searched for a good story, a nice story, a story that would make him love me. But I felt that I owed this man something better, payment for having picked me out at that crowded party. So I told him something true.

"I was three," I began. "Or maybe four. I was in church with my parents. We're Catholic. Or they are. My mother went to take Communion, and I went with her. The church allowed children at the rail, and I didn't like her leaving me behind. I knew that I couldn't have a wafer. They weren't for me, not yet, but I saw how my mother looked whenever she ate one. Like stained glass. Lit from inside. I wanted one. Wanted it so much. The priest put the wafer on my mother's tongue, and right then there was a crash from the fellowship hall. A dropped platter. Something like that. When the priest turned to look, I grabbed as many wafers as I could—four, five—and I ate them all. No one even noticed."

"How did they taste?" he asked me.

"Like nothing. Like God. Delicious."

I stayed another hour—talking, chanting, moving to music from the record player. Then my time was through. Rachel had said that she would sign me in. But I didn't trust her. Not even then. Not completely. So as another member of the group, a Black boy—or no, a man, that man from the show—stood in the circle's center, arms upraised in a private dance, I gathered my coat and slipped away. The blond man caught me at the top of the stairs.

"Going so soon, Alice? Had enough?"

"No," I said. "But I'm in school. Curfew's even earlier on weeknights."

"For a big girl like you?" he said.

I was five foot two, and only on tiptoe. Here, a step down, I barely reached his chest. "For a big girl like me." And then, because I couldn't go on thinking of him only as the blond man, I said, "What's your name? You never told me."

"Peter," he said. "Peter Murray."

This was disappointing, a name like any other. "Good night, Peter."

I ran then, until there were pains in my shins and an ache in my side and a taxi I could barely afford coming toward me, its top-mounted light like a knife through the night.

I should have left it there, put the adventure away in the top drawer of my dresser and taken it out only when I needed the sharp, sweet feeling of a secret. I should have stayed on campus—gossiping, studying, making deals with myself about whether to eat the dining hall brownies. I should have known that freedom was not made for girls like me.

Instead, I was back the next week. Dinner bolted and that same sprint for the train, that same convulsive ride. I had brought a book that one of the seniors, a girl with a kohl-lined eyes, had lent me, the plays of Apollinaire. The words spun and jolted. I couldn't read a line.

I had been this way all week—peevish, distractible—especially in my acting class, a Shakespeare study I had fought to take and then almost immediately regretted. I think I must have known already that acting, the kind of acting taught at schools like mine, was not my calling. I could parrot proper diction, I could feign emotion, but without substance, without depth. This class confirmed it. The teacher, Miss Winnick, an elderly woman with coiled braids and a spine like tempered steel, emphasized mechanics—posture, breath control. With her, I felt like a plastic doll, a thing of blinking eyes and posable limbs. Pull the string and watch me go.

We had each been set a sonnet, mine was Sonnet Sixty, twelve lines on the ravages of time and then a couplet on the consolation of poetry. Nice for poetry. Nice for the poets, who were nearly always men. I had never heard my father's lodge brothers complain about their gaping pores or slack stomachs. But at my mother's coffee mornings, the sitting room thrummed with talk of whatever new cream or dye might wrong-foot time's march.

I hadn't minded the sonnet at first. I was nineteen, still rimmed in baby fat. Time held no terror for me. But the day before, in class, the lines had sounded false, each one a stone weighing down my tongue. I didn't want to say these arcane words—*pebbl'd, sequent, 'gainst*. I wanted to speak how real people spoke, to stand as real people stood. I looked around the room as I recited, thinking that everyone must hear the phoniness. But they only stared back at me, placid, unconcerned.

"Acceptable," said Miss Winnick. "You lost your breath at the middle, but the words were infused with true feeling." No. The feelings had been faked. I had given only lies.

Miss Winnick should have seen me the next night, alone, flashing up Forty-Second Street, a lightness in my chest, a heat between my legs.

That was feeling. That was truth. At the loft, I saw Peter first, deep in conversation with Suzanne. There were other faces, ten or so, that I remembered from the week before. Names returned to me—Jorge, Faye, Molly, JoAnn, Jack. Or no, I was gently corrected, Jax. Stavros was here again, but seated across the oval from Jorge, his long arms wrapped around his longer legs, tight like a tourniquet. A bottle was handed to me, and I sipped from it, not asking for a glass, not asking what it held. The liquid swirled around my teeth and tongue—tinny, tannic. Then the chanting began and the voices were around and in me, stretching past the ceiling, through the roof and up into the stars.

There were other exercises this time, theater games that started when the chanting ended. At one point, a skinny man in denim flares switched on a turntable. Music oozed, and as Peter called out different words—"Desire!" "Power!" "Pain!"—we moved to it, contorting our bodies into the shapes that each suggested. I felt awkward at first. But then hands were on me, smooth ones, rough ones, passing over the thin wool of my sweater, the thicker wool of my skirt, absorbing me into some greater shape. When the music stopped, we stood in smaller circles and said Peter's words again and again, until the words weren't words anymore, just muscle, spit, and breath.

The needle found a new song, slower, with strange brassy frills, and we were paired off, two by two, to mirror each other's movements. Peter took me as his partner. He held his left hand up, and I matched it with my right. Somehow I knew just how he would bend, how he would step. Grace flowed through me, flowed through us both, and in his liquid eyes, I saw myself reflected—white-blond hair, pink skin. His lips were on mine then or mine were on his and his tongue was in my mouth. That returned me to myself. Had anyone seen? No. They were deep into the exercise. Only the child, the boy, was watching. What did children matter?

I was also a child. I know this now.

Out the window near the sink, the sky had turned to ink.

"I have to go," I said.

"Come on," Peter said, reaching out to stroke the curve of my chin, my throat beneath. "Don't be scared of us, Alice."

"I'm not scared of you," I said, stepping back and neatening my hair. "I'm scared of my dorm matron. You'd be scared of her, too, if you saw her."

He let me go then, and I skittered down the stairs. Other footsteps followed, and I turned, thinking it was Peter, that he'd run after me, but it was only Stavros, hurtling past. He looked, I thought, almost frightened.

"Allison," he said. He stood before me, blocking the street door with his spider limbs. "I came here tonight to talk to you. Don't go. Or yes, go. Go now. But don't come here again. This group, these people, you should know—"

"I'm sorry," I said snappishly. "I can't talk. I'll be late. Probably I'm late already." I resented him for knowing something I did not, for being so dramatic about it. "Call me tomorrow, if it's so important. I'll be on my floor after dinner."

"Allison, I was wrong to bring you here. I was wrong to bring myself. The show, yes, it was wonderful. But let us leave it there. This group, they will take from you. They will take from you what you think is right, is good. I see it, Allison—you are giving yourself already. I see how you will give and give until—"

"Stavros," I said. "I really don't have the time. Just call."

Then I slipped out under his gangling arm and away.

Stavros did not phone. Or if he did, I didn't receive a message. And he did not return to rehearsal. I have never known what was done to him, what he had been made to do, though I suppose I can guess. I saw him only once more, nearly two decades later, in the lobby of a suite of doctors' offices in Mid City. I didn't recognize him. Not at first. He was thin, sunken in on himself, and I angled away as I went to pay my bill. But I could see that he knew me, even though I had taken some pains by then—short, sensible hair, glasses I didn't really need—so that few would. I looked at him then. He was gray before his time, but with those same unruly limbs. I knew him, too. As I replaced my wallet in my purse, he came over.

"Allison," he said in a rasping voice. He opened his mouth to smile. Something had gone wrong with his gums. "I was right, wasn't I? That show. It changed your life."

He put out his hand to take mine. I clutched my purse instead.

"What's a life?" I said and left him there.

Another taxi home, paid for with stolen money. It was a risk, yes, but plenty of girls worked the mail room. And Miss Nowak, who ran it, seemed to like me better than most. If I were careful, I could go on like this until summer came, taking the train to Times Square every week, cabbing home just before curfew, living for these few hours alone.

I had made it back just in time. I scrawled my name in the sign-in book and took the stairs anyway, hoping to walk off some of the excitement, some of the heat, exhausting myself back into the mundane. Rachel was in the room, pecking out an essay on her portable Smith Corona, a stack of hardbound books at her side. She didn't look up as I folded myself into the bottom bunk, but her fingers above the keys were stilled. She knew where I had been.

"How was it?" she asked. She had meant it to sound casual, but there was a rasp to her voice, like she was sharpening her teeth around the words.

"I can't describe it."

"Well, you're an English major," she said, facing me now. "So go on and try, huh?"

"I can't," I said, rising just enough to pull off my shoes. "It's like when I tell you about acting class or rehearsal. It doesn't mean anything if you aren't right there. Like, okay, we chanted and we danced and we repeated some words together, which I guess is just *more* chanting, and I know how ridiculous that sounds. But if you'd been there, with the music and the candles and everything, you would have been into it, too."

"I doubt it," Rachel sniffed. "And that doesn't sound like play practice. It sounds like a cult." There was often talk of cults back then, about what they might drive people to do.

"Theaters *were* cults," I said, tugging off my sweater, "if you go back far enough. And what they're doing, this company, it goes all the way back. This is what it must have been like. Before scripts and stage directions and all that. I don't know, it's like—"

I reached out, on impulse, and took Rachel's hand and brought it to my breast, near my heart, wanting to feel hands on me again, wanting her to feel what I had felt. But even as I did it, I knew—certainly, horribly—that it was wrong.

Rachel snatched her hand away. "No!" she said. She said it as though I were a dog that had disobeyed. "God, Allison." She hated me in that moment. And I hated her, too, for seeing me weak and wanting.

I turned to face the wall, taking up whatever book was nearest. The typewriter keys clacked again, faster now. We didn't do that kind of thing, Rachel and me. Not here. Not with the lights on. Late in our freshman year, at a party across the street, we'd found ourselves on a basement sofa, both of us a little drunk, entangled with the same corn-fed undergraduate. And because there had been other girls before her, other darkened rooms, I knew that it wasn't the boy exciting her. The boy, of course, had noticed nothing, too astonished at having not one but two girls to fumble at with his thick, soft hands.

This thing between us, it wasn't so unusual. There were plenty of girls at college like that. In my high school, it had been the same. But you couldn't be too public with it. I didn't want a reputation, and Rachel didn't either. And for good reason. At the college, the girls with reputations were punished, shunned—expelled, even—like the girls a few years back who had lived in this same dorm. They were two brunettes, the rumor had it, alike as sisters. They used to climb to the building's roof to be together and were found there, through binoculars, by some boys across the street. The girls had to leave school. The administration gave some made-up reason. But everyone knew the real cause. What happened to the boys? What always happened: nothing.

After that, it had seemed necessary for all of us in the dorm to prove how boy-crazy we were, how normal. Anything else was an invitation, hand-lettered, to trouble. With Rachel and me, there had been other times. But only away from school, late at night, when we'd drunk too much or pretended to have drunk too much. We had been taught, we had taught ourselves, that what we had wasn't meant for light.

I fell asleep like that—angry, ashamed, still in my day clothes. In the morning, by unspoken agreement, we went on as usual, Rachel shuffling down to breakfast and me to the shower, clutching my little basket of toothpaste and oatmeal soap. Back in the room, I brushed my hair and pulled on a knee-length skirt, a blouse with a wide, soft collar, a red cardigan. The fashion was for blue jeans then, but I'd been in Catholic schools too long and felt naked without a knife pleat.

Taking the gold compact from Rachel's desk, I applied a film of pink lip gloss. This time, I replaced the compact deep into my own drawer and made my eyes go wide as I mouthed what I would say: Your compact? What does it look like? Oh, that one? No, I'm sorry, I haven't seen it in days.

Despite what Stavros had said—or in some contrary, spiteful way, because of it—I could not keep myself from Theater Negative. April had turned to May by then. The trees along Broadway bowed with flowers. The approach of finals should have stayed me, but again I took the subway, again I walked up Forty-Second, this time in a misting rain, my rubberized coat slapping at my thighs, my pink umbrella a tulip.

Up the stairs and into the loft. I removed my outer things. The chanting began, familiar by now, and I entwined my voice with all the others until we were one sound, issued from a dozen throats. The song, the candles, they held me hot and close.

As the last note died, Peter pushed himself up and strode to the center of the circle. He nodded toward one of the men, Jax, and he rose, too. The skinny man, Bill, dropped the needle on the record player. Notes rose, some wordless, moaning song.

There was another sound then, a crunching just beyond the door that resolved into booted feet. Almost immediately, the man in those boots was through it—rain-wet, red-faced, with a thickened body beneath a fatigue jacket. One hand, I saw, held a gun, gleaming mutely in the candlelight. I forgot to breathe then, forgot that breath had ever come easily to me. I knew that I should run. Every part of me was screaming it. But the man stood between me and the door, and my feet were rooted. I could not move.

"Where the fuck is Faye?" he said.

Heads turned to a long-haired, bone-pale woman, the woman who had held me. She was seated at one end of the couch, but as the man approached, she stood, backing away. The candlelight turned her cotton dress to gauze.

"I told you not to come here, Boyd," she said. Her voice had a tremor to it. "I told you not to come around me anymore."

"I go where I want," he said. "Don't you fucking tell me what to do." He moved toward her. The candles caught his eyes. They were too large, too dark. There must have been a dozen of us in the room, but no one moved. We stood still, ensorcelled.

Then Peter stepped in front of him. A foolish thing. You didn't come between a man and his raging. I had learned that young. Someone—JoAnn, it might have been—made a kind of yelp, but Peter did not retreat. "Come on, man," he said. "Whatever trip you're on, you don't have to bring that here. Keep cool, man."

"Shut up," the man said. "You shut up. I'm not leaving till my old lady's leaving with me." He lifted the gun and jerked it toward the woman, Faye. Even all the way across the room, I felt my body start, and I saw Molly, a girl a few years older than I was, with dark eyes and willful curls, sketch a cross into the air. But Peter did not flinch. He stood tall, and Jax moved to stand with him. Bill and Jorge also, though Jorge looked like the breeze would have blown him over. Together they formed a kind of wall, and the man had to move the gun up and around to point it at Faye. If I hadn't felt such terror, I think I would have laughed.

"I'm staying here, Boyd," Faye said. "I told you that. I told you we were all through."

"You don't tell me," he said. His voice was thin, a fraying rope. "I tell you! Don't even have a mind of your own. Wouldn't be nothing without me. Wouldn't have gotten out of Joplin without me. You don't leave me, you hear?" The man shifted his weight. And then, with a sound like thunder, the gun went off.

I don't know if he was aiming for Faye or for Peter or hardly aiming at all, but the shot went wide and high, hitting a spot in the ceiling that drizzled plaster down. Faye screamed and the man screamed, too, a broken, animal sound, and in the confusion, Peter's hand bore down on the man's wrist, knocking the gun to the floor. Jax grabbed for it and took it, cradling it like a corsage. Faye, I saw, had fallen back onto the sofa. Peter stayed with the man, who was on his knees now. Peter whispered to him. The man began to nod, slowly at first and then faster. Then he was on his feet and stumbling toward the door.

"Go," Peter said, audible now. "Go and don't come back."

Peter shut the door after him, bolted it, too. Slowly, we returned to ourselves, to life and breath. I found that I was on the floor, on hands and knees at the edge of the carpet, though I did not remember falling. Was that same song still playing? I did not know. Time had gone syrupy, and I felt liquid, too. Relief had turned my joints to water.

"Should I go out to the corner, call the police?" a tall girl, a newcomer with twin puffs of hair, said.

"No," Peter said. "No police. We can handle ourselves." He went to Faye. "You don't want the police, right?"

Faye gathered herself, wiping one eye with the back of a hand, then the other, her fingers splayed like a peacock's tail. "No, honey," she said. "That's right. No police. And I'm sorry. So sorry. He was savage when I left. I knew it, too. But I didn't think he'd come here, didn't think he knew where I was, even."

"Was he back on junk, Faye?"

"I imagine so. Not sure he was ever off of it."

Peter shook his head. He went to the record player and swiped at the off switch, jerking the needle so that it scratched across the grooves. He turned back to us. "For anyone who's new and anyone who's old and needs reminding, I'm going to say this once: You want to smoke some grass, drop a little acid, fine, man. But anything else—any junk, any pills, any of the hard stuff—you don't do that here, okay? That's not what we're about."

Heads nodded.

"Peter," Jax said. He still held the gun in both his hands. "What do I do with this?"

"Give it to me," he said. He took it gingerly and then handed it off to another man, tall, with a thatch of white hair, an elegant scarecrow.

"Bash," Peter said. "Take this to the river. Throw it in. Deep as you can."

"A gun?" the man said. "Darling, how butch."

I don't know that Bash did what Peter said. Maybe he did hurl the gun into the Hudson, maybe he kept it for himself, a talisman. I don't believe he brought it with him to Europe. He didn't need to. By then, we'd found other ways to die.

"Let's begin again," Peter said. "Let's breathe. Join hands. Whatever you're feeling right now. The fear or whatever, man, use it. Take it in. Take it on." I gave one hand to the new girl, Dede, a dancer friend of Jax's. Bill, the skinny man who looked like a smudged carbon copy of Peter, took the other. I breathed, in and out and in, until my heart returned to something like its normal rhythm. Yet my body still felt strange to me—roused, every cell alive.

"All right," Peter said. "It's still early. But that was a bad scene just now. Do we stop? Or does anyone want to keep going?"

Faye was at his side. "Let's go," she said softly. "Rest of you don't mind, I want the work tonight."

"Good girl," Peter said. And even knowing what Faye had gone through, I was jealous of his praise.

Peter stood up straighter. His eyes were light. "Yeah," he said. "Yeah. Let's do it for real. Let's get up on our feet. Who here knows Genesis? The story of creation? Knows it well."

I put my hand up. Others did, too.

"All right," Peter said. "Jax, you can be Adam. Suzanne, Tree of Knowledge. Faye, you can be the snake—is that cool? And, Alice," he said, turning at last to me, "for you, Eve, all right?" I nodded, wanting to please him.

"I, of course, will play God," he said. He may have meant it as a joke, but no one laughed. "No words now," he said. "Just your bodies. Just the dance."

Bill put a new record on the platter, and we began. Peter swayed, tracing a hemisphere, light and darkness. He moved again, arms high. Sky now. Arms parallel to the floor, this made land and water. Walking in a circle—graceful, pelvis low—he made a sweeping gesture, and I could almost see the celestial lights appear, then plants and creatures, too. He reached a hand to Jax, and Jax took it, entering the circle as though life had suddenly sparked in him, as though he had never lived until this moment. Jax was a dancer, and he could say more with the tilt of his chin than most men could with a whole monologue. What a star he might have been.

Jax's eyes fixed on mine, and without further prompting, I followed him into the circle, pressing my body to his side, my hands to his ribs, birthing myself anew. I did not wait for God to make me. I made myself.

I took Jax's hand and the circle became our garden, with fruit to eat and water to drink and one tree alone—Suzanne, in her long dress, her hair an aureole—forbidden us.

Then Faye approached, not on her belly but at full height, her fingers sliding over my waist in a sibilant kind of touch. She took my arm, leading me toward Suzanne. Faye kissed my lips, a brief joining, feather light. I would have lingered, but I was not myself. I was Eve.

Understanding what Faye intended, I kissed Suzanne on her dry lips, then brought that same kiss back to Jax. The kiss transformed him. Light left his face; his eyes went small. He took off his knit shirt, his jeans. Mirroring him, I stepped out of my blouse and skirt until only my underwear and socks remained. We were naked, or nearly, and we knew it. And there was Peter again, our God, dancing around us, his motions fast and fitful in his anger. He chased us from the circle, which then stood empty, except for Suzanne, her head bent toward her right shoulder, eyes shut. Faye roamed the periphery, a cherubim with a flaming sword, one arm raised, so that we might never return.

Then it was done. And I knew, in a way that was beyond knowing, that it could never happen this way again. It would never be as pure as this, as artless. I had been alive at its creation. Anything that came after would be imitation, sham. The music was louder now. I put my clothes back on. I had to leave if I wanted to make curfew. But I did not leave, just sat in a corner of the sofa, ankles crossed, expectant. When Molly passed me a cigarette that didn't smell like a cigarette, I took it, holding in the smoke as I had seen others do and then letting it filter from my mouth. I wanted to try everything that night.

A few of the actors departed for a bar, Faye and Jax among them. Jax knelt to me, all pomade and sweat, and cupped my face. "Apple a day, baby," he whispered as he went.

Then Peter's hands were on my shoulders, as I had known they would be, his legs on either side of mine. "Come up to the roof," he said.

"But it's raining."

"It's stopped," he said. He took a blanket from the back of the sofa and made for the door. I followed him. We went out of the loft and up a flight of stairs and then up different stairs, curved and decked in rust. Another door and suddenly the night and the city were before us. The rain had stopped, as though Peter had willed it, a god still. Patches of the roof were painted silver and where the water pooled, the reflections of the lit skyscrapers shivered and ran. Peter spread the blanket out and draped himself across it, extending a hand to me. I didn't take it. I felt my youth in that moment, my greenness. I stood there like a statue, a Madonna, if Madonnas were ever carved with their arms folded across their breasts, frozen between this world and the next. But Peter had seen me in my underwear already. And didn't he want me? Wasn't I his favorite?

Besides, this wasn't my first time with a boy. I had lost my virginity, willfully, purposefully, the summer before college. And it hadn't felt like a loss, no matter what my mother and the nun, Sister Brigid, who lectured the senior girls about ladies' hygiene, would have told me. Jim Reilly's fumbling was the price I'd paid to be delivered into experience. I had kept my eyes open, staring over his shoulder at the car's roof, registering each pulse and throb. The tearing hurt less than I'd expected. A few tissues tidied the blood.

I let him do it to me a few more times that summer. Once, midway, I'd felt something close to pleasure, like honey pouring in, filling me up from inside, but then I was returned to the breath, the sweat, the ungainly rhythm of our stomachs smacking together—slap, slap, slap. I didn't tell him how I liked to be touched, how fevered I felt when a girl would slip her fingers into me, how slick I would go. I didn't have the words. So he couldn't do much more than collide his flesh with mine. A shudder, a groan, and then that funny empty feeling as he removed himself from me, tying the rubber off and dropping it out the window of his mother's station wagon. He would drive me home then, unspeaking. He had wanted this, had begged and pawed, like a child wheedling for candy. But I would have sworn he'd been happier when we spent our Saturdays at the movies.

So I took Peter's hand and slipped down onto the blanket.

He kissed me, holding me lightly, as if I were precious, as if we were somewhere close and private. The tang of wine was in his mouth. I tensed for a moment, realizing that no one but Rachel knew where I was, that probably even Rachel couldn't find this place again. But Peter's hands stayed gentle. I let him untuck my blouse and fit his hands beneath it, let his tongue trace the contours of my neck and jaw. I felt golden in his arms. Then his hands were in my underwear and my mind was stars, my breath coming fast and hot.

"Are you on the pill?" he said into my neck.

"No," I said.

Any girl could have it then, not just the married ones. But knocking on the door of the campus nurse—a woman who treated every strep throat and sprained ankle as though it were some personal affront—and asking for it? Impossible. The best birth control, she'd once told a girl on the floor below, was an aspirin held between the knees. Girls who needed real pills, girls who were in real trouble, God knows where they went.

"Don't worry," he said. "I'll take care of you." So I nodded and shut my eyes. Then my underwear was down, looped around an ankle, and my skirt was up around my waist and he was inside me, his breath rasping against my ear. Pressed into that blanket, I was searching again for the honey, the heat. But then he was done, out of me again and spilling himself across my thigh. He took his shirt off and offered it to me to clean myself. I wanted to laugh at this gallantry. Or cry, maybe. As I scooted my underwear up, the door to the roof opened and Suzanne was there in silhouette, the stairwell light kindling the red-gold wires of her hair. I pushed my skirt back down.

"I'm going," she said. "I promised the girl I wouldn't keep her late.

Can you finish with your friend and we'll share the cab?" She left without waiting for an answer.

Peter took his shirt, stained with his wetness, with mine, and put it on.

"The girl?" I said.

"The babysitter; she's watching Zion."

"Who's Zion?"

"My kid," he said. I remembered the boy, hiding behind Suzanne's skirts.

"You have a kid?"

"Kid, wife, house, the whole American disaster." He laughed, only it didn't sound like laughter. Whatever pleasure I had felt went to dust. "But it's cool, babe," he went on. "Suzanne knows how it is. She'd like you, too, you know."

He laid a hand across my thigh.

"No, thank you," I said, hitching my leg to shake that hand away. I said it calmly, as though declining a glass of punch. But my thoughts were white around the edges. A wife? A child?

I hurried from the roof and back to the loft for my things. I nearly tripped over Dede, sprawled across the carpet, as I ran for the door. "Hey," she giggled. "Whatsa matter? There an emergency or something?"

"Yes," I said. Then without quite knowing how, I was in a taxi, speeding back to campus, watching the numbers tick over on the meter, hoping I had cash enough to pay the fare.

"What time is it?" I asked the driver, his face shadowed beneath his soft cap.

He twitched his chin at the dash. "Midnight just about."

I had missed curfew. Missed it by hours. The car stopped. I paid and tumbled onto the misted sidewalk, then moved across the lawn to the window. With careful fingers, I worked the catch and eased myself over the sill, wincing as the umbrella bumped to the carpet below.

Then there was light. Mrs. Pritchard stood at the switch, in a yellow

dress that made her look like a gaily appareled bus. Her eyes were nar-
rowed. Rachel was beside her, in a robe and slippers, head hung down.

"Where have you been, Miss Hayes?" Mrs. Pritchard said. "And don't
you lie to me, my girl."

No lie would hold me now. Not with Rachel there. "At rehearsal," I
said, straightening myself. "With a theater group. A professional one.
They're not school approved, and I figured that I wouldn't get approval.
I went anyway. I thought it was important."

"You thought so, did you?"

"Yes," I said. "But I was wrong. The company, the people, they
weren't—" There was acid in my throat. I swallowed it down. "I don't
need to see them anymore."

"Ah. Well. Do you know what's important to me? Your safety. The
safety of all my girls. I have a duty of care, I do. I can't do that duty if
I don't know where you are, now can I? And this isn't the first time. I
know all your tricks. And now I know what this one here"—an elbow
stabbed toward Rachel—"has told me. How you made her lie for you.
And worse." Rachel, I saw, was crying.

Standing there, damp and cold, my thighs still gummy with Peter's
mess, I knew that I should cry, too. Should humble myself. Should beg.
But I had spent too many years cowering, begging, and it had never
done me much good. Instead, I opened my mouth and screamed.

A meaty hand was thrust across my lips and parts of my nose,
too, so that I could barely breathe. "That's quite enough, my girl," Mrs.
Pritchard said. "You'll have the whole building down upon us, you will."

I tried to bite at those fingers. I was unlike myself or maybe more
like myself than ever—half animal, furious—but the grip held. Hungry
for air, I slackened.

"Can you be quiet now?" she said.

I nodded. Mrs. Pritchard took her hand away. "To bed with you. No
argument. Keep to your room in the morning. I'll come and find you

there. We'll have our meeting with the dean, to see what's to become of you. Nothing good, I'd imagine. And no more than you deserve. Away with you now. The both of you."

I made my way to the elevator, Rachel a step behind, and jammed my finger into the button, wishing something, my finger or the button, would break. The elevator came. We rode in silence.

In the room, Rachel flung her glasses on her desk and ran for her bunk. I undressed slowly—so much clothing off and on that night— unembarrassed now by my nakedness. Nightgowned, I sat down on my mattress. My sweat smelled wrong to me. I wanted a shower, I wanted to be away from Rachel. But Mrs. Pritchard had made the conditions clear.

Above, there were the muffled sounds of Rachel sobbing. I enjoyed it, almost. I wanted her to suffer. When she quieted, I took my cue. "Why?" I said. My voice was even, calm in a way that nearly frightened me. "Why couldn't you just cover for me? Like you said you would."

Another sob. A gasping for air. "I did," Rachel said finally. "I tried. She caught me signing you in."

"You couldn't have made something up? Or found a way to warn me?"

"No," she said, sniffling. "I'm not like you. I can't just lie all the time. And I'm tired of covering for you. You want to go with the crazies all night, that's on you."

She was right in this. I had put myself in Peter's way. I had wanted to feel everything that night, to press myself against the limit of what I could endure. "That's all over now," I said. "If you care or anything."

"Well, I don't," she said. She blew her nose into what must have been her sheet. "I found it, you know."

"Found what?"

"God, Allison. My compact. In your drawer. Did you think I wouldn't look? We were roommates, Allison. Friends," she said, choking on the word, "if you want to even call it that. You came to my house, even. And you stole from me. I don't know who you are anymore. Maybe I never did. But I don't like you and I don't trust you and I don't like who I am around you. It makes me sick, honestly. So I told Pritchard everything. Probably it'll ruin my reputation, but honestly, Allison, I don't even mind." She was hissing now, her whisper wet and barbed. "I hope they make you leave," she said. "I hope they send you out of here tomorrow with just the clothes on your back and I never see you ever again."

Then she was back to crying. I lay below, eyes open, as the sliver of glass through the curtains changed from black to gray to the raw pink of the new day. I pretended sleep while Rachel rose and gathered clothes. She departed, slamming the door. I got up then and put my own clothes on, brushing my hair until it turned from straw to gold, pressing baby oil to my lips.

At nine o'clock, a knock like thunder. It was Mrs. Pritchard, come to bring me to the dean.

4

1997, LOS ANGELES

uditions were held after school in the drama classroom on Thursday and Friday, with students entering and exiting at five-minute intervals. She sat at her desk, a yellow pad in her lap, grateful for the busyness, the distraction, the chance to wield what little power she possessed. Naomi, whom she'd named as assistant director, sat beside her in a folding chair, a twinned pad clutched tightly in one hand, a chewed-on pencil in the other, scribbling away. She didn't always use a student assistant. But Naomi was methodical and orderly, a three-ring binder in pink barrettes. And Naomi's mother, she had heard, was a member of the school's board, the board that would decide the future of the theater department.

The students recited their prepared speeches, mangling the rhythm and the words. A few of them tried English accents, and if they had any talent at all—rare, but it happened—she would have them take the speech again, this time in their own voices, this time as themselves.

"Because this isn't England," she said. "It's ancient Greece. It's not that either. It's a fantasy place, it's nowhere. So you might as well sound like you."

There had been no further notes in her slot in the lounge. No other disruptions to her usual routine. She had never exactly believed that she was safe. But after so many years, she had relaxed her vigilance. Now someone had found her. What did that person want? Who was even left alive? The questions harried her, wrapped thin, wet fingers around her throat. Rosa. Was it Rosa? Had Rosa come back? No. It was impossible. She had fed the paper from her mail slot into the garbage disposal in her apartment, slopping water after it, flinching at the chunking sound the blades made. And what that paper showed she would tuck away in the corner of her mind that held the ruin of her past.

She had problems enough already, right here, right now. She had spoken to Marta and George over a hurried lunch at Art's Delicatessen. Dan Daley had by then told them what he'd told her: Unless the school's endowment recovered, the board would slash the budgets of all the supplementary departments, save athletics. The school could fail, the buildings crumble, but the basketball team would have new uniforms. Marta, her gray bun held in place with chopsticks, said this, with unusual bitterness. George shook his head and said he'd like to drown in his iced tea it was all so terrible. He jerked the point of his tie upward and mimed hanging himself. He was a clown, George, but gentle with it. As he drove them the few blocks back to school, he mentioned that a friend of his was performing a solo show in the black box theater on Wilshire.

"Can I tempt you, Ali?" he said.

"Thanks," she said from the back seat. "But I never see theater. I get enough of that at work."

"Kids ruin it for you?" he said. "It's the same with me. I can't listen to Beethoven on my own anymore. Or even Tchaikovsky. I'm at the LA Phil or it's the best recording in the world, and all I can hear is them screeching away on their little violins."

"It's the still lifes with me," Marta said. "The damn apples. I go to a museum and see a real Cézanne and I just want to puke."

"That's it," she said. "That's it exactly." Though of course that wasn't it at all. She knew better than to let herself too near the real thing. The false schoolroom version of it, that was all she dared.

She would not have said she loved the job. She had never pushed to teach theater, had never wanted to teach at all, really. But a teaching credential was the fastest, most frictionless path out of her parents' house, and to her surprise, she liked the classroom work. It was in its way a kind of performance, but she knew that she would never lose herself while guiding some drowsing sophomores through *White Fang* or *Ethan Frome*.

Her previous placements had all been in English. But when the theater department job at Greenglade became vacant—Greenglade with its lighter schedule and better benefits—she talked her way into it. That had been a decade ago, more. Now, she felt too old and too habituated to start over. And where would she go, with her mother's care to manage? Marta had her husband's income. George had no dependents. They could resign themselves to loss. She could not. She had to make a case for the worth of her department. Which would mean, at the very least, putting some thought to the winter classic.

In her mind, she had cast the play already, more or less, with the popular students as the lovers. Kyle, who had a reputation for romantic cruelty that had made its way even to the teacher's lounge, would play Demetrius. The prettier girls, the ones who could sing, could be the fairies. Patrick, who beneath that height and shamble was a born zany, would play Bottom. The plainer kids could fill out the courtiers and the mechanicals. For Puck, she'd have Nadine, a sophomore who wore her hair in box braids trimmed with beads. Nadine had swagger, a luster to her like headlights on high beam. She worried for girls like Nadine. It was dangerous to shine so bright.

On Friday, Nadine auditioned with the play's final speech, "If we shadows have offended." When she came to "Give me your hands," Nadine rocketed forward, seizing first her hand and then Naomi's. Naomi dropped her pencil.

"Excellent," she told Nadine. "Good instincts. Great energy. You can check the cast sheet on Monday. And with that, Naomi, I think that I have earned a break. Tell the next student to wait, please."

With Nadine gone, she reached into her desk drawer and took the pack of cigarettes. Opening the back window, she lit up, loosing a stream of gray-blue smoke into the brown valley beyond. Landscaping didn't bother with the backs of the buildings. One of these days, an errant spark would hit dry grass. Then the whole school would burn, the tiles cracking and crumbling, stucco turning black.

"Why are you laughing?" a voice said. It was Naomi, anxious that she had missed a joke. That the joke might have been about her. "And can you even smoke in here?"

"Of course not," she said. "But where's the fun in always doing what you're told? Besides, my classroom, my kingdom. And you can keep a secret, can't you?" She waved the pack in Naomi's direction. "Do you want one?"

"No!" Naomi said, sounding appalled. "I mean, no, thank you. Or . . . maybe?" She was biting her lip now, absorbed in some internal struggle. "No," she decided. "I would not like a cigarette. But thank you for asking me." She unwrapped a hunk of gum and popped it into her mouth, chewing fretfully.

"Naomi, so polite," she said. She stubbed the butt against the outer pane and let it fall to the ground below, where it would burn or it wouldn't, because that was the way of disasters. They might happen so suddenly or not at all. "All right," she said. "Let's get this over with. Send in the next one."

Auditions ended at a quarter to five. Just in time for the last students to catch the late bus. She sent Naomi on her way and turned to her computer, delaying the return to the empty condo, the dinner rustled from the plastic tubs of the Ralphs deli counter. Opening the word processing program, she pulled up the cast list, many of its slots already filled, and added in the last few names. She sent the document to the printer, which stuttered it forth in black-gray type, and tucked the page into her bag.

Then, since she'd put it off for long enough, she took from her inbox tray the pink sheets that Mr. Ko had prepared and the silver disc, still in its casing. She removed the disc, holding it by its edges as the surface caught the overhead light and spun it into rainbows. She inserted it into the drive.

An icon mushroomed onto the screen, and she followed the commands that the handout prescribed until the computer began to sing, a rough and shuddering whale song. The disc whirred and paused, whirred and paused, then a steady purring began. The mail portal opened. As instructed, she set up her account and a password. Logging on for the first time, she saw the red circle of an alert. There were messages already. A welcome letter from Dr. Daley. A note from Mr. Ko. She closed the program, powered down the computer, shut off all the lights, and made her way through the abandoned campus, pacing its paths in silence, a ghost walking through her own life.

Saturday was golden, routine. The paper—front page, Calendar, crossword—the dry cleaners, the grocery, the video store, the afternoon spent on the living room exercise bike while the movie of the week hummed and blared. Later, she went to the grocery again, just to have something to do, walking this time, practically a misdemeanor in her neighborhood. A few blocks away, she noticed a pomegranate tree in a house's front yard, its thin branches bowed with fruit. Stealthily, she picked one, then hurried down the block and broke it open. The pith smelled sharp and vegetal. She pried out some seeds and ate them as she walked. By the time she reached the store, her hands were red, as though with blood, which returned her for a moment to that other night—the bridge, the rain. She walked faster. Her life, she had learned, worked best if she kept moving—walking, cycling, swimming at the public pool in summers. All that motion, just to stay in place.

Automatic doors parted for her, and she strode past them, the air-conditioning prickling her skin. She walked the aisles slowly. Picking up foodstuffs and putting them down again. Finally, she bought a fashion magazine and a bottle of zinfandel. At home, she took a tumbler from the cabinet, poured a generous glass, added ice. She slit the plastic on a frozen meal and set it to rotate in the microwave, then ate and drank alone as the smog turned the sunset psychedelic.

On Sunday, as she had done every week for years, she drove to the assisted living center in Tarzana, stopping first at the Winchell's for the coconut crullers her mother loved. She parked and entered, the white box under one arm as she signed in at the lobby desk. The lobby smelled of powder and pine and of worse things that the powder and pine were meant to cover.

On the way to the elevator, Mr. Shirley, the weekend manager, a man with oiled hair and pink skin that flaked like old paint, hailed her. "Mrs. Morales. So nice to see you. Speak to you a moment?" He shoved all the words together as if there were some prize for saying them as fast as possible.

She halted.

"We've sent you a few notices. But just in case you haven't seen them, you should know we're facing increased costs. Labor and food. Laundry, even. There just comes a point when we have to pass some of those costs onto our guests." He paused finally, to draw a gasping breath. "It's a twelve percent increase. It goes into effect this month. I just didn't want you to get that bill and be surprised."

"There's so little that surprises me," she said, passing him and thumbing the Up button.

Her mother was waiting for her, sat at the edge of her bed, neatly dressed in sweater and skirt, a single strand of pearls looped around the tissue-paper skin of her neck. She hadn't bothered with pantyhose, her arthritic fingers couldn't manage them anymore, and above her brown flats, the ankles had swollen. Fluid bulged the joints into pale balloons.

Her mother's eyes slid over her face and to the box. "Doughnuts? Are those for me? Oh, what a treat."

She opened the box. Her mother removed a cruller, delicately, as though the pastry might nip her, and ate it in quick, careful bites.

"Ready for church, Mom?" she asked, setting the box down on the credenza.

"For church? Oh yes. I like to go to church."

She strung a purse, empty except for tissues and a crumbling lipstick, over her mother's shoulder and led her down the elevator to the car. Her mother found their old church, which returned some memories and withheld others, too unsettling, so they went to a closer one now, just off Ventura Boulevard, near the Ralphs. The mass was brief here and in English, the choir often flat. Given the choice, she would not have gone to church at all. But she recognized the pleasure that it gave her mother, the peace it tendered.

Toward the close of the service, she took her mother's sparrow wrist and walked her up the aisle to the railing. When the priest approached her, she declined the wafer. Her mother took it, and as she swallowed, something in her face smoothed and softened. She was made a girl again, in the light of the rose window, a girl in love with Jesus. Jesus would not return her love, but at least he would not shout at her, would not beat her, would not shame her for not giving him more children.

After Mass, they went to Du-par's, a further ritual. The Monte Cristo for her mother, white tuna and grapefruit for her, a slice of blueberry cream between them, her mother chattering away about the hymns. Then they returned to the facility. Her mother shut her eyes in the elevator, barely opened them until they were back in her room.

"You feel like a movie, Mom?" she asked. "Or are you all tired out?"

"A movie sounds nice."

With her mother settled into the armchair, she took the tape from her bag, snapping open the video store's plastic casing and shunting it into the VCR. The title bloomed onto the screen, *My Fair Lady*, and there was Audrey Hepburn, dubbed with Marni Nixon's voice, her mother's own thin soprano trilling over the top of that. They sat happily through the first half, though during the scene at the ball, she noticed that her mother's eyes had turned from the screen and were fixed on her.

"Allison," her mother said. "Is that you?"

"Yes, Mom," she said. Her mother was the only one who called her Allison anymore. She had cast away that name so carelessly, and when she bent to take it up again, it no longer fit, like a sweater that had shrunk in the wash. At Irvine, where she'd gone for her credential, she had introduced herself as Ali. And then there was Manny—sweet Manny—who had given her the name Morales. The marriage hadn't stuck. But the name had. Manny, generous even in the confusion of their divorce, seemed pleased that she had kept it.

"Well, it's nice to see you, dear," her mother continued. "You look well. Though I never like your hair so short."

"It's easier to manage."

"Do you remember how it was when you were little? So blond it was almost white. People used to stop me in the street to look at you."

"Yes, Mom. I remember," she said, returning her eyes to the screen.

"Do you? That's nice."

And then, a few minutes later, she heard a sound like a rat scuttling in the corner. She whipped her head around, but it was only her mother, staring at her again and snuffling softly. Her mother looked sad. And more than sad, she looked frightened.

"Oh, Allison," her mother said, her voice quavering. "It's so terrible what happened to you. What they did to you. Oh, what a terrible, terrible shame. How does a person ever get over a thing like that?"

A person doesn't.

"Shhh," she said. "Just watch the movie."

On Monday, she arrived at school early, the air crisp, if only for this hour, the dew still decking the grass. Setting down her bag, she took the cast list from the desk and bound it to the door with packing tape. The door she left open. She would seem to be busy at her desk, folders spread before her, but she liked to watch the students as they approached, liked to observe their thrill or petulance as they printed their initials next to their names.

After first period, a play-reading elective with an assortment of juniors and seniors, she powered on her computer to key in the attendance. Then she checked the mail program. The red circle indicating new messages flared. She clicked. There was a second note from Mr. Ko, this one even more snappish, listing off typical user errors. Below it was another message, marked as external. Some parent, most likely, making sure that Bryce or Victoria received the desired role. But the username was strange: HighPoint. Mindful that her next class would start in just a few minutes, she slid the mouse along its pad and clicked the message open.

I can't believe I've found you, the message read. **I wasn't sure at first. When I saw your picture on the website, the name was different. But we've nearly all of us changed our names. What a child you were then. A princess in your cardboard crown. Who are you now, Alice? What have you done with your life? What have you paid to live it?**

The message ended there, without farewell or signature. Like the note left in her mail slot, it had not threatened her directly. But she felt its threat all the same. The room had shrunk around her, the air gone thin and scant. She forced her way out the back door, to the lip of the valley with its cement culverts dug into the hill for rain that would not fall. She stopped there, bent at the waist, hands on thighs, shoving breath back into her lungs. The urge to run, to pitch herself down that canyon side and scramble away was almost overwhelming.

Then she heard a high, worried voice. "Mrs. Morales? Are you okay?" It was Nadine, silhouetted in the classroom's door, come to call her in.

"Yes, Nadine," she said, straightening up and putting a hand to her hair. "Of course. Just stretching." She slid past the girl, blinking the sun away until her vision righted. She taught that class in a kind of trance and so on with the next one, saying the words that a teacher would say, nodding as the students butchered Tennessee Williams and Christopher Durang. But really she was somewhere else, several other somewheres: the loft, the London house, that bridge. Once she even checked her hands for blood, but they were clean, dry, the nails painted pearl pink.

She clapped her palms to mask the gesture, though there was no noise to quiet.

Finally, the children left. The next period was a free one. She locked the classroom door, a bar to any student who wanted to complain about their role, and lunged for the computer. And there again, another circle, another message. She put her hands across her mouth. Into those hands, she screamed, a bright and ragged blare. Then she clicked it open.

I'm sorry, it read. I didn't mean to end it there. But I ran out of time on the terminal. I'm between places now. No phone. No fixed address, except for this electronic one. It feels like magic, doesn't it? Sending messages out and through the air. The way we used to think that we could change the world, with just our bodies, just our song. Maybe we did change it. Maybe we only changed ourselves. For the better? I've never known.

I came to see you, Alice. Only the guard at the gate wouldn't let me in. They're so strict where you are. It's like a prison. A castle. How do you stand it? I remember you so free. He let me leave a note. A picture that I carry. Did you get it? I know how it must seem. All these years later, me walking around with a copy of your picture in my pocket. But there's no one else left. Or almost no one. They're dead or lost or out of their minds or so different it's like they killed whoever they used to be.

Are you like that now, Alice? Am I? Will you know me when you see me? You saw it all, didn't you? With those big eyes of yours. Remember that story? The better to see you with, my dear. The better to eat you. I saw things, too, Alice. I was with you that last night. You know the night I mean. I saw everything.

And there it ended. Yes, she remembered the stories: the witches, the wolves, the forest she had never really left. These messages, they were like trails of breadcrumbs. And after breadcrumbs came the darkness, came the oven. Someone had seen her that last night. Her thoughts went of course to Rosa. Rosa blessedly and terribly alive. The messages did not sound like Rosa. Still, it was all so long ago. Twenty years. More. A person's syntax might have changed. Or another person had sent it. Another person had seen them. But they had been alone on the bridge that night. She believed that as much as she believed anything.

She unlocked the door and hurried from the classroom, making her way to the front of the school, which is what she ought to have done as soon as she'd collected that first note, instead of driving to the bar.

Jerome, the usual guard, was at his post, a booth of brick and metal barely shaded by the cedars that stood sentinel at the gate.

"Jerome," she said. "It's Mrs. Morales. I teach theater."

"Sure. I know you," he said. The top buttons of his uniform were undone. He smelled of musk and last night's beer.

"Someone said they came here, the Friday before last, asking for me?"

"Yeah," he said, stepping into the doorway. "Yeah, okay. I remember. Thursday, Friday, something like that. A car came around. I stopped it. You know how it goes. Car doesn't have the sticker or they're not on my list, I call the office. Otherwise, they can't come in. Did the office call you?"

"I don't think so. Or I must have been out. But this person. Do you remember what they looked like? Was it a woman? A woman about my age?"

"A woman?" Jerome said, scratching his belly. "Coulda sworn it was a man. But I just talked to him through the window. And it was sunny that day."

"It's sunny every day," she said.

"True enough. Sun like that, through the glass, makes it hard to see. Don't remember much about the car. White, maybe? Silver? Coulda been there was someone in the back. Told whoever I couldn't let them in, but if they wanted to leave a note, I'd see you got it. Took it to the office on my break. You got it, yeah?"

"Oh yes," she said. "Thank you." The words were glass in her mouth. "I got it."

Back in the classroom, as the air conditioner dried the sweat under her arms and between her breasts, she powered up the computer again. One further message had come through.

You must be wondering who I am, it read. **I'll keep that to myself for now. Or maybe you can guess it. You always were so clever. Would you like that, Alice? To guess my name. A game for you. A riddle. Either way, you should write me back. Write me as soon as you can.**

5

1972, NEW YORK CITY

The office of the dean was large, the size of a seminar classroom. Red carpeting, nearly purple, stretched from wall to wall. The furniture was wood—dark and punishingly heavy. I didn't know a single girl, not even the ones on the basketball squad, who could have lifted the merest chair. There were paintings on the walls. Real ones. In thick frames edged in gilt. Blinds shielded the windows, but some light penetrated, striping the wall above where the dean sat. Mrs. Pritchard had made to come in, but the dean had dismissed her with a look before settling herself behind the bulky desk.

I had never met the dean before, only seen her at various convocations, or at a distance, striding purposefully across the campus. She looked older up close, with lines across her forehead like craquelure in varnish. Her hair, tarnished silver, was twisted into a tight bun, and the fingers of her hands, clasped atop the desk, were elegantly knit. There were rumors about her. How she lived with the woman who headed the biology department. I had never paid those rumors much attention.

"Allison," the dean said, her voice surprisingly deep. "I've asked you to come here because we have serious concerns about your conduct. At the college, we stand in loco parentis. You understand the Latin, yes? Good. Parents trust us with their daughters in the expectation that we will develop their minds and safeguard their characters. This is why we have our many rules. And it is why I do not like to see those rules ignored. Do you follow me so far?"

"Yes, ma'am," I said, looking up at the dean and then back down at my lap.

"I have your academic record here," the dean said, opening a buff folder. While she wore no other makeup, her nails, I saw, were red, in a shade dark as the carpet, a drop of blood daubing each finger. "Your grades are excellent. There's no trouble there." The folder was closed again. "But I have reports from your dorm matron that you've stayed out past your curfew on more than one occasion. Is that true?"

"Yes, ma'am," I said again. I had already told a slanted version of the truth last night. I would have to tell it again to the dean, a sympathetic rendering of what had actually occurred. "Twice. There's a theater company in midtown, a professional one. I went to a show of theirs in April, and I stayed after to speak with them; that was the first time. Their leader, he invited me to rehearse with them on Wednesday nights. I couldn't say no to an opportunity like that. I went. But I didn't feel comfortable coming back to campus by myself in the dark, so I had to wait for an escort each time, which meant waiting until the rehearsals ended. Last night, they ended very late. I am sorry for making you and Mrs. Pritchard worry. But I did not know what else to do."

"A theater company?" The dean picked up the folder again. "But you're an English major, yes? Not a part of the concentration in the arts?"

"Yes, that's right. But I've done theater my whole life. It's what I love. And this company, they're very well known—important, even. I asked Dr. Broussard about them, and she said so." I did not add what else Dr. Broussard had said. I did not add that she had been correct.

"Did it not occur to you to ask for permission to attend? Your studies are of course the priority. But we do make some exceptions. A few of our girls take classes at Juilliard."

"Since it's not my major, I thought you might refuse. It seemed better just to go. And I was sure that I would make it back in time."

"Yet you did not. You broke curfew, which means that you also broke trust. And not for the first time. Even so, this could be forgiven. But I am told that you encouraged your roommate to lie for you. Did you do this?"

I had to step carefully. A foot wrong and the ground would all give way. What had Rachel, traitorous and frightened, told Mrs. Pritchard? What had Mrs. Pritchard told the dean? "Yes," I said, speaking slowly now, hand-selecting each word. "It was something that Rachel and I worked out our freshman year. She said that if one of us was ever late, if we were ever off seeing some boy, then the other would sign her in. She had me practice her signature, and she learned mine. It's what roommates did for each other, she said. I knew that it was wrong. But she'd grown up just outside the city, and an older cousin of hers had gone here. There were so many things she seemed to know about the school. And she had me so confused."

"Confused?" the dean said.

"Yes. I—" I broke off, lifted a hand to my cheek. It was hot, flushed. Good. I swallowed and began again. "I don't know how to say this. I've never told anyone this. Not my mother. Not my priest. I'm not sure how." I inhaled—a hiss—as though the breath burned my throat.

"She did things to me," I said. "Private things. I'm not stupid. I've gone to girls' school all my life. I've heard rumors. Girls who went that way or said they were just practicing for boys. But I never did anything like that. I'm a Catholic. I want to get married. So when Rachel came to my bed, when she did . . . what she did, I told her no. But she said that if I didn't go along with it, she would say that it was all my idea. She's richer than me, her family is. She knows more people here." This last was true and partly why I liked Rachel—for her money, her careless privilege.

"I couldn't tell anyone," I went on. "Because who would have believed me? And even if they did, they would never have looked at me the same way. I could barely look at myself, I was so ashamed. So I did what she wanted. And I'm sorry. So sorry. It was wrong, asking her to sign me in. I know it. But so much else was wrong already that it felt like it didn't even matter. I understand that the school can't protect me if the school doesn't know where I am. But the school wasn't protecting me already, not even in my own room. If you have to punish me for missing curfew, then punish me. But please believe me, I didn't want any of this. Not at all."

There were tears in my eyes. I felt one skitter down my cheek. The dean's head was set at a slight angle, her lips pinched. I had hoped for sympathy. Instead, I saw contempt, for my weakness, for my mess, for speaking of private matters openly. She did not seem to doubt my story necessarily. But she hated me for telling it.

"I see," the dean said in measured tones. "Regrettably, these things do happen. Though of course it is the policy of the college to restrict any such relations between any persons in our charge. Mrs. Pritchard did intimate a liaison, though she understood that you had begun it."

"I didn't!" I said. "Rachel, she's lying—"

"It makes no difference," the dean said, raising one hand to adjust the bun that needed no adjustment. "And we will not discuss it further. I do not make a habit of prying into intimate matters, and the details, whatever they may be, are not in the least germane. Let us return to what we know. You missed your curfew twice. You persuaded your roommate to lie for you. You are a student in good academic standing, but these are serious violations of our code of conduct, and so the penalty must be serious as well."

"How serious?" I said.

"It is nearly the end of the semester, so I think it would be best for everyone if you finish your papers and exams. This I will permit."

"Thank you," I said. I would not be suspended then, not be forced to explain that suspension to my parents. That was some comfort.

"But clearly you cannot continue in your current room assignment. We have a few rooms that we keep for visiting faculty. You can occupy one of them until the semester ends."

"Thank you," I said. "That's such a comfort. I never want to room with her again."

"Quiet, please. I have not finished. You will restrict your movements to your room, the classrooms, the library, and the dining hall. If the dining hall presents a difficulty—I know, you see, how girls can gossip—you can let the house matron know and some solution will be found. You will register with that matron every night, well before curfew. For these next weeks, while you remain in our care, there will be no leaving campus and no further participation in anything extracurricular. Is that understood?"

"Yes," I said. "Thank you." Dizzy with relief at having avoided a harsher sentence, I bent for my satchel.

"One moment," the dean said. I straightened up, the rush of blood painting my cheeks a deeper red. "As I said, your behavior raises concerns as to your moral character, concerns that prevent me from inviting you to return in the fall. I suggest that you take a semester, perhaps the whole year, to examine your conduct. When you have done so, you can apply to me for reinstatement, and I promise that I will review your application fairly."

"You're expelling me?" I said. Fear was all around me now. And in its center, I could feel anger unfurling like a banner. I imagined my hands on the dean's tight bun, how it might feel to rip it from her head. "You can't!" I said. I was on my feet somehow, my nails carving crescent moons into my palms. "I haven't done anything. I didn't want it!"

The dean held up her hand. "Sit down, young lady," she said. "Calm yourself. No more."

I sat. I felt I had no choice.

"Now," the dean continued, "I do not concern myself with your intimate life. Nor should you ask me to. It demeans us both. As I said"—she paused, her eyes darted to the folder on her desk—"Allison, you have violated our code. And if I may, this is not an expulsion. It is a compulsory withdrawal. More than that, it is an opportunity to reckon with your behavior and to make up your mind to behave differently upon your return. I will write to your parents and inform them of the school's decision, though I see no need to share any unpleasant details."

"Don't write," I said. The fight was waning in me. I felt like a child again, scrabbling for solace, for escape. "Let me tell them myself, at least," I said.

"Can I trust you to do that?" the dean said. She studied me. Pushed the folder to the side. "No. I think not. And now perhaps you should go and pack your things."

I took my satchel and made for the door, too depleted now for protest. But as I reached for the knob, one last thought occurred to me, one last way to hurt myself. "What will happen to Rachel?" I said.

"That is none of your concern," the dean said. I knew then or maybe I had always known that Rachel would not suffer the same fate. Her money, her family would protect her.

The dean gave me the location of my new room and the name of the matron who would meet me with the key. I returned to the dorm on legs like knives. From the closet, I removed my leatherette suitcases and packed clothes, papers, pens, toiletries, the oddments of a life. Just before I zipped the second case closed, I tore a leaf from a notebook. Availing myself of Rachel's best lipstick, I scrawled a short goodbye, which I left on Rachel's pillow, facedown.

You know what you are, it read. You know what you've done.

The dean had said nothing about my campus job. Perhaps talk of jobs, of what some girls had to do to afford a place like this, would also have demeaned us. So later that day, after lugging my suitcases into a new, more gracious accommodation, I returned to the mail room, filing the incoming packages and letters, weighing and stamping the outgoing mail. The dean's letter to my parents was not among the piles.

At the end of the shift, I asked Miss Nowak, a middle-aged woman with poorly dyed red hair, if I could pick up any extra hours. It was exam time, so of course I could. The letter might have come through on some other girl's shift, but a brutal luck was with me and I found the letter the next day. The envelope went into the waistband of my skirt, with blouse and vest pulled over it. It stayed there, rustling, until I could slip into the nearby toilets, tear it into pieces, and flush it away. I retched as the water left the bowl, then swallowed the acid down.

My stomach had been nearly empty anyway. I could feel the stares of the other girls when I entered the dining hall. So I collected only the most portable items—apples, bread rolls—and fled with them, eating alone and meagerly at the edge of the bed.

That same day, I called my mother. I knew by then that I would not go home that summer. I had stopped the dean's letter, but the school would send no bill for the next year's tuition and then the secret would be out. I could predict what would follow—my mother's despair, the back of my father's hand or the meat of his fists. He had not beaten me once my body had softened into a woman's shape. But this he would not countenance. Better if I were elsewhere. I had always been a practiced liar, but discovery seemed to have taken that from me, and I could think of no plausible story to explain my withdrawal, only a brief fiction that would buy me the summer months to dream and plan. Without curfew, without rules, I might even discover something of what my life could be, what I could make of it. In the booth, I wrapped the metal phone cord around and around my wrist and pulled it tight. My mother answered on the second ring.

"Mama," I said. "Mama, I have the most wonderful news. I've been selected for a fellowship. It's very prestigious. All the girls in English wanted it, but I'm the only one they chose. They told me just today."

"Oh, Allison," my mother said. There was sunshine in her tone. "How wonderful. And what will you be studying?"

"Drama," I said. "Plays. But listen, there's a tricky part. The fellowship begins in summer. So I can't come home like we thought I would. But it's marvelous, Mama. They're giving me housing and all my food and money besides—a stipend, they call it. My advisor says that if I want to do advanced work in English after, a fellowship like this means

I can pretty much write my own ticket. I know I told Daddy I planned on law school, but could you believe that, Mama? Your daughter, a professor?"

"Allison, I don't know about this. It sounds wonderful, of course it does, but you're supposed to fly home soon. Your ticket, it's already all paid for. I don't know what your father will say."

"Just tell him to change the ticket. I'll use it to come home at Christmas. Or Thanksgiving if you want me sooner. I know you can do it, Mama. You always know just what to say. You'll make it all right, won't you, Mama? Please, please, don't make me say no."

She did not answer. This wasn't the first lie I'd made her tell for me. And I was selfish, in the way that children are. What that lie would cost her, how my father would vent his disappointment, I didn't think of that at all.

"I'll call soon," I said into the receiver. "I promise. But I have to go now. I'm all out of quarters, and there's a study session soon. I love you, Mama. Please be proud of me." I replaced the receiver.

On Monday, I sat my lab and passed it. That night, hurrying back across the campus with whatever food I could pocket, I heard cheering. For a strange moment, I thought the cheering was for me. But no, a governor had been shot and some of the girls in black were rejoicing. The greater world—the voting, the marching—it did not concern me then. I went to my room and locked the door. The following days brought more exams, more essays. Then, abruptly, my sophomore year was done.

I stayed through the weekend, watching from my window as the campus emptied. I thought I might stay longer. No one seemed to notice me. Or to care. I was a shadow now. But a paper slid beneath my door asked for the return of my room keys. So on a bright June morning, I packed the few items I had bothered to unpack, then glossed my lips and swung my suitcases through the gates. I looked back. The campus was lush through the wrought iron, already lost to me. At the curb, a taxi squealed, then stopped. The suitcases went into the trunk. I slipped into the back seat, sticky from the last passenger, and gave the cross streets.

The taxi sped down Broadway, every light a green one. The sun was a jewel. The breeze through the window carried flowers. I had no one. And nothing, except what the trunk held. My future had grown so strange to me. Was I frightened in that moment? I should have been. But I remember feeling free.

In no time, midtown arrived. The taxi left me at the brick building. I stared up at the second floor, shielding my eyes, then hefted a suitcase in each hand. I did not know that Theater Negative would take me in. But I believed they would. I'd convinced myself that I'd come seeking liberation. I had come, I thought, for love.

Peter must have heard me on the stairs, because the loft door stood open and he was there in its frame. His eyes were bleary. I could smell wine on him and worse. He looked older to me in daylight, smaller.

"So you're back," he said, hand on hip.

There were turquoise beads around his throat. I wanted to clutch at them, to clutch at anything. I wondered if he had dreamed of me in these weeks, my skin starlit on the roof. I wondered if he had missed me.

"Thought maybe we'd scared you away."

"I'm not scared," I said. I meant it. Or I told myself I did. "Peter, listen, I need a place to stay. I can't pay much. Not at first. But I can look for a job. Right away. And I can give you something now—"

"Shhh," he said. He put his thumb to my lips and held it there, an echo of that first night. "None of that. Money doesn't matter to us, not the way it does to other people. You're one of us now, Alice. Come on in."

He took one of the suitcases, suitcases I had forgotten I was carrying, and then he took my hand. He led me inside and closed the door, so that no one could follow after.

It was hot that first morning and even hotter in the loft. In minutes, I was sweating through my dress. But Peter didn't seem to mind, and I decided I would not mind either. Faye was there. She showed me to a sagging mattress on the floor and then handed me a glass of juice, spiked with some clear liquor, before falling back asleep. Peter had me then, bent over the sink in the awful bathroom, its tub ringed in dirt, its toilet worse, and later on the roof, with the city steaming and surging below us. So maybe I was paying already.

It seemed that it would never get dark that day, but night came on at last, and others trickled in: Jax, Jorge, Molly, a few faces I didn't yet recognize. There was Chinese food in red-and-white containers and rock and roll on the battery-powered record player, and I danced until I felt empty, holy. We drank wine that stained my teeth red, and when I peered into the spotted bathroom mirror, my mouth looked bloodied. I want this, I thought. I want it all.

The next day—sprawled across a hand-me-down sleeping bag from the army surplus store, sore inside and badly hungover, my hair a nest—I felt different. Had I been wiser, I would have left right then. Told my parents that the fellowship had fallen through and asked them to change the ticket one more time. Instead I got up, brushed my teeth, sponged beneath my arms, then scavenged for what breakfast I could find. Faye woke groaning, groping for her sunglasses. After she'd smoked a cigarette and sent me out for cups of takeaway coffee—"So much cream, just have them slop it right on in, honey," she said—I asked her for the yellow pages. I planned to find some temp agency and hire myself out for office work like the city girls in books I'd read. Faye only laughed. She took off her robe—some tattered silk thing with dragons on the back—and pulled on a pale cotton dress. She wore no bra, and I could see her nipples through it, large and roseate.

We went out. The air clung to my skin like Saran wrap. Faye walked me a few blocks downtown to the Greek diner where she worked part-time. I came home with a polyester uniform and french fries in a paper sack. Faye and I ate the french fries, washing them down with more red wine. Then she held my hair as I heaved it all back up. She showed me how to work the shower, and when Peter came back that night, I was clean for him. I was ready.

I never took to waitressing. It felt too intimate, this business of asking people what they wanted and delivering it to them, harvesting their meager tips. Then there were the grabbing hands, the sick jokes. I laughed and I kept laughing as I ran a finger around the inside of my mouth or under my arm, then dunked it in the customer's coffee or juice. My hair smelled like fryer grease no matter how often I washed it. I wanted to cut it. But Peter told me not to. He liked it long. And he discouraged makeup. "You're more beautiful without it," he would say. He wanted only this meager version of me—innocent, obedient. I squeezed myself into that shape.

What tips there were, I gave him, proudly, though some of the coins I converted back into dollars, ignoring the rolled eyes of Gloria, the elderly cashier who always wore a hat inside. These dollars I folded first into my bra and then later, alongside the remaining money from the mail room job, into the box of sanitary napkins I kept tucked into a corner of a suitcase. Some things had already gone missing from those cases—a bracelet that had been a confirmation gift, my tiny bottle of Miss Dior. I longed to protest the thefts, but any complaint would prove that I didn't belong, that I should retreat to my white-fence suburb. So I stayed quiet. I knew what it was to want pretty things, to take them.

The loft, I learned, was open to all or nearly all, its population shifting from one night to the next. Peter only slept there when he'd drunk more than he should or smoked so much grass that he could barely speak. Suzanne never joined him, though she was always there for Wednesday rehearsals, where she would stare at me from across the circle. I remembered what Peter had said, that she would like me, too. The thought made me queasy. I wanted only Peter then. I would have walked on broken bottles if he'd told me to, swallowed fire. I did not want to share or to be shared. They had a place downtown, I was told, an actual house. He never took me there, only up to the roof or into the bathroom. And still I thought I loved him.

Faye was there most nights, wrapped in that torn silk robe, a bottle of spumante by her side. When she wasn't in the bathroom, way down in the empty tub, having one of her "black spells," as she called them, we played gin rummy for Toll House chocolate chips. She had taken to bringing home tins of food for the cats that roamed the block. She would sit on the stoop, stroking them as they came past, tapping their wet noses if they ever thought to claw her. In feeding the cats, she seemed to be making amends, putting love out into the world without expecting any in return.

Jax stayed over almost as often, coming in late from what he described as "dates," though once he returned with a split lip and a welt that pushed the skin of his cheek toward purple, so he might have meant something else. Jorge was there until July, when he left for a place in Brooklyn, with some new boyfriend, Jan, a Swede with a lazy eye. There were others who came and went, like Molly, with her Medusa hair and strange teas and tarot cards wrapped in black velvet, and Bash, short for Balthazar, the man to whom Peter had given the gun. A refugee from a Shakespeare troupe, he dressed in impeccable whites and liked to corner the handsomest boys and discuss their dharma. Dede, the girl closest to my age, still lived at home. I envied her clean clothes, her clear skin. She could sleep without worrying that a roach would scuttle across her pillow.

JoAnn and Bill Calder, who'd been with the company from the beginning, ever since Suzanne and Peter had dropped out of college upstate, had a place in Queens. It was near a temple, because they were on some Hindu trip now, Faye said. They came by sometimes to drop off food, vegetable curries strewn with spices I couldn't name. When they gave the pots over, JoAnn would steeple her hands in prayer, holding them first at the forehead and then at the heart. But prayer didn't bar JoAnn, a slim brunette who wore tunics that looked like they'd been spun from field grass, from drinking the last of whatever bottle was open. It didn't stop Bill, who had a scraggly blond beard, strewn with gray, from copping a feel whenever he came near. But he didn't try that on with me. This, I think, was Peter's doing. I was still his favorite then.

Everyone else was kind to me, or kind enough. If they were eating, they would offer me a plate. Drinking, they would push a glass my way. Molly read the tarot for me a few times; the readings were frightening and grim. (Faye said not to take it personally, Molly's readings always went that way.) But mostly they left me alone, and on nights when I couldn't sleep, when even sticking my face in the ice chest that we used for milk and eggs didn't work, I would lie apart, behind the bedsheet curtain, and listen as they talked and laughed. They saw me as a child, unformed, and none of them, not even Faye, the kindest and the loneliest, had an interest in forming me, though this was what I'd longed for, maybe more than I longed for Peter, to be absorbed into this world, this wayward life, to be made new.

Groceries arrived, usually with Peter, though we each made small offerings—a bunch of bananas from the street cart, a salami from the Italian market. And there were always JoAnn's curries, though they seemed to give everyone the runs. On Sundays, Dede brought spaghetti in a foil tray. Aside from that spaghetti and my shift meals, I'd never eaten so badly. Not even in the dorms. No one bothered to clean. And after a few half-hearted attempts with Lysol and a bucket mop, I gave up as well. Even the water from the tap did not come clear, spurting out whitish, mineral. We took it in disorderly turns to supply the bathroom with soap and toilet paper, though more than once I'd had to clean myself with the Post.

Yet I was on my own for the very first time, and my memories of those weeks are largely pink-tinged, romantic. I was in love, or something like it. And I believed this place, these people, would teach me who I was. Since before I could remember, I had been two girls—the good girl who did what she was told, and then, in private, the other one, the bad one. But here, I thought, I could live singly. In the meantime, I sent post-cards to my mother, pretending busyness, blurring the ink on the return address, promising to call. I did not call. I could not think of what to say. I could have lied, I suppose, made up some story that would augur my return home. But I did not want to return. Not yet. Some days I would worry at the reckoning to come, but then someone would pour a glass of wine or put a new song on the player or Peter would beckon me and I would let that worry go.

On the Fourth of July, about three weeks after I arrived, there was a cookout on the roof, with hamburgers and hot dogs that tasted mostly of lighter fluid. I had run down the stairs to the corner store and used a couple of my hoarded dollars to buy ice pops for the crowd. They had mostly melted by the time I reached the roof again, but we ate them anyway, posed for pictures with our lips rouged and blued. Was I happy then? Was I free?

Art, the urgency of shared work, would have softened the dirt, the squalor. But this was a fallow time for Theater Negative, I would dis-cover. Or worse than fallow. Whatever spark we had felt in those spring rehearsals had since guttered. The Wednesday gatherings were short and dissolute. There were hints—hints everywhere—that the troupe's best years were gone. Several members had left after that Mexican tour. One had departed to an ashram. One had taken some strange drug and never come down, seeing eyes in every tree. Besides, Faye said, it was harder to shock an audience now, harder to move them past compla-cency.

"Because they are pigs, all of them pigs," Molly said darkly from a corner. "Fat. Bourgeois."

I hated it when they talked this way. Maybe we were all just girls in black, holding up protest signs. The revolution had passed us by. Still, on Wednesdays, Peter would preside, having us play different parts of the

Bible, the Old Testament and the New, the Apocrypha. (Suzanne's Sanskrit was slow in coming.) Here, out of my waitress uniform, I was Susanna, Esther, the angel come to tell Mary the good news. I could never give myself over to a role entirely, I held myself too tightly for anything like that, but some nights, I would catch the shape of a scene, sense how it might be better staged. Once or twice, I'd tried to voice this. Peter silenced me. This was his domain, and he was jealous of it. When rehearsal ended, he would sink into the sofa, arms crossed, unspeaking, while stragglers smoked hash from a water pipe. Eventually, he would haul himself upright and jerk his chin at me, the signal to follow him to the roof, which even after sunset was barely cooler than the loft itself. He would lay the blanket down, then lay me down atop it, sometimes on my back, more often on my stomach, and take off whatever clothing was in his way. Then he would have me, fast and careless.

After that first time, the act itself meant nothing; that honeyed feeling wouldn't stay. But I liked it afterward. He was soft with me then, gathering me into his arms and pushing his sunburnt face to mine. My beautiful girl, he'd say. My baby. Sometimes I let myself believe that he would leave Suzanne, that he would marry me. But even when he spent the night, he never spent it next to me, and by mid-July, in the middle of a heat wave that melted the tar in the streets and turned the cars and buildings molten, he was often gone for days. In his absence, I would find myself thinking of my parents more. I wished for an accident, a catastrophe that would explain away what I had done. They could not be angry with me if I were truly hurt, pale in some hospital bed, my hair a sunburst on the pillow.

Then the catastrophe came. Rosa Salvatore arrived on a Wednesday. We were giddy that day. Jax, though he'd told no one, had been called before the draft board. He'd put on a show for them, he said, had himself classified as 4F. "Unfit, baby," he crowed. "Mental, moral."

"But not physical, my darling," Bash said. "No one could ever say that of you."

I believe that was the only time we talked about the war. There was a rule, unspoken, that the outside world had no place in this room, that it would intrude upon the art we were making, the art we were failing to make.

Then Peter was at the door. He'd brought bunches of flowers, red and pink carnations. And he had brought Rosa, too, who stood before us, untidy, half-wild, like one of Faye's cats in the shape of a girl. Peter introduced her around. He had found her busking in the subway station, he said, singing folk songs in her inch-thick Brooklyn accent. As she passed me, I caught the spicy, cumin-like scent of an unwashed body, and something sharper underneath that, something like decay. That girl could use a shower, I thought. Politely, too politely, I suggested it.

"You got a bathtub?" Rosa asked.

"Yes," I said. "But I'm not sure how clean it is."

Rosa laughed like a car horn. "Cleaner than me."

I pointed the way. Rosa threw down a knapsack and began to wriggle from her dress. As she lifted it over her thighs, I saw bruises there, like squashed plums. There were bruises on her arms, too. We were meant to do Samson and Delilah that day, the Tower of Babel if time allowed. Instead, a dozen of us sat in the main room, drinking beer that was not exactly cold, listening to the sounds of splashing just beyond the door.

"There is something wrong in that girl," Jorge said. He spoke rarely, and even then, his voice was just above a whisper.

"Oh, honey," Faye said. "There's something wrong with all of us."

"Yes," Molly said. She hung upside down from the sofa, her frown a smile. "We are all mad here."

Twenty minutes later, Rosa emerged, hair still wet and clinging to her shoulders, wrapped in my navy towel, a favorite because we only bothered with the laundromat every week or so and the navy didn't show the dirt.

"I washed my dress out, too," Rosa said. "Hope that's okay. Any of youse got anything I can borrow while it dries?"

"I probably have something," I said. Rosa was taller than I was, but she was thinner, so a few things ought to fit. I led her behind the bedsheet curtain. Rosa leaned in close. She smelled like soap now—lemon and myrrh—but that harsh animal fragrance remained. I rifled through a suitcase, pulling out a sleeveless cotton blouse and a skirt with an elastic waist.

"Here," I said.

"You got an extra pair of panties, maybe?"

I could feel my shoulders tensing. Where I came from, underwear was not shared. But I pulled a pair of white briefs from the case and handed those over, too.

"Oh yeah?" Rosa said, laughter blaring again. "These are a goddamn scream."

She dropped her towel and began to pull the clothes on. I looked away, blinking, as though I had stared into a too-bright light. When I turned back, she was dressed. The clothes fit, but they fit her wrong somehow. There was too much fabric or not enough. The pale colors jarred with the sharpness of Rosa's smile, the hollows of her cheeks.

We returned to the main room. Peter took Rosa's hand and led her toward the circle. I knelt on the carpet nearby. I did not like him touching her.

"Okay, Rosa," he said. "I told you a little bit about the work we do. We create performances, and we do it as a collective, so there's no director and there's no writer. We all stage it and we all write it and we all act it out. We're into myths and legends, ancient stuff, stuff that's so deep in our blood we don't even know it. We've been on a trip with the Bible. A while back, we did a piece on Exodus, on getting free, you know? It's about how we're all slaves, man, one way or another." Dede rolled her eyes at this, but Peter did not seem to notice. "How we all need freedom. Now we're looking for a new story to tell. You know the Bible?"

"Had a book when I was little," Rosa said. "Pictures and stories. Noah. The animals. That the kinda thing, you mean?"

"Yeah. That's right. So come on," he said, grinning at her. I knew that grin. "You want to play with us?"

Rosa shifted her weight from one bare foot to the other. "I don't have to strip down?" she said. "Don't have to do nothing I don't wanna do?"

That surprised me. Rosa had stripped for us already. But Peter only smiled.

"Not unless you feel like it," he said.

Peter had us stand and join hands. Clambering to my feet, I could feel that single beer working through me, a sour liquid gold. Rosa came to me, scrambled for my hand. I felt the scrape of nails on my palm, then her fierce clasp. We chanted together, opening ourselves to the universe, calling the universe in. Rosa's singing voice was low, smoky, like a blaze of green wood.

When the tone ended, Peter turned to Rosa. "When we welcome someone new, we like to ask them for a story, something that tells us who they are. Do you have a story you can share?"

Rosa ran a hand along the collar of the borrowed shirt. "You wanna hear about the first time I took my clothes off for money?"

"If that's the one you want to tell," Peter said. He said it calmly, but I could see his body bend toward her. I looked across the circle for Suzanne. She saw it, too.

"Yeah, okay," Rosa said. Her hands were on her hips now. Her tongue snaked out to wet her lips. "Was in elementary school. Third grade. Two older boys, they found me in the playground, said they'd give me a whole dollar if I showed them my snatch. They waved it around. A dollar was a lotta money to me back then. Meant a lotta candy. We went over to the bushes. I lifted up my shirt. Pulled down my panties. Showed them what they wanted. One of them, he looked like he was gonna cry. They started to run away. But I didn't have my dollar yet. So I grabbed for it. One of them, the crying one, he threw the dollar at me. Then he went and told the teachers. I got punished. Ruler on my palm. Had to write lines, too. When I got home, my ma whipped me worse. Called me a whore."

I startled at that. It had been my father. And *slut* was the word he'd used, just for playing in the backyard with the neighbor boys and a garden hose. I'd been even younger, seven.

"But I still got the dollar," she said. She was sticking her chin out now. Her eyes were like black pearls. "I still got the candy."

"Yeah, you did," Jax said from across the circle, at the same time that Faye, next to him, said, "Oh, you poor thing."

"Okay," Peter said. He clapped his hands. He didn't like our attention to drift from him for long. "Thank you for that. And welcome. Tonight, we're gonna do Samson and Delilah. Do you know it?"

He told the story to us, though I needed no reminding. Samson had been a protector of the Israelites, a defense against the Philistines. Delilah, a Philistine woman, had discovered the source of his strength, his hair. She cut that hair. Unmanned, the Philistines dragged Samson to prison. Even weak and blinded, he broke the pillars of his prison and brought it to the ground.

I had expected that I would play Delilah, but as we spread out through the room, I saw Peter whisper in Rosa's ear, and I could guess his words. Bill switched on the record player, and music rasped, low and sinuous. Peter—as Samson—began to stalk the room, shoving some of the men, grabbing at the women, me included, his hand slashing across my chest. He had lowered his center of gravity, made his body dense and animal. He prowled and swiped until Rosa danced her way toward him, circling him. I was reminded of the large cats I had seen once at the Los Angeles Zoo. How they padded around one another, how their tails seemed to twine.

Rosa led him to a wood chair and pushed him down into it, then straddled him, dragging her wet hair across his face, whipping him with it. They were kissing then, and I felt my skin go hot. Then Rosa was up, leaping toward the knapsack she had dropped when she first entered, pulling from it a pocketknife, its handle carved from yellowed bone. Flicking the blade open, she stalked back toward Peter, smiling the kind of smile that drew blood. Peter smiled back, but I could see the tension in him. Rosa straddled him again and moved the knife back and forth before his eyes. Then she took a lock of his long hair and sawed off an inch of it, sprinkling the strands across his face and chest. Peter looked surprised and for just a moment, angry. But finally, he exhaled, shut his eyes, and let himself be dragged to the floor.

The men in the company surrounded him, confining him in the fortress of their legs. He half rose and grabbed at them, stumbling with his eyes closed, feigning Samson's blindness. I watched as he pulled them all down and then the girls hurried in and I hurried with them and we were all there on the floor, breathing, entangled.

There were moments like this in many of Theater Negative's shows. In *The World Tree*, their version of the Norse myths, they had murdered the god and made the world from his body, and in *Blood Moon and Jaguar Night*, inspired—"very, very, very loosely, honey," Faye had said—by the *Popol Vuh*, there had been a similar scene. Maybe everything they did was to find these times, when we were bodies only, when anyone not already onstage would want to join. I'd felt that urge my first night, around the fire, in the parking lot. But as I saw Rosa wriggle in that borrowed blouse, I felt separate, cast aside. With the darkness as a shield, I loosened a hand from my ankle and crawled into a corner of the sofa. A song was playing at some outrageous volume, but no one seemed to listen. No one spoke.

Then Molly began to flail, right there on the ground, her eyes like pinwheels, limbs thrashing. Faye held her tight until the thrashing stopped. The other bodies shook themselves apart, turned back into people. Someone shut the record player off.

"You all right, honey?" Faye said. "You need something? Whiskey? A doctor?"

Molly shook her head, the curls like snakes. "I saw it," she said, her voice a croak. "In the cards and then again tonight. What is to be. It is disaster. For me. For many."

"Hush," Faye said. "You just go on and hush."

I looked around for Peter. But Peter had gone. So had Rosa. I knew where I would find them. And because I liked to hurt myself then, to hold experience like a thorn against my skin, I left the loft, too, and headed for the stairs. They were on the roof, spread across that same saddle blanket. Rosa was astride him, my blouse gone now. The muscles of her back flared as she moved. Her shoulder blades were wings. Peter was beneath her, eyes slitted. I hated him then. I hated her, too. I wanted my mother in that moment. Someone who loved me best.

I'd known—from the way that Molly looked at me, from some stray remark of Faye's—that I was not Peter's first girl. This was a perquisite the company provided, a flow of girls and boys, all yearning, all vibrating with want, taking our first steps toward adulthood on trembling legs. But I was young that summer, and I had believed the things he whispered hot in my ear as he clambered toward release. I shut the door and went back down.

In the bathroom, still humid from Rosa's washing, I changed into my nightgown and brushed my teeth. The loft was quiet now and dark, most of the candles exhausted. Molly was splayed across the sofa. Someone—Faye, most likely—had put a pillow beneath her head. Faye and Jax were at the kitchen window, silhouetted against the sky, sharing a cigarette, its cherry gleaming like a star. It was so hot that night, but I was shaking all the same. I climbed into my sleeping bag and pulled it tight around me. Sometime later, I woke to a shifting sensation. It was Rosa, lying down beside me on the mattress.

"What? I don't—" I began.

"Shhh," she said. "Come on. You don't mind it, do ya, sunshine?"

I did mind. But she pressed her body close.

"Shhh," she said again.

We slept chaste that night. Like sisters.

6

1997, LOS ANGELES

She called in sick that Tuesday morning, making retching sounds over the phone until Dr. Daley's secretary, Ms. Noakes, sounded sick herself and told her to take as long as she needed. After draining most of a pot of coffee and dressing in the soft, pale fabrics that were her uniform these days, she drove to the library, the downtown branch that looked something like a mission and something like a jail. The palms danced as she entered, their fronds like wagging fingers.

It was cool inside and quiet. Bright beneath the overhead lights, shadowed elsewhere. She began at the card catalog, sorting through headings and subheadings until she turned up the likeliest books. A librarian in a sweater patterned with sheep helped her find them. She took the small pile to a long table and settled herself in a stern wood chair. She did not know how it would feel to see those names etched into the pages. Better not to wonder. Better to begin.

Thankfully, her search turned up no memoirs, no diaries or jailhouse accounts. How intimate that would have been, how strange. That left only the published plays, which were soon revealed as useless, and several academic works, which were not much better. One mentioned the company, but only in passing, comparing it, unfavorably, to the more overtly political troupes—the Living Theater, the Free Southern Theater. Another had a single chapter on Theater Negative. She read it, the thorough descriptions of the early shows, the short, concluding mention of *The Grimm Variations*. The book emphasized the company's devotion to collective creation, but only Peter, as director, and Suzanne, as the designer, were referred to by name. She felt the sting of the omissions. All those many boys and girls, prized and then discarded.

But in the third book, she found more. Though short, it was devoted almost solely to Theater Negative, analyzing the company's use of origin stories in the context of the social movements of the 1960s and 1970s, this making and remaking of the world. The tone was broadly admiring, praising the egalitarian structure, the communal aesthetic. As she turned the pages, she found herself wishing that it had really been that way, the motives purer, the shared endeavor genuine. How good that might have been.

In the middle of the book were a series of pictures, glossy ones in black and white. And there they were, returned to her: Peter; Suzanne; Jax, alive still; Faye, naked from the waist up; Molly, with her gorgon's curls; Jorge performing in a town square in what must have been Mexico. There were other faces, unknown to her, from earlier in the company's history. Of Rosa, there was nothing. But at the end of the insert, she found the same photo that had appeared in her mail slot, her younger self in the dress that went see-through under the lights, and behind her, in the shadows, the little house that they had built each night. Built and razed. Below the photo was her accidental stage name, Alice Haze.

Memory flew at her then, fists raised, and she felt it all again, the rage and joy and ache. That girl had been so young, so hungry and untried.

The last chapter spoke briefly of the company's dissolution, then turned to the troupes it had influenced. What became of its members, the book did not say. But certain quotes suggested that the author, Rebecca Liu, had spoken with at least a few of them. The footnotes confirmed it. She flipped back to the copyright page—1991. Not so long ago. And the acknowledgments thanked her colleagues at the University of Wisconsin. She would find Rebecca Liu, she decided, she would phone her and learn what she could.

After borrowing a slip of paper and a golf pencil from the reference desk, she moved to a row of stolid white computers. With the mouse beneath her hand, she navigated to a search bar, then typed in Rebecca

Liu's name and her university affiliation. Seconds later, the results loaded. She had hoped for a phone number, but she found something better. Rebecca Liu had since taken a job at UCLA. A click of the mouse took her to the page for the school's faculty. She noted down a phone number and an address. Twenty miles away. Less.

She stared at the bulging screen, which stared back, unrelenting. A deep breath and she entered new search terms, the names of everyone she could remember from those days, everyone who had been with her at the end: Peter Murray, Suzanne Gold, Faye Storms, Jorge Valle, Bill Calder, Balthazar Dawes, and then, though her hands were trembling now, Rosa Salvatore. It pained her to type those letters, but the searches came up empty or returned only noise. Except for Bash. His name turned up an obituary. A brief illness. No mention of survivors. It was just what the note had said: They were dead or disappeared or living, like she was, under some new name. Dead would be best, she admitted to herself. Dead would make her safe.

Having returned the books to the desk, she asked directions to the pay phone, then searched her purse for quarters. A department secretary answered. She asked for Rebecca Liu then corrected herself, *Professor* Liu.

"She's not currently in the office," the secretary chirruped. "Would you like to leave a message?"

She knew that she should wait, collect herself. But blood was thrumming in her ears. She had to do this. Now. Today. "Do you know when she might be back? It's important."

"Let me see. She has office hours scheduled for noon. Would you like to call back then? Or come in?"

"Yes," she said. "I'll stop by. Thanks."

The Celica took her from the 110 to the 10 to the 405 and then to Sunset, which wound through the city like an unclasped necklace. She left Sunset in Westwood and, after circling the hilly streets, she squeezed into a practically vertical space on fraternity row and stuffed the meter with the rest of her change. She was early and she wandered aimless for a while, peering into shop windows without really seeing the contents. At Stan's, she bought a doughnut, smothered in pink icing, hoping that the sugar would shock her body toward awareness. But even as she licked the icing from her fingers, the fog remained. On this sunlit, California day, the past was all around her.

She entered the campus proper. It was autumn, according to the calendar. But inside the brick gates, it was summer still. Students, golden like the day, sloped up and down in shorts. The building that housed the theater department looked like a castle, its roof crenellated. She found the office on the third floor, behind a door thicker than the tires on her car. Smoothing her dress, she went in. The secretary, an elderly woman with gray hair hacked into a Louise Brooks bob, gazed at her over rimless glasses.

"May I help you?" the secretary said.

"I'm here to see Professor Liu," she said. "I phoned this morning."

The secretary took in the silk and linen of her outfit, the slim chains at her neck, and directed her toward a door at the far end of the room. The door was open, just a sliver. She knocked lightly, and at that touch, it opened farther.

The office was small and neatly kept. An arc lamp lit a framed picture that she recognized as a still from *Dionysus in 69*. The other walls held shelves, packed tidily with books and papers. The professor, a sturdy woman somewhere in her late thirties, sat behind a desk, sleepy-eyed, a highlighter loose in one hand. Her black hair was razored short, like a man's, and she wore a collarless shirt, white like spilled milk and buttoned to the neck.

"Hello," the professor said, gesturing toward the chair opposite. "I'm Dr. Liu. And you don't seem to be one of my students coming to complain about your essay grade. Delightful. Can I help you?"

"I read your book," she said as she sat down. *"Theater and Utopia."* She paused, uncertain how to proceed. She had rushed here, dazed and unprepared, with sugar on her fingers. She felt young again in this moment, reckless. "I was part of all that," she offered. She said it with an anguished kind of pride.

"You were? You don't seem old enough."

"I'm older than I look," she said. "And yes. Theater Negative. I was with them in Europe. At the end."

"Oh, for real?" The professor set down the highlighter and studied her more closely now, peeling away the decades like onion skin. "Sure. I see it now. You're Alice. Alice Haze, right? I tried to find you for an interview when I was doing my dissertation. So you were on that last tour, huh? And you were how old?"

"Nineteen. Almost twenty."

Rebecca Liu shook her head, swallowing like she'd tasted something bitter. "That's too young."

"Yes," she said. "I know."

"I wish I'd found you then. For the book, I mean. There's almost no documentation of that *Grimm* tour. No published version. I guess it all went to hell too fast. A few newspaper things. That's all. And your colleagues, they weren't too forthcoming. I heard a rumor someone shot the show. In England? Or the Netherlands? But I could never find a tape. You don't have a copy, do you?"

"No," she said. She took a barbed breath. "The show was never shot. Not as we performed it."

"Too bad. You left before it ended, right? Or were you arrested with the others? I don't remember seeing your name. But it's a while ago now."

"I left just before," she said. "That was my one talent as an actor, I guess. Timing. So I was gone for all that. And honestly, I haven't thought about it in years. But the school where I work has an email portal now. Yesterday, someone reached out to me there. Anonymously. Someone who knew me then. The messages were strange. They rattled me, if I'm honest. And I want to know who could have sent them. Who's still alive. I was hoping you could tell me."

"Well, I can't tell you much for certain," the professor said. She was intent now, the highlighter capped. "The book came out in '91. It was adapted from my dissertation, so most of the research was done a couple of years before that. My advisor thought it was too soon to reconsider the company. But if you wait too long, no one's around to interview. Even back then, there weren't that many people to talk to. They were unlucky, your friends. But let's see." The professor went to a bookshelf and slid out a metal organizer, removing several folders and flicking through typescript pages, photocopies, loose sheets pulled from yellow legal pads.

"Your colleagues weren't easy to find. After they were released, some of them followed Peter Murray back to the States, where he served that other sentence. Mostly, they scattered. Or dropped from the record. Murray, he ended up doing a back-to-the-land thing. Suzanne Gold was with him. In Vermont, I want to say? Or Maine? I have it somewhere. They were off the grid or mostly off. Said they didn't have a phone. They answered a few questions by letter."

Rebecca Liu held up a paper. "Did you know Fanny Tremblay? She talked to me. I'm pretty sure she's still around. Or as around as anyone can be after that much LSD."

"No, she was before my time."

"That's right. She joined that ashram in '70, I think. Jorge Valle, he was back in Mexico when he talked to me. Didn't have a lot to say. Who else? JoAnn Calder, she must have died right after you left. God, what a thing. And Faye Storms a decade later."

"Faye? I hadn't heard." She thought of Faye, a bottle of spumante in her hand, nearly falling out the kitchen window as she laughed with Jax.

"She was in some weird scene in San Francisco. Sex magic, I want to say. A bunch of them took poison together. In '82 or '83."

"Did you reach any of the others?" she said. It felt wrong to speak their names. But she spoke them anyway. "Bill Caldwell? Jan? I don't know his last name."

"Jan's last name was Sorenson. I couldn't find him. Bash, I talked to him before he died, a liver thing I want to say. He thought Jan had died in the mid '80s. AIDS, maybe. I had a number for Bill. He wouldn't participate—still broken up, it sounded like. Was there anyone else?"

There was, of course.

She tried to keep her voice flat. "Did you speak to Rosa?" she said. "Rosa Salvatore?"

"Rosa? Rose Red? The one who ran away?"

"I just wondered if she ever turned up after."

"Not that I know of. I know the police were looking for her, but she must have found some way to get out or lie low. And what about you, Alice?" On the surface, the professor's expression was composed, even kind. Underneath was something sharper. "What happened to you?"

"What happens to most of us, if we're lucky: I grew up."

"So you never see anyone from the old days?"

"Never." It came out harsher than she'd intended.

"Really?" the professor said. "You left it all behind? Just like that?"

"Just like that." She'd made a clean break. If that break had never healed, that wasn't for Rebecca Liu to know.

"I'm surprised," the professor said, pressing back in her chair. "I always felt jealous of people like you, of that whole scene. By the time I was in college, all the wild stuff had happened already, and the best I could hope for was that maybe someone would wheel a TV onstage or something. All the experiment had gone out of theater, all the danger."

"You didn't miss much," she said. "Believe me."

"Maybe so. But here's the thing I never understood. It's the reason for my dissertation. You wanted to change the world. Not just you. And not just Theater Negative. All of you. All the groups. Paradise here and now. No more rules. Just freedom. Just love. Instead, it all blew up and people disappeared or doped themselves silly or gave it all away. What happened?"

She laughed then, laughed to keep from hitting out, reaching across the desk and grabbing the professor by the neck of her collarless shirt. "Paradise? It's just one more story. There was no paradise. Not really. Not for me. Not for any of us." And that was true. Though there were other truths. She could still remember what she'd felt in the loft on those summer evenings, when they were building something with just their voices and their hearts. But there was no returning. Time—the angel with the flaming sword—made sure of it.

"Look," she went on, "I wasn't exploited. Or if I was, I wanted it. I'm nobody's victim, all right? But all that stuff about no more hierarchies, no more rules? Please. The people in power never really gave it up; they just pretended to. It was like a game to them. The game was rigged. It's always rigged. The world was never meant to change."

"Did you change? Did it change you?"

"Oh, sure," she said. She regretted coming now, regretted what she'd told this stranger. "It changed us all. It drank us, ate us, wrung us dry. Let's just say that there are worse things a person can do onstage than roll out a TV. I should go now. If you have those contacts—the addresses, the numbers—I'll take them."

The professor wrote down a few names and details, then pushed the page across the desk. She thanked her for it. Then she was out in the dazzling sun, which shrank her shadow down to nothing, and back into the car. She hadn't fed the meter quite enough, and a ticket lazed beneath a windshield wiper. She turned the wipers on and watched as they slid the ticket up and down, up and down, until finally the paper tore loose and fluttered to the street below.

At home, she pulled the blinds and flicked the switch that set the ceiling fan whirring, then lay down fully clothed on the bed. So Faye was dead, too. And Bash. And Peter and Suzanne gone to a farm somewhere. Gone to flowers, like the folk song said.

She didn't think that either of them had sent the letter. The jittery, yearning tone wasn't a match for Peter's bohemian self-importance or Suzanne's earth mama cool. Was it Rosa, then? This was her great fear, the night terror that still panicked her into wakefulness. It was also her secret hope. But no. She remembered the body falling. She remembered the glaze of blood.

By the time hunger roused her, the light outside the blinds had declined to rose gold. She slunk into the kitchen and stood frozen in front of the open refrigerator. Finally, she took out a carton of cottage cheese and half a plastic-wrapped cantaloupe, already seeded, and brought them to the table. The familiar motion of scooping hemispheres of fruit into a bowl, of spooning cottage cheese, soothed her. But she could barely taste the bites she lifted to her mouth or even the iced tea she drank, though normally the aspartame was enough to make her teeth ache.

Powering on the TV, she riffled from channel to channel, settling for a while on the news, then fleeing when the news turned grim. She switched the television off. No book could hold her then. No glossy magazine. Instead, she put a CD into the player, the Mamas & the Papas, her teenage favorite, and curled into herself as the sad songs spun.

It was night when the CD ended. Just late enough. She drove to the bar. The crowd was sparse, typical of a Tuesday, the dance floor empty. She took her glass out to the patio, felt a hot breeze graze her cheek. A girl was there, in a USC sweatshirt and jean shorts, her black hair sleek. The girl saw her and gave a slight smile, dipping her head like a duck dabbling for weeds. She approached the girl and gestured with her glass.

"What are you drinking?" she asked.

"Whiskey?" the girl said. She sounded unsure.

"I've heard of it. You want another?"

The girl shook her head. "No. I have to drive later. And I'm not even drinking it, really. It's just to keep my hands busy."

"First time?" she said.

"Yeah." That duckling smile again. "Does it show?"

"That's okay. It's everyone's first time sometime. You didn't want to come on the weekend? It's better on the dance floor then."

"Yeah, I'm not great with crowds," the girl said.

"Me neither. You're at SC?"

"Grad school. Film. Documentaries, or that's the hope. But you're not in the industry."

"God, no. I teach."

"Thought so." The girl drew up into herself, harnessing whatever nerve she had, eyes bright with her own daring. "Think you could teach me?"

"I know a thing or two."

"Your place?"

"No."

"Well, then, mine, I guess?"

"Maybe." She wouldn't make it too easy on the girl. Not yet. She darted her eyes toward the vacant patio. "Sure you don't just want me because there's no one else here?"

"Could be," the girl said. "But if you want to know the truth, I was honestly so scared to come here. Like terrified almost. Took me weeks to work up to it. If you say no, probably I'll never come here again and I'll end up married to some gross guy and I'll have his babies, like six of them, and I'll never make even a single movie. So really, when you think about it, you have to say yes. For cinema."

"Then, yes," she said, draining the last of the terrible wine and setting the glass precariously on a cement planter. "For cinema. Though maybe I should know your name first?"

"It's Gabrielle."

She looked at the girl. "No, it isn't."

"Oh, did you—?" The girl cut herself off. "Fine. It's Monique."

"Okay, Monique. Where to?"

She followed the girl's red Cabriolet up into the hills, along twisting roads that switched back and back. Clematis and passion fruit vines grew here, seeming to brush the Celica as it clambered higher, toward the low-slung moon. This was a wealthy neighborhood. And no surprise. The girl had a silkiness to her that only money bought. She parked in a sloping drive, then followed Monique through a wooden door into a side yard, lined with rosebushes, and out into a backyard with its sunken pool, tiled in green and blue and lit with underwater lights. Monique led her to the pool house, its door unlocked, walking her past a kitchenette and a miniature living room, then upstairs into a bedroom that spanned the building's full length. Its far wall was all windows, and beyond them, the ground fell away to nothing. The lights of the city, bracketed by freeways, spread themselves below. It was dark in the room. The girl sat on the bed, atop a white coverlet, and she knelt before her, like she used to kneel at the altar rail. She bent to her work.

Two hours later, dressed again, with a tape of *Sans Soleil* in her hands, she let herself out of the pool house and made her way toward the side yard. A splashing startled her, and she saw that she wasn't alone. Another girl was perched at the edge of the pool, white calves and ankles dangling in the water. Her body tensed as her mind resolved the image. A girlfriend? An ex? But then the girl at the pool raised her head, and with the help of the underwater lights, she saw that it was worse than that. Because she knew this girl. It was Naomi. Her student.

"Mrs. Morales?" Naomi said.

"Naomi, what a surprise," she said, ironing her voice to evenness.

"It's so random to see you here. You know my sister?"

She kept her distance. Not wanting Naomi to smell the sex on her. "Yes," she said, improvising briskly. "We're friends from a film club."

"Weren't you out sick today?"

"Yes, but I'm feeling much better now." She reached into her coat and flashed the tape. "I just came by to borrow a movie. Come and see me tomorrow, okay? We need to start mapping out *Midsummer.*"

Then she was back in the car, hurtling down the hill, screaming into the windshield as if the scream might crack it. Because she had forgotten: Nowhere was safe. Nowhere she could run to. Nowhere she could drive. She brought the danger with her.

7

1972, NEW YORK CITY

would not have described myself as lonely in those days. In the loft, I rarely had a private moment. Even on the toilet, I had to brace a leg against the door if I wanted to void myself in peace. But immediately, Rosa claimed me as her friend. My unliking fazed her as little as a missed bus. She attached herself to me from that first night. And I suppose I let her, despite the awful jealousy I felt, the jealousy that I was not supposed to feel. The next morning, I let her borrow some toothpaste and my facecloth. Then I told her how the loft worked and what there was to eat and which mattress was most likely free. Here at last was someone who knew even less about this world than I did.

"And you don't have to pay nothing?" she asked as I sliced a banana into cornflakes. The milk had gone sour, so I ate the cereal dry.

"We all pay, but only what we can afford."

"For real?"

"For real."

"And there's no weird stuff?"

"Depends on what you mean by weird."

"Like you don't have to make it with no one you don't want to?" The planes of her face had hardened.

"No," I said. And then, because back then I believed this to be true, "No one has ever made me do anything I didn't want to do."

"Well, okay," she said. She took the spoon from my hand and began to eat my cereal.

So Rosa stayed. She must have found a sleeping bag of her own, because that night, when I came home from my shift, she was sprawled

across it, in a man's T-shirt and what must have been her own lace panties, dry now, painting her toenails a lurid shade of pink. She told me
she'd lifted the polish from the drugstore on Eighth Avenue.

"You want me to do yours, sunshine?" she asked.

And because Peter was not there to make me hate her, I found that
I did.

The next day, Rosa asked me to come with her to buy new clothes.
I told her that I had work, and she asked me when work ended. There
she was at shift's end, sitting at a booth in a different borrowed skirt,
stuffing french fries into her mouth.

"You can pay for this, right?" she said. There was a milkshake, too.
Strawberry, by the look of it. "Like you get a discount or something?"

There were no discounts. But I nodded, counting out a dollar and
a half for Cheryl, the waitress who came on after I did. Rosa took another sip, wiped her mouth with her hand, and we set off. I wanted to
go home and change out of my uniform first, but she said I looked fine
and, besides, I could change later. She grabbed my hand and pulled me
toward Bryant Park with its library lions and then down into the subway. Rosa jumped the turnstile. I traded in my pocket change for tokens
and followed after. The train came, and Rosa spilled herself across a row
of seats and I joined her, my legs crossed primly. Rosa kept hers wide.
Anyone across the aisle could have seen her underwear.

On our way downtown, she asked me about myself, about where I
was from, and I told her a polite version of the truth.

"Heard you were some kinda college girl," she said.

"I was," I said. "I am. I'm just taking a break." And I wondered,
maybe for the first time, if this were true, if I would ever step through
those gates again.

"How come, sunshine?" she asked.

Without knowing why, I told her that, too: how I'd been caught
missing curfew, how my roommate turned me in, how she claimed
we'd been together, just to make it worse for me. I checked Rosa's face

as I said that part. Her mouth opened and she laughed that honking laugh.

"They kick you out for that?" she said. "Where I come from, they pay to see it."

I wanted to ask what she meant by that, but the train had stopped and she'd leaped from the car, leaving me to hustle after her. We came up on the East Side, on a street called Houston. A block over, a block across, and down a few steps into a store so crowded with clothing racks that there was barely room to move among them. It smelled of dust and something loamier, like moss or soil. The walls were painted black and dotted with fraying posters. I stood helpless. I'd only ever bought my clothes at department stores, with my mother by my side. Rosa, however, went straight for the racks, flinging hangers aside like a contained whirlwind. Soon she had a small wardrobe in her arms—jeans, shirts, a sundress, a suede miniskirt, a plastic purse, white with two red cherries.

"I need panties, too," she said. "But I don't buy those antique. You don't want nothing?"

"No," I said. "I'm fine."

"Yeah, fine's no goddamn fun," she said. "Come on."

She went whipping through another rack until she'd found a dress for me, a cotton print in pale blue and pink with a smock top. When she held the hanger to my neck, it fell almost to the toes of my shoes. It was loose, less constricting than anything else I owned, and so sheer that the sun would shine right through it.

Rosa saw me hesitate.

"Nah, go on, college girl," she said. "Put it on."

"Shouldn't we wash it first?"

Another laugh. "Betcha it's cleaner than that uniform. Go on. Just give me the tag."

I pulled the tag. There was a dressing room in a corner of the store, curtained off like the sleeping area at the loft. A few months ago, I never would have taken off my clothes in a place like this, and when the curtain was pulled back, I certainly would have screamed. But it was only Rosa, with a paper bag crinkling under one arm and another to hold my uniform, so I went on tying the dress at the neck.

She appraised me in the warping mirror as she handed me the bag. "Cute," she said, "like one of those Sheep Meadow hippies." She saw the face I made. "Nah," she said, bumping me with her hip, "looks good."

She led me out onto the street and then across Houston and up to a Woolworth's, where she left me on the sidewalk. "Back before you know it," she said.

I wandered to the corner, enjoying the feel of the dress as it brushed against my hips, how cool the cotton seemed. I loosed my hair from its ponytail, recoiling for a moment at the smell of grease, and tried to look like I belonged—on this sidewalk, in this city, in this life. But my back ached and I had a pimple coming on my chin and I didn't quite believe it.

Rosa found me a few minutes later and threw a twist of bubble gum my way. She blew a bubble, then licked it from her lips. "Look what I got!" She opened the paper bag and let me peek. On top of the clothes, I saw a packet of underwear, white like my own. "We can match now, sunshine," she said, laughing. "Like a twin act." I knew she hadn't paid for it.

Rosa insisted that we walk back to the loft. The thirty blocks took about an hour, with Rosa stopping to buy a pretzel, then a candy bar, to pitch a penny into a fountain in Madison Square Park. She gave me a penny, too, and I told her that I didn't know what to wish for.

"Then give it back," she said and sent the coin spinning toward the water. "I got wishes enough for both of us."

She told me something of her life, how she'd grown up in the South Bronx, a place I'd never been, with a crazy mother and four brothers and no father to speak of. She'd left school at fourteen and been on her own ever since. I didn't ask her what she did for money. I suppose I knew. As she chattered, I could feel any lingering dislike dissolve. She was so childlike in her appetites, so honest in her hunger and delight. She was bruised, I had seen it, but none of that seemed to pain her. I wanted to touch her then, so I linked my arm through hers as the day bent itself toward dusk, painting the sky a deeper blue. Music streamed from doorways and cars, and there was the smell of garbage, yes, but over and around it, there were other scents—flowers and gasoline and coffee. I felt almost happy then, grateful for the dazzle of the sun as it hit the skyscrapers' glass. Because Rosa and I were walking through it, arm in arm. This delirious city—which I would leave so soon, never to return—for a moment, it was ours.

Back at the loft, Rosa claimed the bathroom and emerged half an hour later in a red blouse and the miniskirt that barely covered her bottom. Peter had come in, with a sack of groceries, and I saw him drink her in as though she were a glass of something sweet and iced. He saw me, too, and smiled, with a glint of sharp teeth.

"Snow White and Rose Red, huh?" he said. "I like it."

"Betcha do," Rosa said, tossing her wet hair.

While Faye and Jax were busy in the kitchen, chopping and scraping vegetables for the pot, I had my shower, shampooing my hair twice to wash the fryer grease away, trailing soap across my breasts and belly. My breasts felt sore. My period had come. A relief in its way. Dry, with the cotton dress back on and toilet paper in my underwear, I tiptoed to the suitcase for my beltless pads. I found the pads, but the hoarded money, nearly forty dollars, had gone. I understood now how Rosa had paid for the clothes, for the bubble gum. Whatever I had felt for her that afternoon shriveled and decayed.

She was leaning out the window, exhaling a cloud of smoke. I approached her and stood too close.

"Did you take my money?" I asked her, quiet enough so that no one else would hear.

"Thought the deal here was share and share alike," she said. The smoke went into my face this time. I kept my hands pinned to my sides so that I wouldn't push her.

"Not with everything," I said. "I worked hard for that."

"So hide it better," she said.

I could feel my cheeks going red, scarlet to match her blouse. "I want it back," I said.

Rosa stubbed her cigarette out on the sill, then flicked the butt down to the street. "Oh yeah?" she said. Her lips turned down, making a rainbow shape. "Means so much to you. Fine."

She turned back to the room. "Going out for a while," she said, louder now.

"Ooh," Jax said. "Can you get me a bottle of pop?"

"Make it two," called Faye. "Cold as you can get 'em." She went for her purse.

"Nah," Rosa said, with a look right at me as she headed for the door. "My goddamn treat."

"Hey, you want company?" Peter said.

The door slammed. She was gone.

"I'm going to bed," I said.

"Bed?" Faye laughed. "Honey, it's not even eight o'clock. And we're just making dinner."

"Aw, come on," Peter said. "Don't be that way."

"I'm not any way," I said. "I'm tired, and I have an early shift." My breasts hurt. My stomach hurt. My heart hurt, too. And since I was bleeding, Peter couldn't have had me even if he'd wanted. Last month, during this time, I had taken him in my mouth, and that had felt bold, exciting. Now the memory was ugly. If I'd had Rosa's penny, I would have wished that I were home, that home were someplace safe.

I woke at what must have been near dawn. Rosa was standing over me, dropping scrunched up bills onto my face, one by one. Her lipstick, which might have been my lipstick, was half gone. She had that same animal smell.

"There's your money back," she said. "You happy now?"

I rubbed the sleep from my eyes. "How did you get it?" I said.

"You don't wanna know," she said. Her mouth made that rainbow shape again.

"Thanks," I said. I put the bills beneath my pillow.

"We good now?"

"Sure," I said. "Get some sleep."

"Can I sleep with you?"

I moved over on the mattress, and she fit herself to me, back to back. As I fell asleep, I could feel her shaking. She was laughing, noiselessly. Or maybe she was crying. In the morning, I put the new bills in the napkin box and stuffed the box deep down into the case. The cotton dress that Rosa had bought for me, I crammed that at the bottom, too. It didn't feel like mine.

Peter came back two nights later. He had a stack of books with him. From the Strand, he said, a place that I had passed with Rosa on our way to Woolworth's. He handed copies around. Faye and Jax and Molly were there that night. Dede, too, drinking gin and orange juice from a coffee mug. Rosa was in the velvet armchair we'd dragged up from the street, cleaning under her nails with her pocket-knife. She zipped it into her purse and took a book from Peter's hand. The books, I saw, were the same, more or less. They were collections of fairy tales. I'd had a similar book in childhood, its cover patterned with briars.

Peter seemed excited, vibrating to a music no one else could hear. "This trip we've been on with the Bible, it's over," he said. "Done. The Bible's had all the danger scrubbed of it. It's all Sunday school now. But this!" He held up a book, showed it around to all of us. "It's savage. It's death and fucking and hearts ripped out of chests. The dark wood? That's all of us, man, that's the place we go when life can't hold us anymore. This is it, what we've been looking for. And you should thank Alice, because she brought it to me."

"I did?" I said.

"Yes, you and Rosa, too. Standing together the other night, like girls out of a story, this story." He opened the book and ran a finger down the table of contents, then turned it around. "'Snow White and Rose Red,'" he said.

"I don't know it," I said.

"Read it. All of you. That story and the others. This is it. The new show. We'll start roughing it out on Wednesday." I looked at my book, a paperback with a brown-and-white cover, its pages edged in dusty red. I wrote my name, in small, neat capitals, on the inside cover, the name I lived by then, ALICE HAZE.

On Wednesday, *The Grimm Variations*, the last show that Theater Negative would ever make, began. With Peter leading us, the warm-ups gave way to scene work, which we built out through furious, ecstatic improvisations. I had never seen Peter like this, not since that first night atop the car. He was so focused, so intent. He stalked among us, shifting a limb here, whispering a suggestion in an ear, making us match what he saw in his mind's eye. He was so beautiful to me then.

But this beautiful man, he didn't want me. Not anymore. His eyes went to Rosa now. In his gaze, I had felt prized, astonishing. Beyond that light, I was just some hanger-on with pimples on her chin, forking over tips to buy bad wine and worse food. Still I did not leave. Because this was what I had been waiting for, to give myself to the work. And that giving, it was wonderful. Whatever disgrace had brought me here, whatever degradation I had endured to stay, it was, in those few hours, made fair and right. Even now, I can picture how we were: Jax leaping from frog to a prince. Bash preening as a witch. Peter's bear. Faye's blinded Rapunzel. Dede as a troll. Molly as Rumpelstiltskin. I played the princess in that story. And Snow White, too. The tales ran together, like they'd been poured from one vessel, because the stories, Peter told us, were really all one story. I believed him.

That first week, there were two rehearsals. The next week, three. Then it was August and we were working every night, and I had to give up my dinner shifts. All the regulars returned, and there were a couple of new faces. Jan, Jorge's boyfriend, joined us. And Suzanne, who had been absent, arrived with a sketchbook and a metal case of colored pencils. She was the company's designer, and as we moved, she drew us. The second Saturday after we'd begun in earnest, she came in the daytime. She brought the boy, Zion, who played while we worked. As the group broke for a makeshift lunch, she asked Molly and me if we would go with her to the fabric store. This was surprising. She had never spoken to me before. I agreed, though I was hungry, and Molly did the same.

"You'll look after Zion, won't you, Faye?" Suzanne asked.

"Sure I will," Faye said. "Watch him like the sweetest hawk you ever saw." She opened her arms to the boy. Her dress was sleeveless, and I could see the hair curling in her armpits. "Come on, honey, let's make you a plate."

We left, walking in silence, as horns blared and tires screeched and sweat carved rivulets down the back of my blouse. Suzanne, who wore a yellow dress that billowed from her body, knew how to make her way through the crowd. I'd thought her dumpy. And old. Though she must have been younger than I am now. But in motion, she was a queen. She had only to turn a shoulder, to raise an elbow, and the crowd parted.

Though the garment district was nearby, only a few blocks away, I had never visited it. My mother sewed, and she had taught me to work her Singer, but I regarded it as one more chore. When she shopped for fabric, once or twice a year, in the tidy, fluorescent-lit emporiums of Los Angeles's downtown, I tended to wait in the car. But I would not think of my mother now. Now there was work to do.

The store Suzanne brought us to, an Aladdin's cave of color and textures, was like no store I had ever entered. Suzanne fondled various bolts, running the cloth between thumb and fingers in a way that struck me as sensual. I tried to catch Molly's eye. But Molly had her sunglasses on, her face a mask.

I don't know what the clerk—a prim, graying woman in a blue skirt suit—must have thought of us, Molly all in black and me sweating through my blouse and Suzanne in her flowing robes. But as Suzanne began to speak in her regal way about yards of this and lengths of that, the woman lowered her shoulders and did as Suzanne asked. We emerged with oversized bags stuffed with brocade, false fur, a golden cloth that shone like silk, and more besides. Suzanne had bought a whole bolt of muslin, and Molly and I hefted it between us.

"Are you hungry?" Suzanne asked as we neared the loft. "Come on." She turned her steps diagonal, toward a lunch counter window. "Hot dogs okay? They're all-beef. Kosher."

"That's fine," I said.

"None for me," Molly said in her usual flat tones. "I am a vegetarian. I will not kill to eat."

"Well, they must have something that isn't meat."

She ordered for us. Orange drinks all around. Hot dogs with an onion sauce for the two of us and something called a knish, which looked like a man's leather wallet, fried, for Molly. We ate leaning against the wall of a building, the bags and bolts tucked behind and between us. This was another thing my mother had warned me against: eating in public. Men wouldn't like it, she'd insisted. They would think you loose, sloppy. I bit into the hot dog and it bit back, squirting salty juice against the roof of my mouth. It felt obscene. If my mother could have seen me now. But when would she see me? I'd been gone so long already. And still I could see no way home. Queasy, I threw the rest of the hot dog away.

Back at the loft, the air was heavy, thick with incense and dope. Rosa had fallen asleep on the sofa, while Jax lolled at her feet, paging through a movie magazine with Dede.

"Ooh," Dede said. "Just look at Steve McQueen."

"He shift your gears, baby?" Jax said, cackling.

Jorge and Jan stood near the kitchen sink, sharing a crinkling bag of potato chips. Faye and Zion were at the window, playing some game.

Peter, we were told, had gone to the store for beer. We set the bags down at the edge of the carpet. I headed for the bathroom to splash some water on my face. When I came out, Suzanne was there.

"Alice," she said. "A moment?"

I nodded, following her out of the loft, up the stairs, and onto the roof where I'd joined her husband many times, which felt wrong, like a rhyme gone slant. We stood there, in the small shade the doorway provided, and I looked away, out over the city, sultry in the heat. I braced myself, planting my feet sure and wide. I thought she might scream at me then, asking why I had gone with a married man. I did not know what I would answer.

But Suzanne's voice was even, almost tender. "Are you all right?" she said.

The question surprised me. "Me? I'm fine. Why wouldn't I be?"

"I just wanted to make sure," she said. She moved out from the doorway. Reluctantly, I stepped toward her.

"Smoke?" she said.

"Okay," I said. "Sure."

She took a packet from her dress, thumbed two, then lit them, flinging the match to the street below, a casual gesture that reminded me of Peter. She handed one to me, then took a long drag from the other and let it filter out her mouth.

"Girls like you," she said. "You give him something. Something he needs to make the work. I used to give him that. Not anymore. Not since Zion. It's good to give yourself like that. It's beautiful, important. But he goes through girls so fast these days, and he doesn't think what it's like for them, for you, when he moves on to the next one."

"So there have been others?" I said, though I knew the answer already. "A lot of others?"

"Oh, God," she said. "Sure. Everyone pretty much. For some, it doesn't matter. Like Faye. Too flighty, that one. Her feet don't ever touch the ground. But some of you, you take it hard. You should have seen Molly when she first came to us, smile like a flashbulb. I take it he's with Rosa now."

"Yes," I said, stubbing out my cigarette.

"Don't like her," Suzanne said. "I don't trust her. I never trust the skinny ones. God knows where he found her."

"In the subway, busking."

"Is that what he said? Anyway, I just wanted to tell you: I know what it's like. I know it can be hard."

"It's fine," I said. "It doesn't matter. I'm only here for the summer." It was what I told myself then, that this was just a sojourn, a filthy idyll, that I would find my way back to a normal life sooner or later.

"Are you sure, Alice? There's work to do now. A new show. If you can stay for that, you should. I've been watching you. At rehearsal. This work we do, you're good at it. You remind me of me, if I'm honest. Or how I used to be. You're hungry, aren't you? Never had enough of what you needed. You'd swallow the world if you could. I know it's not your usual scene, a mattress on the floor. I get that. I was a good girl once. Nice family. Nice home. But the nice places, the clean ones, they'll never fill you up. You get used to a mattress. Seeing Peter with someone else, you get used to that, too. There's a part of me that even loves him for it. The people who don't want anything? They're the ones I can't stand. It's better to be hungry, Alice. It's better to want. And the work, it might just feed you." She took a last drag on her cigarette, and then that went over the roof's edge, too.

"Come on," she said. "Maybe they left us some chips."

Rehearsals resumed that afternoon and went on until night fell. Molly sobbed. Dede growled and screeched until her throat went raw. Jax, a prince in short shorts, locked his hands in mine and spun me around the room until I was dizzy and couldn't breathe for laughing. I thought of what Suzanne had said, that I belonged, that I was welcome here. Afterward, a party began, and by my second glass of wine, I remember wanting to fling myself up from the sofa and run out into the street, to tell anyone I met that life could be exquisite and strange, that it could burn you, like a candle flame held to your palm in the best, most wonderful way.

But then I saw Peter and Rosa, on the carpet, six feet away, the length of a fallen body, and that delight was bled from me. He was whispering in her ear, and I could feel the bristles of his mustache as though they were scraping my own skin. I wasn't used to it. Not yet. And I felt small and sad and mean. Peter pulled her to her feet, and they moved toward the door, laughing, shoulders colliding. Then Bill was there, with his thin beard and chipped front tooth, a string of wooden beads around his neck. He looked like Peter, but less so, a mimeograph with its edges blurred.

"What's the word, Alice?"

He sat too close on the sofa. I suppose I smiled.

"What a scene, right?" he said. He leaned back and stretched his legs out. He wore jeans and cowboy boots, even in the heat. The candles caught the sweat on his nose. "I've missed this," he said. "JoAnn and me, we needed time to cool down after Mexico. But when it's like this, when it's cooking? Oh, man. It's something else."

"It is," I said.

"And you're into it," he said. "I can tell."

He brought my hand to his chest, to the V of his shirt. His skin was wet and too warm. I wanted to shake my hand free. But his grasp was firm and I was in some ways still my mother's daughter, taught not to cause a fuss, not out where everyone could see. In the past, with other boys, I'd known how to resist. They were supposed to say yes and I was supposed to say no, protecting my virtue. But my virtue had no worth here. So when he moved to kiss me, I did not move away. His breath was sour, his tongue felt too large for my mouth.

"Come on," he said, jerking his chin toward the curtain and the mattresses beyond.

I took a sip of my wine. I had forgotten that I held it. "Isn't your wife here?"

"JoAnn?" he said. "Sure." He pointed to the window where she stood with Molly and Faye. She had a camera hanging from her neck. She was clicking to the next exposure. "But she's not hung up on some old-lady trip. She's cool. She gets it."

I should have told him that I was on my period. Or that I had hang-ups of my own. Or even the truth: that I did not want him, that I would rather have stuck my hand in the diner's fryer basket than touch his body. I did not. And still he saw me hesitate.

"Aw, come on," he said, his voice rising. "You like me, don't you? Because I like you, Alice. Peter told me about you. Said you were cool, free. You're cool, right?" His hand was on my breast now, the left one, cupping it as though he were gauging its weight. "Come on, girl. Don't you want to feel good?"

"Fine," I said. I would make it with him. I would do it for Peter, so that I would not prove him wrong. We rose from the couch and slipped past the curtain. I brushed against the record player on the way and slid the volume notches higher until the sound was like a wall.

Bill seemed to know which mattress was mine. He sat down and I sat with him, primly, like the Catholic school girl I had been. From a back pocket, he pulled out a condom.

"We'll use a rubber, okay? It's a thing with JoAnn and me. I do what I want as long as I don't get any of you girls in the family way. She wouldn't like that." He seemed sad for a moment. The moment passed. He unbuttoned his fly, scrunched the denim and his underwear to mid-thigh. And there was his penis, long and thin, pointing toward the tin ceiling.

I think he meant for me to ready myself, to lift my skirt or squirm out of my underwear. But I would not make it easier for him. So I went away, like I'd done as a child when my father raged. I had learned to abandon my body then, to float above it until he spent his anger and I could return, curling into a ball, protecting, too late, my softer parts.

I was somewhere else when Bill pushed his way into me, the rubber chafing. "Oh yeah," he panted in my ear. "Oh yeah." The wooden beads were in my mouth. Some other girl's mouth.

I wish that this was the last time I let someone have me like this. But once the show was up and running, I was made to see it as an extension of the work, as though, through me, these groping men could touch something universal and divine. We lied to ourselves that way. All of us girls. Except for Rosa. But that night, as Bill moaned, I knew it for what it was. Not a calling, not a miracle. Just a skinny man in dirty jeans making free of my body while I dreamed myself away.

Then a sound came, louder than the radio. A siren, I thought on first hearing, an ambulance. But it was a woman's voice, Molly's voice, shrieking in a tone so high it was almost beyond hearing, the bottom string of a violin vibrated by some endless bow. The sound became words, "Help! Help! Somebody help!" and I was back inside my body, shoving Bill off me, then running, tripping, to the main room, where nearly everyone was gathered at the bathroom door. Being small, I pushed through, and there, lit by the candles atop the toilet tank, was Jax, in the bathtub, in his sleeveless shirt, sallow and unmoving, face slack, lips blue.

"Is he breathing?" a voice said. It was a woman's voice. Faye's, maybe.

He did not look like he was breathing. Jax, all flash and rascal glamor, had never been still a moment in his life. He was still now. There was a new scream then, like a blade slicing the smoky air. It echoed from my own throat. I did not know how to make it stop.

8

1997, LOS ANGELES

She must have slept, though she recalled the night mostly as a series of strobe-lit stills, waking again and again, tangled in the sheets, her limbs sprawled at odd angles. She gave it up around 6:00 a.m., stumbling first into the shower and then, dried and robed, out the door and into the gray light to collect the paper from its mat. With the coffee brewing, she poured a bowl of wheat flakes and drowned them in skim milk, sifting a packet of artificial sweetener over the top like scant snow. The cereal had little taste, and though her eyes moved across the headlines, only a few words registered. She threw the paper down. Pushed the cereal away. Put her head into her hands.

This could not be happening again. She had been a character in a story just like this one. Seen it through to its terrible end. Turned the page. But maybe Peter had been right. Maybe there was only one story. The same story. Her story. But no, she told herself. She was not that young girl anymore, helpless and alone. What had Naomi seen? Her teacher, at night, with a VHS tape. There was nothing wrong with that. And nothing wrong with the rest of it. She and the girl were both of age. And two women together wasn't any kind of scandal, not now. This was the 1990s after all. The school, which liked to think itself progressive, would not make her leave. The school couldn't, not without risking a lawsuit. But she'd always had a horror of having her private life known. She'd never kept a diary. Because a diary could be read. Or confided a secret. Because a secret could be shared. And the memory of what had happened in college, the accusation, however true, that had spun her life out of its orbit, the shame of that was never far away. It wasn't anything to be ashamed of, but still the feeling held.

How could she best protect herself? Should she talk to Naomi? Or should she say nothing, gambling that Monique—if Monique were even her name—would keep her mouth shut? And what was there to do about the messages? Or the threat to her department? Or the problem of her mother's care? It was too much to endure. She had spent those first years back in California walling off her past, stone by stone by stone. But that wall felt so thin now, so fragile. And there was knocking on the other side.

She needed to leave, this moment. Clattering the mug and bowl to the sink, she hurried to dress and gather her things, running, almost, down the breezeway to her car. A light blinked on the dashboard as soon as the ignition caught. Some trouble with the engine. Another crisis. She drove the short distance to the school as the sun summited the palms. The valley oak that roofed a corner of the parking lot had begun to lose its leaves—a deciduous tree in a place without seasons struck her as somehow comic, like an actor miscast. It was, she remembered, the day that rehearsals would begin.

She walked the cement path to the drama classroom and turned on the lights. The tubes flickered, then blazed, their glow stark and white. She straightened the folders on her desk and glanced at yesterday's attendance sheets, filled out by the sub, Leila Massoud, then powered on the computer. She told herself that she was only entering attendance, that she wouldn't check the mail program. But there had been a time, years ago, as her marriage failed, when she would promise herself that she wouldn't go into the bakery section of the grocery store, wouldn't lose herself to sugar and cream. Then she would come to, a pink box already nestled in her cart. It was the same that morning, the computer modem shrilling from the speakers, the red circle of a new message. She gave up pretending and clicked it open.

Alice, it read. **I'm so unhappy. You never wrote me back. Are you**

reading these? Are they reaching you? Don't you want to know my story? I've been thinking about stories. About how they begin and especially how they end. Those tales of ours, do you remember how they ended, even the horrible ones? They lived happily ever after. They lived in peace and happiness. Are you happy, Alice? Are you at peace? I'm not. I'm trying to know my own story. Your story, too. Then maybe we can write our own ending. Even if happiness won't come for us. Not with all our dead. Did you think that I was dead, Alice? I'm not. Though it feels that way sometimes. So write me back, Alice. Or I'll come and find you. Maybe I'll come and find you anyway. I have something of yours from all the way back then. Something I know you'll want to see.

This person, they would come again? To her work? She wanted to shove the monitor, send it spinning from the table to the floor—all plastic, shattered glass, and smolder. She was typing then, anxious, reckless. "Who are you?" But as she grasped the mouse to send the message, a shadow fell across her desk. Dan Daley's hand was on her shoulder. She flinched.

"Just me," he said, as though this were some comfort.

"Sorry," she said. Apologies were a reflex, a defense learned long ago. "I didn't think anyone was here this early. Just catching up from yesterday." She ran one hand through her hair while the other felt for the button that would make the monitor go dark.

"Well," he said. "I'm not just anyone. I saw your lights. Feeling better?"

"Yes," she said. "Must have been food poisoning. One of those twenty-four-hour things."

"That's what you get when you eat dinner every night from the deli section, Ali. You should be like me, find some nice little woman to cook for you."

"Yes, I really should."

"Come here," he said, swiping at her blouse.

She might have given into it, let him have her there, but she couldn't risk a new disaster. "Dan, it's nearly first bell. Someone will see."

"Maybe I want them to see," he said, his lips at her throat.

"No, you don't," she said. She rolled the chair away from him.

"Yes," he said, recovering what dignity remained to a man adjusting himself through the fabric of his pants. "That's right. Listen, I stopped by because we found a technical director for you. For the fall and winter anyway. Tell Noakes when you want him to start."

"I'll do that, Dan. And thanks. Any news from the board?"

"Plenty of news. All bad. But the game's not over yet, okay? I'm doing my best."

"Are you?"

"Damn it, Ali," he said. "Of course I am. Don't you trust me?"

"Sure," she said. "I should get back to it. The attendance sheets from yesterday. All that."

Then he was gone and she was alone. She turned the monitor back on. The picture wavered for a second, then righted itself. She saw her question. Did she want to know the answer? It might be only Bill. Or Jorge. Though Jorge had never said so much to her in all the time she'd known him. But what if it were Rosa, Rosa alive? The mouse clicked. The message was on its way.

The *Midsummer* rehearsal began fifteen minutes after school let out, a short break to allow for snacks and water and the stowing of books in lockers. But Naomi was at the door of the drama classroom as soon as the last bell sounded.

"Naomi," she said, taking the cigarettes from her purse and beckoning the girl toward the back window. "Look at you, so punctual. That's important in a director."

"You told me to come," Naomi said. "Last night." The expression on her face wasn't angry, exactly, but there was a sharpness to it, her features suddenly more adult. "You said we had to plan out the play or something. I would have come at lunch, but you have class during my lunch. Did you forget that you asked me?"

"No," she said. "Of course not." Though she had. Once the message had arrived, she had switched out one calamity for the other. Spoiled for choice, as her mother used to say, pushing a grocery cart up the bread aisle. She lit the cigarette and flicked the match away. "I'm so glad you're here. We're just reading through the play today, as much as we can get through. Maybe you can hand around the scripts? And as we really get going, we'll find things for you to do on your own. You could work with the fairies, if you want. They'll need help with the dances. Or the Athenians at the start. Would you like to stage that scene?"

"Maybe," Naomi said. The girl was standing so close that she could smell her breath—strawberry-sweet. "I could tell, you know."

"Tell what?" she said, the muscles in her shoulders tensing. "That I smoke? Naomi, it's one a day. Two at the most. It's a bad habit, but it's not illegal."

The girl was unfazed. She looked eager, sly. Naomi had made a choice—in life as she never could in scene study—and she would see that choice through. "No," she said. "About my sister."

"Your sister?" she said. Her mind was hurrying now. "That we're friends?"

"Friends? I saw you," Naomi said. "When you went into the pool house."

"And what is it you think you saw?'

"I don't know," Naomi said, looking away, cheeks pinked. Which meant that she did know. "It didn't look like friends."

She pretended unconcern. "What does it matter what it looked like?" she said.

"I think it could matter a lot," Naomi said. "My sister's young, you know? In college."

This surprised her. "She told me that she was in graduate school."

"She lied to you? That figures. She lies a lot. But yeah, she's young. Twenty. She used to be a student here."

"She was never my student," she said. She was sure of this. Or mostly sure.

"I don't think that will make a huge difference. Do you?"

The girl had a point. But she was grown now, an adult. And Naomi was no dean of students, just a girl with bitten nails and bubble gum on her breath. "Naomi," she said firmly. "I don't know what you think you saw or what you believe. I'm certain that you're wrong about the whole of it. And I'm even more certain that this isn't an appropriate conversation for a teacher and student. I'm happy to talk to you about the play and your role as my assistant. A role that is, I'll remind you, a privilege. It demands maturity. Good judgment. I'd like to see you demonstrate that now."

"Well, maybe there are some things I'd like," Naomi said. The girl's mouth was one thin line. But her eyes were alight, shining. "My college applications are due soon. I want a letter of recommendation from you. A great one. I'll tell you what to write in it, and I'll read it before you send it. We can start there."

"And if I don't? Do you really want a reputation as a sneak, a girl who makes up lurid stories?"

"Do you really want to find out?"

She finished her cigarette and threw the butt toward the canyon. She could run at the girl, slam her head into the window's glass, shove her over the canyon's lip. But she'd spent years quieting those impulses. She took a breath and gave it back again. "I like you, Naomi," she said. She was surprised to find that she meant it. The girl wasn't such a goody-goody after all. "You remind me of me. Of who I used to be. I wanted so much then. Everything. By the time you get to be my age, you'll have learned that it's better to want less."

"So you're saying you won't do it?"

"Oh no. I will. I would have written for you anyway."

"Well, make it good," Naomi said sourly. The girl was getting what she wanted and finding that it was not perhaps enough. "And what's that thing you always say? True feeling? Make it like that. Or I'll tell. Maybe I'll tell anyway." The girl might have said more, but at that moment, the door slammed open and a crowd of students surged in, trailing laughter and corn chip crumbs.

She turned from the window with a forged smile and told them to arrange the chairs into a circle. It was time again to pretend.

The rehearsal left her exhausted with the effort of keeping her face neutral as her students confidently assassinated the English language. *Thisbe*, she would say, has a short *i* and a long *e*. Or, I think you mean *wanton*, not *wonton*; it refers to shamelessness, not dumplings. But mostly she let them trample through the play uncorrected. Kyle, his video camera in his lap, his eyes rabbit-pink, was stoned almost to the point of speechlessness.

Now the late bus had left and the sun had reddened, like burnt skin. In the quiet of the campus, she could hear the buzz of the lights and, just beneath it, the desktop's thrum. She should switch it off, she knew. Go home, ride the bike, cook something bland and nutritive. Fish. Broccoli. Rice that boiled in a bag. But she had lied to Naomi. She was still, in some ways, the girl she had always been. She hadn't cured herself of want. She clicked the button to connect to the mail program and waited, hardly breathing, as the speakers shrilled.

A new message appeared, as she had known it would. Though this one was startlingly brief. **You want to know who I am? Then guess my name, Alice**, it read. **Guess it right and you'll be free.**

So a game, then. A riddle. She remembered the stories. To guess wrong was to lose what you loved most. A child, typically. But she had no children. What she loved best was her safety and the spare, air-conditioned life she had built to house it. But that was already threatened. So before she could think it through, she typed a single short word, its letters freighted with a longing that clawed at her from the inside, like some wild cat loosed in her chest: **Rosa**.

She sat, silent, her skin pale under the fluorescents, until the reply appeared. **Try again**, it read. She shut the computer down.

She did not remember walking to the car, stowing her bag, shrieking past the gates. But she must have done those things because she came to somewhere in Encino, driving down Ventura, streetlights stippling the windshield, radio blaring static. Turning in to the parking lot of a Bob's Big Boy, she parked the car, stacked her arms across the steering wheel, and pressed her face against them, eyes closed, breath thin, as the restaurant's mascot leered above. Did this mean that Rosa was dead? Really dead? She'd never believed it could be otherwise. But she had never known for certain. If the writer, this HighPoint, was not Rosa, it meant that the secret of Rosa's end was not hers alone. Someone else had seen her that night. Someone else knew the worst of it. And unless she could convince them otherwise, that someone might tell. She could not waste another guess.

She was hungry, she realized. Famished. She'd skipped lunch that day. She thought of entering the restaurant, ordering a rare hamburger, its juice bloodying the bun. Or maybe a milkshake, with a silver sidecar that would startle her hands with its cold. But she didn't deserve its sweetness. She drove home.

The paper that Rebecca Liu had given her was just where she'd left it, folded into quarters at the bottom of her bag. She spread it out, running her fingers along the creases. A number for Jorge, a number for Bill. And for Peter and Suzanne, a Vermont address. It was early enough, fine for New York—all New Yorkers kept late hours, didn't they?—and for whatever Mexican town Jorge had retreated to. She thought of Jorge as she'd known him. The compact body, the dark stubble, his sulking baby's face. Would he remember her? Of course he would. A person couldn't live through a thing like that and just forget.

She had no idea what a call to Mexico would cost. Probably the bill would ruin her. But she was halfway to ruin already. What could one more bill do? She called the operator first, checking the country code and the various prefixes. Then she dialed and waited as the call rang out a hemisphere away.

The tone sounded strange, the pitch slightly higher, the intervals between the rings too long. It rang four times, then five. A voice answered. A woman's, she thought, though it might have been a boy's. "*¿Hola?*" it said.

She replied in the poor Spanish Los Angeles had grudgingly bestowed. "*Hola,*" she said. "*¿Jorge, esta aquí?*"

"*¿Jorge?*" the voice said. "*Jorge, sí, un momento.*" Which seemed to be a yes.

A clatter, footsteps, and something like a shout. Then a different voice, a voice she recognized, collapsing decades and countries, returning her to her disclaimed youth. "*Hola,*" it said. "*Él habla.*"

"Jorge," she said. "It's Alice." She hadn't used that name, hadn't spoken it in any connection to herself, in twenty-five years. In her mouth, the syllables felt strange. "Alice Haze."

"Alice?" he said.

"Yes."

A noise like swallowing, like vomit being forced back. "I did not know that you are now alive," Jorge said, slowly and with that strange, formal cadence she remembered. "I did not think of it. But I should have known it. People like you, they live on, yes?"

She did not know what he meant by that. But it seemed easier to agree. "Yes," she repeated. "I lived. I'm living. And I'm sorry about what happened to you. All of you. I don't know the whole of it, but I know that it was bad. It would have happened to me, too, if I'd been with you. I was just lucky. Lucky I left."

"Lucky." He said the word slowly, trying it on for size and finding that it fit. "Yes. *Afortunada,* we would say. Alice, you lucky woman, how is it that you have my number?"

"A researcher gave it to me, Rebecca Liu. You spoke to her for her book."

"I remember this woman," he said. "Many questions. Many ideas. These teachers, they read everything and they understand nothing.

They do not know what it is to make this art. I did not tell her much. I could not make her see. And this I think is to punish me for trying."

"You're still an artist, then?" she asked.

"No, no," he said. "That all has gone for me. My father had a store, and it is my store now. So you see, I am lucky, too. *Afortunado.* Not everyone with this time in prison can have a job like this. And I have a wife now. And children. Such blessings, children are. Now you know of my life. But, Alice, it is late here."

"Is it?" She must have had the time zone wrong.

"Late for many years. So I think you must tell me why it is you call."

"I have electronic mail. Do you know what that is? Do you have it there?"

"We have this thing, in Mexico, yes. Though I do not. Not in my home."

"Well, my school has it. And someone has been writing to me. Someone from the old days. I know it isn't you. At least the words don't sound like yours. But I wondered if you knew who else was left."

An exclamation blasted through the receiver, and it took her precious, expensive seconds to hear it for what it was: a laugh. "No," Jorge said. "I do not know the person who writes to you these things. The prison in Germany, the prison you are so lucky to miss, it was a bad place, Alice. After I left it, I did not see or speak to the people from this time. I did not want to."

"What about Jan?" she said, grasping for any help he might give. "Did you stay in touch with Jan?"

"I have told you, Alice. I speak to no one. I am surprised that I speak to you."

"Well, thank you," she said. He had told her nothing. Already she regretted the conversation and its cost. She brought it to an end. "Goodbye, then. And I'm sorry to have called so late. I thought the time was the same as here."

"The same as where?" he asked. And then, before she could answer, he said, "No, Alice. Do not tell me. And since we will not speak again.

I will tell you this: I know that it was you. Alice, you lucky girl. You are the one to tell the police. You made this luck yourself. Made it from my pain. The pain of others."

"I don't—" she began.

He interrupted. "Do not say this," he said. "Do not tell these lies to me. And do not call again." A click. And then the dial tone, wailing in her ear.

She swallowed. Jorge could think what he liked. And he was right. They would never speak again. He hadn't sent those letters. She had no more need of him.

From the refrigerator, she took the wine she had opened over the weekend and sloshed some into a glass. She didn't drink like this. Not during the week, not on an empty stomach. But she wanted the acid, the burn. She was greedy for it. Lifting the receiver, she placed a new call, just eleven digits this time.

It rang twice. Then a machine picked up. "This is Bill," a staticky recording said. Through it, she heard that same splintered voice, calling out across the years. "You, uh, you know what to do," the message continued. "Guess there'll be a beep or something." There was. She left her number and a request that he call back. Not her name, not yet.

A few minutes later, just as she had finished that first glass of wine, the phone rang. She wrenched it from the handset and said hello. "This is Bill Calder," said the voice on the other end, the words crackling like cellophane. "Who is this?" the voice said. "Who's there?"

"Bill," she said. "It's Alice."

"Alice?" he said. "Alice Haze?"

"Yes, Bill," she said.

"Oh yeah? Like for real?"

She stretched out her arm, turned it this way and that so that the overhead light caught the golden hairs. "Real enough."

Then he was crying. "Just a sec," he said. "Give me a minute." He was attempting, it seemed, to collect himself. And then, sobbing still, he said, "Alice. Alice, I'm so sorry."

"Sorry for what?" She thought of his body over hers, the necklace that bumped her chin. That first unwanted time had not been the only time.

"Getting like this. Emotional, you know. It's just that it's been a while. I don't talk to no one from the old days. I mean, JoAnn, JoAnn and I talk to all the time, but that's just in my head. Do you remember her, Alice? At the end. Just before. Do you remember how happy she was?"

"Yes," she said. "I do. So you aren't in touch with anyone else?"

"God, no. Not for years. Had a hard time for a while. Booze, you know? Tried to see Peter and Suzanne. Gave them some of JoAnn's things. But I guess I wrecked that, too. Or maybe we were wrecked already. Peter, he was so angry in that jail. Like a demon, you know. An animal. You remember that?"

"No," she said. "I was gone by then."

"Oh yeah," he said. He was still crying, but more softly now. "What happened, Alice? What happened to us? It was all so good at the start."

"I missed the start," she said. "And I don't know that it was ever very good."

"Sure it was," he said. "Like Peter used to say, it was a gift, something to live for."

They hadn't all lived. But it seemed cruel to mention it.

"Hey, Alice," Bill went on. "You ever think of me? You ever think of JoAnn?"

"No," she told him truthfully. "No, I never do." Bill had not written her those messages. "Goodbye now, Bill," she said. "Get some sleep." She brought the receiver toward the wall. She could still hear him sobbing as she laid it in its cradle.

9

1972, NEW YORK CITY

A hand. Rosa's. Slapping me so hard that my cheek felt like ice, then fire. The screaming stopped. Peter crashed past, shirt flapping around him like a faltering kite. "Will someone turn the fucking music off?" he said. Someone did. Then there was only the sound of Molly wailing. "I see this," Molly cried. "In the cards. I swear I see it a-a-all."

"Fuck your cards," Peter said. "Fuck your doom. We have a problem here. A real one. You found him? How? When?"

Molly couldn't speak for crying.

"Molly," Peter said. His voice was like an aspirin tablet, sweet on the surface, but bitter just below. "I need you to get your shit together, baby, and I need you to do it fast. What happened?"

"I come in to pee. Jax, he is here, in the bathtub. I do not mind this. Jax, he has seen this all before. Just close your eyes, I say to him. But he is not moving."

"Did you check his pulse or anything?" Peter said.

"No," Molly said, her hands in front of her face. "I couldn't. I—"

"Fuck this," Peter said. He stepped forward and took Jax's wrist, pulling it hard, the way he might have jerked a leash to hurry a dog along. Seconds later, long seconds, he let it go. The hand thunked against the porcelain. "Fuck," Peter said. "Damn it all to hell. Does anyone know what the fuck he took?"

No one answered.

"Well, who was he with tonight?"

"Me and Bash, mostly," Faye said. Her voice had gone soft, like worn silk, and I could see that she had drawn her eyebrows on and drawn them wrong, the arches too high. "But we didn't have anything stronger than the wine and just the littlest bit of Mexican."

"How do you know he's even dead?" Dede said. "You're no doctor. My cousin, he works an ambulance. Saves people all the time. People who seem gone. I'm calling the service now."

"No!" Peter said.

But she was gone already, scuffing barefoot down the stairs.

"Fuck," Peter said again. "An ambulance means police. And soon. So quick, Faye, tell it to me straight. Was he back on junk?"

"Not for ages," Faye said. "Least that's what he said. But maybe check his thigh, honey? That's where he used to like to do it. More secret that way."

The shorts Jax wore were cut so high that Peter barely had to lift the hem to find what he was looking for, a blue-brown bruise, maybe more than one bruise.

Faye's face collapsed in on itself. If we hadn't been packed together, she might have fallen. "Oh, that poor, sweet man."

"Sweet prince," Bash said.

"This is bad," Peter said. He slunk out of the bathroom, then drew himself up tall. "Whoever gave this shit to him, we can figure that out later. For now, the police are on their way. So whatever you have, get rid of it. Don't just stand there. Do it! They find anything stronger than a roll of Certs, they'll make it bad for us. And no one leave. You hear me? I'm not taking the heat for this. Not alone."

There was tumult then. The Theater Negative performers and the others who had come for the party, they emptied purses and pockets, some panicked, some resentful, as pills and green-brown leaves went down the drain. I saw one boy, a newcomer in a jean jacket with the sleeves cut off, try to hide something in the kitchen cabinets. Peter stopped him.

"Did you think I was joking, man?" he said.

"Nah," the boy said. "I just—"

Peter hit him in his belly. A short jab. The boy bent double. "Just fucking get rid of it," Peter said. He held himself more easily now. Hitting the boy had restored something to him. Then Rosa was at my side, her knapsack over one shoulder, her white purse strung across her breasts.

"Come on," she said. "Time to go."

"Peter told us not to leave."

"Fuck Peter. Cops are coming. Me, I shouldn't be around no cops. You neither. You want them asking questions, huh? Calling up your parents, maybe?"

"I'm nineteen," I said. "I'm not some baby."

"Oh yeah? Well, a baby's what you look like. Better get going."

"What about you?" I said.

"Cops and me, we don't always get along so good. Come on already."

Then we were down the stairs. Around the corner came the ambulance, squealing like some dying animal. Rosa took my arm, and together we ran.

She led me to a hotel, just a few blocks away, on Thirty-Eighth Street. The night clerk, a man with swooping black hair and a gold canine, knew her well.

"Got a kiss for me, Rosie?" he said.

"In your dreams," she said, but she leaned across the counter to peck his cheek and whisper something in his ear. He reached behind him and handed her a key on a pink plastic fob. "Whole night, huh?" he said. "First time for everything."

"Even girls like me, we gotta sleep sometime. You gimme one of the nice ones, Tony? Room where you set the roach traps?"

"Get outta here with that," he said.

So we did, up the stairs—carpeted in a weave that had once been red—to a stuffy room on the third floor that smelled like cigarettes and lemonade. There were two beds, with a table between them that held a lamp and a pink plastic phone, the numbers worn away inside the dial. The beds were covered in flowered spreads that had been put through the wash so often they had faded to the gray-pink of conversation hearts. I was grateful they'd been washed at all. Rosa set her knapsack on the floor. She unzipped her purse and slid the knife into her hand. She flicked it open, then shut, and laid it on the nightstand between us.

"Just in case," she said, flopping down onto a bed and spreading her arms and legs wide like a kid making snow angels. The springs screamed.

I did not ask her what she meant.

Sitting more demurely I looked around for another door. "Is there a bathroom?" I said.

"Bathroom's in the hall," she said. "Shared. You're gonna wanna lock it. Don't want some perv walking in." I'd been looking forward to a shower, in private. I decided that I might as well do without.

"Are there a lot of pervs here, then?" I said, crossing my legs.

"Pervs everywhere," she said. "Even at the Waldorf-goddamn-Astoria. But this place, it's all right. We can wait it out. Go back in the morning."

I thought then of the loft, the terrible pallor of Jax's skin. A shudder went through me, though I wasn't the shuddering kind. "What do you think is happening over there?"

"Nothing good. Depends what the cops find. Or what they wanna pretend they found."

"You mean drugs?"

She rolled onto her side, facing me, then rolled her eyes to match. "No, sunshine, gumdrops. Yeah, I mean drugs."

"Sorry," I said, without knowing just what I was apologizing for. My ignorance. My privilege. That I had lived so long without having to learn these things.

I asked if I owed her money for the room, though money remained a fraught subject between us. She shook her head and told me not to worry. That she and Tony went way back. "Long as I'm not working and we're out before the day guy comes, he won't charge," she said.

"Working?" I said.

A smile tugged at a corner of her lips. "You really gotta ask?" she said.

"I guess not," I said.

"You can," she said. "Can't all be college girls in penny loafers. Not where I'm from. Tricking got me out the fastest."

"But do you like it?" I said.

She laughed that honking laugh, her long body shaking with the force of it. "You like slinging hamburgers all day?" she said when she could get a breath in. "It's a job, sunshine. Least when some guy slaps me on the ass, I get extra for it. And I choose who I go with, see? I don't give nothing away. Not unless I want to."

"So with Peter, you wanted to?" I asked.

"Sure," she said. "Why? You jealous or something?" She looked at me in that brazen way. A gaze like Peter's, but unlike it, too. Because she looked without wanting, without judging. I was jealous, horribly. She shook her head. "Heard you were his girl before. A guy like that, he's always out for the next pair of tits. Wasn't me, woulda been someone else. Not worth the tears, sunshine. But Peter, he's all right. Anyway, I owed the guy."

"Owed him? Like you owed him money?"

"What is it with you rich girls and your money? Nah, he helped me out when I was in a spot. Real down, you know? Couldn't see how I was gonna make it through. Me, I've always taken care of myself. Ever since I was a kid. And tricking, like I said, it's all right. But it doesn't always go your way. Some of the guys, they're bastards. Don't pay what they say they will or try and take what maybe you don't wanna give. So a couple of months ago, I gave it up for a while, started doing one of the shows instead."

"The shows?"

"Come on," she said. "You walk the same goddamn streets as me, sunshine. You know the ones I mean. Seemed like easy money. Just one guy to make it with. Or a girl sometimes. What do I care? The guy I was going with, Stevie, we worked it together. Turns out, Stevie wasn't so nice. Not once he got on junk. Didn't like it when I told him no."

She blinked her eyes and held them closed an extra beat. Then she went on. "He beat me up, Stevie. Did it smart. Left my face alone. So nobody could see it, long as my clothes stayed on. I ran outta our place as soon as I could. Before he could do it again, do it worse. I didn't take nothing with me, not hardly. Didn't know how I was even gonna eat. The way he worked me over, I had to heal up first. Couldn't do a show. Not how I looked. And some tricks, they see a thing like that, they get the wrong idea. Think maybe they should do it, too. You figure that out yet, sunshine? If a guy thinks some other mook got something special, then he's gonna want it same.

"I jumped a turnstile that first night, rode the trains until some god-damn transit cop caught me sleeping and hauled me up and out. Into Times Square. Right where I started. Felt like that was some kinda sign or something. Like what that crazy Molly talks about. Like I could ride around all night and still I couldn't get away. Couldn't never. I walked all the way to the water after that, out onto the pier. Didn't know what I was gonna do. Me, I can't swim. Never learned. Thought maybe if I just fell in. On accident, almost. . . . I dunno."

"Oh, Rosa," I said quietly.

"Nuh-uh, sunshine," she said, waving a finger at me. "Don't need your pity. Don't need no one's. Probably wouldn't even have done it anyway. But Peter, he found me there. Followed me, maybe. Reached out a hand, asked me what was wrong and the kinda day I was having; I just straight out told him.

"He looked at me after, real still like, like I was a goddamn oil paint-ing. Said he saw something in me, even if nobody else could see it.

Something good in me, he said. Something holy. I'm thinking, okay, a joker, this one. But Peter, he's not laughing. He says he has a gift for me. Some guys, they wanna give you things—a dress, say, or jewelry, makes them feel like they're one of the good ones. I woulda taken it, sold it after. So I ask what and he tells me about the group. What do I want with that? I say. I'm no actress. Never seen a play that wasn't the nativity at Blessed Sacrament. Me, I'm a sheep one year. He says it's not acting, what you all do, it's just telling the truth. I say, I'm not so good at truth neither. But he says I am, that he can see it. The gift, he goes, is the work. The work, it's something to live for. Guess I needed that right then. I went with him."

I was quiet for a while. "I guess that's why I went with him, too," I said.

"Isn't there some story about that?" she said. "One of them fairy tales? Some mook comes to town and all the lost little kids go follow."

"The Pied Piper," I said. "But I don't think they were lost." I didn't say how the story ended, that the children were never seen again.

"Well, maybe that's the goddamn tale we should tell. Come on, sunshine. We gotta be up and out of here early. Better get some rest." She leaned over and switched off the lamp.

I lay on my back, atop that scratchy coverlet, listened to the shriek of the traffic outside, the whirring of the ceiling fan that barely troubled the air.

"Sure you wanna be all the way over there?" she said. Through the gauze curtains, the streetlight found the glint of her eyes, her teeth. "I see how you look at me," she said. "This room, it's a secret, just for us. You like secrets, don't you, sunshine?"

"Doesn't everyone?" I said. My body felt wound tight, a music box with its key turned too far.

"Nah," she said. "You like them more. You like me, too. Ever think of just asking for what you want, instead of sneaking up on it, trying to get it sideways?"

"I just want to sleep," I said, turning from her. But sleep wouldn't take me. Not for hours.

The loft had never been what anyone in my mother's coffee mornings would have described as tidy, but the next day, when Rosa and I returned, sweaty and disheveled, it had descended into new confusion. The curtain separating the sleeping area had been ripped away, the mattresses turned over—blankets, sleeping bags, and clothes mixed with the party residue. The books from the Strand lay open and scattered. I saw a lone page, ripped away, flailing in the breeze from the open window. A box of cornflakes had been upended in the kitchen area, and there were coffee grounds on the counter and hillocks of dried beans. Faye sat amid it all, slumped near the sink, staring at the opposite wall, cigarette in hand. Her eye makeup had carved gullies down each cheek, and her hair hung lank. She looked like her own ghost.

"Hiya, Faye," Rosa said.

"Oh, hi there, honey," Faye said, trying to arrange her face into a smile. "Well, didn't you just miss a night. The men from the ambulance, they came in. Then the police, turned the place over pretty good, they did. Made Peter go with them to the station, seeing as how he said he found him, Jax, I mean. Molly, she went with him. Police, they didn't want to bring her. But you know Molly. Set to wailing. Tried to grab the handcuffs. So they took her, too."

I left Faye and walked to what had been my bed. My suitcases lay open, the contents rummaged. But the box of napkins was still there. And so was the money I'd saved. I repacked as best I could and went into the bathroom to wash my face. I left the door open this time. I didn't want to be in there all alone.

When I came out, I saw Faye's head on Rosa's shoulder. Rosa was stroking one of her hands, making slender circles on her palm. I had never seen Rosa soft with anyone. I cleared my throat in some awful actorly way.

"We should do something," I said. "We should clean."

At the hardware store, I bought garbage bags, a broom, some sponges, and hauled it all back up the stairs. Faye found a Fairport Convention album, out of its sleeve but unbroken, and eased it onto the platter. The morning turned dreamy, dust motes dancing in the sunlight. Faye took a long pull from a bottle of Southern Comfort, then handed the bottle off to Rosa, and for an hour or two, we swept and neatened and scrubbed, then took the bags down to the curb. It was good, somehow, to be among women, to put to rights what men had torn apart.

As the day went on, other company members trickled in. Jorge and Jan first, then Bash, JoAnn, and Bill, who arrived with a stack of tomato pies from the pizzeria on Ninth and bottles of red wine. No one spoke much. Molly came in later that afternoon, with eyes that looked like they had fallen down a well. She went behind the curtain Rosa and I had rehung and lay on a mattress, muttering about "the peegs." Of the regulars, only Dede was absent. And Suzanne. And Peter, of course.

Faye went into the bathroom, emerging with her face washed, her eyebrows redrawn. She left the loft and came back in half an hour later with a thick red votive and wilting roses. She arranged them on the countertop in a coffee mug, then went into her purse and took out a creased photo strip. Her and Jax, both in sunglasses, kissing, sticking tongues out, pouting for the camera. Faye propped it against the mug.

"Love you, honey," she said. She kissed her fingers and brought them to the strip, then to her lips again. She lit the candle. A record had ended and still it kept revolving, the needle scraping against the final groove. No one stood to replace it. We sat and watched the candle burn.

Peter returned in early evening when the light had turned thick and amber. There were bags beneath his eyes, and his shirt, block printed with golden leaves, was torn at the side. He'd brought beer, clanking in a plastic bag. He opened a bottle, slamming the cap against the countertop, and drank half down before he spoke. If he saw the altar Faye had made, he did not mention it.

He looked around at us, breathing us in the way that he did at the start of any rehearsal. But his gaze felt shallow, void. "We're still here," he said finally. "That's the main thing. They kept me overnight, but they didn't have anything to hold me on. Jax's body, they need it for a while, they said. Then they'll release it. He had family, right?"

"A mama. In Detroit, I think, or just outside," Faye said. "Maybe a sister, too. He used to talk about them sometimes when he was blue."

"You got a number?"

"No, honey. But I'll go through his things. See what I find."

"You do that." He took another pull of beer and set the bottle back down on the counter. "I think we all know how Jax died," he said. "The cops, they didn't find the drugs and they didn't find the works. Thank God for that. But if any of you knew he was using and you didn't say, you can get out now. It just about killed him last time. Now it's killed him for good and all. My brother. Your brother. So did you know? Did any of you know?"

No one spoke.

Peter smiled. A smile that stopped miles from his eyes. "Then everyone stays, I guess," he said, opening out his hands. "But not for long. Word got around to the, uh, to the landlord. He wants us out. Says we can have a week. But after that, he's changing all the locks."

So that was our idyll, done. I had nowhere else to run to, no more fictions to invent. I could not keep myself on diner wages, not without a home, a bed, and so I would have to call my parents and beg them to let me come home. And that home would be like a grave. I would never escape it. Not until I was married and some other man's possession. My life in this city, my life in any proximity to art, it was over now. The horror of that felt like hands on my throat, squeezing and squeezing until all the breath was gone.

"But where will we go, honey?" Faye said.

"Go anywhere you want," Peter said. "The whole fucking planet, it's yours. But not here. You can't stay here."

I stopped going to the diner that week. So did Faye. Mostly she stayed on the sofa, suckling from a bottle of bourbon like a baby at the breast and playing sad songs. When that first candle burned down, she went and bought another. The other members of Theater Negative had scattered, even Rosa. I asked Faye if she thought they would return, but she was sunk too far in the bottle to answer. I brought her meals sometimes: jelly sandwiches, fried eggs until the eggs gave out. Faye barely touched the food. Later, I would gnaw at these same plates—the eggs gone gummy, the jelly sunk into the bread—like some scavenging creature. I couldn't bear to shower, not in that bathroom, not in that tub. Faye must have felt the same. After a few days, we both smelled animal, like rot and sex and sweat. I did not call my mother. I would leave it to the last. Until the door was truly barred to me.

Peter came on the sixth day. I heard him before I saw him, his feet bounding up the stairs in a syncopated rhythm, and my hand went to my ponytail, an attempt—too late—to make myself decent for him. Peter wore a white shirt that tied at the neck, though the ties were loose. Sweat had dyed his hair the darkest gold. His movements were fast, fluid, the excitement radiating from him in waves. He had brought a carton of orange juice, and he poured himself a glass, though none of our glasses were anything like clean, and drank it down. The shock of the orange hurt my eyes.

"The others are coming," he said, swiping his mouth with a sleeve. The juice would stain the sleeve, and someone—not Peter—would have to launder that shirt later. "As many as I could reach. They should be here soon. I have news. Wonderful news."

He sat down on the sofa next to Faye, who only then seemed to notice him. "Hi there, honey," she said, adjusting her robe. "Forgive the state of me."

"Today, I could forgive you anything," he said.

"I'll just tidy up," I said. I collected Faye's bottles, washed the cups and the dishes and the egg-encrusted pans. Then I did shower, though I shut my eyes throughout. When I emerged, in a clean skirt and blouse, JoAnn and Bill were there, and Bash, too, eating grapes out of a paper sack. Molly sat cross-legged on the floor, tarot cards spread in front of her. Jorge and Jan were at the window. Faye had changed out of her robe and into a sundress with plastic buttons that shone like pearl. She'd put on lipstick. Too much. Rosa was not there.

Peter beckoned me. "Alice," he said, curling one hand around my waist. "Why don't you go down to the store and get some lunch things, all right? Whatever you want."

He pulled some bills from his wallet, which I tucked into the pocket of my skirt. I hadn't left the building since that visit to the hardware store nearly a week ago, and the sun felt like fire on my skin. But I did as I was told, walking to the market on Ninth Avenue to buy bread, sliced cheese, sliced meat, two tomatoes as round as tennis balls, a head of iceberg lettuce, a bag of salted potato chips, neon mustard in a jar. The checkout girl totaled the items, a teenage boy bagged them. I handed over Peter's bills and took the change, feeling as if I were acting a part, playing the role of a girl who knew how to move and stand and speak.

Turning the corner, the bag nestled against my hip, I nearly ran into Rosa. She was in an outfit I had never seen, a red playsuit that zipped up the front. "Hey, sunshine," she said, sucking on a piece of candy. I had not known if I would see her again, and the sight of her stirred something savage in me. I wanted to grab her arms so hard the skin would bruise. I wanted to bring her mouth to mine. I hated her for leaving, and I could not have said for certain that I wanted her to return. She gestured to my bag. "You got lunch in there?"

I nodded, hefting the bag higher. "Sandwich fixings, some chips. Peter's back. Or did you know already?"

"Nah," she said. "Been busy."

"Well, he says he has news. There's a meeting at the loft. Do you want to come back with me?"

"Gotta eat sometime," she said.

We took the stairs together. In the loft, Jorge was at the record player, swaying, eyes closed, to folk guitar. Dede had arrived. She stood apart from the group, performing some complicated stretch at the window. I put the grocery bag on the counter. Faye and I arranged the food.

"Okay," Peter said, once Faye had brought his plate to the sofa. "Are we all here?"

JoAnn looked around. "Is Suzanne coming?"

"Suzanne, she's gonna sit this one out," Peter said. "For now anyway."

"Sit what out?" Rosa said as she took a handful of potato chips.

Peter bit into his sandwich. He spoke before he'd finished chewing. "That's what I came to talk to you about. I got us a few more days here. Long enough to pack. Because here's the real news: We're going on tour."

"A tour," Faye said. "Where to, honey? And which show?"

"London, to start," Peter said. "I've been on transatlantic calls all week. Cost a fortune. And we're doing *The Grimm Variations*. We can finish it on the boat over. My friend in London, he'll give us a week or so to rehearse, and then we'll debut it there, middle of September. We go to France after. I've got three dates there. Then Antwerp. Brussels, maybe. By November, we'll be in Germany. Most of you know the rules. One case each, no more than you can carry. And no funny stuff, okay? Not even grass. I don't care how well you hide it. Cops over in Europe, they're smarter than the ones here. And the cops here, the 'peegs,' as Molly says, they're bad enough."

"We're all going?" I said. Europe. Europe with a theater company. I felt meltingly grateful that I had not yet phoned my mother. A tour would not solve anything, not permanently. But it meant that I could run for just a little longer. My blood was humming. I could hear it in my ears.

"Yes, Alice," Peter said. "There's a ticket for you. For all of you. I've arranged everything."

There was more chatter then—febrile, eager. We would sail in five days. An airline ticket would have cost the same by then, or even less. But the troupe had gone by boat for its first tours, and that was the tradition. JoAnn took paper and pen from her straw purse and began to make a list of what everyone might need. "Faye, do you remember that time no one thought to bring Tampax and we stuffed our panties with the cloth napkins from the dining room?"

"Then threw them over the side after," Faye said.

"What a day for the sharks," said Bash.

"Are there really sharks then?" said Jan.

"Oh no, honey," Faye said. "That's just Bash having his joke."

"That's it?" a voice said. It was Dede. She was standing with her toes pigeoned at some impossible angle. "A man is dead. My friend is dead. And y'all are gonna just pretend like nothing happened, just go on with your show?"

"Dede—" Peter said, raising a remonstrating hand.

"Nah," she said. "Do what you want." She pulled her feet together. "But when you walk upon that stage, you are walking over that man's grave. He gave you everything, that man. You just gonna go now? Leave it to his mama to bury him alone?"

"Do you know his mama, honey?" Faye said. "I went through his things, but I didn't find a number for her. Didn't know her name."

"You didn't think to ask me?"

"I'm sorry, honey," she said. She gestured to the candle, the browned roses. "Wasn't thinking much."

"It's Elnora," Dede said. "Elnora Jackson. Lives in Macomb County. You mean to say she doesn't even know he's gone?"

"No," Peter said. "But it's okay—"

"Her son dead a week, and this man telling me it's all okay," Dede said, her mouth gone thin. She fisted the straps of their knapsack. "Where's he now? He buried already? You let the city put him out on that island like yesterday's trash?"

"No," Peter said. "God, no. They haven't released him. That's what I was trying to tell you."

"Well, fine, then," Dede said. "You go on and do your European tour." She drew the word *European* out, making a sour mouthful of each syllable. She looked Peter right in the eye until he looked away. "Me, I'll stay here. Phone his mama. See to his coffin. People to sing him home. I was only ever with you because of Jax. Because he said you were so good to him."

"We were!" Peter said, sweat standing out on his hairline. "We are."

But Dede was already gone. Peter put his plate down with exaggerated care and stood from the sofa. "Anyone else?" he said. "Anyone else got something to say to me?" No one answered.

"Okay, then," he said. "We have work to do. We won't worry about the set until we're in London. But, Bill, you should start drawing up the light plot. Suzanne's made a start on the costumes, Faye you can take over all that. Bash, keep working on the dances. We'll make a call on music soon. Then there's the trip itself. Does everyone still have their passports?"

"I have one," I said. We'd taken one awful package trip to Ireland, "the old country," my father had called it, when I was in high school, and I'd kept the booklet ever since.

"I don't," Rosa said. "That matter?"

"Yes," Peter said. "They'll check before they let you on the ship. But we can get you an appointment last minute. I've done it before. Fanny, who was with us, couldn't hold on to a passport to save her life. Sand through goddamn fingers. How many times did we have to get her an emergency one?"

"Twice," Bash said. "At least. That dizzy, dizzy girl. All mirth. And not an ounce of sense."

"So we know the routine," Peter said. "Rosa, do you have your birth certificate?"

"No," she said.

"Can you get it?"

She gave a smile that looked like she'd borrowed it from someone else. "I can do a lotta things."

"Try to get it tomorrow. I'll make the appointment for the day after. Okay, people," he said, clasping his hands and giving them a valedictory shake above his head. The dead, the missing, they were forgotten now. "Clear this food away. Back to work."

I'm sure I slept in those next days, but I recall only constant activity— the record player always going, the empty wine bottles piled in the sink. There was shopping and packing and furious work on what would become the script. I even sewed a bit, making muslin skirts from Suzanne's patterns. To force my one case closed, I abandoned nearly all my books and papers and several pairs of shoes. The other case I gave to Rosa. She'd gone out that first night and slunk back in the following morning, her face pale and bare of makeup, her birth certificate tucked into her purse.

A day later, while Rosa and Peter went to secure her passport, I walked to the Western Union office near Bryant Park. I didn't trust myself to phone, worried that my mother's fretting would somehow move me, make me say too much. It was cool in the office, quiet and bright. I took the telegram form to a bench and sat with it, knowing I had to use the fewest possible words, that even these few sentences would cost several days' tips.

"Mama," I finally wrote. "Invited by fellowship to Europe. All paid. On break from college. Don't send tuition. Will write. Much love. Allison."

Twenty words exactly. I watched the clerk type out each one, her fingers a drumbeat on the keys. I promised myself, right there in the telegram office, that I would take my mother to Europe one day. That we would go together. Every museum, every cathedral that I saw this time, I would show to her in turn. But there would be no museums for me. Only wet streets, smoky rooms, lights so white they blinded. We never took that trip.

That afternoon, I tagged along with Faye and JoAnn to buy supplies. We went to a large grocery several streets away—clean and so chilly that I should have brought a sweater. They let me push the cart. JoAnn filled it with practical things: Band-Aids, rubbing alcohol, sanitary napkins. Faye added small luxuries like chocolate bars and lavender soap, some of which JoAnn took right back out. Then we walked west to a produce market where JoAnn bought bags of lemons and handfuls of some ugly, knobby root.

"It's ginger," she explained as we were leaving. "Helps with seasickness. You can chew it, if you like spicy stuff, or you can put it in your tea."

"The seasickness, does everyone get it?" I asked.

"You ever been on boats before, honey?" Faye said.

"Just fishing trips when I was little," I said. "I was only sick the one time, threw up over the side." This was because my father had thought it would be funny to make me drink his beer.

"Could be you'll be fine. Could be just like glass the very whole way."

I knew what she meant, but I couldn't help from picturing the sea as shards, with waves that would slice your skin to ribbons.

"Just stay outside as much as you can," JoAnn said. "Fresh air. And keep your eyes on the horizon."

"Or just sleep through it, honey," Faye said. "That's what I do."

"I'm excited anyway," I said. And I was, like a soda pop bottle frothing over at the neck. "But there's still so much to do. The sewing alone. It's lucky the landlord let us stay these extra days."

"Luck, huh?" JoAnn snorted. "You don't know who owns the building?"

"No," I said. "Should I? Who?"

"Irving Gold," JoAnn said. She gave the words bulk and heft. But they meant nothing to me. "Suzanne's father. Big real estate macher. How else you think they got that house downtown? On what Peter makes? Please."

"I've never seen it," I said, clutching the grocery bag to my chest.

"Oh yeah? Brownstone on Commerce Street," she said, shaking her stringy hair from her face. "Isn't that a joke? Anarchists on Commerce Street. Daddy didn't want his baby girl to starve, but he did want to rub her face in it a little. He owns that house and plenty others, plus the building where the loft is. Lets Peter use it as long as he doesn't bring any trouble around. Jax dead? The police? That's trouble. Gold gave us the extra days in exchange for Peter fucking off out of the country, I know it sure as shit. Probably thinks he can talk Suzanne into getting a divorce while he's gone."

"Can he?" I said, trying to sound like I knew plenty of divorced people, like the idea of Peter free mattered not at all. "Do you really think they'll split up?"

JoAnn laughed, and Faye joined her.

"God, no," JoAnn said. "Those two, that marriage, they'll outlive us all."

"But he goes with other girls," I said. "And she's an incredible designer. She could do costumes for Broadway if she wanted."

"But she doesn't want that, honey," Faye said, matching her stride with mine and putting an arm around my shoulders as a kind of consolation. "She wants him. She loves him."

"We all do," JoAnn said. "We all love that sweaty bastard."

There were ten of us who went—me, Peter, Rosa, Faye, Molly, Jorge, Jan, Bash, JoAnn, and Bill—crammed like canned pears into three taxi cabs with bags and cases on our laps. The trunk of that last cab wouldn't shut, and Peter and Bill tied it up with rope while the cabbie smoked and fumed and let the meter run, and then we were away, a ten-minute ride across to the highway and then up the few blocks to the terminal.

That morning, I'd put on the same smart pink dress I'd worn to meet the dean of students. No one else had dressed for the occasion—or they had, but in their beads and macramé. We made a strange picture among the families waving handkerchiefs back to the shore. I did not wave. The laundromat had turned all my handkerchiefs gray.

We were gathered with the other tourist-class passengers into a lounge for a mandatory muster drill. Most of the other travelers here were young, exchange students bound for a semester in Europe, or their European counterparts, returning home from a summer in the States. Months ago, I might have made one of their party. In moments like this, the weight of what I had given up sat on my chest like an anvil. Whatever was said about life jackets and fire stairs, I didn't hear it. I should have. A ship like ours had caught fire and sunk in Hong Kong that same year. But that was how my life felt to me just then, like a boat already burning. Treacherous and bright, too far from any shore.

I'd been given a key and was on my way to the cabin when a boy stopped me near the door. He was tall, six feet and more, and achingly slender, like a piece of taffy pulled and thinned. He wore a short-sleeved shirt in fine beige linen buttoned to the top. The collar surged every time he swallowed.

"Don't suppose we're on the same lifeboat?" he said, quirking his lips into a smile. His accent was silken, English.

"I don't know," I said. "I wasn't listening."

I tried to hurry past him, but he kept up with me. "That's terrible," he said. "I was counting on you to rescue me should the pirates board or some iceberg threaten. I faint at the first whisper of disaster."

"I don't think there are too many icebergs in September," I said.

Faye passed us, eyeing the boy up and down and up again.

"Well, thank God for that. Whichever god you like. I'm partial to the Hindu sort myself just now. But before we fall into matters of theology, it seems good manners to introduce myself. I'm Bram," he said. "Bram Simmons."

"I'm Alice," I said. It seemed easier to use that name with everyone.

"Are you off to uni then, Alice? Or no, don't tell me, you're on some terribly secret mission. That schoolgirl dress, that's your fiendish disguise."

"I'm here with a theater troupe, Theater Negative. We're debuting a new piece in London. Then we're off on tour."

"Alice," he said, sweeping his hands. "How marvelous. Ran away with the circus, did you? A boyhood dream of mine. Theater Negative? Of course I know them. Legends, all. And you're to play in London? My God, the maiden aunts will all have heart attacks. Stupendous, really. Put me down for rows of seats. And I don't mind telling you, I'm in the theater, too. All sorts of entertainment, really. My father, Abraham the elder, he has many fingers in so very many pies and——"

He would have said more, but then there was a scream that ripped the air in two, a scream I'd heard before. It was Molly, on the emerald carpet in the center of the room, thrashing her limbs like she wanted them gone from her body. Spit foamed at her lips.

"We must get away," she said. Her eyes were too round, too white. "We have to. The sails. They're black. I can see it. All the dead. So many."

No one was with her; the others must have gone already. So I knelt beside her, taking her hands in my own, trying to quiet her. And she did quiet. Her mouth closed. Her limbs slackened. But when she opened her eyes again, something in them had dimmed.

"You must leave here," she said to me in a whisper that was more like a growl. "You are a danger to us, a danger in this place."

"Molly," I said. "It's me. It's Alice."

"I know what you are." She sat up and took the tarot cards from her pocket, then handed one to me. It showed a woman blindfolded, swords all around her. "A danger, see?" She snatched the card back. "So go. Go now. Before——"

There was a terrible sound then, fierce and low, like the trumpets heralding Judgment Day. It was the ship's horn. We had left the port.

My room, I found, was down an impossible number of stairs and along a narrow corridor that smelled of damp and fish. It was an inside room, windowless and comically small, with space for a bed and a single nightstand and nothing more. A dollhouse door led to a toilet, a sink, a shower cubicle that would barely hold a body. But there were two suitcases there, piled atop the bed, both in blue leatherette. I was to share with Rosa.

She was through the door a moment later and bouncing on the bit of mattress that remained.

"Hiya, sunshine," she said. "Roommates, huh?"

"Not exactly the Waldorf-goddamn-Astoria, is it?"

"Nah, but we're here for what? Four nights? Five? Maybe we won't even have to share. Who's that tall one, from the muster?"

"Bram something," I said, prim now. "He's English, and we've only just met."

"Looked like he wanted to meet you some more. Me, I like them like that, like a flagpole I can climb. Though for you, I guess that's anyone." She laughed, an echo of the ship's horn, and blew a bubble with her gum.

There was no closet proper, just a folding slatted door, behind which were a few wire hangers on a single silver bar. There were also drawers beneath the bed, though they didn't open all the way. I began unpacking while Rosa watched me from behind her sunglasses, flicking her pocketknife open and closed.

"Think we can smoke in here?" she said.

"No," I said. "There isn't even a window."

"See ya later, then," she said. "You can take care of my suitcase, too, you feel like it."

I did feel like it. I have always enjoyed touching other people's things.

"Just let me grab some gum and stuff," she said. She opened her case and rummaged through it. Then she left, her purse swinging.

In her absence, I folded and hung my clothes, found space for hers, then put our toiletries onto the bathroom's lone shelf—toothbrushes, toothpaste, deodorant spray, her baby powder, my cold cream. The baby powder touched me. It seemed so innocent.

We were to take our meals in the grand salon, which sounded elegant, but it was only the same green-carpeted space where we had sat for the muster drill. There was a buffet at one end, silver chafing dishes with blue Sterno flames beneath. The food was barely above college fare—meat in an off-white sauce, a salad that looked sorry for itself. But the plates were real china and the napkins were real cloth and the silverware so clean it dazzled. After the jelly sandwiches and burnt stews of the loft, it felt unbearably luxurious. I finished my plate and two bread rolls and coffee besides.

Midway through the meal, Peter came to where I sat with Rosa and Faye. He'd been promised a lounge that we could use for rehearsals. We would meet there later, he told us, once we'd all found our sea legs.

Rosa looked down at her lap and then back up at Peter. "Didn't know I'd lost them," she said. He kissed her right there, licking a glimmer of sauce from her chin.

After lunch, I climbed up to the deck and stared back the way we'd come. The city, which I'd never visit again, barring a few furtive hours between airline flights, was lost to me already. Water spread in every direction, an endless blanket, bleak and briny. Staring at it, I felt a first twinge of seasickness. Soon that sickness overwhelmed me. The water was not a blanket, it was a wall. Some instinct propelled me toward the railing, where I heaved the whole of my lunch into the sea.

There was a hand on my back.

"Sick up, did you?"

It was Bram, the boy from the muster room. I wiped my mouth with a hand and nodded, though the nodding made me want to heave again.

"No matter," he said. "Happens to us all. My first trip out, retched the whole way. Here, let's get you sitting down."

He led me to a bench, then told me to lie down and shut my eyes. He brought me a glass of water, and I drank it. Then he was back again with a blister pack of little pink pills; I took the pills as well. It was good to be cared for. My head was in his lap, and that seemed the best place for it, and he was stroking my hair, this stranger.

He asked me about the company, and I told him what I'd gleaned from my months in the loft, stories of their early years in New York and those first triumphant tours of Europe, then the sojourn in Mexico and the time in the prisons there.

"But that was before I came," I said. "I missed it all."

"Yes, and good luck to you. So how does a nice young woman such as yourself fall in with this dread crew?"

"They're not so dread. And I'm not so nice."

"Oh, I rather think you are."

"So what's your story?" I said. The nausea had gone by then, though my head felt floaty, helium-tipped. I dared to sit up. "Go on."

He was a student of literature, he said, just as I had been, and had finished his degree at Cambridge. "Rather bungled the examination," he said. "But they passed me all the same." He planned to go into business with his father. His father, as he'd tried to tell me earlier, was a theatrical producer of some note, had produced films, too. Bram had spent the summer in Hollywood, apprenticing at a studio.

"And what did you learn?"

"That you're a very vulgar people, you Americans," he said. "But as it happens, I like vulgarity. It's quite honest, isn't it? Unashamed."

"Is that very different from the English?"

"Oh yes," he said, spreading out his legs so that his right thigh pressed up against my left. "Even among the London crowd. We're shame all through."

"What does that make an American girl like me?" I said, looking up at him. "Shameless?"

"I very much hope so, Alice."

After dinner—rolls only this time and ginger tea—we followed Peter to the room we had been assigned. As usual, we began in our circle, but we barely managed a single breath. The chanting felt wrong there.

"This bourgeois crap," he said, gesturing to the red carpet, the chandeliers, "it's anti-art." (I was sorry to hear this. I liked the chandeliers.) "But we can still work a few things out. We need to cover the parts that Jax and Dede had. Molly, do you think you could play a prince?"

"I do not know," she said.

He went to her and pulled her hair aside, whispered in her ear. "Okay," she said when they parted. Her gaze followed him now, like a flower turned toward the sun. "I will be this prince. And you are right, I have the legs for tights, of course." I couldn't feel jealous. This was his gift. To make us blossom under his touch, to make us believe he knew our worth.

While the ocean rolled beneath us, we ran the scenes. I floated through them, heady from the pills, limbs long. Even in this new, staid room, some of the old magic held. I had made a mess of my life. But that mess had brought me here. We might make some great success. I was so young then. I still believed it could end happily.

We broke up the rehearsal late. There was a disco on a middle deck, but my body pleaded for sleep. I went back to the room, put away my dress, smoothed my face with cold cream, took one more of Bram's pink pills to sleep the waves away. Then I tucked myself into bed, admiring how neatly that bed was made. Because there were no windows, the room turned midnight once the lights were off. Sometime later, Rosa woke me. I was frightened at first, because she was screaming. Or no, not screaming, moaning. She was in bed, and a man, Peter, was above her. I had wondered what might happen between me and Rosa in this bed, with the lights out and the door closed. But the nearness of her, the carelessness of her, it disgusted me, even as I could feel my body respond. I pulled the pillow over my face and willed myself to sleep.

10

1997, LOS ANGELES, IRVINE, CHICAGO, THE NORTHEAST KINGDOM

Naomi, for all her faults, was organized. She brought the forms just after school finished the next day: Stanford, Princeton, Dartmouth, Penn, Berkeley, but that last, Naomi explained, was just a safety. She had already applied to Yale. Early decision, she said. Her college counselor had told her to expect a deferral.

"They all think I'm just another Asian grind," Naomi said. "So I need you to tell them all about my artistic side. I've made a list of some words you can use. We can go over it next week."

She took the forms, each in its labeled manila folder, and laid them on her desk, near the monitor. She had checked the mail program for messages. But there were no new ones that day. "Of course," she said. "I'm sure I'll find lots to say." She let the words hang down, like rotting fruit, a threat she could never fulfill.

"Yeah," Naomi said, snapping her gum. "I'm sure you will." Blackmail had improved the girl. She stood taller, spoke more definitely. Even her skin had cleared. "Where did you go to school, Mrs. Morales? If you don't mind my asking."

She did mind. She would have liked to tell the girl about that first college, about how she had talked her way into theater classes even as an English student, about how she would have made summa cum laude, or magna at the very least, if she had stayed. Instead, she said, "My teaching degree is from Irvine."

"Oh," Naomi condescended. "So you barely left the Valley? Cute."

There were places she had never left. She didn't count the Valley among them. "Yes," she said. She took the pack of cigarettes from her bag and began to tap the pack against her hand, hard enough to sting. "I'll write your letters, Naomi," she said. "As I told you, I would have written them anyway. And I know how to emphasize a person's actual gifts. You're an appalling actor. Truly." She was smiling now, though the smile was hollow, an entrance to a void beneath. "But you're a good student and an even better assistant, and you do have some sensitivity to the text. You could go into line producing after college. Or production management. If you're ambitious, which you are, and if you have family in the industry, which I'm sure you do, you could work your way up to producing proper. But all that is years away. For now, unless you have more forms or some new threat to make, get out of my classroom."

The next morning, as she brushed her teeth, she examined herself in the magnifying mirror. There were fine lines at the corners of her eyes, subtle parentheses around her mouth. The brows were sparser; the lips had thinned. But somewhere underneath that face, she could just glimpse the girl she had been, the girl she thought she had escaped. The image hovered there, a ghost. But who was the ghost, really? She put on clear mascara. A neutral lipstick. She set the dishwasher running. She drove to school, making the turns automatically, without thought. Panic had given way to irritability, exhaustion, an ache in her belly that had the contours of hunger, but was not hunger exactly.

The monitor stood silent on her desk, its screen mute and gray. Her fingers were on the power button almost before she'd put her bag down, and then the dial-up was screeching, one of its notes, her ear told her, was a perversion of the D major she played on her pitch pipe. There were a few messages from the school, including a reminder of Friday's meeting, which she would miss, owing to rehearsal, and then, yes, finally, a message from HighPoint. This one was short. **Another guess, Alice? It's no fun to play alone.**

She had to give him something, she felt, a sop thrown over her shoulder as she ran. Which name should she offer? Jan might be dead, but he might not. Rebecca Liu hadn't known for sure. Who else had been with them on tour? There was that girl Bram had brought. (Benny? Bernie?) But she had not stayed long. So there it was. She typed the name: **Jan**. She remembered his broad chest, his straw-blond hair, that lazy eye. She would have liked to wait for a response, to have sat in front of the screen like some girl in a storybook, sickening for love. But no, the first bell was already ringing. She switched off the monitor.

She was impatient with her students. Each false choice and garbled line felt like a slap across her face. At morning recess, she took three aspirin. The aspirin did not help. After lunch—a bowl of wan matzoh ball soup at Art's—she gave up, trundling out the AV cart and letting the advanced students watch BBC recordings of English actors performing Shakespeare scenes. Maybe it would teach them the rudiments of scansion.

Kyle raised his hand. "Hey, Mrs. Morales," he said. "I have a sick idea. Could we, like, film ourselves rehearsing *Midsummer*? Could we, like, make a trailer for it?"

She sighed. "That's fine, Kyle," she said, removing her glasses and massaging the bridge of her nose. "But keep it clean. I don't need the parents after me. I had enough trouble when your older brother tried to strip during the final performance of *Hair*."

A cigarette before rehearsal began, snuck at the back window, failed to calm her. They were reading through the second half of the play now. If she were a weeping woman, she would have wept then, at the fumbling, stuttering, body-sprayed incompetence. She ended rehearsal ten minutes early, after Carlos, as Theseus, misread *nuptial* as *nipple*.

She blew her pitch pipe.

"Go. Just go," she said. "Out, all of you. Quick as you can. We'll reconvene Wednesday. Start memorizing this weekend. The punishment for unlearned lines is shunning and ritual humiliation."

Naomi lingered at the door, a binder clutched to her chest. "Mrs. Morales, are you, like, okay?"

"What the fuck do you think, Naomi?"

She turned off the classroom fluorescents until the room was lit only by the low sun, which turned the metal of the chairs to gold. Fool's gold. She returned to the computer. Another message waited. **Wrong again**, it said.

I'm sorry, she typed. **I'm trying to think, to remember. I need more time.**

Then, almost immediately, another message. **Alice**, it said, **you've had all the time in the world. You've had your whole life. Mine, too. Don't tell me you've forgotten me.**

Please, she wrote. And then again, **Please.**

All right, the message came. **Just a little longer. But hurry, Alice. It's so late already.** She pressed the button to power off the monitor, and the screen closed like a winking eye, a burst of light at the center, then all to black.

On the way to her car, she found a number of teachers clustered outside the assembly hall, and with some reluctance, she joined them. The mood was funereal. "I was talking to my cousin," George was saying, tugging worriedly at the lapel of his blazer, "the financial planner. He says the market's going to get worse before it gets better. So that means the cuts are really coming."

"And that means firings," said Jed Cohen, the mustachioed senior history teacher and debate coach, who wore Levi's jackets and used to follow the Dead on summer breaks.

"Or worse," Marta said. "It means whole departments closing. My department. No one's closing history."

"They would if they could," Jed said dourly. "California is where you go when you don't care what came before. This place began five minutes ago. If there's a doughnut shop left over from the 1950s, we treat it like the mother-loving Parthenon. And bulldoze it for condos anyway."

"Ali, have you heard anything?" George pleaded. "You talk to Dan."

"Not if I can help it," she said. "But yes. He says it's bad. That it's getting worse. He has this idea that if we show the board members what we do, it might help. Me, I fail to see how two dozen teenagers making iambic pentameter sorry it was ever born will change anything."

"Ali," George said. "You're too hard on yourself. The kids love your shows. The parents, too. My orchestra students, they wait all year to play in the pit for the musicals. Don't you think some of the parents in the industry might care? They're in the business of art."

Linda, standing nearby, gave a laugh that was more like a yelp.

She laughed, too, though not ungently. "They're in the business of money, George. And whether their kids can play the trumpet or paint in oils or make it through 'Gallop apace' one time without giggling, it doesn't matter. That and a million dollars toward a new library will get them into Claremont McKenna. If it's not academics or athletics, it'll be sold for parts."

"I hope you're wrong," George said, scuffing a loafer at the cement.

"I'm wrong about everything," she said. "But not this."

Dan Daley emerged from the building. The others parted for him, shouldering their briefcases and bags. "Dan, do you have a minute?" she said, using her pert, public voice. "I thought about what you said. And maybe we could plan something special around the winter classic. One of my kids, he wants to make a documentary, show everyone what we do."

"I like that," he said. "Let's talk it through." He grabbed her upper arm. To anyone watching, it looked gentle, but his fingers were a vise. "Walk with me. I need to grab some papers from my office."

As soon as the door was shut behind them, she pressed herself to him, one hand to the back of his head, the other at his groin. She touched him through his pants, and he moaned into her mouth.

"How do you want me?" she said. "In your chair? Across your desk?"

"Desk," he said.

She took him in her hand and shut her eyes, trying to bring herself to something like arousal. His hands were unbuttoning her blouse. Then he spun her around, pushing her onto the desk with a hand on her neck so that her breasts were crushed against the wood. He pulled up her skirt and pushed down her panties. Good ones, silk. With the toe of her shoe, she slid them to the floor and kicked them aside. She could do this, she told herself. She could do this once more.

Then he was inside her. She met his rhythm, merged it with her own, didn't flinch when his sweat dripped onto her back or her forehead bumped his nameplate. She thrust a hand between her legs and worked herself. She wanted to come this time.

Then she was there, her breath shortening into a kind of howl. He put a hand over her mouth, and she bit at those fingers as pictures of other bodies rioted behind her eyes. And he was coming, too, with one valedictory thrust and a strangled sort of wheeze. He lay across her back, spent and heavy. The lights buzzed above.

"You bit me," he said. He removed himself from her, gingerly, pulled his pants back up. He didn't offer her a tissue.

She straightened up and turned to face him, tugging her skirt back down. "Guess I just can't help myself around you."

He cradled his injured hand to his chest. "Sometimes I think you don't even like me, Ali," he said, chastened somehow, sick at having gotten what he wanted. She knew that lonely feeling.

"Anyway," he went on, "I should get home. Kelly and the kids and all that."

"Well, don't let me stop you, Dan. I just have to find my underwear."

She could sense his agitation, his wanting to be away from her. "I'm sure they're around here somewhere," she said. She could feel his weight shifting from foot to foot as she searched under his desk and around the wheels of his chair.

He cleared his throat. "Ali," he said. "Could you hurry it up?"

"Dan," she said, straightening. "You're already closing my department and halving my work hours. You want me to go, find the panties yourself. Or if you're in such a rush, you leave first. Everyone's gone by now anyway."

"Okay," he said, hefting his soft-sided briefcase. "Sorry. To lock the door, you just push the button inside—"

"Thanks, Dan. I know how buttons work. Enjoy your dinner."

He left and she listened for the susurration of his feet on the carpet, then stepped back into her underwear. It was fine to be alone in his office, fine to touch his things, to search in his drawers, to run her fingers over his keyboard. After switching off the lights and securing the lock, she made her own way out, past the secretary's desk, through the door, into the tiled hallway lined with the lockers. The doors to the parking lot were set with glass, and as she pushed her way into the musky October night, the left one caught her reflection. Her step faltered. She looked, for a moment, so young.

On Saturday, after dry toast, coffee, and a furious ride to nowhere on the exercise bike while KCRW news and jazz played, she pulled the phone book from the kitchen cabinets. There were things she had put off knowing, things she had sealed away. No more. She found the number for the public library and called the reference desk. Two transfers later, she replaced the receiver. They didn't have the materials she required. Back to the phone book. Another number, another library. Yes, a woman told her, they had that newspaper, preserved on microfiche.

She gassed up the car at a Chevron, her nose wrinkling at the sweet smell of benzene, then with the world sunglass-dimmed, she merged onto the 405 and into the leftmost lane where, for this one hour, she could go almost as fast as she wanted, though the Celica protested every bulge and rut. She knew the route well, though she didn't drive it often.

The later highway, the 73, took her too close to what had been her home, past the ghosts of citrus orchards.

The freeway retreated and Bison Avenue brought her to the tawny bricks of Irvine, her second alma mater, and then to the library, built in the California Brutalist style. It had been almost new when she arrived, the whole campus had. Its concrete looked duller now and brittle, as though it might collapse the next time a Santa Ana blew. It cost her something to approach those doors again, to remember the smiling wreck she'd been when she'd first stepped through them. She went in.

A man directed her to the languages section, where she pulled a dictionary from the shelf, and a different man, a boy, really, a student in stiff jeans, showed her to the microfiche room. This room was new to her. She gave her information to the clerk, a woman in a turtleneck, cigarette wrinkles all around her lips, and waited until the woman returned with several small cardboard cases, each of which held a microfiche reel.

Seated at a console, she opened the dictionary and wrote down the words she thought she might need. Theater was the same, she saw. And so, more or less was Negative. Then there were other words; girl, *Mädchen*; woman, *Frau*; water, *Wasser*; river, *Fluss*; knife, *Messer*; dead, *tot*; stabbed, *niedergestochen*; drowned, *ertrank*. Following the directions on the Xeroxed sheet the woman handed her, she fed the first reel into the machine. The film felt slithery, like snakeskin; it took two tries to make it catch. Then she turned the knob and began to scroll through page after page, issue after issue of the German newspaper, until the gray of the type seemed to spill from the screen and into the room. Her eyes strained. She scrolled on.

At the start of the second reel was that first article, the record of their Frankfurt triumph. She looked again at the pictures, at all of them so beautiful, so young. There were no faces she had forgotten. And further on in the reel, she found what she had sought and feared. The article had run in the evening edition six days later. She was home by then, narcotized with a doctor's prescription, huddled on the sofa, eating soft foods. Thousands of miles away, the body of a young woman, *"der Körper einer jungen Frau,"* had been pulled from the water. She read the article with the help of the dictionary. The body was unclaimed, the paper said, and unidentified. But it was undeniably Rosa. Black hair was mentioned, a blue coat.

She kept scrolling, for another week, then two. At the reel's end, she saw a short item about a member of a foreign theater company dying in prison. She knew this item, had read a version of it from a wire service. She remembered screaming as she read it, frightening even her father. They kept the papers from her after that. She wound the reel through until the end, then slid it from its spindle and packaged it with the first.

The room around her was unaltered, the clerk frowning still. But she had changed. She had lived decades without ever knowing for certain what had been wrought that night. She knew it now. Rosa was dead. That horror had loomed over her all these years, like a wave always about to break. The wave had broken. She felt she might break, too, turn to foam.

So there it was. Rosa had not sent those messages. Rosa had been dead, really dead, all this time. And someone else had seen her fall. Not Bill, not Jorge. Not the others already dead or soon to die. Who was left? Only Peter. Only Suzanne. Mechanically, she brought the boxes back to the clerk and walked back out the doors and into the sun-bruised lot. The car sweltered. The buckle of the seat belt scorched her hand. She rolled down every window and drove, even faster than before, back to the Valley. She was two people: a woman with her foot on the accelerator, her hands soldered to the steering wheel, and also a girl, in the rain, stumbling down stone streets.

On Ventura, she parked at a meter that had a little time remaining and entered the travel agency. She would need a few days and she didn't dare take the time away from work, which meant the Thanksgiving break. It was nearly impossible, the agent, a man with skin so tan it looked pan-fried, told her. And so expensive. Could she possibly travel on another day. She could not. Twenty minutes later, she was out again, much poorer, with the tickets in her hand. The meter showed red.

The five weeks passed with an aching slowness. She hung suspended, counting the hours, the days. Classes seemed to last forever, rehearsals ran even longer, as the students lurched through basic blocking and the fairies giggled behind their painted nails. "Lord, what fools these mortals be!" Nadine, as Puck, said. She nodded over her yellow legal pad. She was one more, believing she could still outrun who she was, what she'd done.

She avoided Dan Daley. Or he avoided her. She brought the letters of recommendation to Naomi, and Naomi accepted them, snapping her gum. One Friday, she begged off dinner with Linda and spent the night at the bar, dancing with a leggy brunette, a Chicana girl in a plaid shirt. They fucked in the bathroom, and she drove home alone, angry though she couldn't have said why, the smell of the girl still on her.

She met the new technical director, Zay, a twentysomething burnout in board shorts and a patchy goatee, on Halloween. She didn't enjoy Halloween. She wore enough masks already. But she'd obliged with a black dress and a witch's hat bought at the drugstore. Zay, who had not dressed up at all, hid behind his sunglasses, saying little in his frayed voice. His hair, his clothes, stank of weed. Still, he seemed to understand the lighting plot she suggested, a wood of pinks and greens, and promised to deliver that and the set pieces within her minimal budget.

On the Sunday before Thanksgiving, she took her mother to church, then to lunch, boysenberry pie this time, and back to the facility. She had rented a childhood favorite, *On the Town*, and it hurt, though only a little, to see the New York scenery go by. Her mother fell asleep in the chair, her head canted so far to one side that her neck looked broken. There was a wheeze to her breath, some extra, choking effort. As the credits played, she helped her mother, gently, to the bed and bent to take off her shoes.

"Would you find my nightgown for me, dear?" her mother asked.

"Mom, it's still afternoon. They'll be serving dinner in an hour. Don't you want your dinner?"

"Dinner? Oh yes, that sounds nice. Can you stay?"

"Yes, for a little while. And I'll see you next week. But listen, there's a trip I have to take. I'll miss Thanksgiving, but I know they do a lovely celebration here."

"You will?" Her mother's face crumpled, like a dress that had slipped from the hanger. "Oh dear. Are you sure? I don't like to think of you alone."

"I won't be alone. Promise."

"Are you lying to me again, Allison?" her mother said, stern suddenly. These electric shifts in mood were, she'd been told, a symptom of dementia. They were startling, all the same. "I don't like that." Then her voice softened. "Do you remember how when you were little you loved that jellied cranberry sauce, the one in the can? How you used to call it *cranbabies*? 'More cranbabies,' you would say."

"Yes, I remember."

"Oh, Allison. I wish you wouldn't go."

"I'm sorry," she said. "I have to."

"I'm just so afraid." Her mother's voice broke at that last word, went sharp and high.

"Afraid of what?" she said, perching on the edge of the bed and holding one of her mother's crepe-paper hands in both of her own.

"That I won't see you again. That you won't come back." A tear escaped her mother's eye, staggered down her cheek.

"Shhhh. It's a few days only. And I see you every week. I always come back."

"But you don't," her mother said. "You didn't. Not really."

"But, Mom—"

"Quiet. Quiet, Allison. No more lies. I need my rest. I'll nap until dinner." Her mother shut her eyes and lay back on the pillow.

On Wednesday, she taught her half-full classes, then went home and colored her hair in the bathroom sink so that no gray would show. She shaved her legs, filed down her nails, brushed and flossed until her gums bled, slathered her face in a cooling mask that dried and cracked until her skin looked like a mud flat. She washed the mask away. And on Thursday, after breakfast, dressed in skirt, blouse, and ankle boots, she parked her car in the long-term lot and wheeled her suitcase, the leatherette long since traded for woven nylon, to the check-in desk. It would be her first time on a plane in twenty-five years.

Since she had come back to California, she had hardly traveled. Her passport had never been renewed. All those years ago, after their cheap church wedding, with no father to give her away, Manny had suggested Mexico for their honeymoon, Puerto Vallarta. She'd countered with Las Vegas. She remembered their first night there, the lacquered black lamps and polyester spread of the hotel room, the laughter and the music just beyond the walls. She'd taken off her sundress for him as he lay on the bed and then begun to cry—hard, racking sobs that bent her body double. He'd asked her what was wrong. She couldn't tell him, hadn't known herself. She'd calmed then, made love to him quietly as flashing lights flared along the walls, gone to dinner on the strip after. That was in the spring. That fall, Manny injured his knee, killing his chances of turning pro. The injury unmoored them both. There were no further trips. The marriage hung on for another year or two while she finished her degree, then foundered. She still received Christmas cards. Manny, paunchy from his years at the dealership, his suntanned wife. Three kids. Or four. A life she could have had. A life she did not want.

Security took no time at all. On the holiday itself, the airport was deserted. Out the window, planes arrived and departed, ground crews hustled baggage trailers here and there, but inside, all was hushed, half

the businesses shuttered. She sat with a magazine until the boarding call
crackled over the speaker, then she was down the corridor and in her
seat. The plane taxied, willing the ground away, until it was airborne,
winging out over the sea, then arcing back toward land. She accepted a
diet soda from the beverage cart, draining it in slow, careful sips as she
watched the movie on the screen in the section's front, some family
comedy. The busty mother looked like Faye, Faye as she used to be.

O'Hare, where she deplaned, was more crowded, studded with fret-
ful travelers stranded by a storm. She forked up a wilting salad from the
airport pizzeria and watched the boards for her gate, praying, to whom
she wasn't sure, that the flight would leave on time. It did. The sky was
dark already when the plane took off and darker still when it landed, the
moon a waning crescent. The baggage carousel went round and round,
finally disgorging her suitcase, which she unzipped, removing her coat.
It was imitation camel hair, too light for the Vermont autumn, but the
heaviest she had.

At the rental car office, she was given a once-white Sonata and, following the directions that the sales rep, a string bean girl hardly old
enough to drive, had written on the back of a claims form, she drove
to the nearby chain motel, the heater blasting full. It was midnight by
the time she parked. She rang the buzzer, teeth chattering in rhythm,
until the night clerk roused himself to let her in. She entered the assigned room without turning on the light. Having removed only her
coat and shoes, she sank into the too-soft bed and slept until morning
light worried the curtains.

The complimentary breakfast—white bread, jelly packets, a basket
of waxed apples—didn't tempt her, so with only coffee sloshing in her
stomach, she began her drive. At a gas station, she bought a map, and
the clerk, his cheeks pitted with chicken pox scars, was nice enough
to help her with the main route. It would take about an hour and a
half, he said. Maybe two hours. She shivered as she strode back to the

car. The day was cloudless, the sunlight fainter than California's. She remembered this eastern light—those giddy campus mornings when she'd stayed up all night writing a paper, that woozy, floating feeling as she left the dorm on colt's legs and crossed the lawn to the dining hall. She was overcome, for a moment, with love and pity for the girl she had been, that girl with so much promise. She reversed out of the station.

There was snow on the ground, just a dusting, like confectioner's sugar atop one of her mother's bundt cakes. The highway had fewer lanes than those she drove at home; its white lines stood starker against the gray. Just out of the city, she briefly glimpsed a sculpture of two whale tails, as though the whales themselves were plunged into the earth. In Montpelier, the dome of the capitol glinting through the pines, she transferred to the state route, then stopped at a roadside diner to pee. The smell inside was sumptuous—maple, bacon fat, coffee's burly tang. But she could not bring herself to eat.

The state route brought her to a small town, with a single main street running through it. She brought the map into a health food store dredged in brewer's yeast and B vitamin dust. The frizzy-haired cashier who rang up her spring water told her how to find the lane. "Beautiful out that way," she said. "Forests, you know? Meadows? The Northeast Kingdom, we call it."

The roads thinned. The pines arched overhead, bent in secret conference. She was awake now, no longer suspended, present in a way she hadn't felt in years, attuned to colors, to sounds, to the furrows of the road beneath. Her eyes caught the turnoff, marked only by a weathered wooden sign, EDEN LANE. She spun the wheel just in time. There were meadows on either side. To the right were black cows. She could hear them lowing through the windows. Up ahead, she could see a red barn and a white house. The drive took a minute. It took a lifetime. Then she was on the gravel, parking the car, climbing the stairs, ringing the bell. It echoed inside the house. She lifted the knocker, shaped like a lion. She banged it. Then banged it again. It had never occurred to her that they might have gone away, traveled elsewhere for the holiday. The thought panicked her.

But then she heard sounds. Muttering, shuffling. "Okay, okay," a voice said. "Had to find my slippers. Don't break the door down." That door shrieked open, and a woman was there. The face, beneath the gray-white hair, was wrinkled and sun-worn, but somehow, even after all of these years, recognizable.

"Suzanne," she said. "It's me. It's Alice. I'm here."

11

1972, THE ATLANTIC, LONDON

The crossing, Faye told me, was a bad one, the waves thudding at the hull like fists. Bram's pills made me dull and drowsy, but they kept me from the worst of it. I saw Bram at rehearsals, often in conversation with Peter. Peter, Bash said out of the side of his mouth, always liked the rich ones. These rehearsals were meant to refine the blocking, but the roll and pitch made us wobble around the salon like drunks. On the second day, Peter gave it up in the middle of the Rumpelstiltskin scene, stalking out of the room, lighting a cigarette as he went. Molly made to follow, but he was too fast for her, too angry. She took out her cards and shuffled them, again and again, her fingers quick, her eyes hollow.

I spent most of that day dozing on a deck chair, a ginger tea at my side. I was avoiding Rosa, though I'm not sure she noticed. She was gone from our room that night. But on the next night, hours after I'd gone to sleep, she was back in our shared bed, shaking me awake.

"Alice," she said. "Get up already. Come into the bathroom."

"Why should I?" I said.

"For Chrissake, just do it," she said. I did, though there was hardly room for both of us, and I had to blink away the light.

"Look at my pussy," Rosa said.

For a moment, I thought I must be asleep, it sounded so absurd. "Rosa, you can't be serious."

"Don't be such a goddamn princess, huh? Just tell me what you see."

She wriggled from her underwear, then lifted the hem of her skirt and put one leg atop the toilet seat. I knelt before her, my face a breath away. I looked, and the looking unnerved me. I had never been this close to another girl, not with the lights on.

"Rosa, is this some kind of joke?" But then I saw them—crawling, skittering things the size of sprinkles on a cake. I nearly fell over.

"What is that?" I squealed. "What are they?"

"Goddamn it. Hoped it was maybe just some rash. But if you can see them, that means crabs, Alice. I've got them, and dollars to doughnuts, you got them, too—same bed and all."

The nausea that was never far away swelled into my throat. Rosa still had a foot across the toilet lid, so I vomited into the sink.

"A social disease? You gave me a social disease? What will it do to me?"

"Fuck's sake, Alice," Rosa said, lowering herself to straddle the lid. "It's just lice. Kind you got on your head in grade school, only lower down. Clean girl like you, maybe you never did get lice, huh? Yeah, well, they itch like hell, but they won't hurt you."

"Are you sure I have them?" I shut my eyes and inventoried my body. "I don't feel anything."

"Probably still laying their little eggs."

I retched again. Rosa laughed and scratched herself. "Not such a clean girl now, huh?"

I rinsed and spat. "Do we need to see a doctor? There's a doctor on the ship, right?"

"Sure. But he's not getting up at three in the goddamn morning for this. I'm gonna shave it, so it don't get worse. You'll wanna do the same."

"Shave? You mean—"

"I gotta draw you a picture, sunshine? God, you college girls are dumb sometimes." She took out the razor I used for my legs and under-arms. "Don't mind, right?"

She turned on the knob for the shower, then stripped off her clothes. I could see her ribs through her skin, the vertebrae of her spine. The water blackened her hair, softening out the curl. I watched as she soaped herself, then scraped the razor up and down her skin.

"I miss anything?"

She looked like a child, like a woman, like a changeling girl. I shook my head.

"Your turn, sunshine."

She brushed against me, handing me the razor. For a moment, I could feel the whole of her body, the jut of her hipbones, the curve of her breasts. The front of my nightgown was damp from the water that clung to her. My arms reached out. I held her there.

"Whaddya want, Alice?" she said.

I wanted never to have met her. I wanted to be delivered somewhere far away, somewhere clean and private, with sheets that smelled of fabric softener. But also, in some feral, animal way, I wanted her, the whole of her.

I let her go and pulled my nightgown off. "You do it," I said. Then we were both in that tiny shower.

She shaved me, as gently as she could. When the razor nicked the top of my thigh, she smiled at it, swiped her finger along the wound.

"So you do bleed, huh?" she said. "Not just ice in there."

"Not ice," I said. Then my mouth was on hers and her fingers were inside me and I felt as though I were falling, as though I would never stop falling.

We dried ourselves as best we could, then stripped away the blankets, pillows, sheets, and tumbled onto the yellowed mattress. Her hair was in my mouth, my mouth was on her neck, her breasts, the softness of her belly. We were together all the rest of that night.

I woke to a new wave of nausea and pressed another of Bram's pills from the strip, swallowing it dry. I took clean underclothes from the drawer beneath the bed, a skirt and blouse from the closet. Even fully dressed, I felt strange, exposed. And the itching had begun.

Rosa was stirring by then. She reached out a hand for me. I shook it off.

"So it's like that, huh?" she said. "You a sorority girl again. You don't gotta pretend with me."

"I'm not pretending anything," I said stiffly. "It just doesn't feel right. Down there. Can I use your baby powder?"

"Sorry," she said, "all out. Just have to get used to it, sunshine."

"Fine. I'm going to the doctor."

Eyes downcast, I asked a steward where to find him, then followed his directions to a suite of rooms on an upper floor. The doctor was a white-haired Englishman, with a nest of broken capillaries across each cheek. Low-voiced, I told him what was wrong.

The doctor made a sucking sound and rattled items in a cabinet until he found a thin tube. "There you are, my girl," he said. "Rub it in, all over, neck right down to toes, and leave it on all the day. That will teach those creepy-crawlies. You young ones, you ought to be more careful in your doings. Some nasty things around. Things a cream won't clear."

I took the tube from him. "Do you have another, please?" I asked. "It was my friend who had it first. We're in a double room, sharing a bed. That's how it came to me."

"Your friend, eh?" He smiled in a way that wasn't nice and gave me another tube. "Yes, yes. If you've had yourself any other 'friends' these past days, they'll need the cream as well." Another steward took me down to housekeeping. I told the woman there that our bedding needed washing, our clothes, that it was a matter of some urgency. Unsmiling, she followed me to the room. Wearing yellow gloves, she gathered the bedding, Rosa's jumbled clothes, the damp towels. Through the haze of the pill, I felt her judgment. She put her gloved hand out. Was I meant to shake it? No, she wanted money. I gave it to her, then I locked myself in the bathroom and applied the cream, which smelled of garlic.

I found Peter and the others in the lounge, practicing a dance that

Bash had devised for the opening, a ballet of abduction. Jorge clapped the time as Peter and Jan and Bill circled Rosa and JoAnn and Faye.

"The violence in these stories, don't forget it," Peter said. "Make it hurt. Make it wound. It's rape, it's death, it's blood, yeah? Jan, grab her harder. Like this." He jerked Rosa's wrist with such force that she nearly lost her footing. "Yeah," he said. "Like that. Make it ugly. Life's ugly, man. Make it true."

He saw me then. "Where you been, Snow White? Come on." He reached for me. I was filthy, disgraced, and still I had to dance.

We broke for lunch. I pulled Rosa aside and gave her the extra tube, telling her, stiffly, that she'd need to let her other partners know. She rolled her eyes. "They can figure it out," she said.

"You won't even tell Peter?"

"Tell him yourself, sunshine. Come on. I'm starved. And you smell like Sunday fucking gravy."

I was able to eat some soup, a few crackers. It was our last full day aboard. Rosa ate only cake. Over a cup of tea, I watched, we all did, as Jan toyed with sugar packets and stirrers, assembling them into what was recognizably a little house.

"The woodcutter's home," Jan said in his sleepy voice. "You like it, yes?"

"Yes," Jorge said, squeezing Jan's arm. I envied their ease with each other, how they would touch right there in public. "I like it very much. You should build for us this house. This is how the stories begin. A house. A *casita*. Just like this." It was the longest speech I'd ever heard him make.

"And then," Jan said, "the wolf is coming." With a swipe of his hand, he knocked the cottage down.

We had just risen from the table when Bram came crashing through the door. "Oh, thank God," he said. "Your gods. Mine. Bloody hell. I thought . . . Well, mustn't say what I thought." He steadied himself on the back of a chair, pushed breath into his chest.

"What happened, honey?" Faye asked.

"A girl, she must have fallen, from one of the balconies onto the deck. There was such a scrum. Couldn't see. I stopped a steward. He said it was one of the girls from the theater. But here you all are."

I looked around the table. Here we were. But no, I counted on my fingers, then counted again. There were nine of us. Molly was absent. Just as she'd been absent from rehearsal. The others must have realized it just before I did, because they were already running out of the salon and onto the deck.

As Bram had said, a crowd had gathered. Some of the girl students had climbed onto men's shoulders, as though this were a pool party. Peter pushed through, and we followed in his wake. A body was there, covered already in a few of the ship's white towels. One was already soaked through with red. At the towel's edge were the ends of Molly's wild curls.

The doctor, the one I'd seen that morning, was there, in conversation with an officer in a white shirt and epaulets. Peter approached, and after a brief conference, the officer lifted one of the towels. Peter nodded, then staggered to the railing. Faye ran to him, weeping, pummeling his back with her fists. He turned and caught her wrists, and they tumbled down to the wood, knit together in their pain.

Bill held JoAnn. Jan took Jorge in his arms.

I turned to Bash. "What do we do?"

He looked at me, his face a wilderness. "There's nothing to do, my darling," he said. "Everything is bent for England. We sail on."

Peter was kept busy for much of the afternoon, signing forms, placing a call from ship to shore. After a dinner that no one ate, we met again in the lounge. There would be no investigation, Peter told us. The ship would call it an accident, to spare feelings. But a few of the students had seen her climb the railing and cast herself into the air. It was terrible, he said. Terrible for everyone. Still, we would disembark in the morning as planned. Molly would stay aboard, in a coffin the ship carried for occasions such as these.

"What will happen to the body?" JoAnn said. "Does her family even want her?"

"Reached her sister in Queens," Peter said. "Said she'd handle it. Acted like the whole thing was just some goddamn hassle."

We were quiet for a while.

"Has anyone gone and checked on Faye?" JoAnn asked.

"I'll go," I said. "Her room is right near mine." Rosa made to come, but I shook my head and went alone. Faye was in bed, on her side, the covers pulled half over her head. I sat beside her, patted what might have been her shoulder. I hadn't known Molly well. I did not know how to mourn her. "Were you close to her, Faye?" I asked.

"The littlest bit," she whispered. "Shut up tight, that one, like a Galveston oyster."

"And she wasn't so close with her family?"

"Oh, honey." She turned and looked at me with something like pity. "We aren't any of us like that. The older ones, maybe. Suzanne, sure. JoAnn and Bill. Bash has a mother who dotes on him, I believe. But the rest of us, I don't know that we'd be here, we had family to go to. Our born family, they can't live with us. Or we can't live with them. You, too, by the look of you. If there's a girl here who didn't know her father's belt or worse, I'd like to shake her hand. The other ones, they come, but they don't linger. Girls like us, we're the ones who stay. This is our family now. We're sisters, you and me. And Molly."

"Faye, do you know why she did it?"

"No, baby," she said. "No, I don't. Molly, she was in a family way in the winter. But that wasn't the reason. Peter had all that taken care of. It's easy in the city. Clean. Had it done a time myself. Nurses were sweet as pie. Held my hand. Molly, she came through it fine. Didn't want it anyway. I suspect that life just goes harder for some of us. Or some of us feel that hardness more. Made for woe. That was Molly. Well, I've cried for her and cried some more. But I'm all cried out now. Why don't you go on and take me back to the others. We'll have a little drink."

We found them back in the salon, singing sad songs. Faye went to Peter, and he took her in his arms. Bram plumped down onto the sofa next to me. He held a bottle of wine. "Alice," he said. "I'm not sure the circus is for me after all. Bit upsetting."

I reached for the bottle and took a drink. "It's all clowns," I said. "Clowns all the way down." I laughed. And once I started laughing, I couldn't stop. Tears were in my eyes. My lungs were burning. Still I laughed.

"Oh, Alice," he said. He took the bottle from me and gathered me to his chest. "Let's get you out into the air."

We climbed to the upper deck. I'd never come here at night. The water reflected the lights from the ship's windows so that it looked as though there were some other ship below the waves. And the stars. I'd never seen so many. All winking. All far away and cold. Bram kissed me then. His lips were soft. I suppose I kissed him back. He was warm and near and promised something other than despair.

His room was above the water line and larger than my shared one, with space for a table, a dresser. He went and sat on the bed. I stood near the door, uncertain. I'd forgotten how normal people did these things. Maybe I'd never known. And I worried that I still smelled of garlic.

He swallowed, his Adam's apple bobbing down and up, and told me to take off my skirt, then my blouse, then my bra. I did what he asked and stood there, in just my underwear and shoes, as he appraised me like I was some trinket in a store window that he might or might not buy.

"You're beautiful, Alice," he said.

I did not feel beautiful.

"Come here," he said. I went to him and, with a firm hand on my shoulder, he pushed me down until I was kneeling. He unbuckled his belt, and I knew what he wanted me to do. I had done as much before. He unbuttoned his jeans and took himself out, thin and pink and veined. I reached for him, but something was wrong. He was hairless there. He had shaved. Then I understood. It was Bram and not Peter whom Rosa brought into our bed.

It was all too sordid then. It sickened me what bodies could want, could do. I backed away, grabbing for my clothes, misaligning the buttons of my blouse.

"Alice," he said. "Wait. I'm sure I can—"

I fled and slept on the deck that night, under a heap of towels, like the towels that had covered Molly. And in the morning, when I woke, sore and squinting, I saw the flagpole above me, its Union Jack whipping in the wind. Against the sun, the flag looked black.

We disembarked, clattering down the gangway and waiting in the drizzle as an immigration official checked our passports and wished us well. There was a coach, a sort of van, to take us to the train. The train brought us to London, to Waterloo Station. We took the underground then, so much smoother than the subway, the black line to the blue. We came up again, the nine of us, into a neighborhood of pale houses and green-leafed squares. Four of the men took the cases of costumes and props between them. The rest of us dragged our suitcases along the pavement. The rain had stopped. It was cooler here, as though London were too polite to swelter.

A man was waiting at the front of some great brick building, black-haired and fat-faced in a tight blue suit. He hallooed when he saw Peter and clapped him emphatically on the back. Peter steadied his sunglasses.

"Nigel, man, how's it going?" he said.

"Very well. Very well, indeed." He turned to the rest of us. "Greetings to you all," he said. "Delighted to have you. Truly. We had another group fall away. Some little contretemps. Left rather a hole in the schedule. So how happy I was when Peter telephoned. It's been what, six years, seven?"

"More," Peter said. "We were here last with *The World Tree.*"

"Yes. And how lovely that was. Now as to your accommodation. We have a few student rooms free, so we've put you there, though you may have to squash in a bit. But that's nothing to you bohemians. I've managed a small account for materials, and you can join us in the catering hall for dinner. Breakfasts and lunches you'll have to sort yourself, all right? We've put you in for four performances, might add more if there's demand, with the box office to share, just as we discussed. But I should warn you, the students these days, they're a funny lot. The work's too radical, they say, or it's not radical enough. Really, there's just no pleasing them. But they're mad for anything American, so really, it should all go rather well. The piece, it's ready?"

"Oh yeah," Peter said. He smiled as he said it, and Nigel nodded, eagerly, like a doll with a spring in its neck.

"And what do you call this masterpiece?"

"*The Grimm Variations.* Show him what you drew, JoAnn." JoAnn reached into her bag and took out a narrow cylinder, a rolled-up sheet of paper secured with a rubber band. She unfolded it to show a charcoal drawing—two girls, children, entering a forest of skeleton trees. The title was above. Below, in letters just as large, was the name of the troupe.

"Do you still have that printing studio?" she asked. "I can make it into a woodblock for the posters."

"Yes, yes," Nigel said, still nodding. "Beautiful. We can arrange all of that with the arts faculty. Now as pertains to the show, you must forgive me, but please remember that this isn't New York City. We're rather behind the times here, I'm afraid. The governors, well, they can be somewhat rigid when it comes to certain matters. Nudity, for one. So let's stay on the sunny side of all that, yes?"

We walked the few blocks to the student dormitories. I'd asked Faye if I could share with her. I did not want to be alone with Rosa. The room was smaller than the dorm double, though larger than the ship's quarters, fitted out with twinned desks, chairs, and narrow beds. A sink stood near the door. Toilets and showers were down the hall, I was told. I washed my face and buttoned into fresh clothes, then joined the others at the university theater, that same brick building where Nigel had met us.

I had forgotten what still spaces theaters were before an audience entered, how empty and serene. Peter was there already, pacing the stage, trailed by Bill. Nigel was with them. New bulbs for the lights were needed, Peter was saying. Some lengths of cloth, green and black. More muslin.

"And tools," he said. "Hammers, nails. You have lumber for us, right? Two-by-fours? Or whatever the hell that is in meters? And hey, can you spot us lunch, just for today? We haven't eaten since breakfast on the boat, and American Express takes fucking years."

Nigel agreed and went to organize it. Peter and Bill left just after. Under Bash's supervision, the rest of us unpacked the cases and began to arrange the costumes in a room with sewing machines and long tables. The props went to another room. There were dressing rooms, as well. And what looked like a woodshop.

"It's like a labyrinth," I said to Faye as we chanced on a set of stairs that led under the stage.

"Sure is, honey. We're lucky we have a place like this to start. Once we're on the road, we just go on and play anywhere we can."

A woman in a belted dress, Nigel's secretary, brought in sandwiches wrapped in wax paper: ham, an egg salad with spicy greens, cheese with a sweet-sour spread. There were blackberries for after. Bash had us run through the dances, without Peter and Bill, without Molly. We were already straining to cover the parts that Jax and Dede had played. Now we would absorb hers, too.

It was evening by the time Peter and Bill returned with bags from what must have been a hardware store and a stack of records. The squawking jazz that Peter liked, some English folk music.

"Shoulda been German," Bill said. "But we listened to it in the store, and it's all oompah, oompah tuba shit."

Peter had brought someone else: Bram. He came straight to me and patted my arm in a brotherly way. "Forgive me for last night, won't you, Alice? Fear I wasn't entirely the gentleman. A day like that. Bit fuddling. But I've asked your man, Peter, here, if I might loiter for a bit. Do a spot of producing, you see. Family business and all that."

"How nice," I said.

There was a girl with him, introduced as Benny, with strawberry-blond hair, wispy as cobwebs, and glasses that took up half her face. She looked as though she would cower under anything as bright as a spotlight, but Bram told us she was an actress, a graduate of the Central School, and that she could take on Molly's parts.

Peter gathered us into a circle. "I've had an idea," he said. "For how to start the show. You can thank Jan. Something he said on the ship. Most of these stories, they start in a house, right, a cottage? So we're gonna make one, every night. We'll have the frame onstage and then as the audience comes in, we'll build it. Add boards, drape muslin for the windows. Then at the end of the show, we'll tear it down again. Because we know better, man. You can't go through all that and just head home after. There's no home anymore. The forest, it's everywhere."

That felt right to me. The others were nodding, too.

"But how large is this house?" Jorge asked. "Do we play our scenes around it?"

"Nothing we can't work with, right, Bash?"

Bash tapped a finger against his chin. "Possible, my darling," he said. "You have the dimensions?"

Bill took a folded paper from his jeans, handed it over.

"Yes, all right," Bash said. "It should work for some of them. Maybe all. But what about on the tour? Some of these halls are smaller, in Germany, in France. Some of them barely have a stage."

"So we do it in the street. Come on, man!"

"I have an idea," I said. Peter never listened to my ideas. So I do not know what made me speak. Perhaps I no longer minded his dislike. Molly, shattered on the deck, had killed all that. I wouldn't be another girl who cared what he thought, who killed herself when she was not loved enough. "The stage isn't the only room. There's the scene shop. The costume shop. More. Maybe we could stage some of the scenes in those?"

Peter looked at me as though I'd changed out my face for another one. "Yeah," he said, slowly. "Yeah. But how?" He shook his head. "Yeah. Okay. I see it. We all start together, we all build together, but then we split up the crowd. They go around to the different stories. Time it out to music. Then we all come back together in the end. Come on, show me the rooms."

There would be three environments, Peter decided, one for Snow White and Rose Red and the Frog Prince, one for Rumpelstiltskin and Hansel and Gretel, one for Little Red and Rapunzel. We'd lose Sleeping Beauty. That had been Molly's role anyway. Peter would have to run back and forth as the bear in one story and the wolf in the other. Bash would play witches all over. Still, it could work.

"How will the audience know where to go?" JoAnn asked.

"They won't," Peter said. "They'll have to figure it out. Find their way through the woods."

We worked through dinner, through the night. I don't know what time it was when we broke. Or even what day. I had lost track of the days. But this was what I had wanted, for the outside world to fall away, to give myself to this one thing only. I crawled into that squeaking student bed as dawn neared. In dreams, I was lost, running, branches scratching at my face, but when I woke, I knew just where I was.

The boards were brought the next day. Jan and Bill began on the frame while Peter went to American Express. He came back with an envelope of cash and gave some bills, colorful and large, to JoAnn to buy us food. Bram went, too. "Otherwise, you'll buy only terribly practical things," he said.

Rosa and I unpacked the costumes. When we returned to the stage, the men were standing up the frame, a skeleton of a room. Rosa stood inside and gave a languid twirl. "Won't keep off the rain," she said.

"Or the wolf from the door," Peter said, kissing her neck messily. "We'll have a pile of planks right here," he said. "Hammers. The audience can help, if they feel like it."

"This is a wise thing?" Jan asked. "To give the people hammers?"

"You worry too much, man," Peter said. "Be cool."

We worked all day, with a break for cheese sandwiches and the sweets that Bram had brought. That night, we were Nigel's guests in the dining hall. It wasn't an especially elegant place, less decorative than the cafeteria in my own college. But the faculty men—and the long table where we sat was populated almost entirely by men—were dressed in suits. They had questions for us, questions about our methods, about our lives, which they asked without pause as they dragged chunks of meat through gravy, their forks held in the wrong hands. We weren't people to them, it seemed, merely curiosities.

"But is it really art?" said a man to my right, his white eyebrows mingling above his red nose. "These pageants you perform."

"A sort of folk art, perhaps," said a professor across the table.

"Carnival," said his neighbor. "Or is it only noise?"

"And is it true that you take your clothes off?" a man at the other end said.

"Now, now," Nigel remonstrated.

"So what?" JoAnn said. They'd served wine with dinner. She'd had several glasses. "Those paintings of naked ladies in all your museums, you'd call that art, wouldn't you?"

"What's art anyway?" Peter said.

"An imitation, an illusion if one consults the ancients," said the first man. "But I've always preferred Kant, who defines it as the purposive—"

"Fuck your Kant," Bill said, his silverware clattering to his plate. "And fuck all of you. Yeah, we're artists. Our bodies are the brush; we're the canvas and the paint, too."

Rosa stood up in her denim skirt, her shirt knotted under her breasts. "Think you're above us, yeah? Had mooks like you above me before. Didn't like it much," she said. There was sweat on her upper lip. "Bet you never made a piece of art in your whole goddamn life! Bet you wouldn't know art if it punched you in your smug fucking face." She stepped toward the first man, but Bash held her back, an arm around her waist.

"Hush," he said. "They haven't even served dessert."

"Fuck dessert," said Rosa. She made another move, but Bash, strong in his scarecrow way, spun her around and marched her toward the door. The rest of us stood and followed.

"Is it always like this?" I heard Benny ask Bram as we scuttled out.

"Oh gosh, pet, no," he said. "From the little I've seen, it's nearly always worse."

Nigel hurried after, catching us in the vestibule outside. "Well, really," he said. "High table hasn't seen such excitement in years. What drama. I must apologize. This older generation, they can be rather set in their ways, really."

"Doesn't mean they can just haul off and insult us," Bill said. "Kant, my ass. I been to college, too, you know."

"Yes," Nigel said, nodding in sympathy. "Of course. Their behavior. The condescension. An outrage. Indeed. Indeed. No reasonable man would stand it. But there's no changing them, I'm afraid. And a rift, well, it would not be without its consequences. Conceding that you are entirely within your rights, do you think you might possibly be persuaded to return?"

"Not on your goddamn life," Rosa said, arms folded.

"Yes," Nigel said. "Quite." The nodding had increased in tempo. "Only I do worry. I oversee the programming of the theater, of course. My fiefdom, as you know. But as to the other dispensations— your housing, the stipend—well, these require approval beyond what I can give."

"Fuck your stipend," Rosa said. "We don't need it. Don't need your rooms neither. I'll pack my goddamn bag right now."

But Peter didn't move. "The stipend?" he said. "Would we have to pay it back?"

"I'm sure it won't come to that," Nigel said.

"So what?" Rosa said. "You can just go get more."

"Not right now," Peter said. His shoulders were hunched, his chest concave. He turned to Nigel. "Fine," he said. "We'll go back in. But we'll sit by ourselves from now on. And we'll be treated with respect." He looked so small to me then. We went back in. Dessert was an apple pudding—an Eve's pudding, they called it. I don't think any of us managed more than a bite.

Five days of rehearsal remained. Except for dinners in the hall and a few snatched hours of sleep, we never left the theater. The rest of London could have sunk into the Thames and we would never have known it. We ran and ran and ran the scenes, with Bram manning the record player and Bill the lights. Peter and Jorge had put the brightest possible bulbs in, so that the main space wouldn't go dark when a scene changed. Instead, the lights would blind you, and by the time you blinked that blindness away, we would be in fresh costumes, readying another story.

In the secondary rooms, there was no grid to clamp lights to, but we did what we could. My scenes were in the main room, but I slipped away whenever I could to watch the others. I wanted to understand how the whole of it worked. Peter was so hassled by then, so fractious, that he let me make some changes—matters of tempo, mostly. And for all the squalor—the unwashed bodies, the plates of half-eaten sandwiches in the wings—I don't believe that I have ever felt more of use.

Then it was our first night. I don't think I ate that day. I'm not sure I breathed. I watched, through a break in the curtain, as the audience filed in, these long-haired, bright-clothed boys and girls. More seats were

empty than full. Theater Negative couldn't draw the same crowds anymore. Suddenly, it was time. Peter stepped out, barefoot, shirtless, in the
cloak he wore for the wolf. He brought the small crowd to silence with a
wave of his hand, and for a moment, I loved him again, for the attention
he could command. He gave a speech of welcome, told the audience that
after the first movement, the work would split in three and they could
follow where they liked.

"All right," he said. "Are you ready for a story?" The girls and boys
hollered back. My heart beat like a trapped bird. The music started and
we were through the curtain, speaking snatches of our lines, hefting
wood and cloth and tools until the house was built. The rest was like a
dream, a dance. The lights turned my dress to spider's silk, my body was
like gossamer, blown here and there. An hour, more, vanished under my
feet. Then the music changed, intensified, the cue for everyone else to
rush back to the main stage. With a signal from Jan, we began to pull
apart the cottage, laughing, leaping, screaming the chant we'd settled
on: "They lived in peace and happiness. They lived in peace and happiness." Then we were lying on the floor of the stage, lumber all around,
breathing together in rhythm. There were hands on me. On my hips.
Across my breasts. I didn't care. I felt perfect, empty, free.

12

1972, LONDON

The police came on the third night, marching down the aisle just as the last board had been wrenched away. Already, the piece had grown wilder, the chanting more ecstatic, the crowd eager and far larger. I remember Faye on Jan's shoulders, bare-breasted, and Bash, fully naked, capering around the stage like some pale, gangling sprite, promises of modesty forgotten. Bash must have seen the officers first, because he paused, frozen, his penis dangling like a hooked worm. Then he ran.

A moment later, the policemen crested the stage. There was screaming among the audience and a scramble for the door to the lobby, but the door had been locked. Peter stood center stage. We stood with him. Bash, now clad in his witch's cape, returned and took his place.

One of the officers, a mustached man, thick as a side of beef, stepped forward. "Sirs," he said. "Madams. We have reason to believe that you have violated the Obscene Publications Act, in that you are performing material intended to deprave and corrupt."

"It's not depravity," JoAnn said, still in her shortie riding outfit, her color raddled and high. "But a pig like you wouldn't understand that."

"Nothing wrong with a little depravity, honey," Faye said, buttoning her dress.

"Yeah, ya moron—" Rosa began.

Peter quieted her. He turned to the men. "Hey," he said. "Hey, there's no corruption here. Not sure what you've heard, but we're a legitimate theater company, Theater Negative. We've won prizes back in New York, Off-Broadway awards, a whole shelf. Prizes at Avignon, too.

Don't believe me? Call *The Times, The Guardian*, they'll set you straight. We're here as guests of the college, invited guests, man. And just so you know, we've been up against this kind of charge before. Lots of times. Never sticks." This was not precisely true. But Peter spoke as though he believed it.

"That's as may be," the man said, unmoved. "But I have my orders."

"At least let the kids go," Peter said, gesturing nobly at the audience. "All they did was buy a ticket. That's not depravity."

"Unless we say that capitalism is the true obscenity?" Bash cooed.

"Come on, man," Peter said to the officer. "Be cool."

There were half a dozen policemen, none of them armed with anything more lethal than a nightstick, and nearly two hundred students. The choice was a simple one. Turning his back to us, the officer muttered a command, and two of his colleagues moved to open the doors. The bright boys and girls rushed through, without a backward glance. Bram, I saw, fled with them. I didn't blame him. On another night, in another dress, I would have joined him. Instead, I stayed onstage and waited to see what would become of me.

When the theater was quiet, the chief officer allowed us to put our street clothes back on. We scattered to the dressing rooms. By the time we emerged, Nigel was there, hands knit in unanswered prayer, arguing futilely. The officers questioned us about the show, about how many performances we had given, about the nudity. Peter and Nigel did most of the talking, with occasional profane interjections from JoAnn. The officers asked Bill to take her backstage.

"She just needs a rest," Bill said.

"You have no idea what I fucking need," JoAnn said. "Never have." But she let him lead her off.

The police intended to take all of us to the station, but they must have realized that we would not go willingly and that to be seen to use force against visiting American artists, however corrupting, would not go unremarked. Peter played his martyr act, convincing the chief officer to arrest only him. The officer agreed. In sandals, his wrists cuffed, Peter walked back up the aisle. He looked like Jesus—or how I had imagined Jesus when I was as a child—gentle, blond, and bearded. Then we were left alone in the mess of boards and nails.

"Yes, well," Nigel said. "Not perhaps the reception we might have desired. And I did warn you. Yes, I surely did. But these are the risks we take, yes? For art, yes? But still, I shouldn't fret. The obscenity act, well, it's very hard to prove. These days, especially. My God, you'd have to outlaw every second book. I'm sure they'll see reason. For now, it would be best, I imagine, were you to go to your rooms and to stay there."

Benny's parents came then. Bram must have phoned them. They escorted her out, shielding her with their bodies, and I wondered for a moment what it would be like to be loved in such a way, to be protected. The rest of us trooped through the rain, parting without speaking. In our room, Faye pulled a bottle of bourbon from her suitcase and wrenched the cap off, glugging it straight.

"Is it bad, Faye?" I asked.

"No," she said. She shook herself like a bird rousing its feathers. "Don't you worry. Time was, they used to get arrested most everywhere. Never came to much, I'm told. Night in jail. Picture in the papers. When bail was made, they used to parade out of the station, right down the street. JoAnn thought maybe Peter was calling the cops himself. Just for the fuss it caused. But that's all it was. Just a bother, just a fuss. A fine, maybe. They always got out quick as lightning."

"Not in Mexico," I said.

"No," she agreed, the smile gone. "Not there. But Europe's different, honey. Laws and such."

"That man, that first officer, he looked at us like he hated us. Why?"

She waved her hand, then slugged again from the bottle. "Lord knows," she said when she'd swallowed. "But hush now. Even if they hate us, it don't mean they can hold us. You'll see. Now go on and sleep if you can. It'll all be better in the morning."

The morning brought no news. We straggled down to the ground-floor student lounge and sat in pairs and trios. We had no food and no money to go and buy any, and I remember an empty, floating feeling as I perched on a paisley sofa, pretending to read.

Peter came at lunchtime, in triumph. Jorge, watching through the window, saw him first. His white clothes were wrinkled and stained at the ankles. But he was risen, returned. Nigel had come with him. Bram was there, too. JoAnn, chastened now, went to thank Nigel, but Nigel waved her away.

"It's no thanks to me. But to this young one, here."

"Yes," Bram said. "I did perhaps mention our problem to Abraham Sr. He phoned up a friend at the Old Bill first thing this morning, and here again is our Mr. Murray, not much the worse for wear."

"This is good," Jorge said with his usual seriousness. He stood taller, his chest broad. "It is very good. That papers have written of us, yes? London will know of us." He turned to Nigel. "For how many nights more will we perform?"

"Erm," Nigel said. His cheeks were red as though he'd brushed them with rouge. "The governors, as you know—well, this excitement, the arrest, it's rather too much for them. They have let it be known that there will be no performance tonight. No more performances at all, I'm afraid. Of course, I disagreed, rather stridently, I should say. They would not hear of it. And I am so very sorry, but they require you to leave these rooms at your earliest convenience. Tomorrow at the outside. I would have you all to stay with me, I really would. But my college rooms, they're nearly as poky as these."

"Come on, man," Peter said. His arms were crossed over his chest, the tendons in his neck conspicuous. "The police, they cleared us. There's not gonna be any more trouble."

"Yes, yes. I do agree. But as it says in the psalm, they shall not be moved."

"Fine," Peter said. "Figures. Knew we shouldn't have come back to England. This place, it's too uptight. We're not due in Amiens for another week, but we'll figure it out. Just give us the box office, and I'll get us on the ferry. No. Fuck. I need to buy the van first. Can you get us one more day, just to sort it out?"

"Oh dear," Nigel said. The rouge had spread. His neck was scarlet now. "Again, I do apologize, most sincerely, but the board has decided that no further monies will be allocated. When you went with the officers, a solicitor was brought in to protect the university in the event of any charges, you understand. And solicitors, of course, are a considerable expense. I really am so sorry. I would give you money from my own purse. But my hands, you see, are tied."

Peter stepped toward Nigel, poked a finger at him. "We had a deal, man."

"We did," Nigel said, shuffling aside. "We do. But if you were to examine the contract, you would find that there are certain provisions there, provisions relating to conduct. The governors feel that you are sadly in violation, and they will brook no argument."

Peter was shaking, his teeth clenched tight as a vise. "Not cool," he said softly. "I thought you were different, man. But you're just like the rest of them."

Nigel winced. "Yes, well. Perhaps you're right. And I am so very sorry. The keys you can leave downstairs. Best of luck, really." He departed the lounge at something like a jog.

Peter crumpled to the sofa. Bash went to him, and the rest of us stood by gracelessly, not knowing where to look.

"Thank you," JoAnn said to Bram, finally. "What you did, what your father did, that was really cool."

Bram demurred, but he looked pleased all the same.

"And if you don't mind doing more," JoAnn went on, "we could use a meal. We haven't eaten since before the show last night."

"Ah yes," Bram said. "Foolish of me not to have thought of it. I know just the thing. Back in a tick. Put a girdle round the earth and all."

He went out, taking Jan with him. Peter went upstairs to change his clothes and then out to the phone box. Bram and Jan returned first, with bags of fish and chips wrapped in newspaper. We ate it with our hands, until our fingers and chins shone with grease.

Peter let himself in more than an hour later, wet from the rain, his shirt see-through. He sat on the floor, his face a storm. There would be no more money, he told us. Which meant no way to get to Calais. No van, no ferry crossing. Other payments would come in time, but none could be offered in advance. He had tried each producer he knew, each official he could reach. None, he said, would help.

"That's how it always goes, man," he said. "They love you when you're hot. Champagne and fucking roses. But we haven't hit it big since *Blood Moon*. And after fucking Mexico—" He shook his head, stood up. "Got on my goddamn knees just to get the tour going. Kissed a hundred asses. And for what? Can't stay in New York. Can't stay here. So what the fuck do we do? I don't fucking know." He slammed his fist into the plaster wall. Again. Again. I had never seen him like this. Not even after Molly. Not even after Jax. So angry and so powerless.

"Anyone wanna sell their hair?" he said. "Or their heirloom fucking jewels? Because I'm clean out of—goddamn it!" he said, shaking out his fingers. He must have hit too hard.

I had the money I'd hidden away. It was for a rainy day. Now the rain had come. Since we'd been in London, it had barely stopped raining. But those hoarded bills wouldn't get us all to France. So I stayed silent, my breath coming short, wondering if this was it, finally, the moment that the running—from dorm to loft to ship to shore—would end.

Rosa was undaunted. "Come on," she said. "You got money, Peter.

I've seen your goddamn house." Had she? Peter had never taken me there, never offered. And even in this new crisis, I could feel jealousy pressing on my heart like a knife's point.

"You mean my wife's goddamn house?" Peter said, cradling his hand. "Her father's goddamn house? I've got nothing but what I earn and what he gives us. Right now, he's giving shit." He sat back down. His eyes were wet. "We're on our fucking own."

JoAnn knelt by him. "That's all right," she said. "We have each other. We'll work something out. We always do. You should eat." Peter shook his head. "Well, at least drink something, then." Faye brought the bourbon from our room. We passed the bottle around. There was no music. No conversation. A few students stuck their heads in—they didn't linger. It was the saddest party in the world.

Bram must have slipped away as we sat there feeling low, because he returned excited, his Adam's apple bobbing like a buoy.

"My friends," he said. "I have news. I told my father of your predicament. Your lack of funds and rooms. And would you believe it? He suggested that you might come and stay with us, the family manse and such. There's beds enough for all. Or nearly. And what's more, he believes that your show, which he has seen already, at my urging, might make a film. A small one and not for all markets, but a film all the same. Which would mean a moderate fee. Certainly enough to deliver you to that ferry. So what say you?"

"A film?" Bill said, his voice fluting. "Like a concert movie? I mean, sure, man. But you heard that asshole. We're kicked out of the theater. Where are we supposed to shoot?"

"Oh, I shouldn't worry about that. Pater, he's full of surprises. He'll find somewhere, I shouldn't doubt. So with your kind permission, we can cram into a cab or two and be on our way. Tomorrow, we'll hire a lorry and collect the rest of your things, the sets and so on. Are they safe at the theater, do you imagine?"

Peter said nothing. Faye nudged him gently. "Did you hear what he said, honey? A place to stay and money, too. A movie, maybe. It's just too good to be true, don't you think?"

Peter roused himself. "Yeah," he said. "Okay. Better than here, anyway. Goddamn mausoleum, this place. Costumes, the set, that should all be fine. Nigel's a candy-ass, but he's no thief. All right," he said. He wobbled as he stood. "We'll do it. Let's pack and get out of here."

We left the lounge. I had a heady feeling that had become familiar, the blood rush of catastrophe deferred. We would survive. We would go on. I'd barely unpacked, so it took only a moment to return my toothbrush and folded nightgown to my lone case. I maneuvered it to the ground floor. The others soon joined, vibrating with my same flushed excitement.

Bram and Bill went out into the road to hail the taxis. Rosa approached me, her cherry purse strapped across her body, her case the mirror of my own. I looked down and away, but she caught my chin in her hand and turned my face back toward her. "Don't trust him," she hissed. She said it quietly, so that no one else would hear. Then Bram and Bill were back through the door, shooing everyone out and away, stealing my chance to ask her whom she had meant.

The house was in the north of the city, on the edge of a large park. It was built from ginger brick, with a tall pitched roof and paned windows. Night was falling as we arrived; the streetlamps shone gold. A man greeted us at the door: shorter than Bram and stouter, with a luxuriant curling beard in dappled gray and black, but still undeniably his father.

He beckoned us inside, and another man, uniformed, parted us from our bags. An assortment of meats, cheeses, olives, and bread had been laid on a sideboard in the dining room. The table, polished wood, and lit, absurdly, with a candelabra, was long enough to seat us all. I should have relaxed, should have eaten the meat and drunk the wine. But with Rosa's whisper still in my ears, I rearranged the food on the plate and barely wet my lips. Beyond the windows, I could just make out a deep garden.

Abraham, Bram's father, was a voluble host with an etched-glass accent. He told wonderful, terrible stories as Bram darted about, refilling plates and pouring wine. I could see the others relaxing, unfurling until Abraham and Bash were comparing kif cafés in Tangier and Faye had her feet in Bram's lap. Rosa held herself apart, her face pale beneath the lipstick.

After dinner, Abraham had his man bring a bottle of port and a humidor of cigars, Cuban, he said, clipping the end of one with a silver-edged guillotine. Bill and Bash joined him. JoAnn, too. Abraham told us that if we wished to retire, beds had been prepared, though a few of us would have to double up.

"But if there's life in you yet," he said, "you might watch one of my films. I have a projector here in the house."

"Sure thing, man," Bill said, his voice slurring from the wine. "Fire it up!" He pushed away from the table, and after two faltering tries, he was up and out of the room. Abraham went after him. The rest of us followed. The projector was up a flight of stairs, in a room with a pull-down screen arranged in front of several leather sofas. Next to the projector was another machine, topped with a wide lens, which must have been used for editing. In the corner was a metal cabinet. Abraham opened it and selected a reel.

"Perhaps we might start with this one," he said. He threaded it into the projector, flicked off the lights, and sat down, an arm around Faye's shoulder. The film began with a title card, "Inside Soho," then opened on a scene of a red-curtained nightclub. A blond woman in a chic black dress and pearls stood on the stage while discordant jazz played. She began to move in time, stripping off one glove and then the other. Then she turned away from the camera as an arm snaked behind her back. She unzipped the dress and stepped free of it. She wore no bra, and when she turned again, her heavy breasts filled the frame. The pearls remained. The camera shifted to the crowd, full of men, drinking, smoking. Some of them held auction paddles. They bid for the woman, and when the auction ended, the winner clambered onto the stage. He bent that woman over a chair. Then a second man approached.

I had heard of films like these. The boys at the college had joked about them, about the parties where they were shown. And I had spent the summer just west of Forty-Second Street. I knew what those theaters played, though I had never visited one. The idea of private things shown on-screen, shown to strangers, it sickened me. I stumbled from the room.

Rosa followed me. "Come on," she said. "Let's go back down. I'm up to my eyeballs, but I could use another drink."

The table had been cleared, but she quickly found the kitchen, where she pulled open doors and drawers until she hit upon some sherry that was probably meant for cooking. She swigged and handed me the bottle. I touched my tongue to it, like a kitten would.

"Was that what you were warning me about?"

"Something like that. Me and Bram, we got to talking on the boat. He told me about the kinda movies his dad does."

"And you didn't say anything? To Peter?"

"Peter doesn't listen to gash, sunshine. You should know that by now," she said. "His old lady, maybe. Nobody else. Besides, there's worse ways to make a buck. You got a better one?"

I didn't. And I felt the horror of it, of what I would be made to do unless I conjured some alternative, unless I fled. That horror was too great. I quieted it with jealousy and scorn. "So you and Bram?" I said, handing the bottle back to her, ungently. "You were talking? Seemed like more."

"Fuck's sake, Alice. Not like he gave you his goddamn varsity pin." She took a big drink, liquid seeping from the corner of her mouth.

"Is that what you do? You go to bed with anyone who wants me?"

"Yeah. So what? Anyone who doesn't want you, too."

"Well, I'm not like that," I said, my voice lower now and small. "I can't do this movie."

"So go home, princess."

I flashed on my father, his fat hands, and shook my head. "I can't do that either," I said.

"So get through it. You're an actress. Act like someone else. Some girl who doesn't mind so much."

I ran from her, or maybe I ran from that other girl, that girl I could become. I flew up flights of stairs, taking the steps two at a time, until I found the room that held my suitcase. I locked the door and slept, if you could call it sleep, with my back against it.

The next morning, I waited until I heard footsteps, then joined the others in the dining room. Abraham, I saw, was absent. A breakfast had been prepared, and I was hungry enough to eat it, though my stomach roiled at the many meats—bacon, sausage, ham, a black cylinder that Bash told me was blood pudding.

"Is it really made of blood?" I said.

"Blood will have blood," he said, forking up a piece.

I filled a plate with eggs and fruit instead.

Peter sat at the table's head. "Guess we should talk," he said.

"Oh yeah?" JoAnn said. "I can start. You brought us here to make a goddamn skin flick, Peter. Fuck were you thinking?"

"Look," he said, wrapping his hands around a glass of orange juice. "I didn't know it was gonna be like this. Bram said his dad made movies. Found out they were blue ones only last night, same as you. And yeah, it's not what we planned. But it isn't the worst thing, is it? I mean, we all love each other, right? Most of us have made love already. Nothing to be ashamed of. It's just bodies, man, just love. No reason we can't make it beautiful."

I shook my head. I didn't want to be seen to go against the group. But I couldn't do this. "Abraham," I said. "He shows these movies. He sells them. What if someone sees me? Someone I know?"

"But you're an artist, honey," Faye said. "For an artist, it doesn't matter what the world thinks. Just what's in your heart."

"But these movies," Jan said. "They are not art."

"Don't be like those college farts," Peter said. "Maybe they are. Or they could be. We could make this art. Yeah," he said, his eyes alight, "we really could."

"I do not think so," Jan said. He put his hand over Jorge's. "My body, I have pride in my body. My body was not made for this."

"Would you even be talking like this if we didn't need the money?" JoAnn said.

Peter thought about it. "Maybe not," he said. "But we do need the money. And I don't see another way to get it. Maybe we should take a vote."

"We don't vote," Bash reminded him languidly. "We're anarchists, my blue-eyed boy. Not Greeks, much as I admire them."

"Well, we're voting now," Peter said. "Who wants to do this? For the company."

He raised his hand. Bill joined him. Then Faye. "Always an adventure with you, darling," Bash said. "Count me in." Jorge removed his hand from under Jan's, raising it. Rosa held hers high, though her lips were pursed and bloodless.

"Fuck it," JoAnn said. "I'll do it."

"I will also," Jan said. "For the company, only."

"Come on, Alice," Peter said. "Don't be frightened."

My face was hot, a fire. "I can't," I said. "I can't. I can't be seen that way." I moved to stand from the table, but I blundered, knocking over a water glass that fell to the floor, bounced from the carpet to the wood, and shattered. I bent to pick it up. I had been taught to clean, to keep things neat. A shard lodged in my finger, and I screamed. Faye pulled me upright. Shushing me, she removed the shard, then kissed the blood where it welled, a red pearl.

"Shhh," she said, "don't you fuss. We'll find a way. We always do."

"Maybe you could wear a mask," JoAnn said. "Wish Suzanne were here. She's good at those."

"Come on, Alice," Peter said, honey in his voice. "We need you." It wasn't true. But I ached to hear him say it.

"All right," I said. I put my finger to my mouth. My blood was sharp and bitter. "A mask. A hood. Something to hide me."

"Okay," Peter said. "So we're agreed. I'll tell Abraham the good news."

We spent that day and the next deciding how the film should go. Which is to say that Peter decided, in consultation with Bram and Abraham. With us, he was confident, swaggering. But when Abraham entered the room, he made himself smaller. We wouldn't do every scene from the play, it was determined, but we would do most of them. The scenes wouldn't need to change, Peter said, not much. The stories were steeped in sex already. All we had to do, he said, was to take what was implicit and turn it inside out.

There was little dialogue in the show, and here there would be even less, though Abraham told us we might ad-lib some, that we shouldn't be too quiet. Our costumes were brought from the theater, and with a needle bruising my injured finger, I helped JoAnn and Faye with the alterations, shortening, tightening. We would wear them that way for the rest of the tour. Bram found a mask for me, a Venetian fancy, dripping with blue ribbons. It covered the top half of my face only. The nausea I had felt on the boat returned, and my right eyelid began to twitch, in time with some frantic, unheard music.

Rosa must have noticed. Early one morning, on the day that the shoot would begin, she found me in the hallway. "Got something for you," she said. She took a small silver case from her purse and opened it, revealing a cluster of flat, orange pills. "Take one," she said.

"I don't want your drugs," I said. "I don't want anything from you."

"Not drugs, sunshine," she said. "Medicine. Doctors give it to rich ladies who need to calm the fuck down. I got them from Bram. The case, too. He's a prick, but like most pricks, he's good for some things. You took his pills on the boat didn't you? This is just another kind of seasick. Go on."

"No," I said.

"Yeah. You don't want nothing from me. You're pure. You're good. Musta had your fingers in my slit on accident. But, sunshine, you got two choices here. You can get through this. Or you can go crazy with it. It's gonna be a bad day or two. A goddamn disaster. But then it'll be over. My advice: Go on. Get through it."

"Fine," I said. I scrabbled for a pill, setting it between my teeth and crunching down. I'd expected bitterness, but the taste was almost sweet. Soon, the world quieted. I quieted. My limbs were feathers, dandelion fluff.

I don't remember much of that day or the next. A blessing, in its way. Men came to the house. A camera operator, a sound man who held a large black microphone, fuzzy like some forest creature. I took the pills when Rosa offered them and spent most hours at this fortunate remove, my body a borrowed dress.

Faye did my makeup, rouging my lips and cheeks. As I was about to stand from the chair, she passed me the blush. "Rub it on your nipples, honey," she said. "Makes them pretty for the camera." I didn't ask her how she knew this.

I had one scene the first day, the story of the frog prince, played with Jorge. We shot it in the backyard, next to an ornamental pond adorned with a statue of a water nymph. For once, the sun shone, a daffodil. I wore a golden circlet, the gold dress Suzanne had sewn, the ribboned mask. I stood at the pond's lip, playing with a ball, until Jorge, all in green, hopped into the frame. At a signal from Abraham, I removed my dress and stood in crown and underwear, a bandage still ringing my finger. In performance, Bash had choreographed a kiss for the scene that felt like a ritual: a brush of one cheek, the other, the forehead and finally the mouth. As we parted, I would take hold of an edge of Jorge's costume, and he would spin away out of the fabric until he was made a man again.

This time, we would not kiss. Instead, I was to take his penis in my mouth. Frogs, I remembered dimly from biology, had no penis. I do not know what Jorge did to keep himself erect. Emptying my mind, I took him in, the circlet sliding from my hair. When he removed himself, to surge, hot and slippery against my cheek, I shut my eyes. I was crying, I think, but the mask hid all that. A transformation should have happened after, from frog to man. Instead, the crew left to ready the next scene. No prince came. I stayed there, kneeling in the dirt, until Rosa found me and helped me to the house. She gave me a drink of water and another pill.

We shot the Snow White and Rose Red scene on the second day, inside the house, in a great room with a blazing fireplace. I had on my white shift, Rosa wore her red one. The mask was a problem, Peter told me. It looked all wrong. But no other could be found. And I would not film without it. So the ribbons and lace were cut away, leaving my eyes ringed in mauled satin.

I do not want to describe what we did. But I have promised that I will. It began with Peter in his bear costume. He took Rosa first and then he turned to me. His thrusts jostled the mask from my face. I put it back. Then Abraham told Rosa and me to make love to each other. Through the pill's fog, I counterfeited what I'd once felt, what I still felt, my mouth on her, her fingers stroking me. I couldn't come. But I pretended it. We tied Jorge up then, cut his prop beard, stripped him, whipped him with our hair. Made him watch, touching himself, as Peter, now out of his cloak, had us both again.

"My beauties," Abraham said from somewhere behind the camera. "Could you kindly look as though you're enjoying it? Just a bit." So I nailed a smile to my face and made noises for the microphone. Rosa faked it better. Or maybe it wasn't fake. Rosa was no liar. And she was never much of an actress.

He finished, on our stomachs, on our breasts. The switch on the camera clicked off. We were handed towels. Our work was done. I went to my room and lay facedown on the bed.

There was a dinner that night. It was Sunday, apparently. And on Sundays, Abraham said, he always had a proper roast. We would have one now. In celebration. The film, he said, was made. It required only an editor to splice it all together.

At the table, there were plates of beef and gravy and vegetables dripping in animal fat. Wine was poured, darker than blood. It tasted like water. I drank it and kept drinking. There were liqueurs after and more cigars. Laughter flashed around me.

JoAnn, who must have drunk a bottle alone, was haranguing Abraham. "But what are you into, man?" she said, drawing out the final word. "Like, what do you believe in, even? Like, are you into women's liberation?"

He smiled his ravenous smile. He had, it seemed to me in the candlelight, too many teeth. "More interested in men's liberation, me," he said.

Bill settled himself on the floor before a massive hi-fi. A record began to play. There was dancing then, the bodies writhing in a parody of sex. I saw Faye loving up on the cameraman, Jorge circling Jan, snake-hipped. Bram began to dance with Rosa, but she whirled away from him and toward me.

"Come on, sunshine," Rosa said, hands around my wrists, yanking me upright. "Dance with me. It's over. You made it."

I didn't trust my legs to hold me, so I leaned against her, let her move me. "Don't think so," I said into her hair.

"'Course you did," she said. "It was what? Two days? Two shitty days out of your whole Suzy Homemaker trip. You're fine. You wanna know a secret? You're just like me, sunshine. The kind that survives. Bomb could go off right now. You and me, we'd be picking rubble out of our goddamn bras."

"Hate my bras," I said. I was slurring my words now. "Hate beige. Bomb can have them."

"Come on," she said. "Get ya into bed. Make up with your bras in the morning."

"Oh, but you beautiful ladies mustn't leave now," Abraham said. "We're going to watch the rushes."

But we did leave. Rosa took me upstairs, unlaced my shoes and tucked me into bed, still in my clothes. I wanted a shower. I wanted to brush my teeth. But none of that would make me clean.

"Sing me a lullaby," I mumbled.

"Don't know any goddamn lullabies," she said.

"Then hold my hand," I said.

I woke alone, hours later. There was a noise from somewhere far away, soft and shrill, the cry of an animal in pain. Pulling the covers over my head would not stifle it. So I swung my legs out of bed and padded down the hall in my stocking feet. The house around me slept and dreamed. I was half-asleep myself as I followed the muffled noise up a further flight of stairs.

At the end of the hall was a door, an inch ajar. I pushed it open; the wood was warm and smooth against my hand. It was dark in there, the shadows thick. But as my eyes adjusted, I could see a four-poster bed. On it, Abraham was moving his stocky body in some awful rhythm, and below him, thrashing, her face forced into the pillow, I saw Rosa.

13

1997, THE NORTHEAST KINGDOM, CHICAGO, LOS ANGELES

The house was snug and warm, the rooms low-ceilinged, with faded tapestries on many of the walls. The floor in the hall looked as though wood from a dozen different trees had joined to make its slats. Suzanne led her to a kitchen, painted yellow.

"Tea?" Suzanne asked, putting on the kettle without waiting for an answer. "Well, go on, sit. You look like the ghost at the banquet. Bone white. But you were always so pale, weren't you? Take your coat off, Alice. Stay awhile."

She sat down, put her purse on the round table. The chair was hand-made, its legs uneven. She put both feet on the floor and glued her knees together. She hadn't seen Suzanne in twenty-five years, and near her, she felt like a schoolgirl again—young, gauche. But no, it was stranger than that. She was at once the girl she had been and the woman she had become, and that doubling left her queasy, adrift.

"Is Peter here?" she asked, keeping her voice steady.

"Peter? No, he went to run some errands. Won't be back for an hour or two. What a surprise you'll be."

The kettle screamed. Suzanne switched off the flame. She took a box of tea bags from one shelf, mugs from another. "Sugar?" she said. "Lemon?"

"No. Nothing."

Then the mugs were on the table and Suzanne was across from her, appraising her with those muddy green eyes, the pupils ringed in gold. "You've changed, Alice. You were so pink back then, all teeth and baby fat. But you've come into your own, haven't you? Look at those cheek-bones, sharp enough to cut. It's been what? Twenty years? God, we were so young then. Even me. I didn't think so at the time. Forty. That seemed ancient. And nothing like a German jail to make you feel the years. Though of course you wouldn't know. What a moment to run out on us. Just before it went to shit. But what does it matter? I've lived a lifetime since. We all have."

"Not all of us," she said. The tea had fogged her glasses. She took them off and wiped the lenses clear.

"No, that's right," Suzanne said. "Not all."

"Were you in jail long?" she asked. She wanted the question to wound.

Suzanne only laughed. Though the laugh was bled of any joy. "Nah. They let me go after a couple of days. They have a thing about mothers there. Zion and I flew back to the States. There was nothing we could do for Peter, for anyone. I left it to the lawyers. Who were useless, by the way. Maybe if Rosa had been there, it would have gone a different way. They were her drugs, after all. But no." Suzanne blew on her tea, sipped. "That girl was as slippery as wet leaves. They kept Peter longer than any of the others, made him pay, thought they could pin that mess in England on him. They couldn't. But the drugs, the shows. It was enough. He came out in 1976. The bicentennial? Do you remember? Bunting everywhere, for this failure of a country. That's when the cops here went for him. Kicking a man when he's down, the American way. My shitbird father wouldn't help. So he was locked up upstate, too. New York was over by then. Had been over for a while. And we couldn't afford it anyway. We were too old to go back to some basement. The company, that was over, too. Everyone had scattered."

"Or they were dead," she said.

"Yes," Suzanne said, brushing the words aside. "Or that. We could have gotten it running again. Found new people. We'd done as much before. But honestly, I was tired of it all. Some college friends had moved up here.

While Peter was away, I came, too. Found this place. Falling down around its ears. I had just enough to buy it, and after all those years building sets, I knew how to fix it up. By the time he was paroled, I'd made a home for us. There's a college nearby. You know that, right? I teach design there. Peter, he heads a performance laboratory. The kids, they love him."

She swallowed, the tea scalding her throat. "They let that man teach?" she said. "They let him around young people?"

Suzanne sighed, then made her mouth tight, wrinkles radiating from her lips. "So it's like that? Alice, please. You knew what you were doing. All of you. Throwing yourselves at him. Tits right up in his face. Show me a man who can say no to that. And he never made you do anything you didn't want to. You had a choice. Always."

"Is that what he told you?" She took another slug of tea.

Suzanne took her own mug to the sink, tipping the liquid down the drain. "Why are you here, Alice? Why have you come?"

"Someone came looking for me," she said. She took another slug of tea. "Someone from the *Grimm* tour. I don't know who. They've sent messages by electronic mail. They've come to my place of work. The messages, they're strange. Threatening, almost, but nothing I can take to the police or the administration. And I don't want to. No one at work knows who I am. No," she corrected herself, "not who I am. Who I was. Who I used to be. My life before. I want to know who sent them."

"Did you think it was me?" Suzanne said, turning back from the sink and leaning on the counter. "Did you think that I would write to you, harass you? I wouldn't, Alice. You were like children to me. All of you."

She supposed that was true. There were all kinds of mothers in this world. "No," she said. "Not really. The messages didn't sound like you."

"So you think that Peter did this? Whatever you think of the man, I can promise you that he hasn't been to see you. I don't know where you live, but I'm guessing it's not anywhere around here. And he hasn't left the state in God knows how long. Used to be a parole thing, then he just got out of the habit."

She put her hands around the mug. The warmth had ebbed. "No, I didn't think that it was you. Or Peter. But I can't think who else was with us. On tour. At the end. I've made a life for myself. Or something like it. I'd like to live it unbothered. So I need to know who did this, who's left alive. That's why I came. I don't want to be here, Suzanne. I don't want to drink your fucking herbal tea and chat about the good old days. Because they weren't good. Not for me."

"Alice—"

"My name isn't Alice," she said.

"Well, what on earth do you want me to call you, then?"

"I don't know!" she said. Her voice had shrilled. "I've never had a name that fit. Not since I came home, I ran, just in time, like you said, only it wasn't a home to me anymore and I wasn't myself and I don't think I ever have been. So I don't know, Suzanne. I don't know. I don't know. I don't know." She made to stand, to run, but her legs were matchsticks. She sat back down.

"Oh, Alice," Suzanne said, stooping awkwardly to gather her in. Suzanne's skin was like parchment. It smelled of lemon peel, resin. "I thought you were so strong. I thought you were like me."

Suzanne held her until she quieted, found her breath again.

"I'm all right now," she said.

Suzanne raised a doubting eyebrow. "Well, we have a while before Peter's due home. We can talk it all through then. In the meantime, put your coat back on. Let me show you the barn."

They walked back down to the drive, then veered right. Suzanne hefted the barn door's latch and groped the wall for a switch. Fluorescent tubes, suspended from the pitched ceiling, buzzed alive. The floor was cement, the walls painted white. Along those walls and hanging from the ceiling were posters, placards, bits of cloth and plaster. She went closer. The barn was a museum, a history in prop and costume and glossy print of everything that Theater Negative had been and done.

These were the masks from *Blood Moon and Jaguar Night*. She'd heard about them. And the giant wolf's head from *The World Tree*, propped next to an even larger bull, a relic of *Gilgamesh*. A rainbow crow, a leftover from *The Trickster Stories*, the Native American cycle, stretched its wings overhead. There were programs from the company's first years, when they were still doing other men's plays—Anouilh's, Genet's—and the front page of a student newspaper from 1953, its type smudged and blurred. She picked out several of the hooded cloaks from *The Exodus Project*, which were hung next to a black-and-white print of Peter atop the Buick as the Pharaoh. The car looked so old and he looked so young. A man. A god. She understood, as she had not understood in years, how she could have loved him.

There were other photographs, a few of which she recognized from Rebecca Liu's book. There was an assortment from Mexico, from the performances of *Blood Moon and Jaguar Night* and others that must have been taken, somehow, in the prison yard. Bill, with even longer hair, flashed a peace sign at the camera. Jorge was behind him, so thin his collar bones jutted from his chest. There were pictures from even further back, from those first European tours. Men and women, mostly unknown to her, with linked arms, standing in front of a paisley-painted bus. Peter, in Pierrot makeup, kissing Suzanne in front of the Eiffel Tower. And a series from what might have been India. Bash and a woman she didn't recognize, garlanded in marigolds, arms open, palms up, smiling like the sun.

"Did JoAnn take these?" she asked.

"Most of them," Suzanne said. "Have you seen over here?"

Suzanne pointed to a collage of images from her own days with the troupe. Jax, with his devil's grin. Molly, with her sunken eyes, a spread of cards between her legs. She saw herself, limp-haired and round-cheeked, passed out on the couch in her pink diner uniform and ankle socks. There were pictures from a party on the roof. In one, she was splitting twinned Popsicles with a laughing Black girl. Deirdre? Dede?

In another, she had her head on Faye's shoulder. She looked happy. Had she been happy?

"You kept all of this?" she asked Suzanne.

"Of course. It was important. The work we did. The work *you* did."

"What was that thing Peter used to say?" she said. "That the work was the gift, that—"

She stopped. Her eyes had found a display in the far corner. The dress she'd worn as the princess, the golden ball she'd played with. JoAnn's Rapunzel braid. On trembling legs, she stepped closer. There were photos from the tour—the troupe crowded together on a bridge in Amsterdam, Faye wielding a baguette like a sword in what might have been Amiens, Bill and Peter leaning against the van, which was more orange than she'd remembered. And Rosa, onstage as Rose Red, the red dress skimming her hips and breasts, her greedy, laughing mouth wide open. Rosa alive. Her heart tried to burst her chest.

The light shifted then. Someone had opened the door to the barn. She turned and there was Peter. His faded hair was long now, nearly to his shoulders, the mustache gone. Stubble, gray and gold, ringed his mouth. Beneath his parka, blue jeans hung loose at his hips. He was shorter than she remembered, shrunken.

"Hiya, babe," he said to Suzanne. "Got a friend here? How you doing?" he said as he walked toward them, his smile easy. "Peter Murray." He put a hand out to her.

She left it to hang. "Peter, don't you know me?" she said.

He took another step nearer and squinted at her through round glasses. "No," he said. "I'm sorry. Should I?" Then something in his face darkened, like blinds being drawn. "Oh shit. Alice. It's Alice, right?"

"More or less," she said.

"Well, shit," he said. He ran a hand backward through his thinning hair. "What's it been?"

"Twenty-five years, just about."

"God, you were such a little thing."

"Big enough," she said. She felt far away, as though she were watching herself through a telescope. "You thought so."

"Hey," he said. He put his hands up. But then he put them down again. "Yeah, I guess I did. Different world back then. These kids now. So fucking serious. Always want to know what's going to count toward their grade. I'm like, it's art, man. Just go with it. And they're like, 'Is that on the final?'" He smiled and waited for her answering smile. It didn't come. "How about you? What have you done with yourself?"

She had no ready answer.

"Someone's found her," Suzanne interjected. "Someone from the old days. Left her letters. That's what you said, right? Someone from back then?"

"Yes," she said. "Someone who was with us on the tour, at the end. It wasn't you, Peter, was it? You didn't write to me?"

"Me? Christ, no. Busy enough with classes and the house and my old lady here. Don't take it the wrong way, Alice, but I don't think about you much. We had, what? Six months together? Seven? It was deep, yeah. Real. And I know some shit went down. But when it comes to a whole life, that's not a lot."

She believed him. The belief hurt. She remembered a vaccine she'd been given years ago, the pinch of the needle and then a worse pain, a stinging cold, seeping all through her arm. "Well, I haven't thought of you either," she said. She said it slowly, barely trusting her voice. "I haven't let myself."

"How come?" he said.

She wished she had a knife then. A brick. Something to make him feel what she felt. "It may not have been a lot for you," she said. "It was for me. Too much. You used to talk about love, remember? About freedom. But it was never love. And I'm no good with freedom. What happened, what we did, it ruined me for anything except the smallest kind of life." She could feel her pulse, thrumming, too fast. She never should have come here. Never stood among these shabby monuments. The room went black. Her hands, they looked black, too. Was that blood? Was it on her coat, her clothes? She screamed—ugly, keening—and that scream broke something in her. She fell. And as she fell, her hands found the gold dress. She tore at it, ripping the seams. She was on the ground then, the fabric shredded, her cheeks blotched and wet.

Suzanne's arms were around her again, in that same awkward embrace. "It's all right," Suzanne murmured into her hair. "It's all right. Or no, it isn't. But nothing's going to hurt you now. Not worse. Not here."

She did not know that this was true, but still she let Suzanne pull her to her feet and take her out of the barn and into the house. The barn had been unheated and it was only in the living room that she realized how cold she was, chilled through. Suzanne saw her shiver.

"Do you want a bath? Something to warm you up?"

She preferred showers, brisk and cold. But she nodded, docile now, and let Suzanne lead her upstairs and into a bathroom with a clawfoot tub.

"Take your time," Suzanne said as she left. "Use what you like."

She closed the door and locked it. There was a footstool in the corner, and she pushed that against the door as well, angling it under the knob. Only then did she run the water and begin to undress. Pulling her sweater off, she caught her face in the mirror. Even through the steam, she looked exhausted, old. But that was only one face. She took off her glasses and there, blurred, she saw another.

She came down an hour later, in stocking feet, smelling of Suzanne's calendula soap. Voices drifted from the kitchen, and she went in to find Suzanne tending to the oven and Peter at the table with a newspaper.

"I'm heating up some leftovers," Suzanne said. "We're late for lunch and too early for dinner, but there it is. We spent the holiday with friends, and Edie, she sent us home with some of everything. Are you hungry?"

She was surprised to find she was. When had she eaten last? So though it felt obscene—a burlesque of wholesomeness—she joined them in the dining room for turkey, stuffing, baked yams, a green bean casserole, slices of apple pie. There was a part of her that wanted to turn the table over, to smash every plate, but instead, she spread her napkin in her lap and ate politely, nodding at their chatter.

When they finished, they settled in the living room. She studied the tapestries, the posters, the accumulated objects. "You've been here how long?" she asked.

"Twenty years," Suzanne said. "Or thereabout."

"So your son, he grew up here? I remember him from rehearsals, he was always—"

Peter interrupted. "We don't have a fucking son." He pushed his chair back. "Going out," he said. "Work to do." There was the rustling of a coat in the hallway, the slam of a door, the sound of an engine warming.

"I didn't know," she said.

"It's fine," Suzanne said. "It's just not something he talks about much. Peter, he's sensitive. He feels things more than the rest of us. Takes things to heart. He'll drive around for a while, come back like nothing's happened."

"And you, do you feel things?"

"Of course," Suzanne said. "But I know how to sit with those feelings, Alice. Or no. Not Alice. What should I call you?"

She paused. "Allison," she said finally. "My given name. Peter heard it as Alice that first night, and I didn't correct him."

"So you just let all of us call you a wrong name all that time?" Suzanne said. "God, I never would have let him get away with that. Well, Allison's a fine name. Suits you. Come on, help me with the dishes. And I don't know about you, but this old lady could use a drink."

Suzanne opened a bottle of cabernet. With the dishes done, they drank it back in the living room, on the sofa swathed in crocheted throws. Suzanne made a fire and in its warmth she felt lazy, torpid. She'd felt that same indolence that blazing summer in the loft, that same sense of knowing she should go—go now!—and staying on anyway. When they were on their second bottle, Peter returned, tossing his coat onto a chair, then going back out and scuffing his boots on the mat when Suzanne reminded him. Peter kissed Suzanne on the lips with a smacking sound and took a slug from her wineglass without asking.

"Hiya, Alice," he said. "Wasn't sure you'd still be here."

"I shouldn't," she said. "I need to head back before it's too dark. But I wanted to talk to you first, about who was there at the end. Check my memory against yours."

"Well, can't say my memory is what it was," he said, lowering himself to an armchair. "In Frankfurt? Let's see. Well, me, of course. And my old lady here. Bill and JoAnn were there. And Bash. And crazy Molly M."

"Not Molly," she said. "Remember? The boat over."

"Oh yeah," he said. A shadow crossed his face. "Well, Faye. She was there, sure as shit. And you and Rosa."

"And Jorge," she prompted.

"Yeah, Jorge. And Jan, he was back by then."

She sat back, counting on her fingers. Ten. "That's my same list. I didn't send myself the messages, and if we leave out you and Suzanne, that's down to seven. JoAnn died; I saw that in the paper. It said something about medical complications?"

"Complications, my ass," Peter said. "Nothing complicated about it. The pregnancy, it went wrong. Up in the tubes. What's the word, Suzanne?"

"Ectopic."

"Ectopic, yeah. They didn't catch it, didn't do the right tests. Or maybe JoAnn didn't let them. So happy to be knocked up, you know? Didn't want to jinx it. Tube burst is what I heard."

"It burst, and she bled out in the cell," Suzanne said. "They took her to the prison hospital, but by then, it was too late. Bill told us later on they wouldn't even let him see her. Sent the body back to her family in the States. But they didn't preserve it. Catholic and they had to do a closed casket. They let Bill out pretty soon after. Guess they figured he'd suffered enough. He wasn't the same, though. Came up here once, drunk as a lord. Peter had to make him go."

"Killed me to do it," Peter said. "My oldest friend. But he was in a bad way."

"I spoke to him," she said. "Last month. To Jorge, too. It's not either of them. At least that's what they told me."

"So who does that leave?" Suzanne asked, pouring the last of the wine into her glass and handing the glass to Peter.

"Faye. But Rebecca Liu said that she died sometime in the '80s."

"Yes, she did," Suzanne said. "That was her way. In over her head even in a puddle."

"And Bash? I read that he died, too."

"Yeah, his liver went," Peter said. "Looked like a canary by the time it was done."

"Do you know what happened to Jan?" she asked.

"No," Peter said. "Stayed in Europe, I think. But I couldn't say for sure. Jorge didn't know?"

"I don't think they kept in touch."

"So it has to be him," Suzanne said.

"Or Rosa," said Peter.

But it was not Jan, and neither was it Rosa. Because Rosa was alive—wet and grinning, bleeding from the breast—only in her mind. The microfiche had confirmed this. She knew no more than when she'd arrived. She felt angry at herself for coming, angrier at Peter and Suzanne for failing her.

"There was no one else?" she asked, plaintive and despairing.

"No one I can think of," Suzanne said.

"Nope," Peter said.

Night had roofed the house. "I should go," she said. "The drive."

Her legs wobbled as she stood. Suzanne saw and patted her hand. "I think you've drunk too much for that."

She wanted to protest, but the thought of the unfamiliar roads subdued her. "You're right. Could I make some coffee?"

"I don't think coffee will do it," Suzanne said. "Not anytime soon. When is your flight back?"

"Not till tomorrow afternoon."

"Well, that settles it. Stay the night. There's a guest room upstairs. Visiting artists, they use it all the time. You can drive back in the morning."

She did not want their generosity. But she had already eaten their food and drunk their wine. Now she would lie in their bed. This was how the stories went. "All right," she said. "I'll leave first thing."

She brought the empty bottles and the glasses to the kitchen. Suzanne made a plate of toast, with homemade apple butter, and a pot of tea. "Ginger and turmeric," Suzanne said. "So you won't have a hangover."

They ate and drank in silence, the silence of having little left to say. "Think I'll go upstairs," Peter said finally, "read for a while before bed. Remind me and I'll fix that busted storm window tomorrow. Night, sweetheart," he said, kissing Suzanne. "Night, Alice." He might have kissed her, too, but she flinched at his approach, and so he only waved. She heard his feet, heavy on the stairs, and remembered nights when she'd followed those steps up the roof, when he'd been strong and golden still.

She and Suzanne took their mugs back into the living room. Suzanne put another log on the fire. "I lied to you this afternoon," Suzanne said straightening up. "So did Peter. We did think of you. It didn't seem fair that you got away clean. I was angry, if you want to know. Livid. At you and Rosa both."

"I had to go," she said. "If I'd stayed, gone to prison, it would have killed me."

"Well, maybe that's what you deserved," Suzanne said. The fire crackled, spat sparks. For a moment it turned Suzanne's hair red-gold again. "But no," Suzanne went on, settling back into the sofa. "I get it. You hadn't been with us for long. You didn't owe us anything. Or you thought you didn't. And you didn't kill that man, didn't have it in you. Anyone could see. You were how old?"

"Nineteen," she said.

"Nineteen," Suzanne repeated.

"You didn't think that was so young. You told me something once. On the afternoon when we went shopping for the *Grimm* costumes. You told me that Peter needed girls like me, that he needed us to make the work."

"We went for hamburgers that day?"

"Hot dogs. Kosher."

"Oh yeah. Isn't that funny? Haven't lived in my father's house for near on fifty years. Haven't believed in a vengeful God for longer. And still I can't eat pork."

"Was that really how it was? A new girl for every show? Two girls? More?"

"It helped him," Suzanne said. "And I didn't care. I knew he'd always come home to me. Me or my father's money. And when there wasn't money anymore, he came home anyway. Then there was the work. The stories. Peter was the one who could bring it all to life."

"But there's no work anymore, right? Are there still the girls?"

"Why does it matter to you?" Suzanne said.

"Because I was a girl," she said. She leaned close. Forced Suzanne to hold her gaze. "He had me for a summer, less. He made me believe that I was special, and by the time I realized I wasn't, that if you lined up all of us girls, all the ones he went to bed with, we'd have stretched across the river into Jersey, it was almost too late for me. I'd given up too much already."

"Really? The ones who came to us, the ones who stayed, usually they came from something worse. Did you really have that much to give?"

"Just my life, Suzanne."

"Look," Suzanne said. "We all make choices. You chose to stay, Allison. And then when it all got real, you chose to leave. I wasn't forced to do anything, and whatever you think, you weren't either."

"Yeah?" she said. "What about the movie?"

"The movie." Suzanne shut her eyes a moment. "The movie was a mistake. It never would have happened if I'd been there."

"How much do you know about the movie?"

"I saw it, or some of it. Peter burned it, mostly. But he saved a reel. Saved it for me. Me and Peter, we don't have secrets from each other. Never have. And yeah, I'm sorry for the movie. That's not what we're about. But you and Peter, you'd been together anyway. And that can't have been the only time you made it with someone you didn't go for. God knows I did. You can't still be unhappy about it."

"I can be unhappy about a lot of things," she said.

"Well," Suzanne said. "That's your choice, Allison. Maybe one day, you'll make a different one. Your room is to the right of the stairs. We're early risers, but if you're up before us, you can see yourself out. Good night, Allison."

"Not going to wish me sweet dreams?"

"We're both too old for that."

Suzanne switched off the lamp and left the room. She sat there a moment, in the fire's glow, then went out to the car for her suitcase and bumped it up the stairs. The guest room was spare, dwarfed by a sleigh bed topped with a white candlewick spread. On the wall opposite was JoAnn's woodcut, the silhouette of the two girls in the dark forest. She touched it. She was still that girl. Why deny it? And this was still the forest. She'd never left it. All those years of running, of hiding, had never led her out. The trip had been a waste. She knew no more than when she'd come. But her time in the barn—amid the pictures and the relics—had reminded her, viscerally, of the girl she'd been, of what that girl might do.

No one knew that she had come here, to the home of these people that she hated. The cashier at the health food store might remember her. But she doubted it. And the cashier wouldn't know her name, her car. She could do it now. Take a knife from the kitchen or a hammer from wherever Peter stored his tools. Maybe she wouldn't need a knife. She'd killed with less.

But no, her blood had cooled. She switched off the light and listened to the house as it heaved and shuddered in the wind.

She slept better than she would have imagined and woke early, to that same threadbare sunlight. Dressing took no time, and after splashing cold water on her face, she tiptoed down the stairs, eager to leave before the others were awake. But Suzanne was there already, minding a moka pot.

"Thought you might want some coffee before you went," Suzanne said. "Milk? Sugar?"

"Milk. Sweetener, if you have it. Equal or Sweet'N Low."

"We don't. I take mine as it comes. I'm sweet enough already, my father used to say."

She made no reply. Her own father had not bothered with endearments. Suzanne handed her the coffee, and she drank it, standing.

"It's not too late, you know," Suzanne said.

"Yes, my flight's not for a bit. But I should get going. I have the rental car to return."

"That's not what I meant," Suzanne said. She put out her hand for the empty mug. "You're young. I know it may not feel that way. But you are. You could still make a life for yourself if you wanted. Have a family."

"I doubt it. And how do you know I don't have a family already?"

"Allison, one look says you're alone in the world."

"Well, I don't want children. I never have. I'm no good as a wife, and I shouldn't be anyone's mother."

"I'm sure that you—"

"No," she said. She said it louder than she'd meant to, shattering the house's quiet. Anger was rising in her. "You aren't sure of anything. Until last night, you didn't even know my goddamn name. Which isn't the name I use now. Well, here's another thing you didn't know: It was me, Suzanne. I'm the one who went to the police, the one who told them about Rosa, about the drugs and what she'd done. That time you spent in jail, all you lost? That was me. So don't you tell me what I should do, who I could become."

Suzanne closed her eyes for a moment. "I know," she said.

"You know?"

Suzanne gestured to a chair. "Here. Sit."

She sat.

"I know," Suzanne repeated. "I've always known. I'm not sure Peter does. He's not the kind of man to think things through. The police, when they came, they knew just where to look. A coincidence? I don't believe in coincidence. Or fate. I thought it was Rosa at first, saving her own ass by admitting to something else. Thought it might have been the two of you in on it together. Her running like that. You right after. But then I knew for certain."

"How?"

"Those shitbird cops," Suzanne said. "After they let me out, they asked me to look at a body, a girl they pulled from the river. They thought it might be Rosa. They took me to the morgue. There was a table. And something on the table, a white sheet over it. God, it was cold in there. They pulled the sheet down, and it was her. She'd been in the water awhile. Her face was bloated, and the color was wrong. Yellow. Like the paper in an old book. I recognized her anyway. And then of course the clothes, that coat. But I shook my head. I said no. I told them I'd never seen her before in my life."

"Oh God," she said, picturing Rosa like that, on the slab in some morgue, ugly and still. "But why? Why would you lie to the police?"

"She hadn't just fallen into the water. There was a wound, in her chest. They showed it to me. Someone hurt her. Could have been any-one. Peter, he was so angry with her, running like she did. Me, I took a sleeping pill that night. Peter could have gone out, he could have—" Suzanne stopped herself. Took a hissing breath. "So I lied to the police, and that girl went into a grave, nameless. I've had to live with that. With that and more. And before you say anything, I don't know if he did it. I've never asked him. It's better not to know. Okay?"

"Okay," she said.

"So if it wasn't Rosa who went to the police that night, that means it was you, Allison. Why would you do that? I understand running. Maybe we all should have run. But why would you turn on us that way? You were angry with Peter about the movie, fine. But you fucked all of us. Me, Faye, Bash, fucking JoAnn."

"I didn't plan it," she said. She would tell Suzanne what truth she could spare. "I just panicked. Rosa was gone. And I thought I'd be blamed for what she'd done, for what happened in London. I thought if I told the police what I knew, that they would let me go. So I told them about Rosa's drugs, yes. And when they asked about the company, the shows, I told them about all that, too. They said that was prostitution, obscenity. And I think now they were right. I think it was. I did what I had to do, Suzanne. I had to save myself. I had to get free."

"Yeah," Suzanne said. She turned back to the stove, freshened her mug. "Freedom's a funny thing. The worst part for me, the awful part, that lie I told, it didn't help Peter. Not really. He went to prison anyway, and when he came out, that spark in him that made the work possible, it was gone. Like it had never been there at all. The museum, in the barn, that's for me. He only comes to see it when I'm in there already. Because he can't stand to be alone. The work he does with the kids now, it's flat. So ordinary. And there are no more girls, Allison. He's too frightened for that. Won't even smoke a jay at a faculty party." Suzanne sat back down. "I get that you had your reasons for doing what you did, Allison. I had mine. Was it worth it?"

"I don't know," she said.

"Well, make it worth it," Suzanne said. She sounded nearly angry. "No one gets what they deserve, good or bad. Not in this life. Not that I've seen. If you turned us in to save yourself, to save your life, then for God's sake, make a life that matters. We've all done terrible things, Allison. Things that can't be forgiven. And we've gone on anyway. Had lives. Had love. You could have the same. You say someone's looking for you. Maybe they are. Or maybe you just needed a reason to come here, to say your piece. Well, you've done that. So now you can leave, move on."

She stood up, too fast. "I should go," she said.

"Yes," Suzanne said. "Drive safe. And don't come here again."

The miles flashed by, the drive reversed, the pines, the capitol, the whales diving down. She returned the rental car and checked in at the desk. Then she was in the air, above the clouds, racing through an empty sky. She was the same woman she had been a few days before. But she felt changed somehow. At O'Hare, she bought a Chicago-style pizza and finished it all, licking her fingers clean.

At LAX, her car was waiting. It shuddered as she drove, the shock absorbers all worn through. The apartment was dark and stale, as though no one had lived in it for years. The aloe she'd taken from the girl in Van Nuys slumped on the windowsill, withered now. She put it in the trash, then brought the bottle of zinfandel from the refrigerator and poured the last of it into a glass. It was her birthday. She was forty-five.

The red light on her answering machine was pulsing, a too-quick heartbeat. She'd missed six calls. The first two were from an administrator at her mother's care facility, the others from nurses at Valley Presbyterian. There had been an event. She thought she heard the word *cardiac*, but she couldn't be sure. She snatched up her keys and ran from the apartment to the car, driving through every stop sign and yield sign and yellow light, wagering, hopelessly, that if she went faster, if she hit the gas harder, if she made the wheels screech at every curve, she might outpace what was coming for her.

14

1972, LONDON, DOVER, THE CHANNEL, CALAIS, AMIENS, PARIS, BRUSSELS, ANTWERP, AMSTERDAM

froze, every atom stilled. It occurred to me to scream, but screaming would summon others, and no one, I thought, should see this. No one else. Rosa must have sensed me there. She managed to wrench her head from the pillow, eyes wild. One of her arms, I saw, was bent back at a wrong angle. Her lips opened, then closed in what looked like a kiss. She was mouthing a word: *Help*.

I saw her purse on the floor, the purse that held her knife. I could use that knife on Abraham. But that would be brazen, messy. Everyone would know what we had done. We would be punished for it. I must have shifted, breathed, because Abraham noticed me then. And in that split second when his eyes widened, I moved.

"Rosa," I said in a harsh whisper. "Up. Now." She raised her hips and I pushed with my arms, and together, we flipped him off her. I leaped onto the bed then and sat across his stomach, pinning him to the mattress. I could feel the flesh of him, through the thin cotton of my underwear, lurching beneath me. Rosa joined me in an instant, lying across his shoulders, one hand atop his mouth to stifle his voice. He was kicking, but his kicks were feeble. He was still mostly dressed. His pants were down, not off, and he hadn't even bothered to remove his belt. A belt that looked like my father's. The buckle, I saw, had scraped Rosa's thighs.

"Will he just let us go?" I said.

"Dunno," she said, quiet and fierce. "How about it, numbnuts? You gonna let us get our beauty sleep?" She moved her hand from his mouth.

"You whore," he said, gasping. "You stupid fucking whore." He maneuvered an arm out from under her legs and hit her in the face, his closed fist a rock. "If I fuck you, if I deign to, it's a privilege." Blood began to drip from her nose. That blood loosed something in me.

"Don't you hit her," I said. "Don't you dare."

"And what will you do?" he said. "You're a whore just like her. You're chattel. So's she. I'll hit her if I like." That fist came up again, clouting Rosa's breast this time. I heard the sound she made as it connected, the forced exhale. She tried to use her arms and knees to hold him down, but he had his strength now. Any moment, he would think to yell, his fury outweighing the humiliation of being found like this, pants down, penis damp and flaccid. I would not let him yell. Abandoning my perch across his stomach, I snatched up one of the pillows from the headboard and crushed it to his nose and mouth. He did yell then. But the pillow stole the sound away. Rosa, still astride his chest, blood streaked across her face, pressed it down farther. He struggled, jerking with his arms, his legs. But we held on until the jerks grew fainter and the thrashing stopped and the body was still and the only sounds in the room were the stuttered rasps of what must have been our breaths.

Whatever rage had spurred me, it fled then. A new and slower horror descended. Gingerly, I took the pillow from Abraham's face. His eyes were open, unseeing.

"Is he dead?" I whispered.

Rosa had rolled away. She sat with her arms around her knees and looked over at me, eyes too wide. "There's those goddamn college girl smarts," she whispered. "Yeah, he's dead. That's what happens when you put a pillow over some bastard's face. What did you think you were doing? Changing the goddamn sheets?"

"I just wanted him quiet," I said. My voice was a pebble, dropped into a well. "I just wanted him to stop."

"Pretty goddamn quiet now."

"Rosa," I said. "We have to go. No one can find us here. We'll clean him up. Clean you up. Put you back in bed. In the morning when they find him, they'll think he died of something else, a heart attack. He was old enough for it. Is any of your blood on him?"

"Too dark to see."

I shut the door, then switched the bedside lamp on. There was blood. On the hand he had hit her with, and then small smears on his shirt, on the sheet.

"Can we clean that?" Rosa said. She joined me, kneeling, on the carpet.

"Maybe?" I said. "But I don't know if it'll dry by morning. What time is it?"

Neither of us knew. Night had swallowed the house.

"So what do we do?" Rosa said.

"I don't know," I said. My body had begun to shake. "Rosa, there's not enough time. The blood. They'll see."

"Shut up," she said. Her gaze was hard. "Lose it tomorrow, next week, sunshine. Not now."

"Can we say that you were with him? That his arm came up, in the moment? That he had a heart attack right after?"

"Nah," she said, shaking her head. "Too complicated. And look," she said. "Look close."

I didn't want to, but I followed her finger. It pointed to the bed, to the still-open eyes. There were red dots, like pinpricks, in the left one. "That's a sign, right? A sign he couldn't breathe."

"How do you know?" I said.

"Don't ask," she said, but a hand went to her own throat. I covered that hand with my own, and we stayed like that for a moment, still and desolate.

"And that doesn't happen with a heart attack?"

"Dunno. Don't think so." Rosa stood. "I know what we can do," she said. "Stay here." She straightened her clothes, took her purse, and left me. I stared at the wall; there was a painting there, framed in gilt, of a woman, nude, looking back over her shoulder. Her lips were parted, in fear, it seemed to me.

I don't know how long Rosa was gone. Her returning step was noiseless, like a cat's, and then she was in front of me. In one hand, she had the canister of baby powder. In the other was a small pouch, in leather or its imitation, that I did not remember from her suitcase. She set the items on the nightstand.

"Help me take his shirt off," she said.

I did. And it was terrible. The body felt too solid.

"Go get some water," she told me.

I rose, opening doors until I found one that led to a bathroom. That door creaked like a tree in the wind. The whole house, I thought, could hear it. But there was no answering noise, no stirring. I filled a glass at the sink, a glass he must have used to rinse his mouth. It shook in my hand. I brought it to Rosa and she took it without thanks, then handed me a spoon, metal and tarnished.

"Hold it," she said. I did.

Carefully, she unscrewed the canister and tipped powder into the spoon. Then she added water. She took a lighter from the pouch, flicked the flame up, and held it underneath. The mixture began to bubble. My hand trembled.

"Stay still, goddamn it," she said. When the powder had dissolved she took a syringe and sucked the liquid up.

"I'm gonna stick him," she said. "Rough, so he bleeds a little. His blood, get it? Not mine. This fix, it's big. It'll look like he took too much. Like his breathing stopped. Just an accident. Nothing to do with us."

"Is that what happened to Jax?" I asked. She didn't reply. "What he took, did you give it to him?"

"You really wanna do this now?" She took Abraham's arm then. Rolled up the sleeve. I could imagine how flabby it would feel. Deadweight. She squeezed and tapped, searching for a vein. It wouldn't come. I thought back to the biology course I'd taken.

"It's because the heart is stopped," I said. "When the heart stops, the blood stops, too. Nothing to pump it. The drug. It'll just sit where you stick it in. It won't go through him. He won't bleed."

"Could somebody tell a thing like that? Could a doctor?"

"I think so," I said.

"Fuck do we do then?" she said. Beneath a mask of control, her face was wild.

I took a stuttered breath. "We work his heart for him," I said. "They taught us how in Red Cross lifesaving. Chest compressions." There was acid in my mouth. I swallowed it. "If I do it right, the . . . the stuff, it'll go into him."

Rosa placed the needle in the crook of Abraham's arm, where she could see a dark line beneath the skin, then pressed the plunger. I climbed back onto the bed and fit my hands, one atop the other, on the left side of his chest where I hoped the heart was. I pressed down, and I could feel, horribly, the bone and fat and muscle moving under me. I pushed and pushed until I was hot all over. Had he been alive, the skin below my hands would have bruised. But it was too late for that.

"It's done," I said.

"Now I'm gonna make him bleed," she said. "The blood on the sheet, it's gotta be his."

She stuck him again, tearing the skin. I pushed, she squeezed, and soon there was a small trickle, enough to smear across his arm. We stopped then as if on some agreed-upon cue, looked at one another, the body between us. Her eyes, I saw, were dark, the pupils so dilated they seemed to have swallowed the iris. There was blood below her nose, darker than her lipstick.

"What happened?" I whispered. "Why were you with him?"

"Was at the party," she said, easing herself off the bed and back onto the floor. "Went back down. Abraham, he was drinking more than anyone. Swigging scotch like it was goddamn water. Peter, he said I should be nice to him, so he'd give us the money, the rest of it. And I go, 'You mean you want me to fuck him.' 'Cause I don't do that. Not unless I want to. And he goes, 'Nah, nah. Like, just be sweet.' So I'm sitting on his lap, laughing at his goddamn jokes, his hard-on up against my ass. Gets late. People go to bed. He says he'll walk me up, just has to get something from his room first. But then he's on me. Hands all over, tearing my panties. He knows I don't want it, and that just makes him want it more."

Her eyes left mine then. Went to her lap. "Shoulda screamed. But that mighta just made him mad. Made it worse. He hurt me, Alice. He wanted me hurt. Guess I did scream then. That what you heard?"

"Yes," I said.

"Don't know if I'm glad you came. Didn't think you had it in you. We're a pair now, huh?"

"I guess we are," I said, though I told myself I wasn't anything like Rosa. Maybe I even believed it. "We need to figure out our story. Get it straight. We'll say that we were with him. Both of us. That way, we can back each other up. He had drugs. Wanted us to take them. We wouldn't. So he took them on his own. He died. Got it?"

"Yeah, I got it," Rosa said.

"Good. Clean yourself up. There's blood on your face."

She went to the bathroom, ran the water. When she came back, there was a clump of wet tissue in her hand. Her face was bare, the blood and lipstick gone. She used the tissues to clean his fist, then stuffed them in the pocket of her dress.

"Get me a handkerchief or something," she said. "One of his."

I went to a chest of drawers and opened the top one, then the one beneath it. I found a handkerchief—silken, pale—and she spread it on the night table, then tipped some powder in. She put the spoon in his hand, then the needle, pressing his fingers to them, then she laid them on the table, too. She nodded to me. I switched off the lamp.

"Gotta go and put the rest of this away," she said. "You okay here?"

I nodded. I wasn't. But I had to be. She came back awhile later and put her hand in mine. There we were, shoulder to shoulder, in that room that smelled of blood and sex and the drug's acrid tang.

I thought of our scene, Snow White and Rose Red, how the girls save the prince, save themselves, how they cut off the dwarf's beard. We had done that. We had been so brave. Where was our reward?

"Whadda we do now?" she said.

"Now we scream."

Time began to hurtle then. My memory of the next hours is streaky, pied. It comes in flashes. The room was suddenly very full and people, men, were on the bed, tending to Abraham, trying to revive him. We told the men our story. That we were with Abraham. That he took the drugs. That his breathing shortened. That his breathing stopped. That we had pressed on his chest, huffed into his mouth. To no end. We wore a mask of shock, but then again, we were in shock.

The men were angry, Bram especially, pacing the room, fluttering his hands as though his fingers were bird's wings. He yelled at us for being so stupid, for allowing Abraham to be so stupid.

"You idiot girls," he said. "Should never have let you in, the lot of you. Soiled goods. Foul. He would never have done this otherwise. You ruin anything you touch, don't you?"

"You touched me enough," Rosa said. Her eyes were hard. "You ruined? Don't put this on me. Her neither. Wasn't us, he woulda found some other gash to show off for. Show what a goddamn rebel he was."

I started to cry then. Because I was exhausted, yes, but also because crying made me seem weak. Not the kind of girl who could suffocate a man. The men were taken in, even Bram, who looked at me with pity and disgust.

There were conferences, in the room and outside of it. At last, we were allowed to leave. Peter met us in the hall. "We gotta go," he said. Bram, avoiding further scandal, didn't want us here when the police were called.

"You get the money?" Rosa said.

"Not all. But enough to get to Amiens if we get a van for cheap. Pack your stuff. We'll go in a couple of hours, when the cabs are out."

Rosa took my hand. "Anything else you wanna ask us?"

"Like what?" Peter said.

"Like, I dunno, 'Hey, Rosa, hey, Alice. Some bastard just died on you, then you got screamed at for an hour. You okay?'"

"Come on, Rosa," Peter said, his shoulders hunched. "Let's just get out of here."

"You're a goddamn prince," she said, her tongue sharp enough to cut. "Think you don't gotta be nice to me no more? That I'm just gonna do what you say no matter what?"

"Think you will," Peter said, fingering the collar of his shirt. "These English guys, they believed you. Not so sure I do, kind of trouble you've been in. So let's get out of this wet sock, crap food, nightmare of a country before they think it through. Get out fast."

We left at dawn, in light rain, lumbering our cases and trunks back down the hill to the high road. We put them into taxis, and the taxis brought us to a car lot that Peter knew. The lot was closed, but there was a workingman's café across the street. We filled it, ordering fried eggs, margarine-slicked toast, endless cups of tea. Rosa and I sat together on one side of a booth, our knees touching. It hurt to be with her, to be reminded. But it would have hurt worse to be without her, to be alone with what I'd done.

The lot opened, and Peter went over, Bill with him. They came out half an hour later and waved us in. The vehicle they had bought was a small bus, with geranium side panels, a white roof, and rusted bumpers. The men began to load the bags.

JoAnn counted the seats. "Have to squish," she said. "Unless anyone wants to ride on the roof."

"No," Jan said. His eyes, the lazy one and the other, seemed hooded, bruised. "This thing that we have done, it has made me ashamed. I will not go with you."

He reached into the cavernous knapsack he carried and removed several reels. "Here," he said to Peter, handing them over, the metal casing clacking. "I have taken these from the house. These I think are all."

He went to Jorge, took Jorge's head in both his giant's hands, whispered in his ear. Faye hugged him. Then he left. We watched him, tracking his steps with our eyes until the mist and buildings hid him. He never turned around, not once.

"What will you do with that movie, honey?" Faye asked.

"Burn it," Peter said. "As soon as we're out of this motherfucking rain."

Bill drove us to Dover along wet highways. His seat was on the left, just like in an American car, and Peter had to keep yelling at him about which lane to use. One windshield wiper was broken. The asphalt blurred into the sky. We stopped once for gas—*petrol*, it was called—and fizzy drinks and sandwiches. For a moment, the salt cliffs dwarfed us, shadowing the car. Then we were at the ferry.

The boat was blinding white and larger than I'd expected. We drove straight onto it, then scattered. Rosa and I went to a railing in the front, let the wind whip our hair into lions' manes.

"What do we do?" I said. I didn't say it loudly, but even over the engine, Rosa heard me.

"We don't do nothing."

"But Peter, he seemed to think—"

"Fuck Peter," she said. "Doesn't know nothing. Even if he did, he's not looking for any trouble, and me and you, we don't want trouble neither. Besides, where you gonna go? Home? You gonna call your daddy?"

"No," I said. "I guess not." I turned my back on the water. We went inside.

Another hour and Calais rose into view, in dingy grays and browns. We disembarked, and after buying a map, we were driving again, toward Amiens. We arrived at nightfall. A dark-haired man was waiting for us outside the municipal theater where we would perform. His name was

Paul, I think. Or Claude. After England, I stopped paying attention, stopped acknowledging anyone who wasn't a part of the troupe. I let the faces smudge, the bodies blur. It seemed safer that way. Safer for me. Safer for them.

We dropped the trunks at the theater, then followed his directions to a boardinghouse. There was food for us there—bread, some casserole of ham and cheese. Then we stumbled up to the rooms. Rosa and I shared a bed that night. For the rest of the tour, we would share every night. Sometimes she would leave for an hour, two, three, to go with Peter or someone else. And some nights I would do the same. But she was always there when I woke. I don't know that I liked Rosa. I know that I did not trust her. But she knew me, the whole of me, and that was a thing like love.

We had two days of rehearsal in Amiens, only just enough time to collect the lumber, to arrange the lights, to adorn the two other environments. We found that if we reversed the order of the Hansel and Gretel and Rumpelstiltskin scenes, Bill could cover for Jan, and Rosa could play the roles that Molly and then Benny had taken. It was messy, frantic. But it worked. No one spoke of Jan, though Jorge looked hollowed out, as though someone had reached into his chest and removed some vital organ. No one spoke of the movie either. That North London house had come to seem like a story in a book. Now the book was shut. The night before our first performance, Peter called us out into the alley behind the boardinghouse. There was a metal trough there, and within it, burning, were the film reels.

"So that's over," Peter said. "It's done, all right?" The flames lit him from below, picked out the bones of his face. "Now we get back to work."

We did. And the work remained a gift, the only gift. During the long, anxious days, as I waited for dusk to come on, I craved the warmth of stage lights on my skin, the comfort of lines and steps already arranged.

In the end, in the joining of bodies just before the final flashout, I let myself go, yielding to unknown hands. In those moments, I was beyond worry, beyond want. I had my period then, and one night as I changed my clothes postshow, I saw that I had bled through my dress. A year ago, a few months ago, embarrassment would have racked me. That night, I only laughed and asked JoAnn, who kept a supply of detergent, for soap flakes to wash the stain away.

She stood over me as I scrubbed the fabric, reducing the stain from brown to red to nothing.

"Mine's late," she told me. "Late . . . and the smell of eggs or coffee makes me want to puke."

"Do you mean—"

"Could be," she said. She put a finger to her lips and smiled behind her finger. We all had secrets, it seemed. I wondered if the baby were Bill's.

We went to Rouen after that and then across to Paris. There was confusion there. The theater wasn't ready, we were told. But that seemed not to be the whole truth. The mood had changed, since '68. The old places did not want us. We were decadent. Trivial. Our politics were felt to be insincere, and this of course was true. We spent a few days in a rooming house on the city outskirts while Peter tried to work it out. Rosa and I talked about venturing out, sightseeing, but we had no money, just the little that Peter had left us for food, so mostly we kept close. Rosa slipped out one night, in secret, without inviting me along, and she didn't come home till late. I asked her where she'd been, whispering so as not to wake the others. She wouldn't say, but when she went to wash, I checked her purse. The knife was there, and a wad of paper money. I do not know what she sold to get it—drugs, herself. She came back to bed, reaching out for me in the dark, her body hot and slick. We fell asleep at dawn.

Another theater was found, in the Ninth, near Montmartre; they booked us for two weeks. We moved our rooms. The Montmartre audiences were of a different sort. The art, the mystery, it did not matter to these people. They were here for sex, depravity. But I did the work just the same. I made it pure, if only for myself. And if I hated them, I put that hatred into the scene at the end when we tore the cottage down. The cottage was meant to be a protection from the forest. But the forest was everywhere. My rage, my grasping hands, the ugliest parts of me, these were the forest, too, and also the only protections that life would offer. So I raged, I tore, I made the house a ruin. Later, Faye would run warm water into a bowl and pry the splinters from my hands with rubbing alcohol and tweezers.

"Shouldn't hurt yourself like that," she said. "A baby like you."

I shook my head. "I have to."

"I know it, honey," Faye said.

From Paris, we drove to Brussels. I remember the ugliness of its government buildings, how they loomed above the narrow streets. Yet the whole place smelled divine, like waffles, like chocolate. And there at the small hotel, as if by magic, was Jan. It was mid-October. He'd been gone a month. He seemed thinner. His hair was in his eyes. Some of that bluff strength had departed him.

On the day he left us, he'd taken the ferry just after ours, he said, then hitched up to Sweden. "But it had changed, my home," he said. His two eyes went in different directions as he spoke. He seemed to be looking nowhere. "Or I am changed. I could not stay." Jorge had written to him during our Paris leg. Now he had come.

Faye ran to him, knit her arms around his neck. "We have to celebrate," she said.

A bar was found, low down, in what must have been the basement of a house. There was wine and dancing, to records and later on to a rock quarter murdering the hits of American radio. Rosa offered me a pill, and I took it, gulping it down with wine from someone else's glass. I had always assumed that I would find my way back—to marriage, to children, to a trim home of my own. But there in the sweat and smoky haze, I knew that I had slipped from the workaday world. Jan could not go home. Could I? Had I trapped myself here, in this squalor, in this half-life? At least I could dance. I grabbed Rosa's hand. We spun each other around the floor.

From Brussels, we went to Antwerp. From Antwerp to Amsterdam. In a time before, I might have hoped to visit the Anne Frank house, to take a boat down the canals. With Theater Negative, I saw a different city—bars, red lights. Suzanne met us there, at the theater. She had her son with her. She put him to bed backstage on a pile of street clothes while she watched the show. During that night's finale, Peter, I noticed, kept himself apart. There was another party after. The boy sat happily under the table. Faye and Rosa fed him bits of pancake.

With Suzanne's arrival, some strain lifted. I do not know how much money she brought with her, but there were suddenly small luxuries. It was properly fall by then. I missed my May Company coat, left behind in the loft for rats to gnaw. Suzanne found us surplus ones at an army shop near the canal, and JoAnn took a picture, on a low brick bridge, of Rosa, Faye, and me, in our matching navy peacoats, the buttons flaring in the afternoon sun. My shoes had worn through; so had Rosa's. Suzanne took us to a shop in a narrow building and bought us wooden clogs, like the ones I had seen the dance students back at school wear, the leather uppers affixed to the soles with staples. We danced out of the store. In such moments, before we went to Germany, to the forest, I could convince myself that I was free.

15

1972, BREMEN, DÜSSELDORF, THE BLACK FOREST, FRANKFURT, LOS ANGELES, NEW YORK CITY

We began our German leg in Bremen. The city had a weight to it, a stateliness. It made me want to square my shoulders, cross my legs at the ankles every time I sat. In the market square, there was a statue of animals standing atop one another, the Town Musicians of Bremen, a story from the Brothers Grimm. This was where the stories had been born.

We performed there for a week. The audience was unfailingly polite. They helped us to dismantle the cottage, but they did it civilly, stacking the wood as they went. Most nights, afterward, they insisted on buying us drinks at a rathskeller, which kept its wine in enormous barrels. Our week overlapped with the Freimarkt, a fun fair, and on our one night off, we went there, sharing gingerbread hearts and candy apples the size of clenched fists. Rosa and I rode a Ferris wheel. The city unfurled like a scroll beneath us. She kissed me and put her hand into the waistband of my skirt, and I gave myself to her, my mouth against her neck, so far above the town. When we came back to earth, Rosa had tears in her eyes. I did not ask her why.

The next stop, several hours south and west, was Düsseldorf. Bill raced the van on the autobahn, howling out the window like a wolf. The wind rattled the lumber on the roof, but somehow the cords held on. It was crowded inside. Zion sat on Suzanne's lap, Faye draped herself across Jan and Jorge both. The radio didn't work, so we sang instead, the Beatles, Big Brother and the Holding Company, the Mamas & the Papas, the Doors. Rosa had a bag of jelly bears. She slipped some to me and some to the boy as we drove on.

Düsseldorf was more modern than Bremen, a city where glass and metal jostled against stone. It was wealthier, too. Money was everywhere here, scenting the air, burnishing the furs the women wore. As a girl, I'd felt envious of furs like those. Now I'd learned disgust. What had died so that these women could cover their shoulders in its skin? What blood, what pain had gone into the coat's making?

Carnival began while we were there, and one morning, we all trooped out to the town square to watch a man climb out of a mustard jar. There were processions through the streets, puppets, cartwheelers, the whole town playing pretend. As I remember it, we ate nothing but beef and cabbage there, everything savory and sour. JoAnn must have starved. The Düsseldorf audience was hungrier, more appetitive. They tore apart the cottage with exacting glee. I looked at some of the men then, the older ones, these red-faced bankers and telecom magnates. They seemed practiced at pulling things to pieces.

One night, one of those men forced himself on Rosa. I did not see it, lost in the forest of other bodies. But I heard a cry and scrambled to my feet, my body primed for calamity. I did not think. I only ran, toward Rosa, toward the danger. Rosa had drawn her knife, which she must have carried in her costume, across the man's ankle. Blood was trickling through his sock, dotting the stage floor like drops of rain. He said something in German that I didn't understand. And then, in English, "Crazy bitch!"

I stood next to Rosa, thigh to thigh. I thought that the others might join me. They did not. Peter went to the man instead, Suzanne to a woman who must have been his wife. "He's a pig," Rosa said. "Put his hand up my panties. Hurt me." She was still holding the knife. I took it from her. It was warm in my hand and heavy. Someone cut the music and brought the lights back up. The crowd straightened ties and fetched coats and dispersed in an orderly way. The injured man and his wife departed with them. Peter, his hands in prayer, his face a mask of contrition, escorted them to the street.

When he returned, he was in conversation with the theater manager. Karl? Klaus? The manager looked stern, his chin outthrust. We were scheduled to perform for several more nights, but I sensed that we were through here. Peter confirmed this. The man, he said, had agreed not to contact the police. But he might change his mind. We would have to leave.

"Oh yeah?" Rosa said. She was barefoot, the skirt of her costume still rucked around her thighs. "What if I wanna contact the goddamn police?"

"You want that, Rosa?" Peter said. "You want to talk to the cops?"

Her spirit sagged, went limp. "That son of a bitch hurt me," she said, quietly now. Her lipstick was smeared, and those lips, I saw, were trembling. "I told him and he just went and did it more."

"Maybe he didn't speak much English," Peter said.

"Spoke it good enough with you," Rosa said. She blinked and held the blink too long. Her eyes were wet. "And you don't need grammar or nothing to know you're hurting someone. Thought it'd be different here. You said so. Wouldn't have to do nothing I didn't want. Wouldn't have to go with nobody unless I said so. But it's all the same shit, everywhere, anywhere, and you don't give one good goddamn."

"Of course we do," Suzanne said. "But there are limits. There are rules. You can't just stab somebody."

Peter talked over her. "We can't have the cops involved, all right? German cops, especially. I'm done with being arrested. I'm too old for that shit now. For the rest of the tour, anyone goes too far at the end with any of you, you yell, okay? Loud as you can. We'll come and work it out. But no violence, okay? No knives. Are we cool?"

That seemed to end it. But later, as we packed the props and costumes and tied up the wood with cords, I saw Peter take Rosa aside. Her back was to the wall, and he had his hands on either side of her head, a threat and a come-on all jumbled up together.

"What did he want?" I said.

She was stowing our makeup, not meeting my eyes. "To tell me how goddamn special I am. How he needs me. How he couldn't do the show without me there. Afraid I'll leave."

"Will you leave?"

She shook her head, too hard. "Nah," she said. "I can take it."

"Here," I said. I returned the knife to her. She stowed it in her purse.

I don't know that I believed her. But I did believe Peter. He needed her. He needed me. The young bodies, the boys and girls, we kept the people coming. He would use us until the work, his gift, had swallowed us whole, eaten up everything inside us that was good and rich and striving.

There was no party that night. We slunk back to our rooms in the rain. Rosa slept at the edge of the bed with her back to me. Her sleep was restless. She muttered, moaned, kicked. I wondered, for the first time, what had happened to the boyfriend she mentioned back in Manhattan, the one who had beaten her. I wondered how many men had hurt her and what she had done when hurt. I knew what I had done to one man. I was glad I had no knife.

The next morning, we staggered downstairs to the breakfast room, some of us dressed, others still in their nightclothes. We ate thick slices of bread spread with butter and topped with golden cheese, drank terrible coffee from an urn. The boy was there, toying with his crusts, but Peter wasn't with him—neither was Suzanne—and I worried that the police had come for them after all. That they would come for Rosa, come for me. But Peter and Suzanne were soon back, hearty and red-cheeked. They had a surprise for us, they said.

We now had several days before we were due in Frankfurt. We would drive there that very day, Peter said, to drop the trunks at the theater, and then, for the weekend, we would visit the Black Forest, where so many of the Grimm stories were set. It would deepen the work, Peter said. The darkness, the sex, we would feel it all around us.

The others seemed excited. And I suppose I was excited, too. How far could we take the show? With forest dirt under our fingernails, with leaves in our hair, how real could we make it? We packed our cases, and within an hour, we were on the highway again.

We brought the cases to the theater in Frankfurt, a city of tall buildings that seemed more American than any town we'd visited so far. We wandered its streets, walked along its river, spent the night in a budget hotel whose rooms had orange carpets the color of vomit and walls so thin I could have kicked through them barefoot. In the morning, we drove into the forest.

It was November then. The red and yellow leaves had already spiraled down into the dirt. But the forest, I saw through the van's window, was mostly fir and spruce, a rich mineral green that deepened to black in the shadows. We stopped for lunch in a town known for its giant cuckoo clock and spent an hour strolling the lanes and main square, sipped foamy beer in a tavern. Under the table, Rosa held my hand.

We drove on, on smaller roads now, to the place Suzanne had booked, a recommendation from a friend in Berlin. The inn looked as though a child had drawn it, a white stucco square on the bottom with a brown oak triangle plunked on top. There was a small lobby and a smaller dining room. The floors were wood, the ceilings and walls were wood. Whole copses must have been hewn, milled, sanded just to make this one chalet. Rosa and I were given a room on the top floor, to be shared with Faye. It sloped steeply on one side, echoing the curve of the ceiling. If I sat up from bed too quickly, I would have hit my head. Jorge, Jan, and Bash had the room's twin. The couples were on another floor. Our room led to a balcony. Flower boxes hung from a railing, though this far into the fall, they held only dirt and shriveled roots. Beyond the balcony was a meadow, and beyond the meadow was the forest.

Excepting staccato glimpses as the van raced by, I had never seen a forest before, not properly. Our family had taken holidays at the beach or in the desert. In Ireland, we had kept to towns. Here, as the late-afternoon sun spent itself across the hilltops, I saw a dozen shades of green. A hundred. More. I wanted to be out among them, the carpet of needles buoying my steps, the branches grazing my arms. I wanted, for the moment, to be wild. Instead, I heard JoAnn on the stairs, puffing as she climbed. She was calling us to dinner.

The next morning, after a breakfast of coffee and buttered health bread so dry and dense I could barely chew it, Rosa and I went out together. Within moments, the forest had swallowed us and we were flashing through the shadows, running in our wooden shoes. We slowed, panting. I faced her, let my coat slide down past my shoulders, kicked away my shoes, removed my tights, and stood there waiting. This wasn't like me. And how she came to me, that wasn't like Rosa either. She was so hungry then. So needy. Sex had always been a game to her. She liked to see what she could make me feel, what she could make me do. But the way she kissed me that morning, up against a leafless tree, she seemed like she would die, stop breathing then and there, if I took my mouth from hers.

Later, we wandered back to the inn, our cheeks red circles, like the porcelain figurines I had seen in the shops. After lunch, Peter urged us outside again. We would do the show, he said. Without costumes, without props, in these same woods where the stories had been set. We would take the forest into our bodies, let it guide us.

"Be the dirt, man, be the trees," Peter said.

"Paint it black, my darlings," Bash murmured.

We went into the woods, Suzanne holding her child by the hand. One clearing was found and then another and a bit of flat ground beside the pond. There was no lumber to make the cottage, but we brought what we could find—sticks, fronds, pine cones, bits of bark. Jan, who had a genius for building, arranged it into a loose, leaning structure, a house for some wood spirit. Then we began.

Months into the tour, I had become accustomed to the lights, the music, the crown I wore as the princess. None of that was offered now.

None was needed. The play became a ritual, a dance. Between me and Rosa, in our scene together, I felt the pull of a golden thread, joining us completely. I do not think of that day, not ever, not if I can help it. But sometimes when the autumn sun hits the Valley's hills, I am returned to that gilt afternoon. It is the last time I was whole, the last time I thought that something true might live in me.

That night, Jan and Bill made a fire in the pit outside the lodge, and we sat around it drinking beer and roasting sausages on sticks—except for JoAnn, who had only bread. A joint was passed around. Bill claimed he'd hidden it in a box of loose tea back in New York. "Tea for tea, you get it, man," he laughed. And Peter didn't think to scold him. We were exhausted, but it was a sweet exhaustion, as though we had spent a day at the beach, sun-warmed, or a night in the arms of some new lover. We would do the piece for audiences many more times—at least, this is what we believed—but the afternoon had been for us alone.

At some point, JoAnn noticed that Faye had gone. Suzanne stayed with the boy, while the rest of us left the comfort of the fire and went back into the forest. We called and called, and finally, in the silence between calls, we heard a low squelching sound. It was coming from the pond. Faye was there, still in her clothes, the water rippling above her breasts. Had the pond been any deeper, she would have drowned. Which is what she may have wanted. Jan and Jorge went and pulled her out. The water fell from her like rope, and she was singing to herself, high and keening, though I couldn't place the tune. We took her inside and stripped her, stripped Jan and Jorge, too, and dried them with the towels that the innkeeper's wife grudgingly supplied. Then we dressed Faye again and put her to bed. JoAnn cuddled against her to keep her warm.

"Why'd you do it, Faye?" JoAnn said into Faye's hair.

"Ask the birds, honey," Faye said. "Ask the birds."

I thought I knew why she had done it. Because it would never be so perfect again.

When Rosa came into bed, she was shaking.

"What is it?" I whispered.

"Dunno," she said. She turned on her side, away from me. "Just took it funny. Her in the water." She slithered down into the blankets and pulled them tight over both of us. "Like it can come and find you anywhere."

"What?" I said. "What can find you?" She didn't answer me.

It rained the next day. We stayed inside, trading what few books and magazines we had, playing cards. Faye seemed to have caught a cold, and she spent the day under a blanket, near the fire, smiling wanly as the innkeeper's wife, tender now, brought her hot, medicinal drinks. After lunch, I took Rosa aside and whispered that we should go upstairs. She shook my hand away and dealt the cards for solitaire. That night, she went to bed before I did and was asleep, or pretending sleep, when I climbed beneath the sheets. But she seemed brighter as we drove back to the city the next day, singing along to songs in her ragged, hooting voice.

In Frankfurt, we were briefly famous. By our third performance, in the red-walled theater just a few blocks from the river, we had become a phenomenon. There were lines around the block to see us, and the last scene was made a joy, a gentle riot. It was just like the old days, JoAnn told us as she changed out of her costume. After that fourth performance, once the stars from the flashout faded, I was hefted onto the shoulders of some burly German man and paraded down the street, singing songs I did not know the words to. Out of the corner of my eye, I saw Rosa in her red dress, also held aloft. Her eyes were dark and shining.

A reporter came the next day. A polite young woman, in a burgundy sweater and sensible lace-up flats, her hair held back in shell barrettes. She interviewed us, in clipped and perfect English, about the show. Peter did nearly all the talking, while JoAnn interjected. A photographer was there, too, a small man in cowboy boots and flared jeans. He sat us for a group portrait on the theater's stage, then had us mime scenes from the play, his camera click-click-clicking as we moved. After the show that night, there was a surprise back at our rooms, a feast: sausages, cheeses, a sponge cake iced in buttercream and filled with cherry jam, and bottle after bottle of sweet and sparkling wine. It was, Suzanne said, with her arm around Peter's neck, Thanksgiving. And we had, she said, so much to be thankful for. We were to go to Munich soon, then to Italy, with a stop in Salzburg on the way. I was eager for Italy. Italy at Christmastime. I dreamed of eating ice cream there, throwing coins into the fountains, running up the Spanish Steps with Rosa's hand in mine.

The article ran in the weekend edition of the general newspaper. The main illustration was that photo of me, in my slip, before the lights. The article told the police just where to find us.

At the close of our Tuesday show, as we emerged in our street clothes, purses swinging, men were waiting in the lobby. Two of them were German and in uniform. The third was English, yet he was different from the London officers who had arrested us at the college, more human somehow, with brown curls gone to gray and circles beneath both eyes, purple like the dusk. His hat was dented, and his overcoat had lost a button, the threads hanging loose in the place where the button had been. He had traveled far to meet us.

His name, he said, in an accent that was almost musical, was Inspector Jones, which sounded funny to me, a name out of a book. He wanted to speak to us about one Abraham Simmons. That name was not so funny.

"Abraham who?" Peter said, trying to make out that he didn't know him.

"Abraham Simmons, sir. A film and theatrical producer," the inspector said. "You're Peter Murray, are you not? And you were at his house, I believe?"

It must have seemed useless to deny it.

"Oh yeah," Peter said. "That Abraham."

"Yes, that Abraham. And you must know that he is dead."

"Yeah, man," Peter said. He shifted his weight from one foot to another. "A bummer, right? Heart gave out is what we heard."

The inspector stared back at him. Peter shifted.

"Not exactly, sir. Mr. Simmons, he was rather a prominent person in certain circles. Circles known to me and my sort, you might say. A man like that, dying in his bed—well, we had to be certain. So the coroner, he ordered an examination. And would you like to guess just what he found?"

No one spoke.

"It was rather a lot of heroin, I'm afraid."

"Yeah?" JoAnn said, stepping forward, arms crossed. "So he had a habit. Nothing to do with us."

"Well, madam, as strange as it may seem, he does not appear to have had a habit."

Bill joined her. "So what? Junk can kill you anytime. First time. Hundredth time."

"Indeed, sir. But what's really so odd, the heroin, that's not what's killed him. The clever men, the pathologists, they're really very good. They went and worked his blood, made all their tests. Seems he was dead already before the lot of it went in."

I went cold then. Ice. I didn't dare to look at Rosa.

Thankfully, Suzanne pushed past us, hands on hips. "You arresting my husband?" she said. "You think he killed somebody? Or maybe it was all of us? You going to take us all in?"

"It needn't come to that," the inspector said. "But there are some conversations I must insist on, Mrs. Murray."

"It's Ms. Gold. Thank you very much. And you can have all the conversations you want, long as you get us a lawyer."

"My apologies, madam. I'm sure a lawyer won't be—"

She cut him off, a finger to his face. "Nuh-uh. My father, he taught me a thing or two. Making theater for twenty years, that's taught me more. No lawyer, no conversation. I'm sure the laws are different here, but not so different. You want to talk, that's the deal." Suzanne's hair was a crown of fire, her eyes twin coals. I couldn't imagine any man defying her. The inspector must have felt the same.

"Very well," he said. "I'm not sure we can rummage one, an English-speaking one, at such a time of night. So we'll make an appointment for the morning, shall we? Ten o'clock, perhaps? At the station." He turned to one of the officers. "The address?"

"Friedrich-Ebert-Anlage," the officer said.

"Friedrich-Ebert-Anlage," Suzanne repeated. "Fine. It's a date. Might even shave my legs." She moved to gather her things. We all did.

"But there is one thing more," the inspector said.

"Oh yeah?" Suzanne challenged him.

"I'm sure you're as good as your word, madam, but it does happen that some people, they don't particularly wish to speak with me. They do a runner, as we call it. I do try not to take it personal, madam, and I'm sure you wouldn't dream, but I'd rather I kept your passport, madam. Yours and your husband's both."

"You can't do that," Peter said.

The officer only shook his head. "I'm afraid I can, sir. Yes, I'm sure of it. But if you prefer not, I can take you in now. There are beds enough at the station. Not so comfortable as what you are used to, perhaps, but beds all the same."

"It's fine," Suzanne said, choosing for us all. "Just let him." She turned to the inspector. "But I want receipts. Got it?"

"Of course, madam. As you wish, madam."

"Then you can follow us back to our rooms. I left mine there."

"Do you want mine as well, darling?" Bash drawled. "It has such lovely stamps."

The officer looked mildly perturbed. "Erm, no, sir," he said. "We needn't trouble the whole of the company, just so long as you all agree to report tomorrow."

This meant that the officer was not yet interested in me, in Rosa. We were for the moment safe. I dared a look at Rosa then, but she would not meet my eye.

We must have made a strange parade, the inspector in the middle and the officers at the back, as we walked across the bridge, the Main seething below, and over to the boardinghouse. I saw the boy tug at Suzanne's sleeve as we passed the brick face of the apple wine tavern where we often stopped after shows. She shook him off. We walked on. Suzanne used her key to let us into the building, the scowling manager having already gone to her bed. Bash flicked on the light. It cast sickly shadows.

Suzanne went upstairs and then came back down again. She slapped two booklets into the inspector's hand, hers and Peter's. "You want the boy's, too?" she said. "You afraid of a child?"

The inspector thinned his lips. "No," he said. "I think not."

"You will have mine also," Jorge said softly. He took it from a pocket of his coat, green with gold lettering. "If you are to come for the one of us, then you come for us all."

But no one else moved to tender theirs.

"Very good, sir," the officer said. He turned his back to us while he scribbled a receipt. Then he and the German men departed. I watched them go, their backs broad, their step firm. The door banged shut, and I let out the breath I hadn't realized I held. The room warmed then. A bottle of red wine was found and passed around, though I did not drink any. I did not know what would come next. But I sensed that I would need a clear head.

"So what do we do?" JoAnn asked.

"We do what we always do," Peter said. The wine had returned some color to him. "We go in tomorrow. We tell him what we know. That scumbag, he overdosed. An accident. Nothing you could do. Isn't that right, girls?"

I nodded. Rosa must have nodded, too.

"So this isn't on us. Okay? Don't care what their fuckin' doctors say."

"Do we tell them of the movie?" Jan asked. "Do we tell the truth of that?"

"No!" Peter said. He waved his arm. Wine sloshed from the bottle onto the carpet. "Fuck do you think? Not unless they know already. Not unless they ask. Otherwise, just tell the rest. He had us over. We stayed a couple of days. He had a little party with the girls. Party went wrong. You got that, everyone? You got that, girls?"

He was looking at me. The wine had stained his lips red. Then he was looking past me, toward the door. Rosa had leaped up, run through it. Unthinking, I ran, too, out onto the street, around the corner. The night was cold. Drizzle fell like needles on my skin. I watched her jacket, the mirror of mine, flapping behind her as she raced. I raced after. My lungs were in my throat, my tongue tasted metal, my legs pulsed to the beating of my heart, fast, then faster.

I caught her halfway across the bridge, my hands in her hair as we tumbled to the ground, just out of the way of the cars.

"Where do you think you're going?" I said. It was dark on the bridge. The lamp above us had blown its bulb. But my cheeks, I knew, were crimson. I was angry with her then. For making a spectacle of herself. For making the rest of them mistrust us.

"Don't know," she said. Her voice was in tatters. "Don't know, okay? I just had to get outta there!"

I shook my head. "How do you think that looks? You running away like that?" I pushed myself to standing, brushed down my skirt. My tights had torn. "We do what Peter said, all right? We tell them

our story. Two girls our size. A man like that? They'll have to believe us."

Rosa's hand shot out and gripped my wrist to pull herself up. Somehow,
the touch revolted me. I staggered back into the railing, then caught myself.
The railing was not high. She was standing now, and I saw that beneath her
coat she wore the blue skirt I had given her that first day.

"Oh yeah, sunshine?" she said. She spat grit from her mouth. "That
what you think? Those men, those cops, they'll believe anything they
want. Been believing things about me since the boys made a train in
junior goddamn high school, since before. Me, I'm not like you. Can't
play innocent, okay? Never been innocent. Never had a chance. And two
girls like us? Turns out, we can do a lot."

She was close to me. I could smell her animal scent, like high meat.
But I was animal now, too. Maybe I had always been this way.

"So what are you going to do, then?" I said. My thoughts were speeding, blurring. "Are you running to the police? What are you going to tell
them? That I did it?"

For a long time, I told myself that this next part was her fault, that
she reached for the knife first, that I had no choice. But I have promised
to tell the truth. And the truth is that I have never been the girl in this
story. I have always been the wolf. Or the girl and the wolf both. Whatever has been done to me, I have done worse.

That night, on the bridge, where no light fell, Rosa stared at me. Her
eyes were wide, panicked, like some skittering prey animal. "You *did* do
it, Alice," she said. She would, I knew, betray me.

I kissed her then, my lips on hers, and in the surprise of that kiss,
I reached for the purse that hung between us and tore it from her. In
seconds, the knife was in my hand. I flicked it open. Rosa backed away.
She was at the railing now. Over her shoulder, I could see the bridge's
filigreed cross, topped with its golden rooster.

"What are you doing?" she said. "What do you think—"

But by then, my arm had plunged forward, through her sweater and into the skin beneath. I was blessed that night, lucky. No cars came by, no trams. And that dull knife struck true, clear of any bone. Even Abraham had not taught me how dense a body is, how solid. I learned it then. Her flesh resisted. But I was strong. Stronger than I have ever been. I drove the blade in up to the hilt. I do not know that I meant to do it, not in any conscious way. I was an animal, with an animal's instincts. Rosa only looked at me, her mouth gaping. Blood bubbled at her lips, or maybe I imagined it. Bracing myself on her collar, I tugged the knife free. Then with both hands, I pushed her over the railing. Rosa, who could not swim.

The charm held. In the rain, the body made barely a splash. I saw it float for a moment, before her coat and shoes dragged it down. I swiped the knife on the inside of my skirt, cleansing it of blood, of the marks from my chilled fingers. I dropped it in after. There was a man beside me then, young in a leather jacket, a spray of pimples across his chin. I thought for a moment that he had seen it all. But no, he held himself too still for that. He said something to me in German, which I did not understand. Then again, in halting English: "Do you lose something?"

"No," I said. "Or yes?" There was a crazed impulse to laugh. Because what had I not lost, not surrendered?

He shook his head, uncomprehending, then handed me the discarded purse, Rosa's purse, white with red cherries. I took it. I ran. Sliding on the wet cement, falling, then righting myself and running again. I did not breathe, I did not think. But my body knew the way. It took me to the apple wine tavern, where I slowed, finally. My hands were shaking. And they were freckled with blood, the right especially. I wiped them clean. Then I opened the purse. Her money was there. I put it in my bra. The purse I hid at the bottom of a pail of food scraps in the tavern's alley, then walked the rest of the way to the rooming house. The rain had stopped, but I was wet through.

As the adrenaline eased, my mind righted. Nausea seized me. Rosa, I now understood, with a scorching kind of clarity, would not have turned me in. Rosa hated the police. She would never have gone to them will-ingly, never have put herself in their power. And even if she had gone, she was a girl from the streets, and I had been, until very recently, a coed from what people would have called a good home. No one would have taken her word over mine. She was no threat to me. But she had made me afraid. And when I was afraid, I did terrible things. I lied, I stole. Now I had killed. Not once, but twice. That horrible man and then this girl I nearly loved. What is more, I had done these things quickly, unthink-ingly. It had been easy. The world went white for me then.

When I came to, I was ringing the bell, beating on the door. I half fell when Faye pulled it open, staggering into the sitting room where the others were still gathered, my feet leaving damp patches on the carpet. I did not know how long I had been away. Minutes. Hours.

"It's Rosa," I said. "Rosa. She's gone. She's . . . she's run away. I—" I swallowed, fumbling for my next invention.

"But why would she do that?" JoAnn said.

I looked at her. "You know why," I said. The words, the lies came fluently. "You heard what the inspector said, that the drugs didn't kill Abraham. He's right. That night, in London, he attacked Rosa. I don't think she meant to kill him. I wouldn't have thought she was strong enough. But she did. A pillow to his face, she said. She came and found me after, told me what she'd done, that we had to make it look like an accident. I told her we should just go to the police. That she could say it was in self-defense. But she wouldn't. Said nobody would believe a girl like her. She made me help her. She said I had to, if I loved her. We took off his shirt, Rosa and me. Rosa had powder, a needle. She put the drug inside him, so it would look like an accident. I'm sorry. I'm so sorry. I didn't know what else to do. And now she's gone."

"Holy fuck," Peter said. He began to pound his hand against the wall of the sitting room, just as he'd done in that lounge in London. The wall was brick. His knuckles bled. "I knew it. I fucking knew it. That stupid bitch. That stupid, stupid slut."

Suzanne took his bleeding hand in hers; she did not do it tenderly. "Stop it," she said. "Not so loud."

"Why didn't you tell me all this before, Alice?" Peter said.

"I couldn't," I said, voice trembling. "I was afraid."

"Afraid of fucking what?" Peter said, his lips thin. "Didn't think you were such a baby, Alice."

"Nah," JoAnn said. "This is on you, Peter. You and your fucking girls."

That Rosa," Bill said. "She's a liar, yeah, a whore."

"You stop that," Faye said. "The poor thing. Killing that man. I'm sure she didn't mean to do it."

"I don't know if that matters," Bash said. "Not to men like our inspector. Well, my darlings, what's to be done?"

Suzanne stood up. "I'll call my father now," she said. "Fuck knows what he'll say this time. But he'll know what to do. Him or his lawyer."

"And I'll go look for her," Peter said. "Come with me, Bill. Maybe we can find her before the cops do. Fuck knows what that bitch'll say if she's trying to save her own skin."

They left. Suzanne went to the telephone in the hall. When she came back, she seemed deflated, like a party balloon with a leak. "My father, he says to wait for now. To go to the station in the morning like we planned. Maybe Peter will find her, or maybe she'll come back on her own. And if not. . . ." She threw up her hands, reaching for the sky and falling short.

Jorge pointed upstairs. "Her suitcase. Her things. We should look there, yes? These drugs, we do not want the police to find them."

"All right," Suzanne said. "Yeah. Go on."

"I'll get it," I said, desperate now to move. "Her case looks just like mine."

I went upstairs, stopping in the bathroom for a thin towel. I did not meet my eyes in the mirror, though I checked my hands again. They were clean. I picked up Rosa's case and took it to the front room, then set to drying my hair.

Jan began. He was careful of his fingerprints. With his hand inside his shirtsleeve, he clicked the latches and pried the case open. "Does anyone have a stick?" he said. "A rod of a kind?"

JoAnn gave him a pencil from her purse. With the pencil, he began to prod, moving aside clothes and underthings. He found the silver case, the gift from Bram. A few orange pills were still inside. He also found the leather wallet with its fresh needle. He ignored the talcum canister. It was too intimate, too white and pink. "There is no more," he said finally. He nudged the pill box. "The police, we may give them this."

"Shouldn't we try to do something for her?" Faye said. "She's had it hard, anyone can tell."

"We've all had it hard," Suzanne said. "And she's just made it fucking harder for everyone else. She killed a man, Faye. We can't help her now. We can only help ourselves."

We sat there in the living room, for an hour, two, waiting for Peter and Bill. I knew they would not find her, not alive. And not dead either. Not so soon. But still, the waiting was an agony. They returned wet, despairing. Faye brought towels, but Peter hardly bothered. "Go to bed," he growled. "The police haven't come for us yet. That's something. So go and get some sleep. God knows what the morning's gonna look like."

Upstairs, I sat huddled in the bed in my damp clothes. Not moving, barely breathing. For a long time, I heard rustling, creaking, whispered conversation. Finally, the noises ceased. I levered myself from the bed, an inch at a time, and tiptoed to my purse. The moon was bright, or bright enough, to guide me. I found a pen, a scrap of paper, and I wrote a note. It said that I was sorry. It said that I was frightened. It said that I was going to the airport, that I would take the first flight home. It said to please forgive me.

I stole out of the room then—my shoes in one hand, a purse with my passport and money, mine and Rosa's, over my shoulder—and down the carpeted stairs. I did not risk my case or my wet coat; these would have slowed me. There was a lit lamp in the sitting room, and movement, a shifting of shadows. I nearly screamed, but it was only Suzanne's boy, jet-lagged still, playing with a doll that Faye had bought him. He saw me, and I lifted a finger to my lips. He nodded, and did the same, mirroring me. Then I was out the door.

The street was dark, deserted. It should have scared me. A young girl, in a strange city, alone. But I knew what I had done. What I might do. Knife or no. Careless of the cold, I jogged up one street and down the next, the pavement and stone vanishing under me, until I came to the boulevard. There was one taxi there, painted a sickly cream, like spoiled milk.

I did not tell the driver to take me to the airport. At the airport, I might be found. I would do the finding first.

"Police," I told the driver as I slid in. "*Polizei*. Friedrich-Ebert." The car started. I shut my eyes, clasped my hands in my lap, feeling the rough wool of the skirt. The texture returned a memory to me: the bloodied knife, my bloodied hands, the white nylon lining. I reached under my skirt and ripped away that lining, shoving it far beneath the seat in front of me when I saw the driver preparing for a turn. To think that I might have walked into that station, wearing Rosa's blood.

It must have been very late by the time I arrived, close, perhaps, to dawn. The station's entrance was grand, like the lobby of some fine hotel. I asked for the inspector, but he was away, asleep. They sent someone to summon him. A different officer took me to a windowless room: a square table, three mismatched chairs. I was cold then, shivering. A blanket was brought to me. I draped it around my shoulders. And still, I could not make myself warm. Before long, the inspector joined me. I sat opposite him, demurely, knees together. I told him what had been done to Abraham that night—that Rosa had killed him when he forced himself on her, that she had made it appear an accident. It was a lie, of course, but I told it simply, with true feeling. Did the rest of the troupe know what she had done? he asked me. Yes, I told him, of course. But they'd had trouble with the police before. They had encouraged me to lie, to deny it all. I would not lie, I told him. It was not right. And as for Rosa, Rosa, I told him, had run away.

He asked for her description, and I gave it, hazarding that they wouldn't think to look in the river, that the clothes and boots would keep her from the surface, for a while anyway. He left me then. I watched him closely when he returned. I wanted to see compassion in his eyes, some fatherly feeling. But his gaze, it seemed to me, was wary.

So I made myself look young, ducking my chin, narrowing my lips, smoothing my hair with busy, worried hands. "There is more that I could tell you," I said.

He leaned closer to me. "Could you now?"

I nodded. A child's nod. "I could tell you where Rosa kept . . . what it was she gave him. And I could tell you about the company. I thought they were so wonderful at first. I thought that if I joined them, my life would be wonderful, too. It hasn't been like that at all." I lifted my eyes to his. "I just want to go home. I want to see my parents. If I tell you everything, all of it, will you let me just go home?"

This finally was what it took—the threat of discovery, of prison, of reckoning with what I was—to restore me to my father's house. Finally, the choice was easy. If only the inspector would let me make it.

"We might do," he said. "Yes. We might at that. Go on."

I told him of the tour, a version, false and true, of what we had been made to do in the show and in the movie Abraham had made. My telling made it worse. Though when I think back on those bodies, on those hands, maybe it was already very bad. My tale meant that a charge of obscenity might stick this time. Even one of prostitution. My story damned Rosa, freighted her with murder. But Rosa of course would not be found alive. What would they think when they dredged her from the river? That she had killed herself? That someone from the company had done it? But the inspector thought me innocent, helpless. I would not be blamed.

There were tears. Many. The inspector gave me a handkerchief and patted my hand and told me that I was a good girl, very good, then went to confer with the German officers. A policewoman, in a yellow blouse and a long green skirt, brought me coffee and a plate of cookies with ruffled edges.

"They're going now," the inspector said when he came back, "the local police, to see what they can find. I'm afraid I can't let you leave, not yet. But I could put you in a cell, if you'd like. You might get a bit of sleep."

I shook my head. I couldn't bear the thought of bars.

"As you like," he said. "Wait here."

I think I must have slept, my head pillowed on my arms. The inspector startled me awake. His cheeks were pink. He looked for the moment like a boy. They had found the talcum container just as I'd said. A search was on for Rosa. The others were being brought to the station. I would like to say I felt regret then, for Faye, who had shown me kindness, for JoAnn and the baby inside her. But this was the exchange that I made. These other lives, traded for my own.

"I won't have to see them, will I?" I said.

"No," he said. "No. I'll see to that."

"Can I go, then?" I said. "Can I call my parents?"

I could call, he told me. But it was the middle of the night in much of America, was it not? Should I not perhaps wait? I agreed, though it pained me. I was racing the hours now. But I didn't dare to question him. I had made him a father to me. I would do what Father said. He told me that he had taken it upon himself to phone the Amerika Haus. I would be brought there as soon as my evidence was typed. The consulate would see to my transport home.

"Thank you," I said. "Thank you so much." I shed tears as I said it. I believe those tears were real.

He told me I might have to return for a trial, here or in England. I told him that I would, though later a lawyer, some acquaintance of my father's, would explain to the officials that I was too weak, too distressed to testify, and the trials would be held without me. There, in the station, I gave my story again while the policewoman scribbled in her pad, then waited, sitting upright, until the typed report was brought to me. I signed it in a child's hand, in my own right name. I had not written that name in months. It looked so odd to me.

It was afternoon when the same policewoman, now in a green coat and hat, came for me. As we were leaving the building, I thought I saw Jorge down the hall, but then I was out the door and into a waiting car that sped me through the city. There was hot food at the consulate, and the Americans there were kind. They pitied me, treating me like a figurine that would break if jostled. A woman on the staff, slim and competent in a trim bob, was assigned to me. In the early evening, she telephoned my parents, speaking in low tones. She said that I was in Germany, that I had been a victim of bad people ("bad actors," she called them, and if I had not been so distressed, I think I might have laughed), that there had been wrong done against me. She told them that I had aided the police in their inquiries, that I was being sent home with their thanks. Then it was my turn to speak.

"Hello?" I said, hoping to hear my mother's voice.

It must have been the weekend or before working hours. Because it was my father on the line. He was angry, I could hear it even through the buzz and sputter of the receiver.

"What were you thinking, Allison? Running off to God knows where. Getting involved with God knows who. A theater troupe? Perverts more like it. Trash. Told us you were away studying. Studying what, huh? How to be a degenerate?" But then his bluster softened. "What'd they do you, these people?"

"Oh, Daddy," I said. "Please don't make me say it." My father did not force me. He had a story that he understood: a girl, an idiot, seduced. "I'm so sorry," I said, sniffling into the receiver.

He put my mother on the phone.

My father must have relayed the story, because my mother, too, was crying. Out of pain or worry, I did not know. She asked me if I was all right, if I was eating. She told me that she had prayed for me and asked if I would come to Mass and receive Communion. She still had hope that the God she loved would comfort me. She did not know that I had given up on gods.

"And happy birthday, lamb," she said, through her tears. "Happy, happy birthday."

I had forgotten that it was my birthday. I could not believe that I was only twenty.

I spent two more days at the embassy, hours that are mostly lost to me. I know my clothes were washed and that I was given other clothes to wear. Food was brought to me, bland and hearty. I ate it. Did I read? Did I play cards? I can't recall. My mind was busy, blurred. How far would the river carry Rosa? When would she be found? Or maybe Rosa was alive. Maybe the wound had been shallower than I'd thought, the river slow and forgiving. Could she have waded back to the shore? Could she yet come and find me? I thought of her like that—sodden, bloody, staggering up and down the Frankfurt streets. So I emptied myself of thought. The workers at the embassy must have thought I was subnormal, a girl half-formed, a girl defiled. I had a new role, the victim of the piece. I played it.

On the third day, I was packed into a car with that same staff woman and driven to the airport. She checked over my tickets and my passport, then hugged me goodbye. I was stiff in her embrace. I had forgotten that embraces could be innocent, polite.

In the waiting area, I sat, straight-backed, hardly blinking, until my flight was called. I did not believe that I really would get away, not even when the plane had lifted off and out the window were only clouds. The stopover in New York was agonizing. I was still convinced that something would go wrong, that the police would yet come for me. Famished, I bought a package of the sweets that Rosa had loved. It sickened me to eat them, but I couldn't stop. Another flight and I was home that same day. My parents were waiting in the terminal. My mother's face was white. My father's red. What must I have looked like to them, stumbling on my pins-and-needles legs in borrowed clothes, my baby fat all starved away? A lost girl. Someone else's child. I fell on them—hungry for their solidity, their ordinariness. We moved out of the terminal and into the day. The sun was like a stage light. It blinded me.

16

1997, LOS ANGELES

t was never dark at Valley Presbyterian, never quiet. She sat in her mother's hospital room as monitors, beeping and screeching, tallied breath and pulse. Her mother was small in the bed, a hummingbird beneath stiff sheets. A canula was in her nose, a catheter threaded below. Her mother's heart had stopped. An orderly at the facility had restored the rhythm, cracking ribs as he went. (She shuddered when she heard this, reminded of how it had felt to press, again and again, on that inert chest.) Paramedics had then brought her mother to the hospital where surgeons had intervened. Now her mother slept on, unaware, though it was not sleep exactly.

She was tired, from the marrow out. But in the squeaking recliner, under the overhead lights, sleep refused her. They were twins of a sort: a daughter who could not sleep, a mother who would not wake. In the next bed, a large woman with a bandaged neck lay splayed on her back, moaning.

The next day, Sunday, while the nurses ministered to the catheter, she slipped out to the hallway and phoned the school, leaving a message on Ms. Noakes's machine to explain her coming absence. Information then connected her to George, to beg his help with the final *Midsummer* rehearsals. Nervously, George agreed. Out on the loading dock, as ambulances squealed past, she lit a cigarette and inhaled it in rushed breaths. Then she stubbed it out. The taste sickened her. She returned to her mother's bed and took up her hand. The nail beds were tinged with blue.

That night, after a futile conversation with the latest doctor, a nurse came in and shooed her away. Her mother was stable. Visiting hours could be stretched no further. Back in the condo, she stripped off the clothes she had worn since Vermont, took a brief, chill shower, and lay down. But even here, in her own bed, sleep would not come. Every time she shut her eyes, she felt herself falling. Finally, she got up, belted her robe, and went into the kitchen to put the coffee on. Out the window, she watched the silhouettes of palms shiver and sway. What would she do if her mother died? Without that tether, what would she become?

The coffee brewed, she poured herself a cup and took it to the guest room, then powered on the computer she used to type out her lesson plans. Grudgingly, the screen began to glow. The trip to Vermont had brought no answers. Neither had the phone calls. She had wondered, for a moment, on the return flight, if Suzanne had been right, if she had dreamed the messages. But no, she hadn't. Which meant that someone else was still alive, still waiting for her reply. She had no recourse left but memory.

She clicked on the word processing program and opened a new document. The white of it scarred her eyes. She blinked. Blinked again. Then she forced her mind back to when she was just nineteen, a naif, trembling with appetite and expectation. She would record it all. And suddenly, yes, there she was, on the subway in her May Company coat on the way to that first performance. Hours later, as the sun crested the Verdugo Hills, she was still writing, the coffee long cold. She clicked to save the document. After another shower, she made the brief drive to the hospital.

It went on like this. The daylight hours were spent at Valley Presbyterian, in the recliner at her mother's bedside, fortified by yogurts from the cafeteria and gift shop magazines. At night, when the nurses made her go, she sped home, thieved a few hours of sleep, then woke to put the coffee on and write again. She had never typed so quickly, afraid that if she paused to stretch her cramping fingers, memory would recede.

On Thursday, her mother stirred. She had stirred before, grimacing while her mind slept on. This time, the stirring deepened, her mother's mouth opened and shut. She let go of her mother's hand and ran out of the room to the nurses' station.

"She's waking up," she said to a gruff woman in candy-pink scrubs. "She's moving. Please come." She raced back to the room, skidding on the plastic flooring. The nurse trudged behind. Her mother's eyes were open now. But they looked frightened, empty. Croaking sounds rose from her mother's throat. Cries, not words. Her thin arms beat against the sheets.

"Can she have water?" she asked. "Can I bring her water?"

"No," the nurse said sternly. "Not yet."

The nurse stepped out and she was alone with this flailing thing that wore her mother's face, who rasped and panted, who did not know her.

"Mom," she said. "Mom, it's me. It's Allison."

Her mother bared her teeth.

The nurse returned with a doctor. In the presence of this man, her mother quieted, moved a hand to her hair. The doctor shone lights in her mother's eyes and tested reflexes. One leg kicked weakly. Then the other. The nurse proffered an ice chip. Her mother swallowed and said hoarsely, "Where am I?"

"You're in the hospital, Mom," she said. "Valley Presbyterian. There was a problem with your heart. But they fixed it." She turned to the doctor, a child swallowed by his lab coat, acne all along his jawline. "It is fixed, isn't it?"

"We performed an angioplasty," the doctor explained. "Which re-stored blood flow. You should be feeling better in just a little while, Mrs. Hayes."

"Thank you," her mother said, unfailingly polite.

Then her mother's eyes met hers. "And thank you, too," she said. "But forgive me, who are you, please?"

"Mom, it's Allison."

"Allison?" her mother said, blankly. "How nice of you to visit."

In the hall, the nurse told her, curtly, that lapses like these were common, a consequence of the anesthesia and the strange surroundings. Her mother's memory, what was left of it, would return in time. And as the hours wore on, her mother did seem more present and aware. But still she did not recognize her.

She drove fast that night. First to an In-N-Out Burger and then home. On Ventura, just past the 405, one hand on the wheel, the other scrabbling for a french fry, she braked abruptly as an animal ran out into the street. It was a dog. Or no, she saw in the headlights' glare, not a dog, a coyote, wandered down from out of the hills. She looked at the coyote, and the coyote looked at her—two creatures, pretending domesticity. Then it ran into an alley. She drove on, wincing from the bruise the seat belt left.

Her mother was better the next day, better still the next. A rehabilitation center would be necessary, for several weeks, the doctor said, but barring complications, a full recovery seemed likely. Leaving the hospital that night, she said a prayer to her mother's God, thanking him for this rescue. Then she went home, and for the whole of a sleepless night, she wrote the rest of it. The worst parts. The house in North London. The bridge in Frankfurt. The knife. The blood.

She sat back from the computer, massaging her fingers and wrists. Mainly, the work had failed. The thousands of words had not returned to her the person who had sent those messages. But they had returned something else—a full incarnation of the girl she'd remembered at Suzanne and Peter's house. The girl she was. In the intervening years, she had become so careful, so adult, so sober and resolved. But she had never outrun this fevered, hungry girl. She never would. She saved the document, then went to bed and slept like the dead.

When she woke, dry-mouthed and muzzy, it was late afternoon. She dressed hurriedly, in jeans and a sweater, and sped to the hospital. Only an hour or two of visiting remained. Her mother was sitting up in bed, eating Jell-O with a shaky hand, watching a black-and-white movie on the small TV clamped to the ceiling. The room's other bed was empty now. She took the plastic pitcher and poured a cup of water, lifting it to her mother's lips. Her mother grabbed for the cup, wanting to hold it herself. The water spilled all down her mother's gown.

"Oh, I'm so sorry," her mother said.

"That's all right," she said. She found a folded cloth and dabbed at the spill. "It's only water."

"No, Allison."

She startled. Her mother knew her.

"Mom?"

"Shhh. And stop fussing at me. I don't care about the water. That isn't what I mean." Her mother's eyes were clear now, twin pools. "I mean, I'm sorry for it all. Your father. How you grew up. I'm sorry that I couldn't protect you."

"That's okay, Mom," she said, her throat narrowing around the words. They had never spoken of these things. "I learned to protect myself."

"Of course you did," her mother said. "You lied. All the time."

"You knew?"

"Allison, I've always known. You made your own way. You did what you felt you had to. When you ran away like that, the shame of it, it killed your father. That stroke, it was . . . what? A year after you came home? Two?"

"Something like that," she said.

"I found him. Do you remember? In the morning. In his armchair. Eyes open. The cigar burned down. A miracle he didn't set the house on fire. And, Allison, I was glad. Afternoons, when the church was empty, I used to go up to the altar rail and pray that he would die. God, in his goodness, he granted that. Or you did. Your leaving. Your blessed return. You're a liar, Allison. A cheat. You show one face to the world and keep another in your heart. I've wished often enough that you would show me that one. If I don't make it through—"

"You will! The doctor said."

"Shhh. If I don't, know that I love you, the whole of you, that I always have."

"Mom," she said, the cloth limp in her hands. "You don't know what I've done."

"So confess it," her mother said. "Confess in perfect contrition. And be free." Her mother closed her eyes then. They spent the rest of the hour in silence, the recliner pulled up to the bed, her head resting on her mother's brittle shoulder, attuned to the fluttering of her mother's frail heart.

On Monday, before the start of school, she returned again to her classroom. She had left a voicemail for Ms. Noakes, saying that she would teach her morning classes, then head to the hospital at lunchtime. If all went well, she would return for that afternoon's technical rehearsal. They were to hold the dress on Wednesday, with performances on Thursday, Friday, and Saturday.

She pressed the power button on the computer, waited for the screen to rouse. The dial-up shrilled, but after a week of monitors and alarms, its ring was almost comforting. She opened the mail program. There were several new messages, all from the school. HighPoint had not written again. No matter. She crafted a message of her own. An answer of a kind. She was through running.

Do you want my story? she wrote. **Come and take it.**

Leila, the substitute, entered just after she hit Send, yelping when she saw the classroom occupied.

"Oh my God," Leila said. "You scared me."

"I just have that kind of face. And sorry to surprise. I thought Noakes would have called you and explained."

"And your mother . . . ?"

"Mending."

"Oh. Wow," Leila said, a hand to her heart. "That's great to hear.

And just so you know, the kids, they've been sensational. God, they're so funny, some of them. So bright. I stayed after a few days to help George with the rehearsals. The show's really coming together. And the design this year, it's a triumph, really."

She looked at Leila. Her blousy jumpsuit, her smile like a double strand of pearls. The woman seemed entirely sincere. How long had it been since she'd felt that way about her students? Had she ever felt that way? "They're lucky they have you," she said. "I'm going to try to teach this morning and then head back to the hospital before rehearsals. Okay to cover me from fourth period on?"

"Of course! Whatever you need. Price of gas and sushi these days, I'll take all the hours I can get."

She taught her morning classes. The students seem to have missed her; a few lingered after the bell sounded, wanting to tell her about rehearsals. She could feel their awkward sympathy radiating like some diminished chord.

After noon, she went to her car, passing Leila on the walk. Jerome stopped her just as she unlocked the door. "Hey, Mrs. Morales," he said.

"Hello, Jerome."

"You remember, back in October, man left a note for you?"

"Yes, I remember. Why?" She could feel the muscles in her shoulders tensing.

"Think I saw him. Last week, around the campus."

"Really? What did he look like?"

"White man. Not so tall. Brown hair. My age. Could be."

"Got it." A useless description, but it meant that he was near, this man. "I have to go," she said. "But if you see him again, will you try to get something more? Like a name? Or the plate on his car? And will you call me if you do? Try my classroom phone, and here's my home number." She dug in her bag for a pen, then wrote it on the back of a Chevron receipt.

Her mother was asleep when she came in. The gruff nurse took her aside. There was trouble in the lungs, a possible infection. They might need to keep her mother longer. She sat in the recliner, reread a magazine. Eventually, her mother woke, and they had lunch together, her mother picking at the peas on the hospital tray, saying little. After lunch, they watched a game show until her mother fell asleep. She kissed her mother's dry cheek and whispered her goodbye.

She arrived back at school just as the student cars and buses were peeling from the lot. In the theater, she saw that Leila was correct in her enthusiasm. Zay and the students on the tech crew had worked a kind of miracle. The lights were hung and the flats painted, with help from Marta, no doubt, in a dozen shades of green, slashed with pink. Offstage, she could see the wheeled platforms that were to represent the palace and the bower. The technical rehearsal went swiftly. Nearly everyone seemed to know their cues, even Kyle, even Margo, the vending machine heiress she had enlisted as Titania. To close, there were sugar cookies shaped like trees, courtesy of Linda, who claimed to have baked them over a Bunsen burner.

On Wednesday, she entered the dress rehearsal depleted. The infection was confirmed. Her mother was on an antibiotic drip and too weak for conversation. It was cool in the theater and dim beyond the stage's lip. She sat in the orchestra. Naomi, still stung by Yale's deferral, sat near her, frowning and snapping her gum. The play began, with George's arrangement of Mendelssohn's overture for piano and violin. The students said their lines, hit their marks. The costumes, pulled and altered by Eleanor Tibbets, the swan-necked junior history teacher who had a passion for clothes, gleamed under the lights.

They stopped for pizza after act 3, and she watched the students joke and caper as they lifted gooey slices to their lips. She took a slice herself. She was proud of them in this moment. It was a brave thing they did, using words that weren't theirs, lending their bodies to some greater whole. It was clumsy, it was slapdash, but she could let herself admit that it was holy in its way. At the end, when the Rude Mechanicals performed, she was surprised to find herself really laughing. And when Nadine's Puck asked for her hands, she clapped and clapped, then elbowed Naomi to do the same.

"Don't tell me what to do," Naomi said.

She looked at the girl, saw the pain behind her frown. "Go on," she said. "They deserve it. And you helped to make this. You deserve it, too."

Naomi clapped.

The students left. Visiting hours were long over. She detoured briefly to her office and powered on the computer. There were no new messages; no voicemails either. She locked the door. The campus at night felt foreign, spectral. Her steps echoed on the path, some acoustic illusion, and in the close-set sodium lights, she seemed to cast two shadows.

Thursday was opening night. That afternoon, after visiting her mother, who mostly slept, she drove home to shower and to change. The dashboard light blinked and blinked. She ignored it. She put on a white linen shift and a matching blazer, painted her mouth with a matte lipstick she rarely used, red as dawn.

Backstage, all was bustle and excitement. Someone had brought a boom box, and Nadine was teaching the fairies a hip-hop routine that had them circling their hips and squatting down low. Eyeliner was traded back and forth, wreathes and tights adjusted. A few of the students had brought her presents—cards, pharmacy chocolates—and she crumpled for a moment in the face of such kindness, then righted herself and gathered them all together: the cast, the crew, Zay and George, Eleanor and Marta, Naomi scowling with her binder. Nadine's hair was newly braided. Kyle had adorned himself with a second shell necklace. Even Zay had bothered. He was clean-shaven now, his curls oiled. She blew on her pitch pipe, a perfect C, and raised a hand for silence.

"I don't have much of a speech to give," she said. "You've all worked so hard, especially in my absence. The set, it's gorgeous. Music, lights, and costumes? Gorgeous, too. Well done. As for you actors, remember if you can that acting is just another word for doing. It can mean pretending, yes, but it can also mean behaving, serving, being. I can teach you a few things—rhythm, pronunciation. Well, not you, Carlos. But I can't teach you how to be. That's all you. And you're good at it. Truly. I had an acting teacher in college. If I'm honest, I hated her. She thought that acting just meant taking breaths in all the right places and standing up straight. Now I wonder if she wasn't onto something. So breathe, please. And keep your heads up. And for God's sake, it's pronounced *nuptial*, okay? You'll do just fine."

"Mrs. Morales," Kyle said, catching her just before she snuck out for a last-minute cigarette. "Still okay if we play the video we made before the play starts? I edited it over the weekend."

"And it's all aboveboard? Nothing to get me into trouble with Dr. Daley?"

"Not unless he's got a thing against Shakespeare."

"I wouldn't put it past him, Kyle. Go ahead."

She smoked a cigarette as the sunset singed the sky, then ground the butt into the lawn. In the lobby, she waved to Linda and Darlene, who claimed to hate the theater but never missed a show. Dan was there, with his wife and their two young daughters.

"Mrs. Morales," he hailed her. "Just the woman I was looking for. We have a few members of the board here tonight, eager to see what your department does. This is Dennis Horovitz," he said, pointing to a bald man, dabbing at his forehead with a handkerchief. "And Chip Easton." Another man, pale in a navy suit. "And Simone Cheng," he said, introducing a woman with a Chanel bag and Sassoon bob. Naomi's mother. Monique's mother, too. She put out a hand. "A pleasure. Your daughter's been such a help to me."

"Has she?" Simone said, appraising.

"And I was sorry to hear about Yale. I've written for her. Enthusiastically."

"I know," Simone said, pursing her lips in what wasn't quite a smile.

They went in and took their seats. The houselights lowered, and two members of the tech crew shuffled onstage to pull down the projection screen. With a crackle from the speakers, Kyle's video began, quick cuts of the actors at rehearsal and outside of the theater, in the sunlight, performing skateboard tricks on the stairs. She half recognized the song the video was set to, something about a symphony, about change. The students smiled for the camera, flashed empty peace signs. She remembered a story that Eleanor had told; Eleanor had shown the students pictures of Vietnam protests, and one girl had asked why so many of the posters had the Mercedes symbol on them.

Then the tape stuttered, and the sound cut out. A new image came on-screen: a firelit room, a man dressed as a bear, two girls. Her and Rosa. She was masked, thank God, and so much younger, a child, though she had thought herself so grown. She was out of her seat and running to the back of the theater, praying that the tape would stop. But no, the mask had slipped, and there was the whole of her tranquilized face. She was in the tech booth then. Two students, a boy and a girl, were struggling to remove the tape from its slot.

"I don't know why it won't come out," the girl said, tears in her eyes.

"Yeah," the boy echoed. "It's really stuck."

"Show some sense," she said. She reached for the projector's thick black plug and yanked it from its socket. The screen went dark. "If you do ever get that tape out, destroy it. Stomp on it. Run it over with your car."

"I don't drive!" the girl wailed.

"So hit it with a goddamn bike," she said.

She ran again, out of the booth and through the lobby doors and around the building to the back entrance. She found the cast huddled in the wings, trembling in their finery. "There's been a problem," she told them. "A technical malfunction. The video. It showed something . . . inappropriate. Where's Kyle?"

"Here, Mrs. Morales," he said it in his usual drawl, but she could see that he was worried. "What do you mean inappropriate?"

"I mean pornography, Kyle."

"Oh shit," the boy said.

"Exactly. Your tape. Did someone give you something to edit in, Kyle?"

"What? No. It's just like five minutes of us goofing in our costumes."

"Who had it? Besides you?"

"No one. I cut it together at home and gave it to Zay last night."

She stood there, stuck to the stage's floor. If Zay, the new TD, had done this, then Zay had been her correspondent, the brown-haired man Jerome had recognized. But who was he? And where was he now?

"Zay, has anyone seen him?"

They shook their heads.

"Not since before the show," said Patrick.

Nadine took a half step toward her.

"Mrs. Morales?" she said. There was green shadow all around her eyes. "Mrs. Morales, are we still doing the show?"

"Do you want to do it?" she asked.

A dozen heads nodded. Even Naomi, in blacks and an unnecessary headset, joined in.

"Okay," she said. "I'll see what I can do."

She made her way onstage. The houselights were at full. Many of the parents were standing, blocking the screen from their children's eyes, although the screen was dark now. She waved for attention, her other hand held across her forehead like a visor.

"Ladies and gentlemen," she said. "I know how upset you must be. How upset I am. It seems that we have been the victims of a prank. A vulgar one. I have some idea of who has done this—let me reassure you that it is not a student—and I will see to it that the individual is found and punished." She went to the screen and pulled the tab that retracted it into the ceiling. "I understand that some families will want to leave, especially those with children present. I see that some have left already. But the students in the show, they have worked hard these past weeks, so if I can persuade you to stay and support them, I would like to do that now." She looked to the wings. "Nadine?"

Tentatively, Nadine walked onstage. She whispered in the girl's ear. Nadine stepped forward and gave the first lines of the epilogue, the shea butter in her hair shining in the lights: "If we shadows have offended, think but this, and all is mended, that you have but slumbered here while these visions did appear. And this weak and idle theme"—she gestured here, to where the screen had been—"no more yielding but a dream."

The audience, those that remained, applauded. Nadine retreated to the wings.

"And now," she said, walking to the corner of the stage where the stairs down into the house were. "I give you Greenglade's unseasonal winter classic, *A Midsummer Night's Dream*." Mercifully, the houselights darkened. George plinked accompaniment; Marcus, a senior already bound for the conservatory at Oberlin, scraped at his violin. The show began.

In the dark, she found her row. Dan was there already. "Mrs. Morales, a word," he hissed.

She bent for her purse and had scarcely closed on the handle before his fingers were around her wrist, wrenching her up the aisle. Then they were in the lobby.

"What the fuck was that, Ali?" he said, still whispering.

She jerked her hand away, then tried to soften the gesture. There was a student in the ticket booth, a pimpled freshman, watching them. "Why don't you ask the TD you hired, Dan? Kyle made a short, and the TD spliced that filth onto it and now he's gone. The kids haven't seen him since before the show. Where did you find him? Where was he from?"

"Fuck do I know, Ali. I don't hire our temps. He came in through the portal, I assume. Noakes did the vetting. She said he had great references."

"Did she check those references?"

He didn't answer. Which was answer enough. "Ali, was that you on-screen?" he said.

She swallowed down the acid in her throat. "Is that what you think?" she whispered. "That I would do that? You think that every blonde is me?"

"Doesn't matter," he said, squaring his shoulders. "Half the board was here tonight. After that stunt, they won't keep the program and they won't keep you. The kids love you. Some of them. But you're not trustworthy, Ali. You're not safe. You'll be lucky if they let you finish out the year."

Her mind crashed back to the dean's red office, to being told she could stay to sit her exams, how the dean had made it seem like a favor, a gift. This time, she would not accept.

"I don't think so, Dan," she said.

"What do you mean, you don't think, you—"

"Stop," she said. She brought a finger to his lips, revolted by their feel. "That last time we were together, do you remember how I stayed in your office after? I guessed your password, Dan. I knew it was either your dog or your wife, and I was right the first time. I found the emails. It wasn't so hard. You were careless, Dan. But people with power, they're so often careless, don't you think? I know you've been taking donations. Large ones. There's no way some of these kids would be here otherwise."

"That's for the school, Ali!" His face was red and puckered now. "How do you think we got the new library?"

"Some were for the school. But not all. I've seen your house, Dan. That time Kelly and the kids were away? I know what they pay you here. And I know what Bel Air houses cost. I copied those emails, Dan. Put them on a disc. Not all of them, maybe. But enough."

His eyes darted for her purse. "No, Dan," she continued. "I didn't bring the disc with me, and it's not in my office. I'm untrustworthy, as you say, Dan. I'm unsafe. But we both know that I'm not dumb. And I'm very good at hiding things. I learned that early. So if you don't make some provision for me and my department, I'll see that every member of the board receives a copy. And yes, Dan, that was me in the movie. I don't think anyone else could tell, but count on you to know what I look like when I'm fucking someone I can't stand. Now go back in. Watch the show. Enjoy. I'm going to the ladies' to splash some water on my face. Then I'll do the same."

He spluttered, reddened, clenched his hands into fists. But then he let those fists go and turned from her, back into the theater. He understood the game, understood that he had lost this round.

She turned the other way, locked herself into the refuge of a stall, sat on the closed toilet. Something, she saw, was sticking out from her purse, a sheet of paper she didn't recognize. She pulled it out. It showed the picture of her under the lights, the same one that had been left in her mail slot. She turned it over. On the back were five words: UNIVERSAL CITY OVERLOOK COME TONIGHT.

In one story, she returned to the theater, sat through the show, led the applause at the end, went home after, locked the door. That woman was careful. That woman was frightened. In the other story, reckless still, the woman went to the overlook. And that was the one she chose. In an instant, she was out of the stall, out of the theater, sprinting over the lawn in her low heels as her purse banged against her hip. She laughed almost, because she had forgotten how fast they could be, she and that girl, how the wind whipped their hair.

She was at her car and then inside it, the seat belt strapped across her chest. She winced where it pressed her bruised shoulder, but the pain gave her no pause. A few turns took her to Benedict Canyon, then to Coldwater Canyon, then onto Mulholland Drive where the city fell away. It was gusting out. Pebbles struck her windshield. From under the hood, a grinding sound came, metal on metal. But just ahead was the brown sign marking the overlook. She pulled off the road onto the narrow parking strip. There was only one other car there, a rusted white Mustang. She killed the ignition. Then to test it, she turned the key clockwise. Again, again. The car bucked and spat; the engine would not catch. She had no way home.

There were no streetlights here, only the moon, nearly full. She stepped over the rocks and dirt, toward the placard, set on its pedestal of stone. The wooden fence was low, the drop abrupt, a sheer cliff garlanded in sagebrush. A tree grew near the ridge, a Valley oak, and as she approached, a man stepped out from behind it. The man was Zay. His hands were in his pockets.

"You came," he said.

"I did," she said.

"Don't you know me, Alice? Or should I call you Ali?"

"Call me what you like," she said. "And no, I don't know you. From before, I mean. You're what? Twenty-five? Twenty-six? Too young to have been around back then."

"I'm not so young," he said. "Look closer."

He walked toward her, his movements jerky, marionette-like. Another step and the moonlight caught his face, rendering his skin and hair and bloodshot eyes in shades of gray. She could smell the weed on him, musty, herbal, oversweet. *Grass*, they'd called it back then. *Tea*. And she saw it then, finally, in his cheeks, in the set of his chin.

"You're the boy," she said. "Suzanne's boy. Peter's. Zion."

He nodded. He was smiling, pleased, but the smile was somehow lightless. "Yeah," he said. "Though no one's called me that in years." His speech was soft and strangely slow. "Guess I gave up on my name, too. I go by Zay now. From my middle name, Isaiah. It's what my grandfather called me. Do you know what Zion means, in Hebrew?"

She thought back to her Sunday school days, then shook her head. "I don't."

"'Highest point,'" he said.

"Like the name on your account."

"Like this overlook. I love these places. Civilization, it's all down the valleys. But the hills around LA, they're wild."

"Wild?" She could feel a quickening in her blood. The wind blew louder now. Zay, Zion, the boy she'd first seen peeking from behind his mother's skirts, took another step toward her. She mirrored him, step-ping away and up the hill. She didn't want him close.

"I've seen your parents," she said. "Last week."

"Oh yeah?" he said.

"Peter, he told me that he didn't have a son."

"He would say that. He made a deal. Or my mother made it for him. When Suzanne and me came back from Germany, my grandfather, he'd had enough. Didn't like the kind of life they were giving me. He said he'd give her money to live on. But in return, he wanted me. She wouldn't do it, not at first. We moved all over. One friend's apartment, then another's. I guess it got too hard for her. She never really explained it. Just said that she had to go away for a while. Brought me to his door and rang the bell and left me. She was gone before it opened."

The words came easily enough. But the rhythm was off, the tone too singsong. "I lived with my grandfather after that," he went on. "Irving. He had an apartment on the Upper West Side. I cried a lot that first year, asked about my mother. He wouldn't tell me anything. After a while, I guess I stopped asking. In high school, I started getting into trouble. Nothing too bad. Kid stuff. Playing hooky. Smoking weed or whatever. Irving was getting older; he couldn't handle it. So I tried living with my parents for a while. But that was worse. They didn't know what to do with me. Suzanne, she spent most of her time in the barn. Know how many pictures of me she has in there? Not one. And Peter . . . I don't know. He seemed angry. But it was like the anger was all stuffed down inside of him. There was a fight one night. A bad one. The kind you don't come back from. So I bought a bus ticket to Port Authority, finished out school with Irving. I even went to college for a while. Studied business like my grandfather wanted." He laughed, but the laugh was bled of joy. He took another step.

"I dropped out my junior year. Came here, thought I'd give acting a try. My birthright or whatever. Irving didn't like it, but he helped out. Made sure I didn't starve. And honestly, I did okay. Found a manager. Did a few five-and-unders, some commercials. Maybe you saw the pizza one? Where they leave the box on top of the car? That one was a national. I mean, it wasn't art, and it would have made my parents crazy. But I was getting by. Then last summer, Irving died. And I don't know, I took it hard. Like there was so much I needed to know, like about my childhood and whatever, and now I couldn't ask him. Couldn't ask my parents either. I guess I got kind of depressed. Bombed every audition until I stopped even going. I was picking up crew work, nonunion. One of the guys that hired me, he said some school in the Valley was looking for a technical director. I thought that might be nice, working with kids. I went to the site to check it out. That's where I saw your picture."

"And you recognized me?"

"Yeah, I did," he said. He was bashful, like a suitor. "The name, it threw me. But even with the glasses, you still looked like you, Alice. Older. But the same. And theater? Come on."

"But why play with me? Why set up this guessing game? Why not just tell me who you are?"

"Because I wanted to see if you remembered me, too," he said. "I wanted to know that you'd thought of me. But you didn't remember me. You met me and still you didn't know."

She could feel anger uncoiling in her now. At this man. "Is that why you played the tape tonight? To punish me for that?"

He seemed hurt by this, offended. "No, Alice. God, no. I found that movie, that part of it, back in high school, in a box in the attic of my dad's old stuff. I brought it back with me to the city, had it copied onto a tape. The footage, it's far out, yeah. But it made me feel good somehow, seeing everyone the way I remembered them. Young, you know? Alive."

"It's sick what's on that tape. And there were children there tonight when you played it."

"We saw worse than that as kids."

"And how did we turn out?"

He held his hands up. "Yeah. Maybe not so great," he said. "But I didn't play that tape to punish you, Alice. I did it to save you."

"Save me? My God. You are a child." So that was how he imagined himself. A prince on horseback. The woodcutter with his ax. "Save me from what?"

"That school. Those people. That's not who you are." Another step. He was close now. She could hear the hunger in his voice. "You burned so bright it hurt to look at you."

The hill was at her back. She held herself tall against it. "Did you think I would stay that girl forever?" she said. "If I had, I would have died with the rest of them. Gone to prison at the very least. Or gone crazy. That light in me, I killed it a long time ago, traded it in for a shitty condo and a shittier car and a job teaching children I can barely stand. And believe me, it is better this way. It is better not to burn. I'm sorry I didn't recognize you, Zay." She had grace enough to mean it. "But you were so young then."

"So were you," he said.

"Yes," she said.

"And Rosa, too."

"And Rosa, too." She paused, swallowed hard. Now they had come to the core of it. "You were with me that last night? You said so in your letter."

"Yes. Remember?" He put a finger to his lips.

"Yes," she said. She put a finger to hers. So that was all. He had only seen her steal from the house. He did not know the worst of it.

"I liked Rosa," he went on. "She gave me candy. Remember? And I liked you, too. Because you were young and you didn't belong, and that's how I felt. Why did you do it, Alice?"

"Do what?" she said.

"Why did you kill her?"

Her legs went slack. She was on the ground then, the dust dirtying her white shift.

He came and knelt by her. That cloying vegetal scent was on his skin, in his hair. "There was blood on your skirt, Alice. On the inside, on the lining. I saw it when you passed. I didn't understand at first. But I scraped my knees often enough; I knew what blood looked like. You ran away that night. And Rosa, she never came back. She wasn't with the others when they took us to the station. So tell me, Alice, what did you do to her?"

She had lied about this night often enough, to herself, to others. She could lie to this boy, too. With her blood on fire, with her heart throbbing in her ears, she said, "Rosa killed a man. In England. Abraham. The one who made that movie. Did you hear about that? About how he died?"

He nodded. "I heard enough."

"The police found out about it. Rosa ran that night. Do you remember?" Her words came quickly now, fast and bright. "I caught up to her a few streets away, told her that she had to come back and face what she had done. We fought the way girls do. Yelling, clawing. I hit her in the nose, and there was blood everywhere. It surprised us both. She got away from me. Ran into the night. I must have cleaned my hands on my skirt. That's all I know."

He looked at her with his bloodshot eyes, said in that singsong voice, "I don't think so, Alice. Suzanne, she likes her secrets. She likes them better shared. Rosa died that night. She went into the water with a hole between her ribs. And when you came back, before you left again, you looked wrong. Like you were sick. You killed her, Alice. Why?"

Because she had loved Rosa. Because she had hated her. Because something was broken in her and had been broken from the start. Even after, on that frenzied walk back to the rooming house, in the muddled days that followed, her concern had never been for Rosa. Rosa, with her bright clothes and her blaring laugh. Rosa, who had suffered so much and still believed that life could be sweet if you only went and tasted it. No, she had worried for herself alone. This was too much to tell. And this boy, he knew too much already.

She offered what she could. "I was scared," she said. "I thought that she would hurt me. Tell on me. People do bad things when they're scared."

"Are you scared now?"

Was she? Her body felt tense, hectic with adrenaline. She felt powerful. She felt alive. "Why, Zay? What are you going to do to me, Zay? Will you tell the school? The cops?" She pushed herself to stand.

"No, why would I—"

She did not wait for him to finish, and whatever words he had, they did not matter now. It had to end here. Ever since that note was nestled in her mail slot, she had known this: She could only run so far. It would be him or her now. Or the both of them, falling together. Trusting that the weed had slowed his reflexes, she leaped for him, lightly.

"No!" he said, scooting closer to the fence. "No!"

Then she was on him, and they were tumbling. He scrabbled for purchase, his breath hot against her neck, but her momentum was too much. It would take them both over. This was escape, she thought, as a rock ripped into her cheek. Out of the forest, finally. One more somersault and they were at the fence. A post caught his thighs, held him. But she slid under, plunging down, until his other hand reached out for her, seized her wrist. She didn't want this hand, didn't trust it, just as she hadn't trusted his father when he'd moved above her, hadn't trusted Suzanne when she'd offered food and counsel. But Rosa had been right; she had an instinct for survival. She let him hold her, let him haul her back from the edge.

They lay there, in the fence's shadow, twined like lovers, breath returning. Zay wiped the dirt from his lips. "Are you gonna try that again?" he said.

"No," she said. The burning in her, it was stifled, quenched. "Not now. Do you see my glasses anywhere?" she said.

Gently, he let her wrist go. "I see them," he said. "Here."

A lens had cracked. She put them on anyway.

Her purse, she found, was still strung across her body, the cigarettes inside. She lit two, passed him one. They smoked together silently. She had expected him to leave. To race for his car and floor the accelerator as soon as he recovered. But he stayed. They were children in the night, the both of them, all the breadcrumbs gone.

"If you're done trying to throw me over a cliff, there's more I meant to tell you," Zay said. "Irving, he left me money. A lot of money. I get it when I turn thirty, which is in just a few months, if probate's through by then. And I know what I want to do with it. I want to make another company, Alice. A better one. You could be an artist again."

She could imagine it so easily. The rented place downtown. The actors, young and beautiful, trawled from Hollywood's gutters. The tours, the car trips, the hotels. A life like that and she could run and run and run. But she'd been running so long. From her father's house, from a bridge in the rain, from herself. And never getting anywhere. Her cheek was wet. She shook the gravel from her dress, used its hem to wipe the blood away. She remembered what Rosa had said, in that tiny bathroom on the ship. It was true. She did bleed. She was human, like it or not, with all a human's frailties.

"You should be careful with that company, Zay," she said. "You should be careful what you do with all that freedom. I can't do it with you. I tried that. And look where it led me. To this overlook, to the bridge where Rosa died. Maybe I would have got there on my own. Maybe I would have found worse paths. But art isn't for me. That was the deal I made. I would give it all up—the intensity, the feeling— because that would keep me safe, keep others safe from me."

"Seems like it didn't work out so great," he said. The end of his cigarette was blazing, a pocket sun.

"No. I can see that now. I should have seen it before. There's no such thing as safety." Naomi could report her. Dan could strike some devil's bargain with the board. Zay could go to the police. And she was her own worst danger—the wolf, the witch, the huntsman with his knife. And also she was the girl, having her heart cut out.

She stubbed out her cigarette and looked out over the valley. The moon had risen higher, overwhelming the fainter stars, but down below, undimmed, were thousands of ordinary lights—headlights, shop signs, lit windows. She felt such sympathy for the people in those windows, for the effort that it took to live.

"Did you find out what you wanted, Zay?" she asked. "Did I answer your questions?"

"Not sure," he said. "But I guess there's no going back to how it was." He flicked his cigarette out over the cliff.

"No," she said. "And you shouldn't want to." She thought of how good it had been and how terrible. All those shining boys and girls. Gone to flowers, the lucky ones.

"So how does the story end?" he said. "Is there happiness? Is there peace?"

"Maybe for some people," she said.

"Not for us?"

"Not for us."

She lit another cigarette, watched the wind, gusting now, thieve the smoke away. Soon she would climb down from this mountain and begin again: beg a ride, summon a tow truck, see to her car, make her apologies at the school, pretend that this was real life. It seemed impossible. But this was what people did. Normal, everyday people.

The girl she was had not wanted the everyday. She had wanted to feel alive, wholly herself, meeting the world with a single face. No disguise. No mask. When Rosa had died, she should have lived enough for both of them. Instead, she'd spent the decades running, hiding, barely living at all. Her time with the company had been too much. The life she'd made in the years after was too little. And it was too late now to try again.

Or was Suzanne right? Was there more life waiting? And was her mother right? Could she confess the horror of what she'd done? Could she live forgiven? That would take her from her mother, from what might be her mother's last weeks. But it was craven not to try. What would Rosa have wanted for her, before the house in London, before the bridge? Rosa would have wanted everything. She wished that Rosa were there with her now, with her foghorn laugh, with her awful honesty. She would take a portion of that honesty, here and now, for herself: Allison, Alice, Ali, all. It was the least she could do for Rosa, dead in some far-off plot, unclaimed. If she told the truth, then Rosa would be given a stone, a name.

That same heat was in her blood now. That frantic impulse. But with it was a sense of overwhelming love. For Rosa, for herself, for everyone who'd ever wanted to make a new world, a paradise, and only made a mess instead. She turned to Zay, with violence and with care, and grabbed his collared shirt. "Go!" she said. Her voice was strong now, louder than the wind. "Go! Down the road. Go to the police."

"The police?" he said, confused. "And tell them what?"

"Tell them what I've done. Tell them what I tried to do to you. I'll tell them more, I will, I promise. The truth. Finally. Whatever I can bear."

"But, Alice, I—"

"Just go!" she yelled. She was crying now, shaking with the force of it. "Go! Before I change my mind."

He left then, jogging for the Mustang in his jolting gait. The headlights flared and then were gone. She sat there in the dirt, hugging her knees, as the night grew cold and still. Was this peace, then? Was this happiness?

When the police car came, a long time later, the lights flashed colors on her wounded cheek. White and red. White and red. White and red.

ACKNOWLEDGMENTS

I've always felt that I came to the theater a little too late. I think almost everyone who loves experimental theater feels that. In college, I studied the seminal groups of the 1960s: the Performance Group, the Free Southern Theater, the Living Theatre, Bread and Puppet Theater, the Open Theater, El Teatro Campesino, At the Foot of the Mountains, and so on. But by the time I had moved to New York, these theaters were long disbanded or hanging on only in attenuated form. (Bread and Puppet was arguably the exception.) Though some remarkable inheritors remained—I think particularly of the Wooster Group, the Talking Band, and Mabou Mines—it felt like the aesthetic revolution had already been fought. I had missed it.

For a long time, I've wanted to write about these troupes whose work I've experienced, with few exceptions, via essay, playscript, and grainy video, to imagine myself back into that world. But my genre is suspense. These real theaters, with their sincere political commitments, would not hold the thriller I imagined. So I invented Theater Negative. Its body of work and its terrible abuses of power are entirely my own creation, as are its members. But if the interested reader would like to seek out some of the real (and to the best of my knowledge, not at all murderous) artists, some places to begin include Arnold Aronson's *American Avant-Garde Theatre: A History*, James M. Harding and Cindy Rosenthal's *Restaging the Sixties: Radical Theaters and Their Legacies*, Richard Schechner's *Environmental Theater*, and Michael Smith's delirious *Theatre Trip*. I was fortunate to study with both Arnold Aronson and Richard Schechner in graduate school. They have my particular thanks, as do Marc Robinson, Martin Puchner, Julie Stone Peters, Shawn Marie Garrett, Bill Worthen, and, of course and always, Martin Meisel.

I owe thanks to many others. Writing is a book is typically a solitary experience, but it is also, like the invented plays in *Flashout*, a collective creation. Let's begin first with my children, Ada and Thom, who are not nearly old enough to read this, but who are daily reminders of the importance of mutual care and love. Thank you also to early readers: Cóilín Parsons; Alex Segura; Morgan Soloski; Judy Soloski, who reminded me of Marni Nixon's role in *My Fair Lady*; Rachel Churner, who told me just how appalling the wine at a lesbian bar would be; John and Skye Adams, for their tremendous patience with my terrible Spanish; and Michael Imperioli, who models the passion and devotion of an artist's life. I want to lovingly acknowledge Susan Mosse, Paula Vogel, and others who spoke to me about their experiences at women's colleges in the 1960s and 1970s. I am also indebted to Estelle Freedman, who shared her essay "Coming of Age at Barnard" with me and confirmed the rumor I had heard about the expelled students.

I am grateful to my *Times* colleagues, who impel me toward better, clearer, more distinctive writing, particularly my discipline editors, Jeremy Egner, Austin Considine, Nicole Herrington, Lorne Manly, Stephanie Goodman, and Mekado Murphy, as well as our department head, Sia Michel. I am happily jealous of the work of my fellow culture reporters and critics, particularly Taffy Brodesser-Akner, who brings so many of us together.

At Flatiron, I am so lucky to be in the care of Megan Lynch, who knew just what I wanted this book to be without my ever having to tell her, and for helping to move it closer to that vision, even if it meant disappearing a few characters. (Sorry, Angie. Sorry, Emily.) Kara McAndrew is perfectly reassuring and beautifully capable, and Chris Smith and Katherine Turro were such stars of publicity and marketing last time around. I can't wait to see what they and Marlena Bittner and Kate Keating dream up for this one. Sara Wood designed this beautiful cover and I'll never tell her how long it took me to realize what you could see if you turn it on its side. Thanks also to Sue Walsh for the interior design, managing editors Morgan Mitchell and Elizabeth Hubbard, production editor Frances Sayers, and production manager Vincent Stanley.

I hope I am not embarrassing Sarah Burnes when I say that she is a hypercompetent ray of absolute sunshine. I am grateful for her enthusiasm and belief, and I feel so cared for by the rest of the team at Gernert, especially Aru Menon, Will Roberts, Rebecca Gardner, and Nora Gonzalez. And thanks also to Sophie Rabineau at WME, who did such exceptional work on *Here in the Dark*. I think this could be a nice one for a mother-daughter team, no?

And lastly, I want to take the theatermakers, professional and amateur, who have so enriched my life. In most ways, I'm not like Allison, for worse and for much, much better, but I agree with her that it is a brave thing you do and holy in its way. Applause all around.

ABOUT THE AUTHOR

Alexis Soloski is a prizewinning *New York Times* theater critic and culture reporter. She holds a PhD in theater from Columbia University. *Flashout* is her second novel, following the nationally bestselling thriller *Here in the Dark*. She lives in Brooklyn with her family.